HOUSE
OF
BEARS

House of Bears
Orysia Dawydiak

Acorn Press
Charlottetown
2009

House of Bears
ISBN 978-1-894838-34-4
© 2009 by Orysia Dawydiak

The publisher acknowledges the support of the Canada Council for the Arts, the Government of Canada through the Book Publishing Industry Development Program (BPIDP), and the Prince Edward Island Depart-ment of Communities, Cultural Affairs, and Labour for our publishing program.

Cover art: Elaine Dillingham
Editing: Melissa Carroll, Richard Lemm
Design: Matthew MacKay
Printing: Hignell Book Printing Canada

Library and Archives Canada Cataloguing in Publication

Dawydiak, Orysia
      House of bears / Orysia Dawydiak.
ISBN 978-1-894838-34-4
      I. Title.
PS3604.A985H68 2009   813'.6   C2008-902975-5

ACORNPRESS

P.O. Box 22024
Charlottetown, Prince Edward Island
C1A 9J2

acornpresscanada.com

*For all immigrants and their children
displaced by war and divided by cultures*

Contents

11   *Prologue*

15   *Copper Creek*

30   *A New Cycle*

40   *Ungrateful Children*

53   *The Cynic and the Hypocrite*

61   *Endings and Beginnings*

72   *An Ally*

83   *The Girl Who Brought Death*

93   *Mother Hens and Queen Bees*

106   *Dead Boys*

114   *Burying a Boy*

122   *The Rivalry*

132   *The Digging Begins*

140   *Reawakenings*

146   *Impotent Angels*

156   *You Can't Choose Your Family*

167   *The Cruelty of Angels*

176   *Inside Jonah's*

188   *In Limbo*

197   *Girls Just Wanna Have Fun*

207   *A Peek into the Closet*

215   *The Gypsy*

227   *Kiss and Tell*

244   *Careful What You Wish For*

255   *Tortured Souls*

267   *Alone in a Crowd*

274   *Dancing Genes*

286   *Starting Over*

296   *Out of the Well*

299   *Reunion*

316   *Gregory Sawchuk's Genealogy Chart*

Prologue

Marushka picked up a stout birch branch from the pile next to the caravan she shared with her sister's family. She set one end of the branch on the ground and held it firmly at an angle away from her body. With the other hand she lifted her skirt, then in one swift motion she stomped a booted foot down on the branch. The snap of wood echoed back from the trees at the edge of the clearing. She stooped to pick up the pieces, and carried them back to her fire. Sparks burst upward when she tossed them in.

She peered into the large copper pot suspended on an iron tripod over the fire. Dozens of bubbles clustered and hesitated at the bottom of the water. She watched as one, then more broke free and rose to the top, bursting and disturbing the reflection of the early evening sky. Marushka lifted her head and squinted. The colours were vibrant this time of the year, the blue sharp and clear above her, the sun's reflection off the leaves throwing shards of gold into her watering eyes. She pulled her maroon scarf over her brow, as if to shield her face. Her skin had battled the sun for over forty years, and was worn to the dull texture of the canvas covering their wagon. It was an old face which held her lively black eyes. She liked to tell her nephew that the song "Chorni Ochi" had been written for her and her Black Sea eyes. Then he would sing the song for her, his sweet, lilting voice making her sigh, close her eyes, and remember the soothing music her young husband once played for her on his violin. Dear Milo, they had such a short time together. When the boy finished his song, she would clasp him to her bosom, kiss the top of his head, and he would wiggle free, embarrassed, and run off to play with his friends.

Marushka looked back down to see the water roiling in the pot. She fetched the tea satchel from the back of the wagon and sprinkled a handful of dry leaves into the large enamel teapot waiting next to the fire. With great care, she tipped the copper pot into the vessel and watched the scalding water make the leaves dance. She righted the water pot and put a lid on the teapot.

Marushka heard the sound of shouting and knew the boys had finished their work in the forest and were running back to their wagon homes throughout the woods and clearings. Her nephew Lazlo raced up a few moments later, panting.

"Auntie," he gasped. "Katia said her baba read her leaves and told her she would be married next year, and she would have five children, all boys. Do you believe that? I don't think her baba has the gift like you do. How can she be so sure?"

Marushka laughed. "We will know soon enough. Why, in another six or seven years you may be married also. What do you think?" She reached over to where he had collapsed by the fire and ruffled his thick black hair, so much like her own when she was younger, wavy and lustrous, often tangled and matted.

"Auntie, can you read my leaves for me? Can you tell me who I will marry, and how many children, and what they will be like? Will they be naughty like me?" He grinned at her.

She smiled back at him. Her nephew was becoming more serious all the time, trying to follow the older boys around, watching as they practiced their smithy skills. He was only eleven, but his childish mannerisms and days of mischief were fast disappearing.

"Here, have some tea with me and we shall have a look at your leaves, if you are certain this is what you want." She tipped the teapot into two large tin cups. The plumped tea leaves rushed out with the gold-tinged water and settled to the bottom. Boy and woman sat on the ground next to the fire, sipping their tea, saying nothing, listening to the evening sounds of the forest as it shifted into night. Birds sang warnings to their fledglings to hurry back; the wind sighed through the tree tops and shook dry leaves to the ground. Finally, Lazlo drained most of his tea, swirled the dregs one time, and handed the cup to his aunt.

Marushka looked inside. She had been amused by Lazlo's request at first, until she saw his earnest face. Most boys his age were not interested in such divination. She did not practice her foretelling arts on her family as a rule, but she could not refuse a request from the boy she loved as she would a son. So she settled in to contemplate the patterns in the cup, half-closing her eyes, letting the shapes form at the back of her brain, letting them speak to a place where they would be deciphered without her conscious interference. Something did not seem quite right. She turned the cup one quarter-turn, then another. It all seemed backward. He had swirled the dregs properly, in the right direction, all should be in order. She closed her eyes, relaxed her face, and dropped her chin to her chest.

His bride was beautiful, radiant with health. She did not recognize the girl, her features soft and wavering. An explosion of crimson made Marushka take in her breath. Something dreadful had happened. To the bride? Lazlo stood alone, a handsome young man, but stooped with grief. A crying baby. But the baby looked round and fit—perhaps he was just hungry. A different young woman now, shorter than the first, running, running through a black forest, her dark hair streaming. Then nothing, just grey mist. Wait, a little girl, pouting, stomping her feet. A feisty one. A daughter perhaps? She did not smile. She was wary, trying to hide. Then a blast of light. A fire!

Marushka cried out.

"Auntie, what is it? What's wrong? Wake up!"

"No, all is well my little one, all is well." She sat now with her eyes wide open, trying to breathe deeply, to still her heart, to appear calm. She reached over to Lazlo and touched his shoulder.

"Sometimes this happens when I go deep inside. I saw your bride. She is lovely, indeed. You two looked so happy together. And do you really want to know how many children?" She feigned a stern look. She was not certain of what she had seen, yet her heart told her she had seen the truth.

"Auntie, tell me!"

"There are two. The first, a fine-looking boy, and the second, a girl. A girl with a lot of spirit. I believe they will bring you much joy."

Lazlo wore a little smile. "Good, two is a good number. I don't know if I could feed five children. Two is fine."

"Ah, my little man, you are already fretting about how to feed your unborn children. There will be time to worry about this later. For now, enjoy your boyhood, your freedom."

Voices from beyond the clearing announced the arrival of Lazlo's parents. Marushka, suddenly weary, pushed herself up off the ground. She dumped her tea leaves, rinsed both cups, and prepared to pour tea for the others.

Copper Creek

Luba pressed her hot face against the cool glass of the bus window. They never got the temperature right inside these things—it was either a hotbox or a meat locker. This one was the former, a sauna on wheels maybe three-quarters full, headed for North Bay and beyond. And of course it wasn't the express bus—her penny-pinching mother had bought tickets for the goddamn milk run. She shivered as a drop of perspiration trickled along her spine and down to the hollow in her back, trapped in the heavy woollen sweater she'd been stuffed into. Probably a bargain basement special. Who else would want this putrid pink cloud of itchy wool? Her mother had insisted she wear it for the ten-hour ride back to Copper Creek, and Luba was too stunned to resist at the time. For Christ's sake, she thought, she was an adult who was still taking commands from her bossy bitch of a parent—not a single protest, just a dopey pup following orders. But now she felt more like a wild stray, locked in a metal cage next to her mother, Volya Kassim, the bulky kennel warden, smelling like garlic and wedged in between her and the aisle.

Still, this had been her only way out from the hospital in Toronto. She'd tumbled down a long, slimy slope into a steaming sewage pit, farther than she had ever dreamed she could fall, and this was her punishment. From living on her own—a university student on a scholarship—to being bailed out by her poor, widowed mother. Way to go, Luba. And that look on Volya's face when she came to pick her up only a few hours ago. Luba felt another wave of heat race up her body like a brush fire out of control—her mother's tight, down-turned lips, her narrowed eyes, her shaking hands. But what was most surprising and unsettling was that for the first time ever her mother was speechless. She could barely look her daughter in the face.

Luba was angry at herself, too, but mostly at Tom. She tried to push thoughts of him away, but somehow he was always there, hanging out in the margins, edging into her mind's line of sight. So she invited him in, imagining his tall, thin back retreating from her in that slouched, loping stride of his, shrinking to a short vertical slit in the darkness before vanishing altogether. That's how she wanted to remember him, as a speck of nothing. She stared hard out the window, blinking several times to force back stubborn tears.

The dreary April scenery of northern Ontario streamed by—dirty white, leaden blue, dead-grass brown, endless snow and granite, scrub brush and fir trees. It never changed. Luba particularly disliked this time of year as she watched people sucked in by spring, by the promise of melting snow, of what lay beneath. They became careless, forgot about the treacherous ice waiting for that one misstep. And then they'd fall hard, flat on their backs, wrenched muscles, cracked bones, soaked through with cold. Why did people love spring so much? What was there to look forward to? Stupid chocolate bunnies and tulips? Then Luba wondered what had happened to the flowers she had left behind at the hospital, like that vase of yellow and white daffodils her cousin Greg had sent her. What a waste. And how the hell did he find out she was in there? Luba had known him when she lived in Toronto as a child, but she hadn't seen Greg in years. She wondered if anyone else knew about what had happened; once word was out it travelled fast.

When she had first arrived back in Toronto for university, Luba avoided any contact with her relatives. And Volya had never encouraged Luba to make connections with her estranged family, not even with her grandmother. But that was fine with Luba; as it was, she'd had her fill of relatives back in Copper Creek, the whole judgemental, carping, meddling lot of them. As the only child of a widow and the youngest of the Tatenko clan, Luba's family treated her like a delicate, thin-shelled Easter egg. She had only one relative she actually liked and related to—cousin Orest who had settled in Toronto a few years before Luba, the last fledgling to launch from Uncle Marko and Aunt Veronica's nest in their northern outpost. She often thought of herself and Orest as two sleek black ravens amongst a flock of fat, squabbling blue jays.

Luba shifted in her seat, cramped and exhausted. Someone behind her was snoring, lucky bastard. All she'd wanted to do was to sleep for the whole trip home, to crawl into a sound-proof cocoon and hatch out when it was all over. But even in the hospital she could hardly sleep—ironic considering it was sleeping pills that had landed her there in the first place. The humming motor of the bus reminded her of the droning night sounds she was subjected to in that pale hospital room, filled with instruments churning and clicking all around her, footsteps echoing in the bare halls outside. And the nauseating smells of disinfectant and bleach. Luba swallowed and the memories came rushing back: she felt the rawness of her throat, remembered the searing pain when she first woke up, the acrid, metallic taste in her mouth, the pounding head and clanging in her ears, the impossible brightness piercing her eyes when she cracked them open, the horrible nightmares when she did sleep. But she couldn't remember any of the doctors' names—there were several who came to interrogate her—or how she'd responded at first. Whatever she'd told them, it was clear she was heading for the psych ward unless she agreed to go home in the care of a relative and get counselling.

So it was home to Mommy. There was only Volya, even though she was the last person on earth Luba wanted to see or be with.

Luba felt a sharp pain behind her eyes as she recalled seeing her in the waiting room, sitting upright and stiff on a metal chair, her shiny black box of a purse clutched to her heavy bosom, her beige coat still buttoned up, her panty hose wrinkled at her stout ankles above the tight patent leather shoes. She wore those shoes only to church, and yet here she was after an all-day bus ride to a strange, frightening city, sitting in a Toronto hospital—her feet swollen and aching—waiting for her suicidal daughter. When she spoke, in Ukrainian, her words clipped, her voice strained, she said, "Well, here you are. Okay to ride the bus now?" No chastising, no hug, no eye contact with Luba the untouchable, the tainted; it was worse than a slap, than a barrage of angry words or insults.

Volya didn't ask what had happened, or if it was an accident, but Luba knew she was afraid to know. Her mother was always afraid of knowing.

As the bus made its first wide turn into the next insufferable little rest stop town, Luba realized she'd been so apprehensive about what her mother would say at first that her silence was almost a letdown. Now, glancing at her mother, Luba found it unnerving that she still had hardly said a word these past few hours. Instead, Volya had begun embroidering once they were settled in their seats. Watching her then, focussed on her embroidery as if Luba didn't exist, she wished her mother would say something, anything, even a sarcastic remark. Luba assumed she was planning what to tell everyone back home, how to cover up her daughter's shame. Suicide was a huge sin in the Catholic books—not that Luba had been an upstanding member of the church by any means—but now she was a confirmed failed Catholic, an unmitigated embarrassment to her mother. Volya's one daughter, her one child, her only anything, and she'd let her down. Again.

The knot that had started in her stomach at the beginning of the ride had spread to her entire body as every cell burned and screamed. Finally, though, her mother folded up the embroidery and slipped it carefully into her green vinyl shopping bag. She then reached into a plastic bag under her seat and took out a wax-papered package.

"Luba, have a sandwich," she said, placing it in her daughter's lap.

Have a sandwich? Luba thought. That was it? As if they were on a picnic at the lake instead of packed in a sardine can hurtling up a highway.

"Here, take it. You must be hungry by now."

Luba could smell the garlicky *kobassa* through the wrapping and began to salivate, but she pushed it away as a pulse of nausea passed up from her stomach.

"Mama, I ate just before we left," she lied.

"That was four hours ago. Look at you, Luba. You are nothing but bones. Your aunt Veronica will give me so much grief when she sees you. All your cousins are nice and healthy and here I have only one daughter, and she is a walking skeleton. What will I say to her? Do you want people to think I have failed as a mother?" Luba shook her head, unbelieving. Her mother acted as if Luba was simply coming home for a visit over spring break.

"Eat."

"What are you talking about? I'm not skinny, I'm normal. The cousins you like to compare me to are fat."

"They are not fat, they are just right and they are happy."

"Happy? Mama, look at Christina—she must weigh two hundred pounds and she's only five feet tall. That's beyond fat, that's obese! And don't give me the excuse about extra weight from the last baby. That kid must be five or six years old by now."

"She is not two hundred pounds! You exaggerate. Anyway, you have no right to be so critical, you know nothing about having babies and the changes in your body afterward."

Luba had lost weight, she knew it, but it wasn't intentional and she didn't want to talk about pregnancies or any other body conditions. In fact, she wished she had the nerve to tell her mother to lose fifty pounds, but the man across the aisle had been scowling at them since her mother's voice had risen, and a comment like that would get the fireworks going, no question.

She turned her head back to the window to find that all the dull colours and shapes outside had drained away in the dusk. A sign flashed by: North Bay 24 kilometres. She closed her eyes...kilometres, miles. Why did they have to go metric, all that conversion no one could remember. She only knew it was ninety-five more miles from North Bay to crappy Copper Creek.

"Your cousin Orest was never fat, as you like to call it. You saw him before Christmas, right? Is he still as thin as he always was?"

"He's just the same, he's fine." But Luba knew he was not well. Too many late nights and drug parties.

"His parents have not heard from him for over six months, such a thoughtless son. It does not matter how old you are, your parents want to know you are okay." Luba caught the edge of her mother's glare.

"Next time I see him I'll tell him to call home, okay?"

Volya grabbed Luba's arm and leaned into her. "Where exactly did you see him last?" Her breath was sour. Luba drew back.

"Hey, take it easy, Mama, he's just busy. I saw him playing at a downtown club—he's the drummer for the Harbour Rocks, you know, his band. Plus, he works for Uncle Bohdan during the day. He's a busy guy." She didn't wish to divulge any more details. Orest was a dope-addicted high school dropout and a construction worker by day, the boy no one in the family liked to talk about, the where-did-we-go-wrong kid. He didn't write or call, send birthday cards or go to church. She envied his lifestyle on the road, playing in clubs across the country, even some US gigs.

"Maybe he is sick." Volya released her grip. "Maybe he takes drugs. Those rock-and-roll kids do it all the time, I see it on the TV." She nodded her head, then narrowed her dark eyes. "And what are you doing at night clubs? You are supposed to be studying."

"You can't study all the time, Mama. Even students need to take breaks. We dance, we have fun. It's good exercise."

"There are bad people in those places, dangerous people, all that drinking and fighting."

"Don't worry Mama, all my friends are from school. We go out in groups, we stay away from the *bad* places."

Luba then patted her mother's soft, dimpled hand, still holding the wrapped sandwich. As annoying as the nagging was, it felt like comfort food to Luba—*perohy* with wild mushroom sauce, or fresh blueberries smothered in sour cream and sugar. Maybe, Luba thought, if she was lucky they would leave her messy Toronto life behind and her mother could stop treating her like one of those fragile china dolls she had on display at home. Or like the bride doll she was given for Christmas one year but then had to store in a closet cupboard, high up where Luba could never reach her—Snow White in her long slumber. Luba forgot about the doll until she rediscovered her as she prepared to leave for university. When she asked her mother why they had given her the doll when she wasn't allowed to play with it, she was told, "Because you were so insistent on having one, but you were too young to play with it properly, so we saved it for you, for when you were older and wouldn't ruin her." Volya then added, "We paid a lot of money for that doll." Luba insisted the doll be given to a little girl; the girl she chose was delighted with the two-foot, blue-eyed blonde dolly in her perfectly preserved starched white crinoline dress and veil. She hoped the girl would actually play with the doll.

"Please eat this sandwich," Volya pleaded and Luba caved.

"Now, about that boy you were dating. Tim? Is he still your boyfriend?" Volya was trying to tease and fish for information at the same time, but she couldn't hide her disapproving tone.

"That was Tom. No, we're not going together any more."

Volya grunted and nodded.

Luba tried to sound nonchalant, but she felt anger rise into her throat and her face flush when she spoke his name. That dickhead. How stupid she had been to be taken in by him, to have ever trusted him, to have cared for him. No, she corrected herself, she just thought she had cared.

He was someone her mother wouldn't have approved of, a boy with questionable morals and without a solid future. But he was so cool, tall and slim, with tight-ass jeans and dirty blond hair falling into his steel-blue eyes, a strong nose and luscious lips. And what a kisser. He was unpredictable, she had been warned by her friends, but that was part of the mystique. Her own life was so boring, regimented. She was tired of vanilla. She needed dark chocolate and chili.

"You should find yourself a medical student, or a lawyer. They make good money."

Luba scowled.

"Do not look at me like that. I want you to be comfortable and not have to work as hard as I do. Marrying a wealthy man who is kind to you is not such a bad thing." She leaned over and took her embroidery back out. Luba instinctively reached up to switch the light on for her.

"Thank you," said Volya without looking at her daughter.

"And you should know, by the way, I'm not getting married," Luba declared.

"I did not plan to get married, either, you know," Volya said, deftly knotting the end of a thick blood-red thread she had pulled from a twisted skein. Her puffy fingers moved fluidly, as if programmed to work on their own, not requiring any direction from their mistress. The skin on her knuckles shone, worn smooth from thousands of hours of scrubbing floors, toilets, and the insides of unfamiliar refrigerators—a lifetime of hard work. But her hands also created intricate foods, like the neatly stuffed and tucked cabbage rolls, the perfectly formed and filled *perohy* that Luba loved, the *paska* Easter breads with their elaborate decorations made from dough. And, of course, the exquisitely painted *pysanky*, the Easter eggs her mother made every year with lines so straight and designs so precise, it didn't seem possible that human hands could have created them. But these were also the hands that could strike quickly and painfully when her mother was unable to contain her anger and frustration with Luba and the world. Luba could still remember her stinging cheek from the last slap three years ago. She'd wanted so much to punch her mother back then, but instead ran off to stay with Aunt Veronica for a few days.

The bus lurched and started a wide turn into another small hick town for a rest stop. Volya flattened the white embroidery cloth on her lap, then picked up one corner and poked a heavy steel needle through the material, tugging on the thread to make sure it didn't come through. Luba marvelled at the red and black border she had already completed. The cloth was at least five feet long by two feet wide—another dresser scarf she guessed. Volya must have hundreds of embroidered towels and runners. Every surface in the house was covered with them, so why was she making another one? There were so many other hobbies her mother could take up that didn't require much physical exertion either, like reading, keeping a small flower garden, or proper parenting. But as her mother continued to work the fabric, Luba knew it was what her mother loved to do, that and fatten people up with her rich cooking. Right now she could tell her mother was about to launch into another tedious story from her childhood; the poverty, the mean father, the drudgery, the horrors of the war. Normally this would have Luba rolling her eyes, sighing and wishing she could get beamed up off the planet, but today, oddly, this relieved her. At least they wouldn't be talking about Luba any more.

"I was twenty-nine years old when I married your father, quite old in those days. You were born when I was thirty."

Luba knew this one.

"Most girls got married as soon as they could, to get away from home, but not me. Your Aunt Zenia was married at eighteen, and Uncle Marko at twenty. No, I was too worried I would end up with someone like my father, so I did not encourage the young men." Her voice faltered for a moment and she cleared her throat. "Oh, there were some who were interested in me when I lived in England, you know, but they were all foolish boys."

"Aha, you had suitors!" Her mother had never mentioned this before.

"You should not be so surprised. I used to be young and pretty, like you. Never as skinny, though, except during the war." She shook her head and studied the cloth in her lap, beginning to sprout roses in one corner. "And we did not go around like you kids do today. No kissing in public. No kissing at all unless you were engaged."

"You're kidding me, right?" But Luba knew she was serious, her prim and proper mother from a strict Eastern European tradition. Luba thought back to the photos of her mother as a young woman just after the war. At that time she was what people would call a handsome woman—big-busted, slim hips, thick black shoulder-length hair arranged in careful waves, and an olive complexion on an oval face with an aquiline nose totally unlike her siblings. And she was short, unlike most of her family who were tall and fair, so, like Luba, Volya must have felt a bit out of place in her family. Now, thirty years later, sitting next to her daughter, Volya was much heavier, her hips well-padded, her stomach a shelf for her embroidery. She resembled their Copper Creek female relatives, all rolled and kneaded and puffed up like the deep-fried, sugar-dusted *pampushky* they adored. Nothing like her sister Zenia, though.

Luba had her mother's colouring and her nose, but she seemed to have inherited her aunt Zenia's taller, slimmer build and her better taste in clothing. Still, other than that, Luba didn't seem to have anything else in common with her mother's family. She stood apart with her dark complexion and her nearly black, iron-straight hair, which covered her most annoying feature— her bane as a child—ears that stuck out from her head. No one else, including Luba's father, had those ears, or her unusual smoky amber eyes, which just supported her notion that she didn't belong to this family. It was Tom who had remarked that he'd never seen such a haunting colour. Her eyes reminded him of a wild jungle panther, or a wolf of the steppes.

If Volya weren't her mother, biological or otherwise, Luba would never have chosen to sit beside her. For one thing, her mother's dowdy, outmoded clothing drove her nuts. Luba preferred casual clothes in dark colours accented with large silver hoop earrings and wrist bangles. She wore her hair long and loose. To Luba, her mother looked like the immigrant she was. She couldn't understand why her mother didn't pay more attention to current dress fashions and fabrics. Volya was an excellent seamstress, so it wouldn't cost that much more to dress a tad more stylishly. Today her mother wore a shift with slashes of purple, green, and orange on white. Oh, and nickel-sized yellow spots that she had accented with a string of fat yellow beads and two yellow discs clipped to her ears. Thank God for the overcoat, Luba thought.

Volya continued, "Your father was a gentleman, and very kind. That is why I married him. But he was a labourer and a sailor and we did not have much money. Money is necessary, Luba. Love is expendable. So I want you to find a kind and rich husband." Volya stopped embroidering and pointed her needle at Luba. "And if you do not find one, I will find one for you." Her stern expression masked a smile beneath. Something rare for Volya, a real smile.

It was Luba's turn to frown. Yes, her father had been kind. She certainly had no bad memories of him. But kind was not a word that would ever stick to Tom. When she first met him at the Bear's Den where Orest's band often played, she saw bad boy written all over him. He slouched low in a chair, cigarette hanging from the corner of his mouth while he drummed in time to the band on his spidery stretched-out legs. She was the one to approach him on a dare from one of her girlfriends. Not something she'd normally do, but the third tropical sunrise had turned her brain to a Bacardi mush. He curled his lips at her when she flopped into a chair beside him and appraised him with her wildcat eyes. His warning growl did not deter her. She was the hunter, he her quarry, and she won the bet didn't she?

She recalled enough of their first night together to know she had to see him again. He was a pal of Pete's, lead guitarist for the Harbour Rocks, so when she ran into him the next weekend and he walked up to her with a grin and a warm "Hello, gorgeous, we meet again," she was smitten. He never had to call her; she knew she could always find him hanging out with the band. A male groupie. Why not, she thought, they were a great bunch of guys, except maybe for Pete. What a head case he was. Luba had never met anyone so self-centred or verbally abusive— worse than her mother.

She asked Orest one day why they all put up with Pete. He ran his hands through his long tangled hair before answering. "He's obsessed, ultra focussed yeah, but he's brilliant, man. Doesn't matter how the rest of us play, he makes us sound good. Yeah, his attitude is the pits, but he's the one who holds the band together, gets the gigs, makes it all work. Anyway, if he ever gives you any trouble little cousin, you let me know. You don't need to put up with any of his shit. Same goes for Tom. He treating you okay?"

Luba remembered feeling defensive about Tom, then. She didn't say anything to Orest at the time, but whenever she complained in private about Pete, Tom lashed out at her. "Cut him some slack, for God's sake!" he'd shout. "He's had a rough life, you don't know the half of it. We grew up together. I know. Just let him be, ignore him, all right?" That was an order, not a plea. Luba tried to tell him that she understood how people could get messed up with a rotten upbringing. She was thinking of her mother's childhood stories, and how paranoid and touchy her mother could be. But Tom would cut her off. She could never understand Pete, he insisted, but he refused to explain why, and would sulk and shut down if she pressed him.

Luba realized too late that she would never be able to compete with Pete for Tom's loyalty. The kindest thing he ever did for her was to leave when she needed him, to show what scum he was really made of. Still she couldn't help but wonder what if. Luba caught herself. No, there could be no what ifs. She'd tried to do herself in for that piece of shit. How fucking stupid was that? Luba's head felt feverish, tears threatened to ooze out, but she knew they wouldn't. She couldn't cry in her mother's presence, she couldn't risk her scorn. She needed to switch topics—no more Tom. She brought up the only subject she figured might shut her mother up: her mother's father, that tyrant Boryslav. Yes, she thought, they should talk about the ugly men in Volya's life, not hers.

Luba cleared her throat and again felt the tender damaged tissue. "Grandfather Boryslav was a nasty character, wasn't he?"

Volya paused in the middle of a cross-stitch and stared straight ahead for a moment. Then her hand resumed directing the needle from hole to hole in the porous cloth, the trailing thread leaving behind one rose after another—a ruby bouquet on a blanket of snow.

"Yes, he was." So now she didn't want to talk. That was perfectly fine with Luba.

Copper Creek. Pop. 13,231. As they passed the sign, Luba felt a heaviness in her stomach like she'd just swallowed a pound of rusty nails. She wondered why anyone would choose to live in this deadbeat town, a burned-out star at the end of the universe. And how did they come up with that exact number of people living in Copper Creek anyway? All the ones she knew were write-offs. They probably needed to update the worn, green sign—there couldn't be more than a few thousand citizens left. All her friends had evacuated as soon as they could, like rats jumping off a condemned toxic ship. Now she almost wished she had chosen the psych ward option. She slumped in her seat with the strange sensation that her will had been sucked out of her body. They were only minutes away from home—her mother's home on Maitland Street.

Volya had been jabbering for the last hour of the trip. She had finally put the embroidery away and decided to update Luba on all the local and family news. As they closed in on the home den, Luba watched her lips flapping, going on about this cousin, that niece, someone's aunt visiting from Ukraine. Who cared? It was all pointless gossip, like all the soap operas her mother was addicted to. While Volya listed who was getting married and who had died, Luba began to picture herself turning into a soap opera zombie in her mother's home. Volya would like that, someone she could control, who wouldn't talk back or cause trouble, like an old toothless, declawed cat. Maybe Luba should give in. What else was there to do?

"Veronica wants us to come over for supper, but I told her you'll need to rest from the trip. Besides, she has a houseful over there. Zachary and Phyllis and their youngsters are visiting from Timmins. My, those children are wild. I keep telling Phyllis she needs to be firm and not give in. Young people do not know how to raise children any more. They let them do anything they want. Spoiled brats. And rude, too. No, I am not going over there. I will just get a headache listening to those children scream." She paused. "You can go over if you like, I suppose."

"No thanks, I'll just stay in. Anyway, it's too late to visit." They pitched forward as the bus slowed and turned a corner. Copper Creek Bus Depot just ahead.

"Luba?"

"Yes, Mama?"

"Shall we keep our lips buttoned about any silly mistakes we have made? People here would not understand."

Luba stiffened. "Sure, whatever you say."

A wave of diesel fumes floated up from the bowels of the bus and Luba's stomach lurched toward her throat. Welcome home.

Luba couldn't wait to leave the bus depot with all the rumbling motors and nauseating fumes. Her body still echoed the engine vibrations and her ears buzzed as she dragged a suitcase toward the taxi stand. Volya was an old pro at this. She didn't own a car—she didn't drive. And thank God for that, Luba thought, considering how neurotic Volya was as a passenger. Luba hadn't bothered to get a license herself. You didn't need a car in Toronto; it was easy to get around on public transport—and as easy to disappear there. They slipped into a cab and were soon leaving the commercial heart of Copper Creek for the older part of town where Volya lived in one of the many small stucco and wood bungalows. It was dark, but Luba recognized all the intersections under the streetlights, and the low, squat public school she used to attend, now surrounded by a new chain link fence. When did that go up? She hadn't been home since last summer and any changes seemed more like open sores than improvements in such a small town.

They stopped on Maitland Street in front of one of those nondescript little grey houses. Luba began to tremble. The house seemed sinister, the windows black, empty eyes, a grim mouth formed by the porch rails along the steps leading to the door. She was afraid of being swallowed up if she went inside, afraid that she would never emerge again into the light. Why did she come back here? She hadn't thought things through; they must have drugged her. Luba waited until the cab driver had hauled their suitcases from the trunk before she reluctantly opened her door. She could barely move her limbs. She felt like one of those radiologists wearing a full suit of lead. It was then that her head began to throb.

"Look at you, twenty-two years old and you walk like an old lady," Volya said, then turned to fuss with her key. Luba wished she had the energy to turn around and get back into that cab and go anywhere else. When she looked back, the cab was rounding a corner then vanished with a flash of brake lights.

"Come on, come on, get inside, it is still cold out, you will get sick."

She waved at her daughter to hurry then lifted up Luba's suitcase as if it was a feather-filled paper bag and disappeared inside the house. Luba felt dizzy as the odours of the home assaulted her nose. It was a battle between musty old walls and cheap, lemon-scented cleaners—cleaners 1, mildewed walls 0. The floors were spotless, of course, and the glare of the kitchen light reflected sharply off the shiny linoleum, making her squint. She kicked off her shoes and automatically slid her feet into a pair of knitted nylon slippers, the same kind she used to wear to slide across the floor when she was a kid. Her mother kept several pairs by the door for visitors, neatly lined up like a row of colourful cheerleaders with pompoms in their hands. Luba chose the turquoise pair trimmed in orange, oddly the least obnoxious colour combination.

Then she hauled her rock heavy suitcase to her old bedroom. It was all made up, tidy and sterile, just like a hotel, as though no one had ever lived here before, as if no little girl had ever played there with her dolls and checkers and Snakes and Ladders game. The bed cover was white chenille, perfectly tucked in, not a wrinkle to be seen. The walls were the same odious pastel pink. No amount of begging or tantrums ever resulted in having them painted a colour Luba liked—fuchsia when she was younger, indigo as a teenager. The only concession was the glow-in-the-dark universe of stars, moons, and planets on the white ceiling, a Christmas gift from Aunt Zenia when she was thirteen. At night Luba would stare at the galaxy above her and imagine she lived on a different planet, leading the thrilling, exotic lives she read about in books. Her night stand was still nestled next to the bed, complete with its sticky drawer. Luba noticed the deep scratch was still there, too, stained with brown shoe wax to cover the blemish, the way it looked when her mother first brought it home from the thrift store. The overhead light was the same god-awful suspended square of frosted glass. The only change to the room was the loveliest touch of all: a picture on the wall over the bed headboard, with an embroidered towel draped along the top and sides. She had never been allowed to hang any prints or posters, or her own artwork lest she damage the plaster walls. And now she faced a framed Madonna portrait, complete with golden halo, hands pressed together in prayer and her red heart exposed on the outside of her blue robe while her eyes rolled heavenward. Jesus, was this her mother's idea of a homecoming present?

Luba removed her jacket and tossed it on the bed, then flopped down next to it. How the hell could she stay here? The room was a tomb; the person who used to live here was gone, morphed into an alien being. There were no warm, touching memories for her here.

She closed her eyes for a few minutes to fight the claustrophobia, then got up and walked into the living room. Switching on a corner lamp, Luba gasped. More change. What had her mother done? She vaguely remembered a conversation about redecorating, but she hadn't paid much attention at the time, probably trying to rush her mother off the phone so she could go meet Tom Dip-shit. Looking at the room now, she could sum it up with only one word: yellow. It was as though the sun-fairy had crash-landed and thrown up all over the room. And no wonder, since it suffered from a serious case of jaundice—a gold brocade couch and armchair, mottled yellow-brown carpet, yolky curtains edged with cream lace, lemon-coloured walls, and canary lampshades. Even the white embroidered coverings had turned sallow. Gross. Luba felt like she was inside a huge scooped-out lemon, with the scent still punching at her nose.

"Luba, do you want something to drink?" her mother yelled from the kitchen. "I am boiling water for tea. I have milk, apple juice. What would you like?"

"Uh, tea is fine."

Grateful to leave the living room, Luba walked into the kitchen to find her mother bent over the burner, stirring a large, steaming pot.

"What are you cooking?" Saliva poured into Luba's mouth.

"Just heating up a few *perohy*."

"Can I do something to help?"

"You can put out the plates and cups. Do you remember where they are?"

"Of course I do. Unless you moved things around." Luba started for the cutlery drawer.

"No, nothing has changed in here. Did you see the living room?" she asked, turning around and smiling. Luba nodded as she gathered up forks and knives.

"So, do you like it?"

Luba placed the cutlery on the table, slowly. A heavy plastic sheet covered the same old, immaculately preserved embroidered tablecloth beneath. "Well, it's bright. Quite a change from the dull beige and browns you had before. Yup, this one sure is brighter."

"You do not like it."

"No Mama, that's not it."

"Well, I did not change it for you. I do not need your approval." Luba could feel her mother bristling behind her.

"It's fine, Mama, I'm just not used to it yet." She turned around for the plates, avoiding her mother's eyes, too weary to argue.

"Never mind. You have always been difficult to please, so particular about everything."

"What? Me? I don't think so."

"Yes, you have been. As a child you never smiled."

"Huh?" Luba sighed. "Look, Mama, colours are personal. Everyone has their favourites. I like red, someone else may like blue. So what? *Vive la différence.*" She plunked the unbreakable Corelle plates on the kitchen table. The overhead light blazed off the plastic into her aching eyes.

"I would never paint the walls red. How ridiculous! That is not a living room colour. This place is not like one of those bars you like to go to. Red is not a decent colour for any wall in a home." She stomped to the table, frying pan in hand, and scraped a heap of *perohy* onto Luba's plate. "Sour cream?"

"I didn't mean you should paint your walls red, I was just trying to point out that we all have different colour preferences, period." Luba poured boiling water into the waiting teapot.

"Enough about colours. Sit down, child. Eat. Here is some *kobassa* I sliced up for you. You need to eat protein."

"That's way too much food, Mama."

"Eat already!"

"I have a headache. Do you have any aspirin?"

Volya's eyes widened, "Are you allowed to have aspirin?"

"Allowed? Of course I can have aspirin. What do you think?"

"I think you have had enough pills."

"I only want one or two, for Christ's sake!"

"Do not take the Lord's name in vain in my house!" she shouted back at Luba.

"Well don't treat me like an invalid."

"They told me no pills." She turned back to the teapot and brought it to the table.

"I'm not asking for sleeping pills, which, by the way, is what they meant. And I don't want the whole bottle of aspirin, just one or two." Luba sank into her chair, her legs trembling and weak.

"No need to be sarcastic," Volya said, pouring the tea into their cups. "No one tells me anything, especially not you. How am I supposed to know? You never talk to me, tell me about your life or what is happening." She dropped into her chair across from Luba, her lips pursed, her eyes narrowed.

"How do you think I felt when I got that phone call from the hospital all the way in Toronto? When they told me you were in emergency, that you nearly died? Huh? In the middle of the night! I was so scared. What could I do? An old woman alone. All night I stayed up, praying and crying, wondering what had happened to my daughter. Did someone try to kill her? Was she mugged? Why did I not know before? I was sick. That is how I felt. A mother should never have to live through something like that." She began to raise her cup, but her hand shook so badly she spilled hot tea on herself. "Ah, look what I have done!" She stood up and hurried to the bathroom shaking her hand.

Luba heard the water running but remained where she was. She didn't care that her mother had hurt herself. Her stomach had hardened into rock again and she tried to push the plate of food away, but it stuck to the plastic. She swallowed and felt the rawness of her throat. It had been two weeks since that tube had been forced down into her stomach. How long would it take to heal? Getting up, her legs wobbled beneath her. She had to get out of there, but her mother blocked the door to the hall, a wet towel around her scalded hand. Thrusting out her other hand, she gave Luba two small white tablets.

"If you need more they are in the medicine cabinet." She wouldn't meet Luba's eyes.

Luba took the pills and rushed into her room, sick that she'd actually chosen to stay with her mother over the loony bin—irrefutable proof that she was certifiable.

A New Cycle

Luba sat on the floor of her mother's living room, surrounded by dusty photo albums and musty cardboard shoe boxes, leafing through loose pictures with scalloped edges. When she had walked into this room two days before, she felt only revulsion. Now she didn't notice the colours so much. Outside it was bitterly cold, while inside, in her mother's home, it was yellow; it was warm; it was safe. She was a little girl again; it was easier this way. Besides, if her mother wasn't going to treat her like an adult, she needn't bother acting like one.

Luba found the photos amusing, especially those of herself as a baby and a toddler. But they also depressed her a little. There were so few pictures of her father—he was the photographer in the family, and his absence was haunting. After he died Volya had put his old Brownie camera away. Luba was eight at the time, and often felt guilty that she remembered so little about him. She tried to make out his features in the black-and-white photo of her christening ceremony. He was a slight man, with light brown hair, and short, just two inches or so taller than her mother. Luba was taller than him. She turned the print around to read the faded script on the back—Copper Creek, 1956. So long ago, and yet her mother was so angry still.

Luba returned to work. Her only task was to dust all the knick knacks in the house. And there were a lot, especially in the living room. For Luba it was more like a scavenger hunt as she discovered more old family albums on the bottom shelf of the tall bookcase that housed a small scale Ukrainian craft museum. The lower shelves held a variety of wooden carved plates and figures, most inlaid with tiny, bright beads and shell in intricate patterns; a huge Easter egg collection as well as carved wooden eggs, some inlaid with beads, others painted with brilliant flowers on a black background; a collection of ceramic dishes with red and black geometric designs on white. A higher shelf was home to a chorus line of tiny dolls dressed in identical em-

broidered costumes. She had always found this macabre, like an army of ma-
levolent double agents, about to be released into the world, all the faces shiny
and smiling, eyes opened wide, affecting innocence.

She sighed with relief when she replaced the last dusted egg in its basket.
The fragile pysanky had survived her cleaning, thank God. Only her mother's
prized bear family on the top shelf left to do. Beautifully carved from Carpathian Mountain birch, they were stained in tones of antique bronze and
gold. Not exactly the ursine family Goldilocks had run into. One was on all
fours and looked harmless enough, but the other was rearing up, her claws
raking the air, with two cubs tucked in just behind her. She stood on legs
solid as tree trunks; she would never budge, she would fight forever, Luba
mused.

As a young girl, Luba often asked about the carved figures because she
knew her mother was afraid of real, fur and flesh bears. When they lived in
Vancouver her mother told her frightening stories about people running into
grizzlies up in the mountains. Some of the hikers escaped, others were badly
injured or mauled to death. Volya had no idea how many nightmares Luba
suffered after hearing these tales. She also liked to tell Luba about the time
she was eleven years old, and she visited a Gypsy camp with two girlfriends,
hoping to get their fortunes read. They passed by a small bedraggled brown
bear, chained by a leg to a tree. The girls stopped to stare at the sad creature,
noticing that the fur around his manacle had been rubbed off, and his skin
was raw and bloody. A thin dark man in dirty ragged clothes suddenly appeared and held out his hand, asking for money to make the bear dance for
them. In his other hand he held a sharp, pointed stick. The horrified girls
ran off, and plotted to sneak back in the dark to release the poor bear. He
looked like a half-grown cub, and had probably been starved and beaten. But
of course, they were too frightened to return to the camp, especially after
a Gypsy woman tried to steal Volya later the same day. Luba was terrified
when she first heard that story, but over time she came to believe that her
mother was probably exaggerating. After all, Volya was only a girl then, and
she probably didn't remember what really happened. Or she made it up to
entertain Luba, and to rationalize why she disliked Gypsies so much.

Luba's reverie was interrupted when a sharp thud beyond the curtain
made her jump. She stood up slowly, scared to approach the picture window.
There was no one. Then a slight flutter on the ground below caught her attention. A small sparrow lay on the lawn, breast up, head twisted back, one
speckled dun wing spread out as if waving good bye. She thought she could
see a drop of blood at the corner of its pale beak. The windows had been too

clean, too clear. Her mother was superstitious about such things; she claimed that a bird hitting the window heralded a death in the family. Well, thought Luba, she had recovered from her near death, maybe the sparrow would as well. She doubted it, but she'd check back later, and if the bird was indeed dead she would throw it away before her mother saw it. She didn't need Volya any edgier that she already was.

Volya was a professional house cleaner, and swiping her finger across the top of the TV, Luba thought it ironic that her mother's house had any dust at all. But she also knew that cleaning houses for a living was exhausting work, and probably demoralizing as well. Volya was fond of pointing out that her lack of employment options was due to her lack of education. She didn't want Luba cleaning toilets for living, as if there was any chance of that. Volya was usually home by five pm each day—one place to clean in the morning, one in the afternoon—so Luba was surprised to hear her mother's voice, animated as if she was having a conversation. It was only noon. Then she recalled that her mother had invited her sister-in-law, Veronica, to come over to paint Easter eggs. Or, as they would say, "Pysati pysanky"—to write Easter eggs. It was more like writing than painting, applying hot wax with a metal-tipped stylus sometimes shaped like a beak. The modern commercial ones had fine metal tubes, like a delicate quill pen. Luba hadn't made pysanky in years; she was too busy hanging with her friends when she was a teenager, then she was gone and left all those traditions behind.

She recalled one of the photos she had just looked at, from the early sixties album, she thought. She was grinning up at the camera, at her dad, one front tooth missing, proudly holding her first decorated egg. That was a happy time, all the other little girls and their mothers lined up along a table, some looking up at the camera, some focussing on their waxing and drawing; a few tears when partly finished eggs were dropped; the laughter and light conversation flying over their heads as the mothers enjoyed one of those rare breaks from the drudgery of their homes and lives. Aunt Veronica was at the very back in that photo, with Orest. Luba couldn't remember her cousin being there, but she was only about five or so at the time. She wondered if he had wanted to come, or maybe he was sick and his mother wanted to keep an eye on him. He was never the healthiest kid and seemed to miss a lot of school.

Luba hadn't seen her aunt yet, although they had spoken once on the phone. Aunt Veronica's voice had a breathless, pained quality. She was always exhausted from running after her grandkids but they had finally left yesterday, back to Timmins—another fine northern metropolis.

A few seconds later Aunt Veronica's round, jowly face popped around the corner, feigning surprise at seeing Luba. "Oh my dear little dove, how are you? You are so thin, how do you feel?" She lifted her niece from the ground with her two huge paws, and Luba found herself enveloped in a strong, fleshy embrace.

Luba barely had breath to reply, "I'm okay, Auntie, really."

Veronica pushed Luba an arm's length away, still gripping her shoulders. Next to her, Luba felt like a waif, a mere pup. Hence her private name for Aunt Veronica: Jabba Woman. She could hear the notes of the Star Wars movie theme tinkling in her head and envisioned the enormous blubbery character. Every part of Aunt Veronica jiggled when she walked, but in spite of her extra weight, her aunt had a lithe, youthful air and moved like a large, graceful panther.

"I can see why you have been hiding her, Volya," she scolded. "Trying to fatten her up, the poor little dear." Once again she drew her niece close. Luba gasped, breathing in a mixture of mothballs and sweet perfume. Veronica finally released her, flopping onto the couch.

"Come, sit next to your favourite auntie, and we'll get caught up on all the news."

Luba watched her mother setting up the kitchen table to decorate pysanky. Volya wheezed as she gently lowered a heavy cardboard box onto the table covered with old newspapers. Luba wondered at that. Her mother had rarely been sick, she was the healthiest person Luba had ever known. One by one she lifted out jars of colourful dyes and set them down. Easter was always a big deal for their family. The adults took it seriously, the religious ceremonies, major rehearsals for the long Easter mass, the blessing of the traditional foods afterward. It was not as much work as Christmas, but there was still a lot of preparation. And it seemed to Luba that the women did everything for these celebrations; baked, decorated, bought gifts, cooked elaborate feasts. The men simply enjoyed. At Easter the women prepared paska, a delicate, sweet egg bread ornamented with braids, flowers and leaves of dough. The aroma was heavenly when it emerged from the oven, brown and shiny with egg-white shellac. Luba loved paska—she had some toasted for breakfast that morning. Her mother always made plain loaves for everyday eating, and even though the bread dried out quickly, slathering it with butter fixed that right up. It was almost as good as fresh warm paska—kind of like refried perohy which Luba preferred to freshly boiled.

After the women put in all their long hours of work, the men drove their families to church and male priests led the ceremonies. Good old patriarchies, alive and well in their Ukrainian Catholic church, Luba thought. She wondered how long it would continue this way. It didn't seem quite right, although she had never heard of any girls or women in her family complaining.

"Luba, will you join us?"

Her mother had arranged the jars in a row according to colour. Typical of Volya to be so organized and particular, but there was a good reason for this sequence. First yellow, then orange, red, blue, purple and black. The last three looked the same, except for stains inside the lids. Luba recalled the first and only time she defied her mother's instructions about which colours to use first. Because the entire egg had to be dyed before trapping that colour with hot wax, if you dyed it red first, you could not go back and dye it yellow or orange. Luba was impatient and wanted the red, and at first was most upset she could not use any of the lighter colours afterward. She ended up with a red, purple and black egg which, she decided, was far more interesting than the traditional version, and suited her mood at the time. Luba's colour and design tastes had always clashed with her mother's, even as a child.

Volya peered into each jar, swirled the contents, sniffed, then wiped the tops. Veronica had already settled herself in a chair, her back to the wall, her dimpled elbows on the table. She was sorting through a pile of cards with photographs of completed eggs in many designs and colours.

"Uh, I think I'll just watch. It's been too long," Luba said.

"You will remember as soon as you start. Trust me. And if you forget something, Veronica or I can remind you. It is, how do they say? Like falling off a bicycle, you never really forget."

"I've already fallen off, Mama. It's the riding part I'm not sure about."

She gave her daughter a puzzled look. "You will remember." Volya resumed her preparations: a white candle secured in a holder for each person, a couple of blocks of fragrant beeswax, several kistkas with different sized tips to choose from. Luba picked up a medium sized kistka. Kistka, kistka, what a strange word, she thought. At one end of a small wooden dowel, the attached metal piece was shaped to scoop up a small chunk of wax which would be melted in a flame, then drip down a tiny funnel ending in a fine tip for drawing. Luba jabbed her tip directly into the beeswax, then held it in the flame of her candle. The wax sputtered and melted, dripping off the tip, back into the flame. She loved that sweet beeswax scent, so familiar, so comfortable. She lowered the kistka to the newsprint, tapped the excess wax off and started to draw. A fat black streak followed the tip of the metal in a straight line, then a curve to the edge of the paper.

"See, you remember," her mother beamed.

Luba picked up a card with the colour photograph of an exquisitely decorated pysanka. Each time Luba studied the patterns she was amazed that human hands could have drawn those smooth, unwavering lines around and across the curved and bumpy surface of an egg. A cross was the prominent feature on this egg, in white, red and gold, and through the centre was a sheaf of wheat, another common motif.

"Veronica, is that a new dress?" her mother asked, a master at working and talking at the same time. "Did you make it yourself? What an interesting pattern."

"It is the same material you bought at the Bonimart sale before Christmas. Remember, Volya? You made a dress out of it as well."

"I made two dresses, but I sent them to Ukraine. They love that kind of stuff."

"Your cousins back home are lucky to have you sending them such nice clothes." Veronica turned to Luba and seemed to wink. It was hard to know for sure since her fleshy cheeks came up so high that they covered most of her blue eyes. Volya scowled. She could detect sarcasm in any voice. Veronica's body quivered with laughter and Luba admired her aunt's ability to handle her mother, how she never let anything bother her.

Ignoring her last comment, Volya picked up a block of the newly unwrapped beeswax. "I just love the honey smell of fresh beeswax." She inhaled deeply and closed her eyes. "It reminds me of home, back in Ukraine. We collected our own honey, and took wax from the hives."

"I did not know you kept hives," Veronica said as she tested one of the kistkas in front of her. "I thought you were the cow's shepherd."

"I was. I did everything. But yes, Kalyna was my special responsibility. More than once she got me into trouble, especially with my father. Sometimes I fell asleep while I was supposed to be watching her." Volya reached for a clean, white egg and began to draw fine steady lines in hot wax, flipping the egg around while her drawing hand appeared to remain still. Luba watched, mesmerized. And she listened. As a teenager she used to be bored and irritated when her mother told those stories from way back when. But right then, with her aunt sitting next to her, she was transported to what she remembered as a time filled with no worries, no unpleasant family history, and no thinking required.

"Sometimes I hated that cow. But other times she was my best friend. The village children used to make fun of me, of my dark skin and eyes. They called me tsiganka, a Gypsy—hated thing. So, the day I fell asleep and Kalyna wandered off and into the village, the other children painted her black with mud.

What a sight!"

"You were lucky you had a cow," Veronica muttered and picked up a clean egg.

"I thought your father was a blacksmith," Volya said.

"Sure, so we had his services to trade for what we needed. But milk was scarce, a cow would have been a welcome treat. Oh well, I have made up for the lack of it since then." She smiled at her niece and patted her belly. "Now Luba, do you drink milk? When you eat like a bird you especially need milk to keep your bones strong."

"Yes, Auntie, I drink milk. And I eat lots of cheese and butter, too, don't I Mama? And bread and potatoes and perohy. Don't worry." She picked up an egg and pointed to a design out of her reach. "Can I see that one? It looks simple enough that even I might be able to finish it today."

The dying and waxing finally complete, Luba held her lumpy black egg next to the flame. Not too close or it would get scorched, just near enough to melt the wax. As she rubbed off the soft black goo with a clean tissue, the trapped colours were revealed, one wipe at a time—vibrant red and yellow, lively turquoise, rich purple. She squinted at her egg, spotting the places she had missed with the kistka. They showed up as black, the last colour the egg was dipped into, which dyed every part that was not protected with wax. Dying eggs. How odd, she thought, those two words together. An Easter tradition now, but before that a pagan rite of spring to celebrate rebirth with brightly dyed eggs. The church said Jesus died to be reborn, but Luba didn't believe that actually happened, it was too incredible. And for such a hopeful season, it was a rather brutal story. Luba much preferred Christmas. Well, the idea of Christmas—the actual celebration was a bit depressing: her mother running around buying, baking, cooking, buying, writing Christmas cards, buying. It was especially hard when you didn't have much money to shop with, but the pressure was always there. It seemed to her that the traditions around death and rebirth and even birth were not all that different from each other.

"Oy!" Veronica gasped as her egg slipped out of her fingers. Somehow she managed to catch it before it hit the tabletop. "That was close. Always when you are nearly finished, never early on when it would not matter." She wiped perspiration from her forehead with the back of her hand.

"If you kept your hands near the table you would not have that problem," Volya advised lifting a dripping egg out of the red dye and laying it on a fresh paper towel. The egg bled crimson onto the white towel.

"It's gorgeous, Auntie." Luba admired the completed pysanka where it sat for them to critique, cupped in her fleshy palm. Veronica rolled it over so

Volya's keen eyes could appraise it.

"Very nice, Veronica."

"Not nearly as good as yours. Your mother has the steadiest hand I have ever seen, Luba. You will not find any mistakes on her pysanky. She even knows how to pick the best eggs. See this pale spot on my first egg, where it did not take the dye properly?"

"That is because I know how to handle them. I never touch them with my fingers. The oils from your skin stick to the egg and then the dye will not adhere. You should use a tissue, Veronica." Volya was melting wax from her last egg so quickly it seemed to hatch in her hands. The eggs didn't dare disobey her, that's why they were so perfect, Luba thought; her mother's focus was almost frightening.

"I cannot use a tissue, Volya. It would be too slippery—I would drop them all. Anyway, it does not matter. This one I will lay in a basket so you do not see the splotchy side."

The three women were all concentrating so hard that they did not hear anyone enter the house until the outside door slammed shut. Uncle Marko walked heavily up the steps and loomed in the kitchen doorway. He was a tall, heavy man with dirty blonde hair and watery blue eyes, and the whites of his eyes were always pink, whether or not he was drinking, which was often. He looked nothing like his sister, Volya, but was the exact image of their father, Boryslav.

"Luba! How is my favourite niece?" he bellowed into the small kitchen.

"Marko! Do you have to shout? She is right here and she is not deaf," Volya growled at him. He did not pay attention to her, nor did he move out of the doorway. He probably didn't want to remove his shoes, Luba thought, or put on those ridiculous slippers—he knew the rules. Luba gingerly placed her egg on a tissue then stood up to greet him. She smiled to herself—she was his only niece. He enveloped her in his long arms and squeezed hard.

"I'm fine, Uncle, thank you. You're looking well." He reeked of cigarette smoke. She had never liked the smell of cigarettes. Once in high school she tried one from her friend's pack, but all it did was make her feel nauseous.

"I am well. Life is good, no complaints. So you are making pysanky with the old ladies? That is good, good. Nice when the young people learn our old traditions. You know why we Ukrainians make pysanky? I expect not."

Luba smiled wearily and sat back down at the table to listen to another Ukrainian story.

"Today we use them to celebrate Easter and the resurrection. But thousands of years ago, before we were a Christian people, the old tribes dyed eggs to say farewell to winter and welcome to spring. They believed the eggs would protect them from evil and they planted the coloured eggshells in their fields so the crops would be bountiful. But best of all, the young maidens would have a very special pysanka to help them win the love of a suitor. So, Luba, if you have someone in mind, all you need to do is present him with a beautiful pysanka and he will be yours. Ha, ha, so easy. But I am sure you have no need of any such device to win a lover. Not someone as lovely as our Luba."

Without glancing at Marko, Volya waved a hand to dismiss him. "Oh get away with you and your silly stories, Marko. Since when were you such an expert on pysanka history? Or love! Hmph!" She was melting the wax off her fourth intricate egg. Luba had completed only one.

"You would be surprised at what I know. You never give me enough credit." He coughed several times, then bent over and covered his mouth.

"You cough like that and say you are well?" Volya glowered at him. "I told you to see the doctor. All that smoking is bad for you."

"No point in seeing a doctor when you already know what my problem is, Doctor Volya. She knows everything! Ha, ha. She is so smart. That is why she cleans houses for a living. Mrs. Smartie." He hacked again.

"Marko!" Veronica protested. "Go outside and wait for me there. I am already finished. I just need to get my coat."

Luba heard her uncle grunt just before the door slammed shut.

"I was going to make tea, Veronica. I sliced some fresh poppyseed cake for us," Volya offered, acting as if Marko had never come.

"No, no thank you, Volya. It is getting late and I need to make supper for Marko. He is on midnight shift this week. I should go. But look, I have three new pysanky. A good afternoon's work," she said, breathy and flustered.

"Here, put them in this half carton to keep them safe. Will you varnish them at home?"

"Yes, I have it all set up in the basement. Marko made me a drying board with nails, like the one you have. Goodbye, sweet Luba. Will you come over to our place for lunch after the Easter service?" she asked Volya.

"Perhaps. We shall see."

Luba looked out the kitchen window and saw her uncle leaning on his car, smoking. He did not open the door for his wife, just slipped into the driver's seat, his cigarette hanging from the corner of his mouth. Like her mother, Aunt Veronica did not drive.

"That no good lout of a brother," Volya grumbled behind her. She had started to put away the jars and clear off the table. "He is so ignorant. He has always been rude and thoughtless. Luba, do not just stand there, help me clean up," she ordered. Luba smirked but did as she was asked. He was not the only rude person in this family, she thought.

"Poor Aunt Veronica," Luba said, crumpling up the newspaper. "Why does she put up with him?"

"Because she does not have any choice. She knows what it is like to be on your own. Look how hard I have to work. Better to put up with a grumpy alcoholic than live in poverty. Anyway, she is a good Catholic and ridiculously loyal—she would never leave him." Her mother had already switched to cooking mode, washing and cutting up lettuce. She was like a machine, moving effortlessly from one task to another.

"You were still pretty young when dad died. How come you didn't remarry?"

"I had no interest in marrying again. It is just one more person to take care of. It gets complicated." Her flashing knife pulverized the crisp green onions into a limp heap.

"What about love? What if you fell in love with someone?"

"Love? I had no love to give anyone. And anyway, who would have wanted a forty-year-old immigrant woman with a child? No, I did not need a husband then and I do not need one now. Especially not one like Marko. There are too many husbands like him around." She turned to the sink. "We are having pork chops today. I hope that is okay with you." She did not look up, did not expect an answer.

Luba nodded anyway. She wondered if her mother had ever loved her father. She wondered if her mother had ever loved anyone at all.

Ungrateful Children

Volya closed the French doors, stepped back, and squinted at them. They were a new addition to the Brenton home where she was cleaning today, and what a mess the carpenters had left behind. But finally all the dust had been vacuumed up and the last fingerprints on the bevelled glass squirted away and wiped clean. The effect was spectacular, Volya had to admit, like a magnified version of her treasured cut crystal vase. Still, it seemed a huge waste of money to have such fancy doors in a regular family home. Frivolous spending. She sighed, perhaps not so regular after all. Volya turned away and trudged towards the children's rooms. Empty the waste bins, then finish with the kitchen. She rubbed her back and groaned as she made her way up the wide staircase.

She wondered what Luba was doing at that very moment—probably watching TV, or reading those awful magazines. A daughter who did not appreciate what others sacrificed for her, who thought her own life was so hard. She did not really want to listen to Volya's stories about growing up in Ukraine, she was so wrapped up in herself. That look on her face, the smirk— she thinks I am exaggerating, she does not believe me, Volya thought. I can see her thinking, "I'll humour the old woman." I know what she is doing: she wants to avoid talking about herself. She does not want me to ask about what happened, what she did. And perhaps I do not want to know. Anyway, it was an accident, there is nothing to talk about.

Luba was spoiled like all the others, she supposed. Canadian children had everything right in front of them. They could reach out and take what they wanted, when they wanted. It was easy to close your eyes and your ears when you had so much to eat you could grow fat, or obese as Luba liked to say. To have a roof that did not leak, a truck to deliver heating fuel, clothing in your closet to choose from. Too many choices, really. It was her own fault that Luba had been pampered, but she could not bear to say no to those things she herself had been denied as a child. If only she could afford to send Luba back to Ukraine, her daughter could see for herself how lucky she was to live in Canada. Maybe then she would realize how hard Volya worked for her, or how important it was to value and enjoy what she had. They still had so little back home. She sent packages—clothing for the women and children, cloth for sewing, bandages, shaving supplies, soap, candies, chocolates, and small toys for the little ones—but they wanted more, and the latest fashions, no less. Luba needed to see that hunger, to feel that pain. Then again, Luba's pain was a mystery to Volya, untouchable. How could a child who had everything in the world be so miserable? She had never known want like Volya had, and she never would. She had a nice little apartment in Toronto, friends, a good future ahead of her—unless she did not finish her education. Even so, a person without an education, like Volya, could still make a decent living.

I support myself by cleaning houses, Volya thought. Let Marko laugh all he wants. There was no shame in honest work. Her job was not nearly as dirty as his. Sure, he made more money, he risked his life every day down in the mine. She could never do something like that. But she did okay. Most of her customers were good people with busy lives and a lot of money. It was hard work, but it was decent.

Volya tipped Marguerite's waste basket into a larger bin. What was this? A perfectly nice pair of girl's underpants, pink with white lace. Had she thrown them out by accident? As she examined them more closely, she noticed the lace was torn in one spot. It would be so easy to sew them up, she thought. Rich people were so wasteful, such a sin. How she would have loved to own a pair like these as a girl. They did not even know what nylon was back then, when plain soft cotton underwear was a luxury. She remembered the winter of 1935, when her sister Zenia and she had to share one pair of winter underpants. Luba laughed when she told her that story; she had no idea. It was certainly not funny at the time. She remembered Zenia groping through a pile of clothing in the darkness of early morning, the two girls often bickering over who got to wear the underpants on which day. She would feel each piece with quick agitation and toss it aside.

"Where are the long underwear?" she shouted from the rafters where the children slept. "Volya, are you wearing them? It is my turn today."

Volya was already downstairs, shivering under her thin coat after dumping an armload of firewood into the wood box, trying to remain unnoticed. She stood quietly by the stove to keep warm, rocking from side to side on her cold, wet feet, her back turned to her mother, who was setting a steaming loaf of rye bread and a lump of pale butter on the table. There was no place to hide in such a small house. If she closed her eyes, Volya could still see her home clearly—a sturdy beech table and four unmatched chairs in the middle, a bench carved from willow pushed against the wall beneath one of the two small west-facing windows, and a sewing machine neatly tucked beneath the opposite window. A large clay stove heated the entire house. She remembered the sensation of her Mama's eyes on her as she huddled by the stove.

"Volya, are you wearing them?" she asked, her voice stern and warm at the same time. Volya wrapped her arms more tightly around her shoulders, wishing she could squeeze herself invisible, but said nothing.

"You can wear the trousers under your skirt," her mother suggested. She patted Volya's bowed head, then ran her fingers through the girl's unkempt hair.

"Give the underwear back to your sister—you had them on Friday. And make sure you comb your mop before you go to school. I do not want you looking like an orphan." She picked up a knife and prepared to cut the cooling bread.

"Mama, I do not want to go to school. It is too cold today," Volya whimpered and put her hands back over the stove to warm them.

"Volya, we have been through this before. There is nothing for you to do here and you will only get in your father's way. Anyway, you have no choice." Volya turned to glare at her, but she knew it was no use to argue. In fact, she would rather not be in that small house when their Tato was home and much preferred to be at school where she could avoid him and his changeable moods. But she hated wearing the rough wool trousers under her skirt; they chafed her legs and they smelled like manure. The soft, white-ribbed cotton underwear was the one piece of clothing that did not rub her skin raw, that allowed her to forget who she was for a short while.

"Volya, I will not tell you twice."

Volya stomped to the ladder and climbed back into the loft where her indignant sister waited. Instead of removing the disputed clothing, she crawled back into bed with her little brother, Lubomyr. He was four years old that year.

"Mama! Volya went back to bed wearing my underwear," Zenia hollered and reached over to yank the cover off her sister.

"Mama, Zenia pulled my hair and kicked me!" Volya screamed and fell back on her startled brother. "Look what you have done, now Lubomyr is crying." She shoved Zenia and they both tumbled; the whole loft shook with their scrapping.

A wooden spoon suddenly appeared through the bright opening into their room upstairs, and a dark head followed.

"Girls, quiet down at once or you will wake Tato. He will not be in a good mood and you know what that means." They stopped immediately. A grouchy father was the last thing anyone wanted to deal with. Volya peeled off the coveted undergarment, scowling while Zenia sneered at her. Then she turned to comfort her sleepy, sniffling brother.

"There, there little dove." Volya wiped his tears with the worn sleeve of her grey wool jumper. "I will help you get dressed, then you come have some breakfast with us before we go to school. When I come home, we will play," she promised her pouting brother. His round face broke into a big smile as he threw his chubby arms around his sister. Volya was determined to help raise this boy to be someone sweet and caring. Not a bully like her older siblings, Zenia and Marko.

Walking into the modern kitchen of the Brentons' home, Volya thought about how different her life may have turned out if she'd had another child, a son. The Brentons did not know how fortunate they were with a girl and a boy. And he was a doctor, so the chances were that their children would have the best of care and would always be healthy. They could have lessons for anything they desired, wear beautiful clothing, eat the best food, enjoy summer camps and class trips to Toronto. Volya regretted she could not afford the piano lessons Luba had asked for, nor send her on school trips out of town, but Luba could never understand, or perhaps she did not wish to understand. Instead, she responded with childish tantrums, even as a teenager.

Volya opened the fridge door and surveyed the shelves. She could sniff out anything that was just starting to go off, her sense of smell keen as a ravenous lion on the trail of a fleeting gazelle. Her nose could detect the faintest essence of wilting lettuce locked up in the crisper. Today she fished out a lump of mouldy cheese, and a newly opened quart of milk, already souring. They stuffed the fridge with too many groceries, she thought, and food started to go bad well before the expiry dates. What a waste of good food and money. They probably had no idea where their milk and meat and vegetables came from, these sophisticated city people. Volya thought back to their cow back at home. They were lucky to have Kalyna; at least they had a steady supply of milk and cheese—unless Marko was the one milking her.

Volya remembered how the door would blow open then bang shut as Marko rushed inside. He was so rough and thoughtless, always barging in. He still did that as an adult. "That stupid cow!" he would say, waving his fists. "She kicked the bucket over again. I refuse to milk her any more. That is a girl's job anyway."

"You idiot. Do not complain later because there will be no cheese this week." Mama grabbed the bucket from him.

"What do I care, I am not milking that beast any more!" Marko stood over the stove to warm himself before he sat at the table. He reached for a piece of bread from a pile on the plate. Volya wanted to smack his hand as she watched from above. He was always thinking about himself first.

"Wait for the rest, Marko. We are not heathens here. And go wash your hands, first," Mama scolded. "There is warm water next to the stove."

Zenia had already gone downstairs, but Volya remained in their room above, still annoyed that she had to wear those horrid trousers. She watched as Marko stood next to Zenia by the stove. They looked like twins with their fair hair, blue-grey eyes, and willowy stature. They favoured their father, handsome and tall at six feet, not their short, plump mother. Tato used to boast that he and his two eldest had Viking warrior blood, passed down from the early invaders and first princes of Ukraine. The first-born pair had also inherited their father's temperament—easily angered, selfish, pushy, inconsiderate. All three warriors were constantly bossing her around. Volya hated being younger than Zenia and Marko; they often ganged up on her with insults and physical abuse when their mother was not watching. It did no good to complain—the two of them did not seem to respect their mother either, especially as they grew older and taller than her. The only thing that united the three older children was fear of their father, who never hesitated to hit them when they irritated him or he was out of sorts about anything at all. Of course Volya believed she was brutalized most often, and the only sympathy came from her mother who was usually helpless to intercede.

Her mother, Sylana, tried to comfort Volya however she could. When Volya complained that the other children called her a filthy Gypsy, Mama told her she also used to be teased about looking like a Gypsy when she was much younger. Then her hair was deep chestnut, and so curly it was always tangled. She said that although Gypsies had a bad reputation for being sly tricksters and stealing children, among other things, they were just different from the people who had settled in villages and cities. They tended to travel and not have permanent homes, they were clever copper smiths and traders of goods they brought from exotic places, and they were loyal to their families.

"The other children are ignorant, Volya. They do not know any better, so it is best to ignore them."

"But why do they say those things?" Volya asked, confused. "They all say the same horrible things about Gypsies."

"Because they are mimicking what they have heard from others. Repeating rumours is a sin, Volya. It is unkind and unfair. We know better." Sylana looked very sad as she stared into Volya's earnest eyes.

"But Mama, how do you know about Gypsies? I have never seen one."

Her mother sighed deeply. "I knew some Gypsies long ago, little one. They were good people. I saw how they cared for their children, how they lived. It is not the life we have chosen, but it was not a bad life. They are just people like we are, and many of them are Christians."

In spite of these talks with her mother, Volya was not totally convinced. Her mother was the only person who had ever defended the mysterious Gypsies. Her own father even cursed her as being a Gypsy, especially when he was drunk, although she never heard anyone refer to her mother that way.

About two years later Volya finally had an encounter with travelling Gypsies, and she began to understand why people sometimes feared and despised them. She and two friends were allowed to visit a caravan set up beside a neighbouring village. They were accompanied by several adults from Brinzi who were hoping to purchase a few pots and see what other useful wares the Gypsies might be selling and trading. Volya and her friends dared each other to see the fortune-teller in her gaudily decorated tent. Nadia went inside first, while Volya and Oksana awaited their turns just outside the opening. They watched a young woman who sat next to the tent sewing tiny coral beads onto a velvet headdress. The girls had never seen such fancy beads and shells, and satin ribbons in colours they had only heard about. Volya wondered if she should spend the little money she had on ribbons rather than the fortune-teller. She was apprehensive about having her fortune read anyway, and she was about to speak when a hand clamped down on her arm.

An ancient, stooped woman peered into Volya's face, with eyes sunken so deep they looked like two black coals. "Where are you from, little girl?" she asked.

"Br-Brinzi," Volya replied, trembling.

The old woman grinned and her eyes disappeared completely. She tugged on Volya's arm. "No, I think you are one of ours. Come." She tugged harder.

Volya cried, "No!" and pulled back, looking to Oksana for help.

The woman sewing beads stepped forward and put a hand on the old woman's arm. "Baba, let go. She is a visitor."

At that point Nadia and the fortune-teller emerged from the tent, and all three girls left quickly. Though Volya was badly shaken, they never told their parents what had happened for fear they might not be allowed out of the village again. Volya decided then that some of the stories she'd heard about Gypsies were probably true. Perhaps her mother had never run into the treacherous ones, the thieves and kidnappers. And when a genuine tsiganka had mistaken Volya for one of their own, she could finally understand why she was often taunted with that name.

Her mother may have been teased in her youth as well, but she had lost her Gypsy colouring on maturity. By the age of thirty-four, Sylana's dark hair was salted with white, and she wore it in braids coiled on her head. More so than Volya, Lubomyr resembled their mother with his very dark curly hair and hazel eyes. Volya's features were unique in the family; her aquiline nose, wavy black hair, and deep-brown eyes gave her a serious, brooding expression. Volya supposed she did brood—she found a lot to worry about.

"Zenia, take the pail back out and see if you can get any more milk from Kalyna," Mama said, handing her the bucket. Zenia was about to protest, then she looked up and pointed at her sister's head hanging over the edge. "Volya can do it Mama, she is the best at it."

Volya was without doubt the most skilled milk maid in their family, but Mama pointed to Zenia's legs and said, "You are wearing the warm underwear and Volya has already brought in the wood. She will milk tomorrow." Without a word, Zenia pulled on her heavy coat, grabbed the pail and shuffled out the door. As it slammed shut, a loud groan was heard from behind the curtain that separated the parents' sleeping area from the kitchen. Suddenly the room became uncomfortably quiet—please let Tato stay asleep until we go to school, Volya prayed.

When Volya walked in her own door that afternoon, she still had cleaning on her mind. "Luba?" she called. There was no answer. She looked in the living room and noticed the basket of clean laundry was still there, the ironing board set up, but no iron—just as she had left it. Her daughter moped around all day, and did not lift a finger. Volya decided to have some tea and rest a while before her show began on TV. She could not understand why young people seemed to have such a poor work ethic, especially in their own homes—so different from when she was young.

Volya had tried so hard to be a good girl, to please her own Mama when she could. From an early age, she knew that her father was unpredictable in his moods and she was afraid of him. She learned that when he was gone for a long time, which could have been one day or four, he would return in a sour humour and they all had to tread carefully around him, or, better yet, remain out of sight altogether. Volya seemed to anger him easily and most often. Tato seemed to hate her. But all the children knew what it meant when their father lost his temper, and each of them had spent many nights crying and bruised. Except for Lubomyr. Her little brother always had the most pleasant disposition; even Tato could never be annoyed or angry with him. At least, that was how she remembered it.

Mama also treated her differently from the others, but in a special way. She would give Volya small treats and favours when the others were not around. They never saw it, and Volya made sure to say nothing to them. She was grateful she had one ally in the house at least. Zenia and Marko teamed up; they were close and they treated her with contempt. They played together, and plotted and whispered together. They would try to make her run and scream by pinching or kicking her. Volya learned to stay out of their way as well as Tato's. She never really felt jealous, but often wished she had another sister so that they could be friends. Mama was the one she always looked to, the one Volya observed for any signs of what she needed, what she wanted. Volya even began to anticipate her moods. Zenia and Marko called her the "watcher," the "sly one."

Mama was a calm, quiet woman most of the time, and Volya truly wanted to be like her. She did not gossip like the other women in the village, and preferred to keep to herself and their small garden behind the house. Volya was happiest when it was just her and Mama and Lubomyr together at the house. Then her mother would hum or sing while she worked in the kitchen or garden, or while sewing and mending clothes in exchange for some money as well as food—flour, sugar, salt, meat, lard. Volya noticed that everyone who spoke to her mother did so with respect, that they treated her well and never raised their voices. She seemed to bring calm to agitated neighbours who came to complain about various ailments, their children, husbands, other people in the village and life in general. Volya wished that had she could have such an effect on others, that they would actually want to come to her for advice and comfort. Instead, she seemed to attract trouble, both at home and elsewhere.

Her mother's calm nature did not protect her from the wrath of her husband, however. Volya's father was a drunk. She flushed admitting that to herself now, though the man was long dead. Tato was a farm labourer when he was sober, and as a young child Volya could not understand why he was so popular in the village. He was filthy, irritable, and tipsy a lot of the time. And he usually reeked of alcohol, urine, manure, sour sweat, and other offensive odours she could not identify. Volya was born with her olfactory acuity, and she did not know that others did not get bombarded with scents the way she did. The other men slapped her father on the back when they saw him, called him kolega, a good man. She learned later that he operated a still and sold liquor to bring in money, hence his popularity. He was a bootlegger. A good one, too, apparently, since buyers from other towns nearby often stopped by, asking for him. His vodka was well-known in their county and beyond. Fortunately, the still was housed in a shed located in the middle of a small stand of trees about two kilometres away from their home. The Polish landlord's rent was paid in liquor. Her mother saw very little of any profits, so she never relied on him for anything. Volya admired her mother's independence, but she did not understand why Mama stayed with Tato when he was so mean to her and the children.

Volya put down her cup of tea and shuddered, recalling the first time she realized her father had hurt her mother. She was about five years old and did not know how the argument started, only that she had been sleeping in the loft and heard a crash, then a muffled scream. All three of the children were awake by then and peering down. Tato had his hands around Mama's throat, and she was trying to push him away, her mouth gaping and her eyes wild. She seemed to be gasping for air. Zenia began to cry, then Marko started shouting, "Mama! Mama!" Suddenly, Tato looked up at them, his lips drawn up over his teeth, like an animal gone berserk. At that moment, Mama somehow broke away and ran for the door. Volya remembered Tato coming towards them, shaking his fist, growling and swearing. His hands were bloody, and his face was smeared with black dirt; the devil himself was coming after them. Volya began to scream when he put his foot on the ladder leading up to the loft. Then two men burst in the door and dragged him away while he continued to struggle and bellow curses.

Shortly after, one of the neighbour women came into the house with Mama, and told the children to hush, everything was fine. They clung to each other, sniffling and watching from above while the woman washed Mama's face. The basin was dark pink with her blood. Later, Mama came upstairs to comfort them, and sang to them until they all quieted and fell asleep. Her face puffed up and turned splotchy blue with bruises, which faded to green and yellow over the next few days. Volya was certain she would die. But when she did not, and the beatings were repeated, Volya began to grasp that this was a pattern they had to get used to and endure.

Years later, when Volya asked her mother why she stayed with Tato, Mama explained that God did not allow a wife to leave her husband, that they were good Catholics. Besides, they needed a house to live in and Mama could not afford a roof of her own. It made sense to Volya at the time, but it also made her sad. And guilty. She often felt it was her fault that Tato beat Mama, but she did not know why she should think that way.

Volya poured herself another cup of tea and switched on the TV. Her favourite afternoon show was just starting as she settled herself on the sofa. Yesterday it ended with a phone call from Simon, Gloria's long-lost, supposedly deceased, father. Her mother had told Gloria that Simon had died in a car crash in Italy when she was just a little girl, but Gloria had always suspected her father was still alive, somewhere. She had looked for the death certificate and had even made inquiries in Italy on the sly; her mother's explanations always seemed suspicious to Gloria. Now her wedding day was approaching and she dreamed about the father she recalled from her childhood, about walking down the church aisle with him.

There he was now, on screen, Simon, clean-cut, chiselled features, greying hair. All those actors were such beautiful, handsome people. Volya thought about Yarko, also long gone but truly dead. There would be no miraculous phone call from beyond for them. He was not quite as handsome as those Hollywood types, but still a good-looking man. He adored Luba, and she him. Volya was grateful that he was such a shutterbug and had taken all those photos of their small family. Only a shame there were so few of him. He was a rare man, to have been so devoted to her and Luba, so kind, so thoughtful. There were very few things she did not like about him—rare indeed. She had only known one man before him who approached those qualities. She did not think of Yarko often, but when she did she realized that she missed him, his gentle, open spirit. Perhaps if he were still in their lives, he could have kept Luba from drifting off, from becoming so combative and contrary. He would have managed to keep the peace between them, somehow. Perhaps he could have prevented Luba from slipping into that dreadful place, the unhappiness that still seemed to consume her. No matter how she tried to help Luba, to guide her, all her suggestions were rebuffed. She only wanted Luba to be happy, but that girl was so stubborn. She was miserable now, but she would have to learn to deal with her sadness. We all have to, Volya thought.

Ah, there was Crystal, Gloria's mother. Coiffed, blond hair piled on her head; probably two cans of hair spray to make it all stay in place like that. An ice queen, that woman. No wonder Gloria did not trust her—she was always scheming. But then Crystal had her own sorrows: the child she gave up years ago, the cruel stepfather, the wealthy mother who disowned her. And the baby that died, that would have been unbearable.

Nearly losing your only child was torture enough, Volya had discovered. Luba had no idea how much pain she had caused, how the thought of losing her had made Volya question what her own life was worth without her daughter. But Luba would not talk to her, not about anything serious. She was a master at deflecting attention from her own problems. On the bus, Volya nearly choked when Luba asked about Boryslav. To Luba, Volya's childhood experiences were just stories, like the dramas on TV. She had humoured her daughter then, selecting particular events, avoiding the most painful ones. She could play Luba's game. To say the words out loud was to dwell on and relive the past, and certain memories were best left locked inside.

The year 1935 was the one Volya remembered most clearly. She was nine years old, and the memories were as vivid as the characters whose lives unwound on the TV in front of her. She recalled the time she fell asleep by the stream, and some of the other children had painted her cow black with mud. She wanted so much to cry, but she heard the snickers from behind a rock wall and she knew those hateful children were watching her. Volya bit her lower lip hard, picked up a switch, and whacked the backside of the muddy cow. "Go on, Kalyna, go on!" she hissed at the confused animal. The cow swung her head in Volya's direction, letting out a pathetic bellow, and, like a pack of raucous crows, the hiding children shrieked and guffawed. Volya still remembered how angry she was, how she picked up a fist-sized rock and was about to heave it at the cow, but then made herself stop. Kalyna had done nothing wrong; it was those awful children. She raced after them.

"I will get you. Just wait until I catch you miserable brats!" she yelled and heard noises of scrambling as the threatened mischief-makers dispersed. She hurled the rock as hard as she could when the last two came around the corner, and managed to hit a boy as he scurried by. He screeched like a wounded cat, but Volya took little notice and headed for home, the cow obediently following her. Back at the stream behind the pasture, Volya tried her best to wash off the tar-stubborn black clay. Like two soggy ghosts, girl and cow were both still dripping and stained grey when they arrived home for milking. And, like a ghost, Volya slipped into the house with the full milk bucket. Fortunately, Mama was busy at the stove and minding Lubomyr, so she did not notice her daughter's sorry state. Zenia made a disgusted face, pale with flour, when she looked up from kneading bread dough. But she said nothing as her sister plunked down the frothy milk bucket and ran back outside.

Volya tried to clean herself up beside the well, although she knew there was no chance her clothes would be dry before supper. It was a warm spring day, however, so she scrambled squirrel-sure up to the thatched roof of the small barn where Kalyna stood below, udder relieved, safely tethered and chewing hay. She was sorry now for hitting the cow. Her temper had gotten the better of her again. On the roof which gently sloped toward the western sun, Volya lay spread-eagled and prayed that the clouds would not move in. No one ever bothered to look for her up there. She was just another lazy barn fly soaking up the last heat of the dying day, and as Volya's eyes took in the empty blue space in front of her, she imagined herself falling into the sky, leaving the filth and heaviness of the earth behind. Those children were mean, and had no idea how much their pranks could get her into trouble. Volya closed her eyes, dizzy with thoughts spinning out of control. She felt herself floating, like she could fly, set free of everything that had ever held her down.

No one commented on Volya's appearance at the supper table. Tato was not back from the village, but they did not wait for him; they never knew when he might be home. Mama had stopped looking for him during his frequent absences. But, just as they were finishing their meal, Tato burst into the house, yelling, "Where is she?" The children all jumped up from the table and, as if blown before a foul wind, scattered into the corners of the room. Lubomyr burst into tears, then hid his face in Volya's damp skirt. Volya shook so hard she was afraid she would pee her pants.

"What is the problem, Boryslav?" Mama stood up slowly and faced the angry, red-faced man. His grimy undershirt was unbuttoned half-way down his chest, one suspender hanging off his shoulder. He stepped toward Mama, waving a white fist, tripped, and caught his balance on the table. His lurch sent a bowl of partially eaten soup off the edge. It smashed when it landed, leaving a gash of bleeding borsch on the floor. Seething, Tato grabbed the table edge with both hands, then swung his head around slowly, a python scanning for its prey. His watery blue gaze locked on Volya.

She could feel the blood draining from her face as she tightened her hold on Lubomyr. Tato raised his arm and pointed at Volya who continued to tremble in the corner. "You have brought shame on this household, on my good name!"

"What are you talking about, Boryslav?" Mama demanded, her voice shaking slightly.

"That miserable daughter of ours threw a sharp stone at Myron's little boy. Now he has a huge cut in his leg." Volya gasped. Could it be true? Tato often exaggerated, even told untruths—the alcohol confused him. But she had thrown a rock and hit a boy. "Are you going to deny it?" he shouted, and started toward her.

"Boryslav, I want to know all the details—" but before she could stop him, Tato grabbed Volya's arm and began to drag her toward the door. "Stop! What are you doing, where are you going?" His free arm swung out and caught Mama full in the face. She staggered backward from the blow, her mouth bleeding. Little Lubomyr began to howl again as Mama wiped her mouth then followed them out the door, her fists clenched. But her bravery soon faded. She would not meet Volya's eyes as she stood there, a silent witness, while Tato began beating his youngest daughter. Volya wailed for leniency, but her father responded by hitting harder. Feeling doubly wounded, she watched her paralyzed mother through her tears, a rigid form bathed in the dull red reflection of a dead sun.

The Cynic and the Hypocrite

The pews of St. Peter's Ukrainian Catholic church were as uncomfortable as ever. Hard cold slabs of wood, joined at an angle unnatural for the human body. Sitting near the back of the church, just under the choir loft, Luba shivered inside her light coat. Her mother was upstairs with the rest of the choir, a few feet closer to Heaven, preparing to sing the Easter Mass. Coming to church today was unavoidable, but Luba had still dragged her feet until her mother burst out at her in exasperation. They had definitely returned to their normal, combative relationship. Luba stifled a yawn. She didn't appreciate being in a cold, drafty, unhappy room full of strangers when she could be wrapped up in a warm quilt in her own bed. Next to her, people were quietly shuffling in, sliding into pews, and kneeling on prayer benches. Luba hoped her mother didn't notice that she had skipped the praying part. What was the point? She already felt like a hypocrite just showing up in church. If there was a God, he already knew where she stood. No doubt the congregation had its share of other impressionists and actors trying to convince the world of their pious nature. Luba only needed to convince one person, though she wasn't putting much energy into her act this morning.

Luba tried to keep from looking around, from meeting anyone's glances. She didn't want to talk to any of these people. Most of them weren't even her mother's friends, just curious to know what Luba had been doing. Like why was she back in town when the semester wasn't over yet? Her mother had already told a few people that her daughter had pneumonia, but Luba was tempted to tell someone the truth. Anybody. Maybe to be mean, maybe to embarrass her mother, or maybe just to talk about it. Volya had not brought it up, had not asked her about it. Her mother was obviously ashamed of her and what she had done, and how it reflected on herself as a parent.

Luba always wished she could be spontaneously sassy like Janice in her psychology class. Janice had been married for two years when an aunt asked her when she was going to have a baby. In the middle of a family reunion, in front of several elderly relatives, Janice answered, eyes wide and innocent, "Well, we tried sex once, but didn't like it." No one ever asked her that question again.

Oh Christ, was that Mary Bebiuk with the three little kids? God, she looked old. And tired. She used to be in Orest's class, Luba remembered, and he had a crush on her in high school. Trying not to look too obvious, but sizing him up, Luba settled on the fact that she didn't recognize Mary's husband. Must be an import, she thought or, heaven forbid, an Anglo or French Canadian. He looked very placid and dull. Good father material, she supposed.

Finally Luba's pew filled with people she didn't know, and she was grateful. She checked her watch. Nearly eight o'clock. Let's get this show on the road, folks, she muttered under her breath, then quickly crossed herself as the person next to her glanced her way. She didn't know why she should bother trying to blend in when all these rituals meant nothing to her. In fact, she had decided long ago that the church was not benign, that it harboured a sinister hierarchy.

Luba's earliest recollections of church and God were frightening ones. Her catechism classes were taught by nuns with joyless faces, tight inside their black-and-white armour. The most terrifying experience came when a priest asked her a question during class one Saturday morning. She stood up, but before she could answer, he roared out at her, "Sit down you Godless child! I should excommunicate you for such impudence!" Giggles all around her. Luba began to tremble and looked at her classmates for clues to what she had done that was so awful. The usual troublemakers gawked at her with awe, others were shocked. None dared speak to her until after class, when they informed her that she had stuck her tongue out at the priest. Horrified, Luba realized that she must have licked her lips, something she often did when she was anxious.

The idea that she could be excommunicated from the church for a nervous tic added another crack to the crumbling foundation of Luba's religious beliefs. At the tender age of seven she decided that God's messengers were often fallible, bad-tempered men and women who lacked good judgement. How could they accuse her of something she had not done? Why were they so mean to Stephen who couldn't help stuttering? He wasn't being cheeky; he was scared shitless. They all were. She couldn't trust anything they said after all that. Because the church meant so much to her mother, she carried this burden in silence as long as she lived under the same roof, and played along with all of the rituals as best she could. In the confession booth Luba made up sins that seemed appropriate to other kids her age; she sure as hell wasn't going to tell some untrustworthy man she hardly knew any intimate details of her life. So the layers of guilt grew once she realized she repeatedly committed the sin of lying during confession—how twisted was that? At least her mother didn't insist that she go to confession this Easter Sunday, even if Luba had attempted to commit a mortal sin. Thou shalt not kill. Thou shalt not talk about it.

The large ornately carved and painted oak doors at the front of the church swung open, finally, and the entire congregation arose as two priests stepped forward, each holding a large cross next to his heart. As their tenor descant began, Luba drifted off. The ancient Slavonic chants of the Easter Matins were as strange to her ears as ever, yet oddly hypnotic. She pictured a quiet, shadowy place, lined with cold slabs of stone, shafts of light from small openings in the wall high overhead; a monastery she had visited with a friend who was studying early church music. Grace, a music major, had talked her into going one spring weekend last year to this secluded religious community near Georgian Bay. Luba sat at the back of the chapel, a cave scooped out of natural limestone, and listened to the peculiar melodies and unusual harmonies while Grace recorded the music and took notes. For all the apparent monotony of the notes, it soothed and calmed her. It was just before final exams, she remembered; she had met Tom not long before, and she had been arguing with her mother about not coming home for the summer. She was sorry to leave the monastery that day, and yet agitated that she had felt so comfortable in a churchy setting, like a wayward rabbit enjoying shelter in the entrance of a coyote den. She got out in time, but she wouldn't have minded going back. The peace, the solitude, the haunting songs beckoned her. What she wouldn't have given to be there now, all by herself with just the chants and solemn chanters for company.

Her somnolence was interrupted when the air above her suddenly filled with a melodic blend of many voices. She felt sonic waves wash over her, and the hair on the back of her neck and head prickled as if she was now surrounded by ghosts who had risen from the cemetery next door. The sensation flowed over her scalp, onto her forehead and into her eyes, a warm, burning feeling that caused her eyes to tear. Where the hell did that come from? Luba blinked hard, reached for a handkerchief to catch the drip from her nose as the harmonics continued overhead.

Then the phrases she did understand returned, as did the tedium of the mass: "Hrystos voskres eez mertvih, smertyu smert podolav"—Christ has risen from death, he has defeated death. Once again, she felt small, insignificant. This place seemed to have some kind of hold over her. She was taught that Jesus died to give all sinners a second chance. So, was this her second chance? Had she died once already? Or did trying to die not count? Or was suicide the ultimate unforgivable sin? Luba looked around her; she wasn't convinced she wanted to be saved. The opening songburst came to an abrupt end, a priest mumbled, everyone sat down. Sheep, they were a flock of brain-dead sheep, Luba thought, not a one thinking for him or herself.

At long last, the communion had begun. Only minutes to go now. It seemed everyone in the church was lining up in front of the two priests, a parade of ants, two by two, to collect their reward and scurry back to their spots to await a magical transformation. Now Luba could watch them, see who was here, who she recognized, what they were wearing. After all, they went out and bought new Easter outfits just for this big day. Luba smirked; most of these people were just like her, or worse. While their hands were folded over their hearts to make it look sincere, Luba knew a lot of them went to confession and communion once a year, at the Easter service. And as the choir sang on, angels in the loft, the Christians emptied their souls of evil and filled up with Jesus, all the while knowing they would sin before the end of the day in spite of their best intentions. How pathetic. Just like the priests hiding in their rich satin robes, waving fancy goblets of mock flesh and blood in the air.

It was the hypocrisy Luba couldn't stand. For instance, Father Buchkovsky had a reputation for being a ladies' man. He hired only young, attractive housekeepers, always single, preferably new immigrants who were grateful for any job. He talked to women's boobs, not to their faces. He was an average man. Human. So why would anyone ever confess anything to him? As for her mother, Luba had little respect for people who blindly accepted all these church rules, treated the priests as gods, then broke the rules themselves. She could count on her mother to gossip, be critical or yell at her before the sun set. But then, her mother was human. At least Aunt Veronica acted like a true Christian.

Volya sinned even before they were off the sacred property. She caught up to Luba on the stairs as they headed down for the blessing of the food baskets.

"I saw you from upstairs," she hissed at Luba. "You cannot believe how embarrassed I was. Mrs. Polchuk saw you, too, and Mr. Kravchuk. How could you do this to me?"

"What are you talking about? I just sat there. I didn't do anything." Luba was confused by the sudden attack.

"That is exactly what I mean. You did not kneel down and pray. You did not kneel down at all. You did not even cross yourself! Why did you even bother coming to church? I am so embarrassed!" She was turning purple, stifling her rage as they walked down the last steps into the basement.

"You are the one who wanted me to come to church. I don't kneel. My knees get sore and I lose circulation in my legs. And I did cross myself."

"What nonsense! Old ladies with arthritis can kneel. God help you. What am I going to do with you?" Her hands flew up in despair.

"Just leave me be, Mama. I have my own faith. All these rituals are meaningless and silly." The words flew out of her mouth before she could stop herself, but luckily someone had spotted her.

"Luba! Is that you? How are you my dear?" Mrs. Polchuk put her arm around Luba's shoulders. She never thought she'd be happy to see this gossiping old peahen. Volya pasted on a strained smile and the two women chatted as Luba slipped over to Veronica and Marko. Veronica patted her hand as the priest chanted and sprinkled the food with holy water. Everyone else remained silent and reverent.

Back outside in the morning sunshine, her uncle bellowed, "Come on, we'll give you a ride home." Volya and Luba climbed into the back seat of the big blue Chevrolet, tense and quiet.

"The choir was perfect today!" Veronica told them, twisting around in the front seat with breathy effort.

Volya scowled. "Not perfect at all. Did you not hear old Slavko when he went flat? The director was so mad. It ruined that song."

"You are too critical, Volya," her brother admonished. "You all sang beautifully. All those rehearsals paid off."

"Yeah, Mama, I thought it was wonderful. It's always my favourite part of the Easter service. You guys sound like professionals."

"So, we sing better than the Toronto church choir?" She looked at her daughter with narrowed eyes.

"Not better, just as good, though."

"When did you ever hear them?" she challenged. "You never go to church, how would you know?"

"Well I did hear them, and I have been in that church," Luba retorted.

"Just once, I suppose?" Volya's face was a dark storm.

"Just because I don't go to mass every Sunday doesn't mean that I'm a bad person."

"It is a mortal sin."

"You mean it's worse than being judgmental, talking behind people's backs, gossiping, criticizing? What ever happened to the Golden Rule—do unto others as you would have them do unto you? Unless I'm mistaken, that's written in your Bible."

"You have a lot of nerve quoting from the Bible when you are not a good Christian yourself!" her mother spat, her lips quivering. "Do not preach to me! What you did to yourself was against God's laws and you should be ashamed and repentant. You have no respect for your family. You have no respect for your own body. You are a thoughtless, godless child. What have I ever done to deserve such treatment?"

Luba began to shake. She couldn't believe her mother brought up the subject they'd both been avoiding, and voicing it in front of her aunt and uncle.

"Volya!" Veronica twisted around again. "It is Easter Sunday. Please stop picking on Luba, for heaven's sake. Are you coming to our house for lunch? You may as well come with us now, no point in going home and sending Marko for you later."

No one spoke for a moment.

"Luba, darling, put on the shawl I have back there, you look pale. Volya, do not say another word—you are making the child ill. Marko, they are coming straight to our house. Turn here."

Dear Aunt Veronica, Luba thought. The one good thing Uncle Marko ever did was to marry her.

"That was a long phone call." Volya's eyes were suspicious slits, her lips turned down. "You talked nearly an hour. Who was that?"

Luba looked up from where she sat on the couch by the phone, closed her Redbook Magazine, and sighed deeply. Her mother had been in a foul mood since they had returned home from her aunt and uncle's place. Luba had recovered from the fight, or at least put on the appearance that she didn't care; she was out of practice since she'd been away from home. And for the first time since she'd been home, Luba yearned for a drink: vodka, rye, rum, anything. But of course there wasn't a drop of booze in her mother's home. The woman who had suffered the brutality of an alcoholic father could not tolerate the stuff anywhere near her, or people who drank, even socially. So for now Luba tried to remain calm because her mother would always find fault in her no matter what she did, and there was no point in sulking.

"If you were timing me, you were listening to the conversation, so you must know who I was talking to," she said in an even voice.

"I am just asking you a simple question. Why do you have to be so rude to me? I am your mother; I can ask you anything I want to. And I can listen while you are talking on the phone in my house. But I was not listening—I have better things to do!"

Luba didn't reply. She knew a sarcastic rejoinder would escalate into another shouting match, and she didn't have the stomach for it. Her mother was always, unequivocally right and she was wrong. Luba reopened the magazine and pretended to read.

"So, who were you talking to?"

"Will Buchler. You probably don't remember him," she muttered.

"Of course I remember him. You think my memory is so bad I would forget the boy who took you to your graduation dance? That was only three years ago. I do not understand why you choose the boyfriends you do."

"What are you talking about? First of all, Will was not a boyfriend. He was a friend. He still is my friend. And what's wrong with him anyway?"

"He is German," she stated with undisguised contempt and turned to leave the room.

"So? What's wrong with being German?" Another of her mother's endearing traits, Luba thought, her prejudice against nearly every racial and religious group outside her own.

Volya wheeled around, hands on her hips, and marched back into the living room. "Have you forgotten already, what the Germans did to us during the war?" She seemed truly angry as she plunked herself into the sofa chair opposite Luba and leaned toward her daughter, her face a grey cloud about to burst with hailstones and lightning.

"I know what the Nazis did during the war. But that has nothing to do with Will, or his family. Why would you hate Will because of what the Nazis did? That's ridiculous! It was decades ago."

"How do you know that his family was not involved in the Gestapo, or the SS, or being collaborators? Have you ever asked him or his parents?"

"No, I haven't asked. It's not the kind of thing one asks over dinner. 'Oh, hey Will, did your parents ever murder anyone? You know, during the war.' Why would I ask them something like that? I don't even know his parents all that well."

"You see what I mean? You don't know. I know what the Germans are like. It was not just the Nazis who were cruel and vicious to foreigners, and to their own people. I can tell you some horrible things about German civilians, too."

"So maybe they did awful things during the war. That was then, that was the war. What does that have to do with Germans today, Germans in Canada? The next generation of Germans? And what about the Jews? You hate them, too. What did they ever do to you? Look at how many were slaughtered in concentration camps. Why do you hate so much? I don't understand it."

"No, you do not understand. You will never understand. You did not have to live through the Nazi occupation or through the war. Young people today will never understand us. You just have to believe us because we were there. We saw it, we lived it!"

"If understanding means accepting your hatred of people you don't even know, then I'll remain ignorant, thank you very much. What you don't understand is that I have friends who are German, Jewish, Black, Chinese, Protestants, and Buddhists, and they are decent people. And you know what? They don't hate me or each other because of the colour of our skin or the sound of our names or the churches we do or don't go to. They have no interest in starting another war. Hating each other isn't going to save us. You're being stupid!"

Volya was silent for a moment, her lips stretched tight across her face. "You are never to call me stupid. I am your mother. You will learn, one day, you and your friends. I just hope it will not be too late for you, that all our suffering was for nothing." She heaved herself out of her chair and left the room.

Luba sat there, like she usually did after an argument—choking on dirt, not allowed a final word. She bit her lower lip, felt the burning behind her eyes, and knew that tears would not come. She could not cry in her mother's house. Not a tear had been shed since she was fourteen. She remembered the feeling then of being so desperate to go on a school trip to Toronto, but so terrified to ask her mother. When her mother said they could not afford it, that those poorly supervised so-called field trips to the Royal Ontario Museum were just an excuse for wild teenage parties, Luba lost it. She had slammed the bedroom door shut and sobbed into her pillow for hours, trying to block out the sound of her mother laughing in the hallway. Laughing at her misery! Laughing at her weakness, at the power to make Luba cry. What a silly girl she was, her mother had taunted her, to cry over a thing of no consequence. She could still hear her mother's heartless chuckles, dismissing her tears. Never again, Luba swore.

Stifling her tears was not that difficult to do. Volya could make her daughter angry, frustrated, disgusted, but she could not make her cry. Luba was the one who had power over that now. Luba knew that it was she who could make her mother's life miserable if she wanted to. Volya had certainly taught her daughter well, a fine role model, indeed. Volya Kassim had better watch that she didn't push too hard.

Endings and Beginnings

From where she sat on the south-end bus, Luba got a good view of the old town. Shabby and dingy were the words that came to mind. The snow was nearly all melted, except for the dirty rust-tinged piles along several streets, like garbage that had been kicked out of the way. Nothing changes here, Luba thought. The same restaurants: Mae's Diner on the corner of Elm and Linn with the familiar faded green-and-white striped awning out front, and Canton Palace capped by the fake red-and-umber pagoda above the darkened windows. The bus chugged up a steep hill, past a series of narrow, crowded houses, smaller than her mother's, all clinging to the side of the ravine like a mangy old cat, claws dug into the rock. Tiny neglected front yards were either overgrown with withered weeds or paved over with concrete; missing roof shingles exposed the black tar paper beneath. Every house was a shade of beige or pink, finished in brick, stucco, or vinyl siding weathered like the spine of a long-dead beast, picked clean and worn to a bony roughness. It could have been a ghost town, Luba thought, not a soul to be seen in that neighbourhood.

She had managed to avoid leaving the house for the last few days and only went out for church and to visit her Auntie; she didn't want to talk to anyone who might recognize her. Her best high school friends had all left Copper Creek as soon as they could, just like she did, dispersed all over the country and further. There was no one left in town she wanted to communicate with, even if she did feel like talking. Then that damned hospital psychiatrist telephoned from Toronto. No, it was his secretary or receptionist, some underling. The doctor wouldn't be making such a menial call to ask which counsellor she was seeing. A mandatory follow-up after a suicide attempt, she'd said. Nosey annoyances, the whole lot of them, her mother included. Luba didn't feel like anything was her own here, not even her time. So there she sat, trapped yet again on a leaky old bus, nauseated by diesel fumes as the bus clanged and grumbled and wound through the streets. Everything was second-rate in this place.

What could this psychologist possibly tell Luba that she didn't know about herself already? She'd studied psychology—the one class she got an A in last term. She may have actually enjoyed a career in the thing, being able finally to slot her mother and various other relatives and friends into their appropriate categories of neurosis. But she'd have to be returning to school for that to happen, which she was not.

Luba stepped off the bus at the Uptown Pharmacy. Jesus, such an original name, she thought, dragging her feet along the sidewalk into the building. Amidst a list of names covered by a smudged sheet of glass, she read Bella Davies, MS, Psych, SW, second floor. That was a lot of letters next to her name. Great. She was going to be a real charmer. Searching for the office, Luba imagined Dr. Davies—a short grey-haired woman with black cat's-eye glasses and a heavy German accent. She'd ask about daddies and dreams and decide all Luba needed was a hug and a penis. She pushed a buzzer next to the name on the second floor.

"Good morning—Luba?" A tall young woman with straight, shoulder-length blond hair offered her hand to Luba. The receptionist, probably.

"Yes."

"I'm Bella Davies. Won't you come in, please?" Luba hesitated a moment, not quite believing this elegant woman was who she said she was. Then she stepped into what looked like an ordinary living room except for a desk at the far left. There was a sofa covered in a dark green velvety material and a couple of matching easy chairs facing it, but no stark cold leather. Bella Davies, MS, Psych waved her arm at the furniture. "Please sit anywhere you'd like."

Aha, Luba's first decision. She wondered if her choice would give the psychologist some critical information about her. But Luba couldn't make up her mind. She felt like she'd walked into a Hollywood movie set and a camera was following her every move, and Bella was an airline hostess, not a shrink.

"If you're not sure, you might find the sofa a bit more comfortable. But it doesn't really matter." She smiled at Luba and sat down herself. Luba had no idea how to read this woman. Choosing the sofa, she stared at Bella, who wore a dark brown pantsuit with shiny pin stripes, and a collarless gold blouse underneath. It accentuated her long, graceful neck. There was a smooth gold pin on her right lapel, shaped like a flying bird. Her eyes had a golden hue, and Luba couldn't help but wonder if this woman bled golden blood. She looked like something you should lock away in a safe. As Bella glanced down at a notepad on her lap, her gold button earrings flashed. She finally looked up, still smiling.

"I'd like to begin by asking you to please call me Bella. I like to be as informal as you are comfortable with. Is that all right with you?"

Luba nodded but said nothing.

"So, Luba, how did you feel about coming here today?" she looked directly at Luba, more serious now.

"I didn't want to come."

"Honest answer, I like that. Do you feel perhaps like you were forced to come?"

"I was."

"It's protocol. Since a psychiatrist referred you to counselling, your medical records were forwarded to me, and I have reviewed them. I know a little about you, so perhaps you may want to know about me, what kind of therapy I practice, and in particular what I usually do in cases such as yours."

"I guess so."

"You can ask questions anytime, and you can decide if you think this therapy program might be useful to you. How does that sound?"

"Fine."

"So, ask away."

"How long have you been doing this?"

She smiled. "Six years now. I graduated from Queen's University in 1972 with a Master's degree in clinical psychology and went right into practice in Toronto. I moved up here a year ago."

"Why? This place is a dump." Luba couldn't believe anyone would voluntarily leave Toronto to live in a hole like Copper Creek.

"I'm from Timmins originally."

"Oh well, that's a large metropolis compared to this place. My friends and I used to call our little hamlet the Abyss of the North. And not just because it's a mining town."

"I don't mind Copper Creek. And I really enjoy my work here."

"Maybe you need the shrink."

Bella laughed. "What about you, Luba? How did you find Toronto?"

"I miss it."

"Why?"

Luba sighed. "You know—the clubs, the theatres, art shows. Civilization." Luba stopped and looked down at her hands. She was twisting an embroidered handkerchief her mother had made for her. She used it to blow her nose on occasion, even though she knew her mother would be appalled, or perhaps because she knew that. Such a simple act, but so empowering.

"Any good friends there? Maybe from school?"

"A few, I guess." Luba stopped again. She hadn't thought about anyone from Toronto since she came back home—except for him of course. She didn't know why.

"Do you find it upsetting to talk about your friends?"

Luba shrugged, not looking at Bella. She didn't say anything for a while. When she finally raised her head, she thought Bella looked sad, her hands resting on her lap. She noticed her fingers were long, like her legs and neck, and she wore a simple gold ring on the middle finger of her right hand. Luba could picture Bella pirouetting in a ballet of Swan Lake. Luba began re-twisting her snotty handkerchief.

"Have any of your friends called since you returned to Copper Creek?"

"Nope."

Her eyebrows curved up in a question mark.

"I asked them not to call," Luba explained

"Any particular reason why?"

"I don't know. I guess I didn't want to talk about what happened."

"What about your boyfriend?"

Luba looked up. "Ex."

"Sorry."

"Look, I don't know where he is and I don't care." Luba's handkerchief untwisted as she ripped it out of her left hand. She stuffed it into her right pants pocket.

"You look like you care."

Luba reddened. "I don't."

"Do you feel betrayed by him?"

"I don't feel anything about him." Luba crossed her arms over her chest. She could feel her heart racing beneath her arms and a flush rising up her neck again. Why couldn't they leave him out of this?

"You sound angry, Luba. Which is perfectly understandable, considering what happened to you," she added.

Luba looked at her with narrowed eyes.

"Nothing happened to me. I happened to myself."

"I see. But I understand you thought you might be pregnant at one point. Is that right?"

"If you already know all this stuff, why bother asking?"

"I'm just trying to get some things straight."

"Great."

"But you are defensive."

"Sorry, I'm just tired."

"No apologies here. Back to it. How did you feel when you thought you might be pregnant?" she asked in a voice so soft and low, Luba could barely hear her.

"Fantastic. What do you think?" she mumbled.

"I don't know."

"I didn't want to be pregnant. It was a mistake. Tom was high. I was drinking and passed out. I don't remember what happened after that. The next morning I woke up in Pete's bed, alone and naked."

"So, you don't remember having sex?"

"Nope."

"And did Tom explain what happened?"

"Not really. They'd been smoking joints for a while before I got there, and god knows what else they had taken earlier. Tom says he passed out on the couch, but I figured he just forgot to use a condom."

Luba couldn't believe she was talking about that night. She hadn't told anyone about it.

"So, that's when you thought you got pregnant?"

"It was the only time it could have happened. But Tom had the nerve to say he never slept with me that night. He just couldn't remember. It was a really great night all around."

"Who is Pete?"

"He plays bass guitar in my cousin's band. He's a moron. Pete told me he slept with me that night, but I know he's a liar. He just said that to piss me off because he knows I hate him."

"Is it at all possible?"

"It's bullshit, okay?" Luba was furious, picturing his taunting, laughing face with the stupid goatee.

"Okay."

"Sorry, again."

Bella smiled. "What did Tom say when you told him you might be pregnant?"

Luba felt her throat constrict. "Not much at first, but he sure wasn't too thrilled. We'd only been going out a few months, we were serious, kind of. Me more than him." Luba choked up, remembering the look on his face, as if he were disgusted with her, as if she had played a cruel trick on him. "So he asked me what I planned to do. I said I didn't know."

"What did you want him to say?"

Luba pulled the handkerchief out of her pocket for another round of twisting. "I was confused. I just wanted him to be supportive, to be concerned. I didn't want him to propose to me or anything like that. I started to think I could have this baby, if he was willing to help out. I wasn't doing so well at school at that point, my grades were awful, I'd been thinking about quitting anyway. I just wasn't happy in the pre-med program, I didn't belong there."

"And what did he say to you?"

"Abortion. That was it, one word. So then I broke down, I just lost it. And I guess I got to him, and he backed off and said if I really wanted to have this baby, I should, it was up to me and he'd help out." Luba paused and looked up at Bella's quiet, thoughtful face.

"Go on."

"Then I get this note from him saying he can't go through with it. He's too young, and anyway, it's not his baby. That asshole." The handkerchief and her hands had become a blur in her lap. Bella had put a box of tissues next to her on the sofa. How mortifying—crying in front of a stranger.

Bella waited for a while before she resumed.

"So, what happens next for you? Tom is out. And there is no baby."

Luba sniffled. She was relieved that Bella didn't mention the pills or her time in the hospital.

"Dunno. Next topic, please."

"Fair enough. Do you want to stay in Copper Creek?"

"Definitely not!" Luba grabbed another tissue, then dropped it and smoothed out her handkerchief, folded it once, and blew hard into it. Bella smiled.

"Is that Russian embroidery on the hanky?"

"No, Ukrainian. You know, Ukrainians hate to be mixed up with Russians, or Poles, or any of those other Slavic nationalities. My mother would have a fit."

"Sorry."

"No, no, it's okay. The explanation is just a habit of mine. My mother actually embroidered this for me, but I'm not supposed to use it. Crazy, huh?"

"Do you also embroider?"

"Uh-uh. Watercolour, acrylic painting, some sculpting, yes, but not the traditional crafts so much. Anyway, my mother's given me all the embroidery I'll ever want. I don't know what I'll do with all of it." Luba didn't expect to ever own enough furniture to display it all. And most of it was too gaudy for her tastes, anyway.

"So it's just you and your mother in your immediate family?"

Luba nodded.

"And did you participate in your Ukrainian community when you were growing up? Folk dances, church?"

"Oh yeah, the whole works. I was forced." They told her what to do, and she did it to keep the peace. Peace equalled miserable Luba. War equalled miserable Luba. Irrational math, skewed curves.

"Any other family members here in Copper Creek?"

"My aunt and uncle, my mother's brother, live here, but all their kids, my cousins, have left. Some of them live in Toronto. And my other aunt, my mother's sister who she doesn't get along with, and her family and my grandmother also live in Toronto. But we're not very close. I mean with the Toronto relatives."

"I understand you were eight years old when your father died. Do you remember him very well?"

"Not really. He was away a lot, working on the big ships. My mother used to explain that he was sailing all around the world. She'd show me the postcards he sent and read them to me when I was little. She never seemed to worry about him being away on those long trips, sometimes months at a time, so I didn't either." When he was home for his short visits, Luba recalled the wonderful gifts he brought back from exotic lands: delicate fans from Japan, tiny dolls from Africa and China, a boomerang which her mother had to remove after Luba smashed some of her knick-knacks by accident. She would never forget that awful scene. But her favourite gift was a paint-by-number set. After that he always brought her art supplies, when he saw how much she loved to draw and paint. She was forever grateful to him for noticing that about her.

"He was thoughtful and kind and he made me laugh. He made my mother laugh, too, and that's not easy to do." Luba could picture him doing handstands on a beach, and falling over like a clown, wiggling his toes. And her mother actually laughing until tears came streaking down her red cheeks. It was a happy day in a fuzzy past.

"Your mother sounds like a serious person. Does she have a sense of humour?"

"Maybe in a sick sort of way." She hadn't laughed at all since Luba had been home.

"What about you?"

"I guess so. But there's not much to laugh about right now."

What a thing to ask, Luba thought, after Bella had just made her cry.

"Well, Luba, I think we have a goal for you to work towards. You've probably been told countless times that you are a talented young lady with a bright future ahead of you. And here you are, in a town you dislike, unhappy with your situation, and not much to laugh about." She paused and smiled ever so slightly.

"So it looks as though we have something to work on, don't you think?"

"I guess." Luba was not completely sure where she was heading with this line.

"That's great. Is this a good time for you to come back next week?" Bella stood up and walked toward her desk, scribbled something down, and handed Luba a piece of paper.

"You want me to come back?"

"You don't have to come back to see me, but you'll need to see someone in counselling."

Luba nodded her head. "Okay, then."

Bella smiled, her gold eyes and earrings flashing in unison, as Luba stood up and followed her to the door. "See you Friday, Luba."

Luba stepped out of the building and had to squint in the sudden glare of sunlight. She was not quite sure what had just happened in there, but she was coming back for another round in a week and, oddly, she was already looking forward to it.

A few days later the Tatenko family received terrible news from Toronto— Orest was dead.

"I cannot believe this is happening to our family. First you, then Orest. A-ya-yay!" Volya sat hunched over in her favourite chair in the living room, bowed head in her hands. Luba couldn't tell if she was crying or not. She'd been in that state since the dreaded phone call, alternating between tears and rage. Orest had been found by one of his band mates in a Windsor motel room, dead of an apparent drug overdose the morning after a successful show. Aunt Veronica had collapsed when Uncle Marko first told her and was in the hospital for a day, and still on sedatives four days later. He had not stopped drinking in all that time and was impossible to deal with. Anatolia had come up from Toronto and Zachary was arriving the next day to look after their grieving parents. Luba was also surprised—not at Orest's demise, but at how little it all bothered her. She was half-tempted to pay Uncle Marko a visit, have a drink or two with him. She'd been dry ever since she'd left Toronto; it hadn't been easy. But she knew there was no way to disguise it from her mother who could detect alcohol off a person's skin twenty-four hours after they'd stopped drinking. A freakin' bloodhound, that woman.

Through all this drama, the television was always on; tonight it was The

Love Boat. Luba switched it off.

"What are you doing?"

Luba had never seen her mother's face so distorted, her eyes were red and dry.

"You're not watching it. Why have it running twenty-four hours a day? It's really irritating." Luba stood beside the set, staring down at her mother.

"I will tell you what is irritating—you are irritating. Turn it back on."

"I'm going out. I can't stand all the noise around here." Luba started to walk out of the room.

"Fine, go!" As Luba walked past, Volya grabbed her arm. "Where are you going? Not to Veronica's?"

"Of course not!" Luba jerked her arm free. As much as she might have wanted to be with her aunt, to comfort her, she also could not bear to face her and talk about Orest. First the police had asked her a few questions, wanting to rule out foul play, she supposed. Then her uncle went at her. Where did she see him, who were his friends, did he take drugs? She told him as little as she could, hating to think that Aunt Veronica would learn the truth about her son. Orest never meant to hurt anyone, she was sure of that—especially not his mother. Why, she thought, did she have the misfortune of being the last relative to have seen Orest alive? And why did she have to be here when this happened?

"So where are you going?" Volya repeated.

"To see Will Buchler and his German family. Maybe I can ask them where they were and what they were up to during the Second World War."

"You think you are so smart!"

"Oh, I don't know. After all that questioning by the police, I think I have a pretty good idea what the Gestapo were like."

"Don't be stupid! They need to find out how Orest died. Somebody probably killed him—some drug addict." She slumped back in her chair. Suddenly she looked old to Luba.

"I'm telling you, it was probably an accidental drug overdose," Luba told her.

"I cannot believe Orest took drugs. Did you see him taking drugs?"

"Mama, like I told the police, the crowd he hung out with was into drugs. Amphetamines, alcohol, cocaine, other stuff, I'm sure. Anytime I saw him, he was tripped out."

Her mother gave Luba an impatient look. "On drugs, Mama. He took meth to stay awake for his late-night gigs. I guess once you get hooked on it, it's hard to get off. You guys have to face up to it—Orest was a junkie. I'm sorry.

That's just the way it was."

"Why did you not tell us? We could have helped him!"

"Oh yeah, what were you going to do, drag him back here to dry him out? The guy was twenty-six years old. He was an adult. Plus, Uncle Bohdan might have known something was going on. I mean, Orest worked for him."

"He would have told Veronica and Marko—he would have done something to help. They knew nothing about any drugs. They never said anything to me. He is my nephew. He was my nephew. Poor Orest. How could something like this happen to such a nice boy?"

"Look at our entire family. There are tons of addicts. Wasn't your father an alcoholic? And look at Uncle Marko. I bet it's genetic."

As soon as the words slipped out, Luba realized she might have gone too far. But her mother just looked dejected.

"Your uncle Marko has had a hard life, Luba. We should not judge him so much. But I cannot understand why Orest turned out liked this. All his brothers and sisters are doing just fine. Most of them are married and have children and good lives. What happened to Orest? Oh, the poor boy."

Luba slipped outside quietly while Volya sat absorbed in misery. She didn't have any answers for her mother. In fact, she had questions of her own. In spite of the fact that she rarely saw him in the past six months, she liked Orest well enough. He invited her out a lot when she first moved to Toronto, introduced her to all sorts of interesting people, mostly musicians. They treated her like his kid sister and most of them were fun and seemed like decent, caring people. Except for Pete. He was a pig from the start. Orest had been very protective, though, and he didn't let Pete get away with any of his usual misogynistic crap. She, however, was having a hard time feeling sad about his death. What the hell was wrong with her?

Orest acted tough, but he wasn't. He had rescued a scrawny orange kitten he found eating out of a dumpster near a construction site where he worked. One back leg was hanging limp—it was badly broken, crushed—and Orest brought him to a nearby veterinary clinic where they had to amputate the limb. But he paid for the expensive surgery and had the cat neutered a short while later. Stumpy they called him. She could still picture Orest cuddling the cat to his stubbly jaw.

Luba didn't know when he started taking meth to stay awake. Maybe he was already hooked when she first moved down there. She had tried it once, before a midterm exam she wasn't ready for. Tom got it for her. It did the trick, but she felt terribly depressed for the next two days. She made up her mind never to use it again. The last time Luba saw him, Orest was down, deathly pale and shaky, starved. It wouldn't have taken much to push him over the edge. She understood how easy that was for the willing. But, unlike Luba, he wasn't getting a second chance. At least he didn't have to struggle any more.

Luba hoped someone kind and dependable was taking care of Stumpy.

An Ally

Luba stood in front of Bella Davies' door and wondered what they were going to talk about today. And what she'd be wearing. She looked down at her worn jeans, bagging out at the knees, the navy V-necked sweater pulled over an olive cotton shirt. She'd found the sweater and shirt at an army surplus store in Toronto. Tom said the green turned her eyes to hazel, though she wasn't sure it did much for her skin tone. Now, standing in front of the door, she felt her heart racing, her face flushed. Moments before she had kind of been looking forward to this second visit, probably because of what was going on at home, or at least that's what she told herself.

"Come on in, Luba," Bella smiled brightly, tilting her head so her golden hair spread in a perfect fan over her right shoulder. She wore a black silk blouse and loose black pants with a large gold chain belt wrapped around her hips. A finer chain of gold links circled her slender neck. She waved her hand toward the chairs and Luba chose the sofa again.

"So," Bella started as she sat across from her, "how did the week go for you?"

"It's been crazy. My cousin Orest died last weekend." Luba watched Bella's face for a reaction. Bella leaned back in her chair, her expression sombre.

"What happened?"

"They say it was a drug overdose, maybe a suicide."

Bella's eyes rested on Luba's.

"Suicide?"

Luba looked away.

"And what do you think about that theory?"

"I don't think he did it on purpose. He was hooked on meth."

"I see."

"His mother is such a wonderful, kind person. She's just a wreck right now.

I mean, I can hardly believe it all myself. Orest was in a great little band, he had tons going for him. I think my aunt will need some counselling," Luba finished, breathless.

"I'm so sorry to hear this, Luba. Were you close to your cousin?"

"Not really. I mean, he left town when I was only thirteen and we didn't hang around together. I got to know him a little after I moved to Toronto for school. He was a pretty decent guy. The problem is that I was the last of our family to see him alive, so I'm kind of the living monument right now. They all want answers from me."

"So your family is upset, but you're not?" Bella's face showed no expression as she twisted the bottom of her gold chain with her hand.

"Well, yeah, it's upsetting, I guess. I mean, it was a shock to hear about Orest dying, but it doesn't affect me really. Is that bad or something?" It was bad—Luba knew it was. She'd been fond of Orest. She should have felt worse than she did.

"No, Luba, I'm not making a judgement here."

"But?"

Bella shook her head. "But... it's just that sometimes when we're overwhelmed with feelings we become numb. We cut ourselves off from everything. It's a protective mechanism—it's very common. I just want you to be aware of it. Eventually those feelings have a way of catching up to us, often when we're least expecting them."

"I don't know, Bella. I can tell you that I have not been numb this week. My mom and I haven't stopped fighting since I got here. We may kill each other yet. Numbness would be welcome."

"What is the main issue with her?"

"Do you have five years? She's so critical! I can't take a breath without being told I'm doing it all wrong. And when she's not lecturing me, she goes on and on about the old days when she was a kid. It's depressing. Then there's my poor aunt hanging around and she's so distressed, it makes me upset to be around her. I've kind of been avoiding her, actually. I feel guilty every time they look at me, like I was responsible for Orest's death."

Bella leaned forward, elbows on her knees. "What do you mean?"

"My mom says I should've told them that Orest was taking drugs. I know it wouldn't have helped. He wouldn't listen to any of them, anyway. But I didn't say anything, so..." She shrugged. "I just couldn't rat him out. Our family is too nuts. What could they do?"

"And you're feeling guilty because you are not feeling much of anything about his death?"

Luba looked at Bella then. She was good. "Well, I guess I'm also pissed off that his family didn't know their own kid. Orest had problems—they could've tried harder to reach him. Been more supportive early on, I dunno. But then I feel selfish. Maybe I should've done something, said something to him. Poor Aunt Veronica."

Luba was picturing Aunt Veronica's eyes, shiny and hard with tears, boring through her as she gripped Luba's shoulders. "Where did you see him the last time? What did he say? What did you talk about? What are his friends like?" Luba felt so cold inside; her aunt was a strange desperate woman shaking a rag doll, trying to squeeze out a few drops of bloody information, and Luba couldn't help, or wouldn't. An odd sensation, as if Luba wasn't in her own body. She had to force herself to speak, to tell her aunt that she knew nothing, that she was sorry and wished she had called him more often. Veronica let go and her head drooped. "No, it was not up to you to look after him. That was my job. I have lost him, lost him. It is all my fault." Her body convulsed as she collapsed into the nearest chair. Luba stood there, unable to move, to offer comfort.

"Will you go to the funeral?" Bella asked

"Yeah, I'll have to. I hate funerals."

"Have you been to many?"

"First one was my dad's, which I can hardly remember and really didn't understand what was going on. I was so used to him being gone, it only hit me much later when I realized he was never coming home again. That was sad and awful, but in a muted sort of way. I was ten years old, I think, for the next funeral. I came home from school one day and my mother was crying because a close family friend had just been killed in a car accident. I knew the man, but not all that well. I remember sitting at church with a bunch of other girls my age and they were all crying. I felt really bad that I wasn't crying, too, so I forced myself. But when we went outside, all the adults were telling us not to cry. It made me crazy; I was so confused. I hate funerals."

Then another thought struck Luba. "And all my cousins will be there. They'll probably grill me, too, and want to know what I'm up to. Christ."

She looked over Bella's shoulder and realized there were lace curtains in the window and a tree outside that was just starting to bud. It blocked the view of the downtown, so it was easy to forget where she was. Luba could just make out a chickadee flitting from branch to branch. She would have given anything to be that bird right then, and not some screwed-up depressive maniac trying to pretend that her cousin's suspected suicide didn't remind her every minute of her own failed attempt. Then she remembered the bird flying into the window, its limp, broken body in front of her. She'd forgotten to check on it, to see if it had really died. The bird marks a death, her mother would say.

Bella brought her back.

"What will you say to your cousins if they ask you about school?" She looked directly at Luba.

Luba examined the orange seam on the front pocket of her jeans. It was beginning to unravel. "It's my business. I'll probably lie though. I'll just tell them I decided to change programs at school, but I don't know which one I'll apply for yet."

"And do you have an idea of a program you'd be interested in?"

"I don't plan to go back to school, not for a while anyway." Luba noticed her hands had become fists in her lap and her knuckles were white. She opened her hands and spread her sweaty fingers, wiping them on her jeans. Somehow, her mother would have to get used to the idea that she would never be a doctor, or even a nurse.

"Do you think if you had an alternate plan instead of school it would satisfy your family?"

"Nope. They want me to finish university, get a high-paying job, marry a nice, rich Ukrainian guy, have a bunch of kids, go to church, and then I'll be a success."

"And how would you define success for yourself, Luba?"

"Not turning into my mother for starters. Not living in Copper Creek. Not being married with five kids. Not being poor. I dunno."

Bella leaned forward and smiled. Luba stared at her then and realized that Bella's eyes were actually green-gold. She had never seen this colour before. She was mesmerized.

"Luba, I'd like to give you a homework assignment for our next meeting. I'd like you to think hard about some positive images of what you'd like to be. They don't have to be practical. Try to identify people you admire, figure out what it is you like about them, whether it's their lifestyle, the clothes they wear, the way they talk, the talents they have, their character qualities. Write it all down."

Luba shook her head. "It's going to be a busy week with all the cousins coming and the funeral."

"Try," Bella said. Her voice was firm, her eyes encouraging.

Luba felt foolish. "Okay."

"I don't think it will be an easy assignment for you, but it might be fun." She smiled at her then.

Luba made a grimace and shrugged. She'd rather be solving calculus equations than working on a life plan. Nothing she'd tried so far had worked, and neither would this psycho crap. Miss Bella Perfect couldn't possibly understand how difficult this would be for Luba, especially now with her entire family about to close in on her. It would take time and emotional energy to prepare a story to satisfy their curious, prying minds. And then stick to it.

"Look Veronica, there is no problem. When Zenia and Bohdan get here they can have Luba's room, and Luba can move downstairs to the rec room. Greg will be staying at the Starlight Motel—that was his choice—and no one will be in the way. Besides, you do not need Zenia meddling with everything over there. So, did the flowers for the church arrive yet?"

Meddling, Luba thought, overhearing the loud, one-sided conversation. How ironic that her mother, the biggest meddler of all time, was accusing anyone of meddling when they hadn't arrived yet. Volya was practically melded to the phone receiver with all her helpful interferences.

So, her long-gone Aunt Zenia and Uncle Bohdan were coming all the way to the northern wasteland from the great metropolis of Toronto. And their son, Greg, but not the other two boys. Luba didn't know any of them well. She knew Greg the best, perhaps, because he was the only one of her Toronto cousins who had ever taken any interest in her when she and her mother had lived there. Thinking back to those years, it was amazing he had: he was about ten years older than she was. She remembered being shy around him, a tall, blond guy with twinkly grey-blue eyes, so handsome and funny. He used to tickle Luba to get her laughing. He even took her to a couple of movies when she was around eleven or twelve, just before she and her mother left Toronto for Copper Creek. The Day of the Triffids was the sci-fi thriller she remembered. Greg had laughed all the way through the movie, but Luba was totally creeped out and couldn't sleep for two nights afterwards. Later she felt proud she'd seen it because it was a campy, low-budget film. Not exactly film noir, but on its way to becoming a cult classic. Last fall Orest told her that Greg, who'd been out west for a few years, had returned to Toronto with a girlfriend. So much for the rumours about him being gay. For some reason, this disappointed Luba. She rather liked the idea of another maverick sheep in her family flock. Apparently Greg and his woman had bought a big house together and were living in sin—that would be her mother's assessment, and probably Aunt Zenia's, too. Well, good for Greg. Not everyone had to get married and start popping out kids. There were too many people on the planet already.

And no one would ever see Orest marry, either. Luba still couldn't grasp that Orest was gone forever. She tried to imagine what it might like to be dead, or what it might have been like if it was her they were making all the arrangements for. No doubt her mother would be terribly upset, at least at first. She'd be dramatic about it, wailing, calling people on the phone, crying all the time, soaking up the sympathy. And how long would that phase last, Luba wondered. Her mother had to be in control, and by now she'd be ordering everyone around as they prepared for the funeral. At the moment, she seemed downright cheerful, but perhaps she wouldn't be as enthusiastic if it was Luba in the casket. Then again, who could know for sure. There would be no one for Volya to nag and harass. She'd probably be as miserable as Aunt Veronica. Poor Auntie, constantly leaking tears. Luba didn't know what to say to her aunt any more. Every time Aunt Veronica cried, Luba was sick to her stomach—she couldn't bear to see her aunt in such agony. It was so unfair. As for Uncle Marko, he hadn't been sober since Orest died, leaving Veronica to do everything in that family, which included nursing a disgusting drunkard.

Luba remembered going to a wake in Toronto for a friend's step-dad. It was more like a party. Singing and eating, drinking and toking up, and even dancing. An all-night full-out binge. Not much wailing and grieving going on, but Luba had too much to drink to remember those details. Karen hardly knew her step-dad and she partied along with everyone else. Her mom cried a bit, but not for long. Mostly they talked about the good times, which led to more stories that didn't have anything to do with the recently deceased. It was a hoot. Luba didn't suppose their dour Ukrainian culture could be persuaded to celebrate death that way. Custom required dark attire and morose spirits.

She thought briefly about the assignment Bella had given her. Positive thoughts, positive thoughts. You couldn't force positive thoughts. Luba liked to wallow in the negative. Why not, she thought? It was a family tradition.

"Luba, did you finish the downstairs bathroom?" Volya suddenly appeared in the door of the living room, waving a dust rag in one hand and gripping a can of furniture polish in the other. "Why are you reading magazines? There is a house to clean. Our guests could arrive any minute!"

The page Luba had been staring at came back into focus. An ad for lacy black underwear, worn by long-legged, voluptuous models. She slapped the

Cosmopolitan shut, her hands sweaty. "Mama, this house never gets dirty. Anyway, I finished the bathroom over an hour ago, and I vacuumed the rec room. Check it out."

"I will," Volya promised and marched off. Luba heard her stomp downstairs to do the inspection. Volya was a compulsive cleaner, a neatnik beyond anything Luba had ever heard of. Volya would have done well in the army, she thought.

Luba heard a door slam outside and got up to see who had arrived. She didn't recognize the sleek silver car parked in their driveway. She heard her mother's pitched voice.

"Greg? Are you here already? So nice to see you again, come in, come in. You must excuse me, the house is a mess. We have not finished our preparations for all the visitors. Come in, come in, you must be tired. Such a long drive from Toronto. Have your parents left already, no? Have you been to see your aunt and uncle, already? Are you hungry?"

Luba heard a muffled reply, a short laugh, and footsteps up to the kitchen door. She got up to greet the first of the onslaught.

Greg filled the doorway—Luba had forgotten how tall and solid he was. But he looked the same as she remembered him. And his smile was just as sunny. He even had her mother beaming, a nearly impossible feat.

"Hello, little cousin," he finally said in the same playful way that Luba recalled from years ago.

Luba laughed. "Not so little, eh? I'm a few inches taller than the last time you saw me." Greg chuckled, reached over and tousled her hair like he used to do.

"Hey!" she protested.

"Step inside, Greg. No, leave your shoes on, such beautiful shoes. Luba, get out of the way so he can come inside. I will get some lunch ready." Volya literally shoved Greg into the kitchen and toward the table.

"Oh, no thanks, Aunt Volya, I ate about an hour ago, at one of those famous roadside truck stops. Nothing for me, okay? You go ahead, though. I'll just sit with you if you don't mind." His Ukrainian was flawless when he addressed her mother—much better than hers. Greg planted himself on a kitchen chair looking very much like he belonged, like a neighbour used to stopping in for tea every day.

"Some coffee, then? Tea?" Volya persisted. "I just baked some nice, light krusty. All air, no calories." With her hands on her broad hips, she gave a gusty laugh at her own joke.

"Yeah, Mama, those little babies are fried, not baked, then coated with icing sugar."

Volya gave her a cross look, so Luba added, "They are tasty little suckers, though. You have to have at least one, Greg. It would be rude not to." She winked at her cousin.

"You cannot force people to eat like that, Luba," Volya admonished.

Moments later, Greg and Luba were stuffing their mouths with moist cabbage rolls dripping tomato sauce, and plump potato-cheese perohy smothered in sour cream. They both groaned and held their stomachs as Volya sliced more garlic kobassa, piling up their plates again, but she didn't stop until the two of them, as one, stood up and took their plates to the sink.

Back at the table, Greg leaned over to Luba and whispered in English as if conspiring, "I've been sitting in a car all day. Why don't we go for a walk in the fresh air?"

Luba wanted to avoid a one-on-one with any of the cousins, but the idea of leaving the house and her frantic mother appealed to her. Volya's back was turned to them, already up to her elbows in soap suds. No way were guests from Toronto allowed to help with the dishes.

It was still cool in early May, even on a sunny afternoon. They headed toward a neighbouring subdivision filled with older, smaller homes. Most of them glittered with blue-grey or pearl-coloured stucco, but there was the odd brick house, and one or two drab wood-shingled bungalows. The sun shone too weakly to brighten up the pallid afternoon colours. But it was heartening to see new grass already trying to push up through the dead brown carpets on the front lawns. Luba couldn't help but inhale deeply when she smelled growing things in the air all around her. She felt her chest cavity stretch and expand, then collapse again. She threw her head up toward the sun and closed her eyes briefly to feel the transient heat through her eyelids. It felt surprisingly good at that moment.

"How are things?"

She was jolted back.

"Okay, I guess. How about you? I mean, the news about Orest must have been quite a shock." Luba glanced at him obliquely. His head was down, watching the cracks in the sidewalk as they ambled along.

"Yeah, it was a shock, especially for my dad. I don't think my parents had a clue about Orest's private life."

He hugged himself as they crossed a quiet street. No traffic, no children to be seen during this early weekday afternoon.

"You saw him a couple of times this past winter, didn't you?" he asked.

"Yeah, a couple of times. Didn't talk for very long, though," she added, so he didn't interrogate her, too.

"So, you saw what he looked like. I mean, he wasn't well. Not exactly sick, but unhealthy-looking. He was over at my parents' house one day when I stopped in. Couple of months ago. I hadn't seen him in years."

"I figure he didn't get much sleep or good food," Luba offered. "He looked tired, and pale. Like me after cramming for exams." Why did she have to say that? The last thing she wanted was to talk about herself.

"He was more than tired, Luba." Greg looked at her with a strange expression.

"Well yeah, he OD'd didn't he? He was always on something when I saw him," she said, but Greg didn't react.

"I see a lot of kids on drugs in my family law practice. It's really, really sad, but after a while, you start to see patterns. Certain types of people, certain types of families seem to have the most problems with chemical addiction. And that includes alcohol. It doesn't just happen to the poor or disadvantaged. I used to be shocked at how much of this stuff was going on in the wealthy families, too. Maybe worse." He paused, seemed slightly breathless. This sounded like a well-rehearsed speech. Luba had a suspicion about where he was headed.

"You know, Greg, you must be tired after all that driving. We can go back." She slowed down, but his hand on her forearm made her shiver.

"I feel just fine, cuz, unless you're tired?" He looked at her questioningly.

"I'm all right. Don't worry about me. I'm fine," she answered in what she hoped was a definitive tone.

He seemed to accept the message and nodded. "Good. I really wanted to talk to you."

"Okay."

"Did you know that I drew up a genealogy chart for our family last year? I figured I'd have it printed out for everyone and give it to them at Christmas this year. But with Orest dying, I don't think it would be such a good idea any more."

Luba nodded her head in agreement. She heard him catch his breath.

"And to think we almost lost you, too."

There, he'd said it.

"I wish I'd called you, but I didn't even know you were in Toronto until a short while ago. I should have known, tried to keep in touch with you." Greg's voice cracked and he put his arm around Luba's shoulders. At the same time, the sidewalk cracks blurred in front of her. Damn! How did he know? She felt guilty all over again, but she would not apologize to him for something she did to herself.

"Sorry, Greg, I really don't want to talk about this, okay?" she muttered, head down.

"No, I'm sorry that you felt so bad and so alone. I do know that feeling, believe me. No one should have to feel so bad. Anyway, I'll drop it, but I just wanted to tell you that you can talk to me anytime. I mean any time at all." He squeezed her shoulders then dropped his arm. "Okay?"

Luba nodded. "Okay." She wondered if her eyes were as red as his. She couldn't believe that Greg was crying over her. Perhaps it was Orest's death affecting him as well.

"Sometimes it's hard to keep my work life out of my family life," he said. "I come here and see my aunts trying to take care of everyone like we were all still helpless children. I suppose I can't stop being a family advocate-slash-social worker and they can't stop being mothers."

"I wish they'd try."

He laughed. "Don't hold your breath. Anyway, I had a lot of time to think about things in the past few years, and especially about my family. And patterns I see in families that I work with. Grandfather Boryslav was an alcoholic, so are two of his children, and I believe both my brothers are as well. Unfortunately, Orest got into different chemicals, the kind that killed him quickly. Then again, maybe he was luckier."

Luba pulled her head up to the sun again and wiped a sleeve across her eyes. "So, you think maybe I have a problem like that, too?" She didn't look at him.

"I'm not saying that, Luba. I really don't know you since you've grown up and left home. I guess I was pretty upset when I heard what happened to you, I had no idea.... You know, hearing about you and then learning that Orest was... gone. I kind of expected Orest would go in a violent sort of way. But you, you were so quiet, so serious, the A student, so sure of what you wanted—"

"You mean, so sure of what my mother wanted."

Luba kicked at a small chunk of loose concrete near the curb, then stepped off to walk down the street to her mother's house.

"No one knows me anymore."

"Does that mean that nobody will ever know Luba Kassim?" he asked in a lighter tone.

"Depends on who's lookin' to know."

They both laughed.

"You know, Luba, Aunt Veronica thinks of you and me as her other children. She's gonna need us right now."

"Yeah, I know. I love her, too. I once asked her to adopt me, you know. I think she was mortified."

"She probably was," Greg chuckled. "And flattered, I'll bet."

"And you know what else? I believe my mother would love to adopt you, the way you can put food away. Oh yeah, she'd put meat on those scrawny ribs of yours." Luba reached over to pinch him, payback for all the tickling of years past.

"Hey!" Greg gave her a little shove and they spontaneously broke into a run, two leggy colts racing back to her mother's corral.

The Girl Who Brought Death

"Is this the street up here, Aunt Volya?" Greg asked.

"Yes, put your blinker on, turn right here," Volya instructed him, sitting in the front passenger seat, clutching her everyday brown vinyl handbag. The Wilsons' house was at the end of a long street at the edge of town, a sprawling bungalow, one of Volya's easier cleaning jobs.

That morning she awoke to find Luba up already and puttering about in the kitchen. Luba never got up before Volya, but there she was, preparing breakfast for herself and Greg. Volya had insisted he come over and not pay for that awful restaurant food. She knew what went on in some of those kitchens; she had worked in several over the years.

"So what are you two planning today?" she asked them.

"Oh, just driving around. I want to show Greg my high school, some of the old hangouts. Then we're going to see if Aunt Veronica needs anything."

"Make yourself useful over there, Luba. You can offer to help her clean the house, for instance. Or make some sandwiches." Luba would never think to do such things on her own, she thought.

"Mama! Of course I'll offer to help, stop treating me like a little kid."

"If you acted more like a responsible adult, I would not have to keep reminding you. Left at the next street. Greg, slow down!" Volya braced her arms against the dashboard as Greg braked and the car came to a gentle stop.

"There you go, Auntie. Just call us and we'll pick you up when you're ready to come home, okay?"

"If you are sure it is no trouble. But if Aunt Veronica needs you there, I can get home by bus. Thank you, Greg."

Volya watched them drive off before she turned toward the house. Greg was a thoughtful young man, and she hoped some of that rubbed off on Luba. She wondered about the girl he was living with. Zenia most likely disapproved of her, but Volya believed there was more to it than the two of them simply living in sin. Her sister was much too hush-hush about it all; she had always refused to discuss anything to do with Greg's personal life, and, in fact, rarely mentioned him at all. Volya had heard the rumours about him, and whether they were true or not, she felt she could not judge him given the mothering he'd had to endure.

Anyway, since Greg had arrived, Volya noticed that Luba seemed more cheerful, more open. She was still broody when her cousin was not with her, but at least she had finally seen Luba smile. How strange that a funeral brought laughter to her daughter. Of course, she did not dare suggest that Luba should be morose—she'd had enough of Luba's sour moods and long silences. Still, Volya could not tell if Luba was upset by Orest's death. Most of the time she seemed more angry than sad. Perhaps it reminded Luba of what had happened to her just a few weeks ago, but Volya would have expected her to be frightened more than anything else. Maybe Luba was afraid, and that made her angry. Or perhaps she felt guilty that she had lived and Orest had not. What a horrible thought. How could Volya even think such a thing?

Then again, they had all been infused with guilt at an early age. The church taught that all babies were born with Adam and Eve's original sin, that the blemish had to be washed away in a watery ceremony. Sometimes Volya felt that guilt ruled her entire life, that she was born with an extra dose of it. She was physically bathed in guilt before birth, suspended in a poisoned womb. Why else had Tato hated her so much while Mama always made excuses for her, tried to protect her? Of all her siblings, she had been marked from the start, despised, rejected, then partnered with a dumb cow who had been her solace and her friend. Had Mama known this? Volya never particularly cared for animals, but Kalyna's company was always preferable to Zenia, Marko, and Tato's. And they had all been only too happy to leave the cow's care to Volya.

She still remembered the spring of 1935 when the time came to breed Kalyna. Volya's father insisted on accompanying her and the cow to the farm with a bull, something he had never done before. Nor had she ever been alone with him for any length of time, and the thought of it made her highly anxious. She had already left their cow at Vasyl Petrushko's farm, but the usual stud bull had gone lame, and Petrushko suggested that his customers take their cattle to Eugene Barinov, five kilometres further north. Volya's father was furious when he heard the news, sitting on his usual tree stump chair behind the shed of one of his drinking friends. He already resented Petrushko for turning him down for a lucrative building project on his big, fancy farm; he became incensed when he heard that the man had called him a derelict swill-belly and a wastrel. Boryslav fumed; just because the man had been educated in Poland and was a wealthy landowner, it did not give him the right to judge and insult honest, hard-working people from the village. It was already late afternoon when news about the lame bull reached him, but he decided they must leave immediately to fetch the cow and take her to Barinov's farm.

"Where is she? Get the girl ready, we're going now!" he shouted at the family as he charged through the door. Zenia, who was washing dishes, jumped up, arms dripping soapy water and ran outside, calling Volya's name. Volya had seen her father stumbling home and had hidden in the barn. She waited with Zenia, just outside the partially opened door, trembling and wondering what she had done wrong this time.

They heard their mother plead, "Boryslav, do not be unreasonable. It is late, it will be dark by the time you get there."

"No, we have to go now or that damned cow will never be bred! Where is that girl?" he lurched around the house, as if to flush Volya out of hiding.

Mama quietly pulled a large heel of bread out of a wooden box, then wrapped a square of white cheese in brown paper. She placed these along with two small apples into a canvas sack, folded the excess cloth over, and tied a string around the bundle, leaving a loop for a handle. Boryslav, growling like a ravenous bear, yanked the door wide open. Volya could feel her sister shrink behind her.

"There you are!" Tato spit on her as he spoke. "We're taking the cow to Barinov's. Right now!" Volya shook under his loud voice. Mama handed her the parcel of food and gently turned her around.

"If you need to spend the night, Mrs. Barinov may have some room at the back of her house. They have a big house and they are good people. You behave now." She patted the back of Volya's head and gave her a warning look—she must not aggravate Tato.

It was darker than the inside of a heifer when they arrived at the Petrushko farm. Volya so longed to be invited into the warm, cheery-looking house as she stumbled up to their porch. Her feet burned with blisters from wearing shoes that no longer fit. Tato, who always carried a half-litre bottle tucked into his belt, had been drinking since they left home. As the vodka disappeared into his belly, the steady stream of curses grew to a torrent. He strode up to the door of the Petrushko house and slammed his hand flat against it.

"Petrushko, you come out here!" he demanded. Volya hung back, shivering, tucking her hands under her rough woollen sweater.

The door opened and Volya saw the silhouette of the farmer as he stood nose to nose with Tato. Vasyl Petrushko, who perched on his sill six inches above the porch, was that much shorter than Tato, but he was a heavier man and as muscular as his bull. He feared no one.

"Tatenko! What are you doing here at this late hour? Is something wrong?" He seemed genuinely surprised.

"I'm here for my cow. We're taking her to Barinov's this very moment!" He stepped back and tottered. Petrushko grabbed his shoulder to steady him.

"I think you should go home and come back in the morning. It is far too late to be driving a cow. You will get lost in the dark. Go home and sober up before you go running across the country. You might end up in Lviv, ha, ha!" His huge voice filled the great outdoors and bounced back from the trees which seemed to laugh with him. Volya could hear his wife's tinkling laughter from inside the house.

Tato broke away from the farmer, muttering. "Where is she? I'm taking her now."

"Suit yourself, Tatenko. She is in the far pasture, behind the barn. Do you want a lantern?"

"No." Tato stumbled off.

"Stay out of the front field. The bull is in there and he is in a foul mood," he warned and waved to Volya. "Is that you, young Volya Boryslava? You know where she is. You can show him, but watch yourself out there," he added, shaking his head as he shut the door.

Volya started toward the barn, slowly, unsure of her footing in the darkness. The night sky was clear and the moon, a mere sliver, was just rising above the trees to the east. She heard Tato cursing as he tripped not far ahead of her.

"Where are you, you little brat? Show me the way!" he commanded. Volya hurried a little, but kept her distance all the same, always fearing the swat of a hand attached to those long, careless ape arms of his. Tato continued to shuffle forward toward the barn.

He grunted, "Here's the gate," and she heard him fumbling to untie it.

Volya froze where she stood. She opened her mouth to say, No, not that gate, but the words stuck in her throat. She remembered staring into the blackness, paralyzed, as the gate scraped open along the ground.

"Kalyna!" Tato shouted, as if she would respond to him like one of his children. "Where are you, you cursed beast?"

"No, Tato, she is not there," a whispery voice finally escaped from Volya's dry throat. "The bull..." A faint snort erupted from the darkness, then a low moan, like a distant fog horn. The earth rumbled slightly, followed by the sound of a gust of wind pushing leaves across the pasture. Then another, louder snort and a bellow blasted through the air. Volya heard a heavy thud to her left, then felt warm liquid splatter her face. She thought she had been killed; all became silent.

Her Tato, Boryslav Tatenko, was only thirty-four years old when he died that May night. Most of the villagers of Brinzi mourned him; even some of his distant customers attended the funeral. Mama wore her black with quiet, relieved dignity. But to everyone's surprise, it was Volya who was most affected. She refused to join in any singing games at school, nor did she linger to talk to her friends when classes were done. She rushed home to do chores that awaited her, she stopped complaining about work, she did not even mind when Zenia and Marko teased or insulted her. When Lubomyr cried, she no longer comforted him, and when he cried harder, she refused to hear him at all. She became deaf to everything outside herself.

It wasn't until some months later that Volya became herself again. During a lesson when their school teacher, Miss Pawluch, discussed the origin and meaning of their names, a great weight was finally lifted and Volya's haze began to clear. She remembered running home that day, picking up her little brother, and waltzing around the yard with him. He was delighted to have his beloved sister back.

"Do you know what my name means, Lubomyr?" she asked her giggling brother.

He shook his head, curly locks flying.

"Freedom. It means freedom. Is that not the most marvellous word? And you are my precious love dove, Lubomyr. Luba, lubov, that is love, love of mine. What a lovely boy. What a sweet brother, Lubomyr."

Volya could feel Mama's eyes on her through the window. She imagined that Mama was sewing, and had stopped to bow her head and cross herself.

"Thanks be to God," she would have said, wiping her eyes and picking up her embroidery again—a table runner for the church, with three blood red roses in each corner.

Volya pressed the start button on the dryer then walked into the kitchen to retrieve her cup of tea. Even cleaning women were allowed a break after three hours of non-stop stooping and scrubbing and straightening. What was it that Greg had called her—a domestic engineer? She had immediately pictured a train operator wearing a chef's hat and apron over a striped shirt. Greg was a well-educated lawyer, but from time to time he said the oddest things. She settled herself at the kitchen table and grasped the tea mug with both hands. In front of her, on the freshly wiped-down wall, the month of May stared back: a calendar spring scene, cheerful with a bright palette of flowers sprinkled throughout a well-kept fancy garden. Even this life-affirming vision could not dispel the darkness that had gripped Volya's mind that day. Death, she mused, has always been part of the great cycle. We are born, we live, sometimes only for a short time, then we die. What a waste. Or was death a blessing? There had to be something better after all the suffering.

Volya did not regret her father's death, though at the time she felt responsible for it. She knew he was a horrible man and his drunkenness killed him, not his nine-year-old daughter. And she did not believe anyone could have cured him, dried him out as they now said, made him a gentle and loving father and husband. Though he did not harry Marko and Zenia like he did her, she could not recall any show of affection toward them either, unless he did so in her absence. No, if he was capable of being kind to them, he would have used such blatant discrimination to torment her further. He was simply a totally self-centred man. But still, she had not screamed for him to stop. When she was feeling really awful, blaming herself for having failed everyone who had counted on her, she thought she may have willed him into the pen, into the horns of the bull.

Perhaps, if her father lived today, here in this country, he could have been treated for addiction. She did not know. It seemed to her that once an alcoholic, always an alcoholic. Look at Marko. If she was Veronica, she would have left him long ago, no matter what the church said. Marko was like their father in so many ways, but he was not abusive—well, not physically, anyway.

Alcohol and drugs. Orest was taken from them; Zenia was surely an alcoholic as well—she and Marko were still so alike. She wondered about Zenia's son, Bill, and maybe even Adam, carrying on that sad family tradition. With Volya's acute sense of smell she could always tell when they were drinking, no matter the occasion, at church or home or chance meetings. Thank god she did not inherit those tendencies. Perhaps this was due to her olfactory sensitivity; the mere whiff of alcohol turned Volya's stomach, and she kept no liquor in her home. She hoped Luba did not drink—she had never seen her drunk. And the sleeping pills, surely that had to be an accident.

Sometimes Volya wondered about her little brother Lubomyr. He had been such a joyful child, he would never need to drink or take drugs to be happy. She longed desperately for him, wished she could speak to him now. Volya was sure he would understand her, not judge her like Marko and Zenia did, like her daughter did. And with such disdain, too. No, he would be fair and he would listen patiently and sympathize. He already had those qualities as a child. He was not selfish like his older siblings, but was always prepared to give, to share, to love with abandon. The only person who ever totally adored her, and yet she, his big sister, his protector, had betrayed him. She could not bear thinking about it. Little Lubomyr.

Volya thought she could imagine how Veronica might be feeling now. She blamed herself for Orest's death, but it was that lout Marko who had driven Orest away. He and his father were forever sparring, two heavy-antlered elk clashing over and over, with no resolution. He never even finished high school, poor boy, but at least he found work with his uncle Bohdan in Toronto. Meanwhile, Bohdan was probably blaming himself for not keeping track of his nephew. But who could fault her brother-in-law, with his hands so full, trying to keep Zenia happy, two alcoholic sons and another who was a socialist. What a load that must be. Volya was amazed that Zenia had not sucked the lifeblood out of Bohdan yet, that he remained so faithful. She could not understand it—Veronica stayed with Marko, Bohdan with Zenia—two siblings modelled on their selfish, alcoholic father. If Yarko had been alive, she believed they would still be together, living in relative harmony. Neither of them had addictive temperaments. So why was it she had so much trouble with her daughter? Whatever happened, she did not want to be blamed for driving Luba away. Yet she would leave sometime, and how could Volya protect her then? It seemed the closer you were to your loved ones, the easier it was to harm them.

Volya sniffed and blew her nose. She poured more tea into her empty cup, mentally checking off all the items on her to do list, trying to refocus on her work, trying to push out all the dark thoughts crowding her mind. But she could not stop thinking about her little brother, Lubomyr.

The year Tato died was the most dreadful year in her life, Volya thought. That September, she came down with a fever which lasted for days. On the third day she broke into a red, blotchy rash, and, by the fifth day, a yellow cast had covered her skin.

Much later Mama told her that their neighbour, Mrs. Shapka, stopped by to offer her grim advice. "Sylana, you must prepare yourself. No child can survive such a long illness with such a high fever. Remember old Zamillo had hepatitis, and look what happened to him. And little Marusia has never been right in the head after her fever. Better she should have gone to God."

"Go on with you! Do not say such wicked things! She will recover. She has a strong will, a strong heart. Volya is a fighter. She will not die!"

On the sixth day of her illness, the fever subsided. Volya was able to talk coherently again and Lubomyr was allowed to spend time with her. "Victor said you were going to die, but I knew he was wrong," he told her triumphantly. "Are you going to stay yellow?" He looked worried.

"I do not think so, little dove," she whispered back, her voice still weak and uncertain.

"Do not call me little dove. That is a baby name. I am big now, I can milk Kalyna," he stated, sitting up straight and proud next to her.

"So, you want my job?" Volya smiled at her pudgy little brother, imagining his short fingers tugging on the teats.

"No! I am going to help you. You need me," he said with great confidence.

Though Luba enjoyed her brother's company when she was tending the cow in the field, she found his attempts to help with milking to be more than annoying. She had still not completely recovered and was feeling weak and tired one day when he managed to tip the half-filled bucket onto the ground.

"Oh, Lubomyr! You are more a hindrance than anything. Look what you have done! Go play with the other children for a while so I can clean up your mess and finish up here."

He pouted and looked like he would burst into tears. "The big boys don't want me to play. They call me names."

"Then go inside with Mama for a while. Just get out of my way, I don't care what you do," she said in exasperation and turned her back on him.

She forgot about him for the next while, and after milking her, led Kalyna out into the field by herself. Volya remembered resting against that old oak tree next to the orchard, eyes half-closed, rolling a stripped willow switch between her palms. She dozed on and off, glancing up at Kalyna from time to time as the cow ripped out mouthfuls of grass and swished flies away with her tail. She was daydreaming about what it might be like to live in a city like Lviv. It was hard to imagine, since she had never left their village. Volya had heard that city people did not keep gardens or cows, and had to buy all their food at shops. Even bread. And she had heard that they also bought their clothing at shops because nothing was home-made.

A peculiar noise interrupted her reverie. The shrieks of children at play, perhaps? Had someone fallen into the stream? At that time in the fall, the stream was low and could be easily waded. Confused, she listened to the high, shrill screams, as if some small creature was being torn from limb to limb. Then Volya remembered Lubomyr.

Volya dropped her cow switch, pulled up her skirt, and ran as fast as her legs would allow. She bolted up the pasture hill, breath tearing out of her, then down the other side toward the stream. She looked around wildly.

"Lubomyr!"

But the screams had died away. She now heard nothing but the water gurgling and her own gasping.

"Lubomyr! Where are you?" she shouted. Still nothing but the water sloshing past. Volya looked in every direction, trying to decide where to go next. Then she heard a faint sound off to her right. Sobbing? She dashed off again, nearly tripping over an exposed tree root. When she found him, Lubomyr was crouching down in the middle of the stream, his arms dangling in the water. He moaned between his sobs. She did not remember walking into the stream but when she reached her little brother, she found live wasps clinging to his clothing and crawling in his hair. Volya got him to lie down in the water while she batted away all the wasps she could find, suffering several stings in the process.

When she brought him home, Mama immediately set out to find a special clay to plaster on Lubomyr's stings. After stripping him down, they counted forty-seven welts. Lubomyr swelled like a fall pumpkin and became quite feverish that night. Volya and her mother sponged his face and body with cool, wet cloths through the night. He was delirious, like Volya had been not so long ago. Volya heard him call out her name several times, and each time she cried. She should have let him stay with her, she thought. Why had she been so mean to him? That night Volya slept next to Lubomyr, who tossed and turned, flinging his arms and legs, kicking her many times. In the morning he seemed a little quieter. She wasn't sure if he could hear her, but she told him stories anyway until she was hoarse. Sometimes his eyes opened wide and Volya thought he was listening to her. But then he hollered words she could not understand, and she realized he was still delirious. Volya continued to sleep next to him, but was constantly awakened by his kicking or yelling. By the middle of the third night, they were all exhausted. Volya fell into a deep sleep. She dreamt of huge, monstrous insects that crept into their house at night, searching for food. For some reason, she could not see anything—she was blind. She called out for Mama. She called to Lubomyr to hide himself. Finally, her sight was restored but she could not find Lubomyr anywhere in the house. She searched for him under cupboards, outside in the barn, up in the trees, back at the stream where he'd been attacked by the wasps. Then she realized they had carried him away. The great insects had found what they were looking for.

Volya jerked awake from the dream in a sweat. Sitting up in bed, she felt the cold air rush around her. She shivered. The dawn was just breaking, and Lubomyr lay peacefully beside her. The giant insects had not carried him away after all. She placed her hand on his forehead. It was cool, no more fever. She smiled with relief as she looked down at him. He was so still. She felt his cheek. It was cold, as cold as deep well water. She took in a sharp breath, her heart racing.

"Lubomyr!" she shouted at him. "Lubomyr, wake up!" She shook his limp arm. There was no response. "Lubomyr!" she screamed, gripping his shoulders. Mama was suddenly by their side. She took his head in her hands and tried to open his eyes. She felt his throat for a pulse. Volya had stopped breathing for a moment, then began to hyperventilate. She grabbed for Lubomyr's hand.

"Lubomyr?" she whispered. Mama wrapped the little boy in her arms and began to wail with long, low, heart-rending sobs. Volya felt arms around her shoulders. Zenia, who had been watching in horror from across the room, had joined them.

"I killed him," Volya wept.

"You did no such thing," Zenia comforted her. "It is not your fault. It is God's will." She repeated the adult answer to all deaths, crying as she did so.

"Then I want nothing more to do with God," Volya gasped. "He is not my God. I want my Lubomyr!"

Volya put her cup of cold tea down on the table and wiped her wet face with the back of a hand. Over forty years had passed since her precious little brother's death. It made no sense to carry that guilt all these years, and yet, it was all she had left of him. She could not give that up. And then to nearly lose her daughter, his namesake—that was just too much.

Mother Hens and Queen Bees

Yesterday he was nearly a total stranger, and now Luba found herself eagerly awaiting Greg's return from Aunt Veronica's. He was singular and distinct from her other cousins, Aunt Veronica's kids—more like a close older brother she had not seen for several years. After a few hours with him, Luba felt like they'd never been apart. It was weird and yet comforting. As for the rest of her cousins, she felt awkward with them; they had nothing in common. She was a long, rectangular chip of onyx surrounded by brightly coloured, fat marbles that kept clunking up against her then rolling off. Faced with seeing them or staying home with the resident Dragon Lady, sitting put seemed like the best option that morning. Greg would come to her rescue soon. Luckily, her mother's gift for gab had her on the phone most of the time and off Luba's back. No one ever called for Luba.

When Greg's silver Volvo slid into the driveway, Luba could barely contain herself. "Hey cuz, is it crazy over there?"

He gave her a devilish grin. "I'm back for some peace and quiet. They are all there. And Christina—"

"Oh, good, you are back in time for supper," Volya interrupted him unabashedly, and automatically beelined for the stove where a four-course dinner had been ready for an hour. "So, they all arrived? How is everybody? Did Christina's husband come?"

"Yes, they're all there except for Phyllis. And Ralph was able to come after all. He traded shifts with one of the other doctors." Volya didn't stop moving, and in no time the table was laden with steaming bowls of caraway-speckled sauerkraut, fat sausages, potatoes running with melted butter, and overcooked faded peas.

"Sit, sit, eat!" she commanded, and snatched Greg's plate before he could protest. "Two scoops of nice hot mashed potatoes?"

"No, please, Aunt Volya, just one. I ate a little at Auntie's—"

"Why did you do that? Your poor aunt has a houseful and I have all this food."

"I..."

"Here you are, two scoops. Take lots of meat, you need your iron. You are much too thin and too pale. Both of you!" She scowled and muttered to herself while Luba took a plate heaped with food, stifling a snicker.

Greg pointed to her plate. "Eat up, scrawny—you have to catch up to me! I'm zdoroviy, healthy and solid!" He illustrated it by lifting his golf shirt and pinching a small roll of waist between his thumb and forefinger—all skin and no fat.

"You think being skinny is so funny," Volya began to lecture. "Young people, always dieting, it is not healthy. I was skinny when I was a girl, but not because I wanted to be. Starvation is not funny."

Greg's expression changed immediately. "Those were terrible times," he said sympathetically.

Volya nodded. "You can never know how terrible. But now we have all this freedom to do what we please, especially the young people, and most of you are wasting it. Look at poor Orest. And you, Luba—so smart, but here you are throwing away your education. And for what?" She shuffled back to the sink, shaking her head.

"Don't worry, I'll pay you back."

"I do not want your money! I want you to have a good education so you do not have to work like a slave, like me, or like your uncle in the mine. You need to go back to school."

"I'm not going back there. I need more time—stop pressuring me!"

"Is that counsellor person useful? How could she be? She is being paid to tell you what I can say for free. You just do not want to hear it. Greg, you talk some sense into her." She turned back to them, wiping her hands on her apron.

"Mama, can we just eat our supper in peace?" Luba noticed Greg's sad eyes, his flushed face. How embarrassing, she thought.

"Fine. Go ahead, eat." She untied her apron, her lips pinched together, and walked into the living room where she turned on the TV. Luba shrugged an apology to Greg. He returned an understanding smile. They ate quietly while The Price is Right contestants wagered and clapped in the next room.

Later, when Volya had gone next door to visit a neighbour, the two of them moved to the living room.

"When was the last time you were in Copper Creek?" Luba asked Greg.

They were planted in front of the television, but not paying much attention to Laverne and Shirley.

"For Phyllis and Zachary's wedding. Long time ago, eh?"

"You weren't here for Anatolia's?"

"Nah, I was in Vancouver then, in the middle of a big case and couldn't get away. Anatolia and... James, was it? They split up last year, or was it the year before?"

"Two years ago, I think. Your parents were up for her wedding, though. I remember them telling me that you were next."

"You mean my mother said that. Yeah, she keeps hoping. It ain't gonna happen," he said with a wry smile. Luba felt uncomfortable, not sure if she should ask him to explain, so she glanced back at the TV.

He seemed to notice her silence. "I'm sure you've heard rumours about me. That I might be gay?"

Luba nodded her head but didn't meet his eyes. "Uh-huh."

"Well, it's true."

She turned to look at him.

"I hope I'm not shocking you. I don't discuss this with the rest of my family, because they don't want to hear it."

"And the woman you live with?" she asked, not sure how to frame the question.

"Leo—that's her name. Short for Leonida. She's my best friend. She's also, as luck would have it, Ukrainian. Originally from Edmonton."

"How did you meet her?"

"She and I worked together in Calgary, and let me tell you, it's one big conservative cowboy town, and if you're different, well let's just say you're not so welcome. Neither of us was comfortable there, so we moved to Toronto when we found jobs there."

"She's, umm, different too?"

"Leo is what you call a bisexual—she can go either way and likes men and women both, but currently she's happily unattached. We have separate rooms, but we share the house. Well, technically I own the house and rent her a room. Works well for people who want to believe we're straight, but doesn't confuse our friends, because, frankly, most of us have to make compromises a lot of the time. It can be a real bitch out there."

He grinned at her as Luba let out all the air she'd been holding in.

"Cool," was all she could manage. "Cool."

Just then the phone rang. "Hello, Volya?"

"No, it's Luba."

"Ah, Luba, you sound just like your mother. It's your Aunt Zenia. How are you, my dear?"

"Fine, Aunt Zenia. And you?"

Luba tried not to laugh when Greg rolled his eyes and scrunched up his face.

"A little tired, but I'll recover. We're over at Veronica's and will be there in a few minutes. Is your mother in?"

"No, she's just next door. She'll be back soon, though."

"That's okay. Just let her know we'll be there shortly if she gets home before we arrive. It will be so nice to see you! And on such a sad occasion, oh my. Bye, darling."

"Bye," she said and hung up. "Your parents are on the way over."

"Great," he snickered.

Suddenly Luba felt herself go hot. "Do your parents know about what happened to me? In Toronto, I mean? How did you find out?" She stared at him, feeling panic rising in her chest. "My mother has been telling everyone I had pneumonia."

Greg shook his head. "Not to worry. That's exactly what we heard. That's still what my parents think. I have my own sources, but you know your mother would never let her sister in on something like that."

"But do you really think people will buy that story? That I landed in the hospital and quit school because of pneumonia? Isn't that a stretch?"

"Not really. Syphilis would have been a more interesting story, but pneumonia will work."

"Greg!"

He laughed and she couldn't help but smile. "Besides, they believe I'm straight. They must be gullible."

She laughed then, too.

"Actually, have you thought about what you want to do?" He regarded her more seriously.

"Yeah, I've been thinking about it. I can't stay here, that's for sure. I've been trying to write down some things—homework for the therapist I'm seeing," she grimaced, but Greg looked at her with encouragement. "When I was a kid I used to dream about being an artist."

"I remember seeing some of your sketches. And school artwork. You've got a gift, no question. I always figured you'd be an artist, so you could have knocked me over with a cat's whisker when I heard you were in a pre-med program."

Luba snorted. "Yeah, I should have had my head examined. It was not a good fit. I was never meant to be there. Just because I got good grades Mama thought I was heading for medical school. Somehow I let her convince me."

"So, what are you thinking: fine art, painting, and that sort of thing? Graphic design?"

"Not fine art, I'm not that talented. More like graphics, or maybe interior design. I sent away for some information on Ryerson's programs just after Easter. The interior design courses are the ones that appeal to me most. I might even be good at it."

"Ryerson's a great school."

"Yeah, and not so easy to get in. I may not have all the prerequisite courses, and I still need to put together a portfolio if I want to apply."

"You may be able to use some of your U of T courses. And you kept your artwork, didn't you?"

"Yeah, it's here packed away, just needs to be assembled."

"Great. Well I hope it works out. If you come back to TO, do you have an idea where you'd want to live?"

"God, no, I'm just in the fantasy stage right now. I guess I'll have to find another apartment."

"Well, if your fantasy morphs into reality, we have a guest room in the house while you're looking. I'm sure Leo wouldn't mind. Anyway, something to think about. And we're only ten minutes from the Ryerson campus by subway."

"Thanks, Greg." The idea intrigued her—she'd never had housemates before.

The outside door opened just then and they heard two women's excited, clattery voices talking simultaneously. Greg and Luba looked at each other. Aunt Zenia had arrived.

They peeked around the corner to watch Aunt Zenia pointing to parcels while Volya lugged a suitcase up the stairs. Her aunt stood several inches taller than her mother, slimmer and delicate-looking, wearing a fitted caramel-coloured mohair coat with matching high-heeled leather shoes—very classy. Uncle Bohdan, a bald man who was a head taller and three times thicker through the girth, struggled past both women with two more suitcases.

"Which room?" he asked, breathless but smiling broadly. "Ah, there you are! Hiding?" He had spotted them. Greg pushed her out and Luba greeted her aunt and uncle.

"Oh, my darling, you are all grown up. Dear, dear Luba. And here is our Greg. Look Bohdan, doesn't Luba look terrific? Are you feeling better, darling?" She gave her a tight hug and did not let go for the longest time. Luba glanced over her shoulder to see her mother scowling.

"She is too thin. So is Greg," Volya complained.

"Of course not, Volya, don't be so old-fashioned. Girls these days have to keep their figures. How else are they going to catch a good-looking rich husband? Right, Luba?" Aunt Zenia laughed harder as Volya's lips tightened a notch.

"Which room?" Bohdan stood in the hallway, sweating in his navy wool coat, the two heavy suitcases still dangling at the end of his long arms.

"You take that middle bedroom, there, just behind you. That one, yes. Luba, did you move your things?"

"Yes, Mama, the room is still clean like it was twelve hours ago, six hours ago, one hour ago—"

"No need to be sarcastic," she snapped, and pushed past everyone into the room where Uncle Bohdan was heaving bags onto the bed.

Aunt Zenia winked at her. "Still can't take a joke, can she?" Her English was perfect with barely a trace of accent, unlike Volya with her simple vocabulary and awkward phrasing. Slipping off her coat she handed it to Luba whose nose wrinkled from clouds of perfume floating up from the fabric. Her mother was probably choking on the strong scent.

Greg had already put the kettle on.

"The boys send their greetings and apologize for not coming," Aunt Zenia announced as she set herself in a chair at the kitchen table. Her eyes had not stopped moving as she took in the decor—the marbled brown arborite counter tops, cupboards painted beige with white trim, the chrome and beige plastic chairs, the worn but polished off-white linoleum floor, the small table covered with a heavy sheet of plastic, protecting a white table cloth, printed with an imitation embroidery pattern in orange, red and black. Luba suddenly saw the room as a stranger who walked in for the first time and she was embarrassed by the cheap, gaudy furnishings and by her mother who bustled from counter to table, bringing platters of her special pastries, rohaliky, krusty, and makivnyk.

"Do you still have that old toaster, Volya? Why, it was already an antique when you had it in Toronto."

"It works, so why should I buy a new one? I do not make toast every day, you know."

"Well you might want to replace that cloth cord. It looks like a fire hazard. Bohdan can replace it for you while we're here."

Volya did not reply as she poured water into the teapot, her back turned to them. Bohdan merely raised his eyebrows at his wife as he reached for a piece of poppyseed cake.

"Come, sit next to me, Luba," said Zenia. "My goodness, you have turned into such a beauty. Hasn't she Bohdan? You have your mother's colouring, but your father's build. How tall are you?"

"Five-foot-seven." Luba looked nervously at her mother, who was filling tea cups by the stove. She could sense Volya's agitation.

"I thought so, an inch taller than me, five inches taller than your mother. How lucky for you."

"And five inches shorter than me," Greg chirped. He was smiling, but Luba knew he was trying to head the duelling sisters off at the pass.

"Now, our boys get tall genes from both sides, mine and Bohdan's. They are so busy and never take time to play. Adam was just promoted to chief city planner and has no vacation time. He works so hard. And Bill has no one to substitute for him at his clinic. In fact, the other dentist is on holidays right now, down in Arizona. His practice is going so well I expect he'll be buying out the clinic and hiring more staff by the end of this year. And their new wives are lovely women." She turned to Greg. "Aren't they, Greg?"

"Sure, Mom. Lovely women."

"And where are their first wives?" Volya asked in a sharp tone, not turning around.

"They don't know anyone, so what was the point in them coming?" Zenia snapped.

"Orest was at their weddings. They knew him—they should be here."

Luba couldn't believe her mother was challenging her sister this way. They were talking about ex-daughters-in-law.

"For heaven's sake, Volya. They are not even in the family any more. And they both remarried," Zenia protested.

"Susan has one of your granddaughters—she is related." Volya just couldn't let it go. Luba wanted to shake her.

"We told them about the funeral. If they wanted to come, they could have. It was their choice."

"Tea?" Greg offered again, and stepped between the two sisters with the pot.

"Thank you." Zenia sighed and turned to her son. "Did you see your cousin, Christina, over at Veronica's? I notice she has lost weight since that last baby. It took her a while, though."

"Why are you so critical about people's weights? Just because you starve yourself to look like that Twiggy girl does not mean everyone else should!"

Volya glared at her sister.

Zenia dropped her spoon with a clatter. "I am barely in the door and already you are jumping all over me. You are the one who is being critical, not me." Her face was a narrower, sour reflection of Volya's. Usually there was no physical resemblance at all, but for the first time Luba saw the two as related, and for a moment she stopped breathing.

Bohdan jumped in. "Let us not get into an argument, please. You just got here. I am sure everyone is upset about Orest. I, for one, am just devastated—I had no idea. You know, Volya, he quit his job two months ago. He came over to tell me he needed some time to tour with his band. He did not look well at the time. You remember, Greg, you were there that day. I just thought it was the flu." He sat down exhausted. "He was so thin. I did not know the signs. I should have asked more questions, but...." He dropped his head and put his two big hands to his face.

"None of us knew, Dad." Greg had put his arm around his father's shoulders. Luba stepped back into the hallway, out of sight of everyone in the kitchen, her face and eyes burning, her head throbbing. She slipped into the bathroom and took a couple of aspirin. This was going to be a long visit.

When she returned to the kitchen she saw that the two sisters remained silent, grim. They sipped their tea and nibbled the sugared treats, studiously ignoring each other. Why couldn't her mother be more civil? All this time Luba believed she was the only one her mother attacked and criticized. Just then, watching Zenia, she didn't feel so alone. She had a new ally.

"Thanks again for driving me down, Greg. You didn't have to do it."

"It's no problem. I have a few errands to run for Aunt Veronica anyway. Besides, it's nice to get away from Funeral Central for a while."

Luba had been worried about this next session with Bella all night—she hadn't done her homework. Well, at least it wasn't school, she told herself, but standing in front of Bella's door, Luba could barely bring herself to knock.

"Come on in, Luba. What a gorgeous day we have today." Luba decided to take a different chair. Bella didn't seem to notice. As usual, her therapist was dressed impeccably, this time in a dark green pant suit with gold accents. And today her eyes were a deep mossy green, as if she had applied makeup to her irises. She could have been a model.

"You have such gorgeous clothes. Did you buy them in Toronto?" Luba blurted out.

"Why, thank you. No, I usually buy my clothes here, but to be honest, sometimes I almost wish I could wear a uniform, even though I used to hate them."

"When did you wear a uniform?" Luba asked, amazed. Bella rarely spoke about herself.

"In grade school, very long ago." She sat forward and was opening her mouth to speak again.

"Did you go to a Catholic school?"

"Well, yes, but that's irrelevant. Let's talk about you, Luba."

"Yes, but if I know some of your background, it might be easier for me to relate to you. I mean, if you were raised a Catholic, you'd understand my background better, right?" Luba was floundering.

Bella knitted her brows and gave her a strange look. "Well, that's not generally how counselling is approached. Of course, each client is unique and flexibility is a good thing." The corners of her mouth hinted at a smile. "I wonder if perhaps you are stalling. Do you not want to talk about yourself?"

Maybe it was the chair. "I think I'll change chairs, if you don't mind."

She waved her hand like a wand. "Go right ahead." When Luba was seated back on the couch, Bella resumed. "How are things going at home? Have you been to the funeral?"

"No, that's tomorrow morning."

"How do you feel about it?"

"I haven't really thought too much about it. We have a bunch of relatives from out of town visiting, so I've been busy with them. And helping my mother."

"And how do you get along with your relatives? Any that you especially like or dislike?"

"Well, I'm very fond of my Aunt Veronica. And one of my Toronto cousins is visiting and spending time with us. We seem to get along pretty well. Then there are his parents, my aunt and uncle, also from Toronto. Whenever my mother and Aunt Zenia are in the same room we all wonder who will kill each other first."

"So they argue a lot?" she asked.

Luba nodded.

"How do you feel when that happens?"

"I dunno, I feel embarrassed I guess. I don't understand why they fight so much—it's over such childish stuff."

"Is that how you feel when you and your mother argue?"

Luba paused for a moment. "You're sounding quite Freudian today."

Bella laughed. "I'll have to work on that."

They sat in silence for a moment and Luba started thinking about how bizarre it all seemed. She hated talking to her mother and now she was stuck for an hour each week with a woman who would talk about little else. It made her feel childish and petty, as though she should have some real inner turmoil to offer up, not simply family drama.

"This must get so boring for you."

"What do you mean?" Bella said, genuinely confused.

"Middle-class, average Joes and Janes coming in to your office to chat about how tough it is to relate to their parents. I mean, I wish I had some multiple personality disorder or something more serious."

Bella smiled, "I think by the end of this you'll see you have a lot to deal with."

Luba wasn't sure if she should be happy with that or not.

"So let's get back to your family dynamics," Bella said, smiling. "Do you think your mother likes to fight?"

"Oh yeah, but fighting really doesn't describe it. She's self-righteous and everybody else is wrong."

"Is she ever right, according to your perspective?"

Luba paused before she answered. Was Bella being sarcastic?

"Look, it may sound like I'm exaggerating, but this isn't some mommy-daughter spat. My mother and I have never gotten along, and she hates being challenged by anyone."

"So your mother picks on others, too?"

"My aunt. Well, they sort of pick fights with each other, although of the two I'd say my mother is more petty. Almost cutthroat."

"What do you do while they're arguing? Do you try to stop them?"

"No way! I don't want to be accused of choosing sides. I just try to stay out of the way. I'm really hoping they can keep it together for the funeral."

"Are you expecting trouble at the funeral?"

"I hope not. Greg and I will probably try to keep our two mothers apart so we don't have any scenes. That would be horrible."

"So you and Greg hit it off. You say he lives in Toronto?"

"Yeah. Greg's okay, you know, kind of like a brother, I guess. We've been talking a lot, about everything. About me. So, I suppose I have two therapists now," she said hesitantly.

Bella's smile seemed ambiguous. "What about the homework assignment, Luba? Have you come up with anything?"

Damn. "Well, to be honest, I didn't do much about it. I tried, but I just couldn't think of anything positive about anyone." She paused and pressed her lips together. "Wait, I just thought of something."

"Yes?"

"My cousin, Greg. He's positive about nearly everything. That used to make me mad, in other people, I mean. I usually hate being around uber optimists because they sound fake. But he's sincere, upbeat, he seems happy, he cares about people. He really seems to care about me, and for the first time I don't mind that."

"You usually mind if people care about you?"

"Well, I don't know, I guess it makes me question their motives."

"How so?"

"It's hard to explain. It's like people say they care because they think they should, like it's some kind of obligation."

"To you?

"No, an obligation to be a good person who is supposed to care about others."

"Do you think there are some people you trust who care about you because they just do?"

Luba thought about this. "No. Most people who said they cared about me were just trying to get something out of me or to manipulate me. I couldn't trust them."

"But you trust your cousin."

"Yes."

"And what about your mother?"

"My mother? How can I trust someone who used to make me kneel on dried peas for punishment?" Luba rubbed her knees.

"Outside of your cousin, and Aunt Veronica who you're fond of, are there any other people whose traits you admire, even just a little bit? Friends? Teachers?"

"Not really."

"No one at all? Perhaps a high school teacher? No close friends, confidants from school?"

Luba squirmed in her chair and closed her eyes. Who was her favourite teacher? Her eyes popped open. "I know. Mr. Gilbert, my art teacher. He was tough, a perfectionist, and really hard to please. Hardly anyone ever got an A in his class. And he was the kind of person you wanted to please, even though he looked like a grouch and he never cracked a smile. He would stand behind me in class and kind of hum. It was weird, but sort of soothing. He never said much, but he started to talk to me halfway through the year, asked me to stay after class, gave me some extra pointers. At first I thought he was being too critical, then I realized he rarely paid attention to anyone else's work. And just before I graduated, he asked me what I planned to do. He said I was gifted and he hoped I'd be able to use my God-given talent some day. The look on his face when I told him I was enrolling in a science program..." Luba shook her head and laughed. "He knew. He knew I wouldn't last. But it was a good feeling, knowing someone with high standards had confidence in my artistic abilities at least. Yeah." She looked down at her clasped hands.

"That's good, Luba. Anyone else?"

"Actually, there is one other person." Luba paused and felt herself blushing. "You."

"Oh, and what do you admire about me?" she asked in a matter-of-fact tone.

"Well, you're a professional woman, and I admire that. You listen, you're calm and intelligent. And have a hell of a super wardrobe."

"Are these the qualities you'd like to see in yourself?"

"Well, I'd like to be an independent professional some day. I'd love to be confident, smart, and have money. I'd like to be beautiful."

Bella sat back, and Luba's heart started racing.

"This is how you perceive me, Luba, but is it possible that you are creating a fantasy image?"

Luba felt sick. "I didn't mean anything by it—just forget I said you."

"No, I'm flattered. But I just want you to understand something. What we," and she pointed to herself, speaking softly, "perceive in other people is often what we want to perceive. We see what we need to see, and so your seeing your mother as awful may be a reflection of you needing to see her that way."

Luba was miffed.

"I know that sounds belittling, Luba, and I'm not saying you're making things up in your head. I'm saying that interpretation comes from a place inside of you. Your mother is no doubt very difficult, but she is also important to you."

Luba shifted in her seat, feeling uncomfortable, remaining silent.

Bella smiled. "And for the record, I think you already have some of the traits you seem to admire in me."

Luba looked at her then and felt better. Maybe, just maybe Bella thought she wasn't a total moron. She scrambled to redeem herself. "I've been thinking about going back to school. This time something I'm really interested in, and pretty good at, I think. Maybe an arts program at Ryerson, if I can get in. I've put an application together."

"That's wonderful!"

"Yeah, things are kind of falling into place. Now I just have to survive this funeral."

"Shall we plan a session for the day after the funeral? Say, eleven a.m.? If anything comes up, you can always give me a call and we can change the time." Bella stood up—a tall, green willow.

"Okay." Luba walked out in a daze. Were things really falling into place for her, or was she just fooling herself? Inside Bella's office anything seemed possible, but back out on the grimy street, she felt herself deflate. The dragon's den with its sniping siblings awaited her, a funeral she wished to avoid lay straight ahead, and escape from this hell-hole was fraught with obstacles. This was her reality.

Dead Boys

"Luba, are you ready yet? Greg has been waiting for half an hour already." Volya rattled the bathroom doorknob. "Luba!"

"Five minutes, okay? I'll be out in five minutes. Geez."

Volya snorted and stomped off to the kitchen. Through the window she could see Greg buffing his car. Watching him in the sunlight, patiently awaiting her daughter, she decided Zenia didn't deserve a son like that. So courteous and thoughtful, hard-working and successful. When would Luba stop being a teenager?

Volya was still smarting from the evening before. Wait until she had that girl all alone; once the funeral was over and company gone she'd give Luba a major talking-to. Why did Luba have to make everything so difficult? She should have known by now what clothing was or was not appropriate for a funeral. That black shirt with the tassels looked like she was dressing up for a nightclub. Fortunately, Zenia happened to have an extra skirt that fit her. What type of woman did not own a single skirt? Or pantyhose!

Luba shuffled into the kitchen, scowling.

"Do not look at me like that," Volya snapped.

"I'm not a morning person. You know that, and you just can't leave me alone for ten minutes?"

"No, you are just lazy. I have never seen anyone sleep as long as you. I am glad Zenia and Bohdan went to Veronica's earlier so they could not see what a bone-idle daughter I have." Without another word Volya and Luba walked out to the car in the driveway where Greg helped Volya into the front seat.

"Thank you, Greg. You are so considerate, just like your father," Volya said in a loud voice, but Luba's eyes were focussed on the ceiling of the car, her expression still sour.

"My mother sure is an early bird. I think Dad would like to sleep longer, but she won't let him."

"She probably cannot sleep after Bohdan gets up. Nobody can sleep, except for Sleeping Beauty back there. He blows his nose and the roof shakes. And he walks like a moose. At least Zenia is quiet—unless she is laughing. What a cackle, she sounds like a witch when she gets going."

Greg snorted and Luba slapped a hand over her mouth.

"What is so funny?" Volya asked.

"Takes one to know one," Luba said under her breath.

"I am not joking. You think I make jokes, but your mother has a loud laugh, always has. She could wake the dead." And then Volya was silent, catching herself and what she'd just said.

Greg turned his head to look at Luba. "So, you ready for this?"

"Hey, watch the road! You want to kill us all? Then there will be a big funeral," Volya caught herself again.

"Honestly, cuz, where did you buy your license?" Luba spoke up from the back.

"And what's your problem, cuz? Twenty-two years old and you don't have a driver's license yet. You couldn't buy one if you tried!"

Volya began fidgeting with her purse. "We should have left earlier. Drive faster, Greg."

"Auntie! You want me to break the law and tarnish my perfect record?" He grinned.

"You will not get fined. Not for rushing to a funeral. Anyway, you are a lawyer—no fines for lawyers. I can make sure of it."

Inside the church, the rest of the family was already seated near the front. Greg joined his parents in the pew behind Veronica and Marko and their children. Luba and Volya sat next to Greg, but left a looming space between each other. Volya pulled out the kneeling bench and tugged on Luba's arm until they both knelt for prayers. From the corner of her eye, Volya observed Luba signing a sloppy cross and she closed her eyes tight. What was wrong with that girl? Dear God help her, she prayed.

As Volya murmured her Hail Mary, the sniffles and sobs all around took her back to the night before and a bad dream that had awakened her. Afraid to return to sleep, she made herself a cup of weak tea with milk and sat at the kitchen table, almost wishing she could stomach something stronger to help her forget. In her nightmare, she had been searching for someone lost, looking inside strange houses back in her village of Brinzi. And then she saw it: a heap of bodies in the village square, next to the communal well. Several women, her mother Sylana among them, whimpered and cried, tugging at the arms and legs, peering into pale, grey faces, some with opaque eyes still open, mouths gaping, ears hanging by skin or missing altogether. All dead and frozen like cracked porcelain dolls. She then heard the snickering of the Nazis standing over them.

Sitting at the table, sipping tea, Volya was back in the fall of 1941. She had turned fifteen in June, and had heard that the German army was coming to liberate them from the oppressive Russians. Volya remembered how excited they all were, laughing and dancing outside, singing victory songs. The word that preceded the Nazi arrival was that they were looking for young men to help them fight the Red Army; Marko hoped to join their youth league. He could not wait to leave the village and go travelling to places like Italy and France. But their hopes of freedom were dashed when the Nazis began taking their harvested crops, their cattle and sheep to feed their troops, and bullied anyone who did not co-operate with them. All suspected Bolshevik sympathizers were executed in public with a gunshot to the back of the head. Marko joined the underground youth resistance along with all the other village boys, and the Nazi recruitment efforts faltered. Volya's mother was terrified.

"I beg you, stop this nonsense. It will only get you killed, and all the rest of us once they learn what you are up to. This is war, not a time for children's games. Please, for the love of God, do not go!" She grabbed the sleeve of his worn grey coat, too short for his long arms.

Marko, who towered over their mother, already bore a strong resemblance to Tato. He pulled away from her, slapping at her hand. "I am not playing games, you foolish woman! I am doing this to save all of you from the Nazis and the Bolsheviks. I will not roll over and lick their boots like you. Get some self-respect!" He ripped open the door and slammed it behind him, off to another clandestine meeting.

"Oh, Lord," she wailed softly. "What will become of us? Who will take care of us?"

Volya shivered in the loft above, where she had been watching as usual. She hated to see Mama so agitated, but she was upset often those days. Still, Volya could not help but agree with her brother this time. They were, after all, at the whim of these German invaders. No one ever knew when the Nazis might march in and help themselves to what little food they had. There was nothing left in the garden by mid-summer, and Kalyna had been taken the previous fall. If someone did not stand up for them soon, the Nazis would take everything they had.

Mama repeatedly warned her two daughters to stay out of sight of the German soldiers. She was terribly worried that the soldiers might take a fancy to her girls as she suspected they had done to many missing girls in nearby villages. Zenia, in particular, with her honey-coloured hair and lively blue eyes, had just turned eighteen. She was willful and selfish even then, and naive. By refusing to stay home she caused their Mama no end of grief. Volya, on the other hand, never left their property.

A crash later that night woke up both her and Mama at the same time. Volya sat up quickly; someone was sobbing and a male voice was cursing downstairs. She crept out of bed and peered down from the loft. Zenia and Marko had just come in, and Mama had joined them.

"I told you not to go out. No? Now look what has happened. Dear God, what will we do?" Mama was holding Zenia, who wept into her mother's shoulder.

"I would have left earlier if I knew the soldiers were coming back. They surprised me!" Zenia cried out. Then she whimpered, "I will see Bohdan next week when he returns. We have been talking about marriage, so I will tell him I am ready now. That is what I have to do." Her voice cracked.

"Damn women," Marko spit. "Stupid, stupid, never use your heads!"

"Shut up, Marko. Leave us," Mama told him.

Marko raised his arm as if to strike her. Mama glared at him and he growled back at her, then he left the house, slamming the door again. Upstairs, Volya closed her eyes tightly and covered her ears. She had heard stories about what Nazis did to girls, and sometimes to boys they caught alone. She did not want to think what might have happened to Zenia; at least she got away from them. She was too mean to get rid of that easily, she thought spitefully.

Two days later there was more bad news. Marko ran into the house, breathless.

"They have Levko! In Lviv!"

"What does that mean? Who is Levko?" Mama asked.

"The regional head of our youth group, our man! The Nazis have him. They will probably torture him."

"He will give you up!" Mama screamed.

"No. He will never give them any names." However, Marko did not look as certain as the words he spoke.

"Aya yay!" Mama wailed. "Of course he will talk. You cannot know what torture will do to a soul! You ignorant boy, you are as good as dead yourself!"

Before Marko could retort, the door broke open again and two of his friends ran in. "Biliy is calling a meeting at his store. Come on!" They grabbed Marko's arms and disappeared as suddenly as they had entered. Mama dropped into a chair, stunned. Watching her then, Volya knew her brother was lost. That day, all but two of the boys who had previously belonged to the underground resistance signed up with the Nazis. Within a week, they were all gone. The Nazis assured families that the boys were in Italy for training. Her brother had been forced into the devil's lair.

Zenia and Bohdan married quietly and left for Germany in late October. They had learned there was a demand for labourers, and felt it would be safer there. Volya wanted desperately to go with them, but Mama would not leave as long as there was a chance Marko might return to the village. Volya lost count of the times the Nazis brought remains of young men and even children to the village. Each time Volya and her mother ran to see if Marko was among the dead. Volya never wanted to go, but Mama could not bear to go alone. She implored her mother to leave Brinzi and join Zenia and Bohdan in Manheim. But Mama hung on.

"As long as there is a roof over our heads, and we can find a few kernels of wheat to live on, we will stay here. This is our home."

After seeing all those dead boys, Volya could not imagine that Marko was still alive. She would stare at Mama in disbelief. Her mother's skin was stretched tight over her bones, not much different from the starved skeletons of boys and men dragged into the village centre. In fact, they were both feeble from lack of food. Volya was certain that Mama was losing her mind from worry and lack of sleep. Finally, Volya and her mother were forced to leave the next spring, when the German soldiers burned down all the houses and barns of Brinzi. They all left for Germany on carts and trains, not knowing what had become of Marko and the other boys and young men.

Father Buchkovsky stepped up to the lectern and cleared his throat. He spoke in Ukrainian at first, then switched to English. Volya wondered how long he had been speaking while she was in reverie and tried to refocus on the ceremony.

"I think most of us will remember the happy Orest of twelve years ago, how enthusiastically he took up the accordion to accompany our young Ukrainian dance troupe."

In front of her she could not help but notice Anatolia's heaving shoulders as she wept silently. The poor woman, Volya thought. She was the most reserved of Veronica's children, and had already lived through her share of sorrow—two miscarriages and a no-good philandering husband. But Volya had never heard her complain and Anatolia would never say anything bad about anyone. Pure of heart, that one, like her mother Veronica.

"Orest was an accomplished percussionist, first with the high school band, later with his own garage band called the Crickets, although I'm told I should not confuse this group with another professional, slightly more famous, band." He smiled at his joke and one person chuckled.

Volya found herself staring at the profile of Nicholas. How sad he looked—what a tragedy to lose a younger brother. A handsome young man, dark-haired like his mother, tall like Zachary but more slender, probably because he was still unmarried and did not have a wife cooking for him. Since he had moved out west years ago, she did not know him any more. She wondered what was going through his mind.

"Of course, like all young people, he eventually found his true love as he tried different paths, following his own unique interests and talents, falling in and out of love with music, and with girls, of course." He paused and scanned the audience.

What was wrong with Father Buchkovsky? Was this some modern new way of conducting funerals? This was not an entertainment. This was a solemn occasion, or it was supposed to be. Volya's lips tightened as he continued.

"Orest went on to play with different professional bands in Toronto. He had found his true calling."

Who was whimpering now? Zenia of course, all for show, no doubt, to be followed with a waterworks display. She just had to be the centre of attention, even at her nephew's funeral. The woman had no shame.

"Orest Tatenko was a young man with great promise. At some point he chose a path that cut short his budding career and youthful life. We are not here to judge him, but to mourn the waste of a good life, the loss of a loving son, brother, nephew, cousin, friend. God has already accepted Orest into his new home...."

More crying now, even wailing. Christina, perhaps? She had always been so emotional, and it was worse after the second baby. In fact, Veronica had hinted that Christina was seeing someone for professional help. Ah well, it happened sometimes. Here was Luba, no good reason she could see for her depression, a healthy young woman and she had to get counselling; doctor's orders. Dear Lord, she hoped no one would find out; the vicious rumours that could start.

The priest stepped down; the pall bearers lined up and the casket was closed.

"Zenia, don't go on so," her husband soothed her as Luba, Volya, and he crammed into the limo, but Volya could sense his own agitation and nervousness as he wedged in between them. He appeared to be choking in his tight white shirt and hand-knotted tie, and tiny drops had formed on his wide flushed forehead.

"I agree, Zenia, you have cried long enough. You can stop your show any time now," she snapped.

Zenia huffed in surprise. She narrowed her watery blue eyes and pressed her lips together. "That is so typical of you, Volya. You have no feelings whatsoever!"

"That is not true."

"No? When was the last time you called Mama? Or wrote to her? Don't accuse me of being insincere when you have cast your own mother off like she was already dead!" She blew her nose almost as loudly as her husband, honking in Volya's direction.

"I do not have to answer anything to you! I am sick of your showing off, pretending to be better than everyone else. You are in no position to judge me. You abandoned Mama back then and you know it. And who was left to pick up the pieces? Me, that is who. Always me."

"You selfish cow. That's not true and you know it. I got married!"

"Sure, after flirting with the Nazis, then leaving us in danger. We were lucky they did not go after us, after me!"

Zenia gasped and stiffened. Her husband turned to Volya and said sternly, "That's enough Volya. Don't say things you can't take back."

Meek, docile Bohdan had never spoken to Volya like that. Perhaps she had crossed a line, but she could not stop.

"So you have more money, so what! That does not make you a better person. I am tired of hearing about your professional sons and how wonderful they are and how much money they make. As if you made them that way and earned those degrees yourself. You are smart, all right. A smart scavenging old crow."

"You self-centred, selfish Babayaga! You can't even talk to your own mother. How can you expect Luba to talk to you?"

In the front seat, Luba reddened.

"Mama is not fit to talk to. All she spouts is nonsense—has for years. How can anyone get to know her now that she is a senile old woman? What is the point?"

"She was not spouting nonsense when you up and left Toronto ten years ago. Was she, Bohdan? She was fine. You just did not want to listen to her. You broke her heart. Do you hear me? You broke her heart when you left! You were always her favourite child and you abandoned her. You are the most cruel, vicious person I know—"

Bohdan, his deep pink cheeks and pursed mouth resembling a puffer fish, finally cut in. "Enough. Zenia, for God's sake. And Volya, you should be ashamed. We are burying a boy in a few minutes. Have some consideration."

No one cried or spoke—they barely breathed. Outside, the clouds were heavy and low and threatening to spill. A suitable day for burying a boy.

Burying a Boy

Luba hadn't been to a Catholic funeral in a long time: the smoky pungent incense, the chanting priest circling the altar, droning on and on. And though she knew it was a possibility, she was still unprepared for the open casket. She was startled to find herself staring at him, lying stiff as a sleeping Ken doll in a crisp white shirt, black tie, and dinner jacket, ready for a prom he would never attend. She shuddered. This wasn't Orest—it was a slicked-up impostor who glowed with clean-shaven, unnaturally pink skin, his hair neatly cut and combed. Did his family really think of him this way? This wasn't Orest, she repeated to herself. If she had to look at Orest, she wanted to see him the way he was a year ago, high and happy after a bar gig in Toronto, his lips chapped, his hair tied back and a sweat-soaked bandana wrapped around his head. Luba wished she had the nerve to get up and slam the casket shut. He would have been so disgusted at what they had done to him. She would never let them do that to her.

After the insufferable funeral service, Luba found herself in another hell on the ride to the cemetery. When she finally tumbled out of the limo, she gulped in several breaths of air and scanned the grounds for Greg. Luba saw him standing under a budding elm tree with her cousins Anatolia and Christina, and she nearly ran to join them. She grabbed Greg's arm.

"Please, don't ever leave me alone with those two again!" Her voice was a coarse whisper. He patted her arm and gave her a hug.

"This was awful for everyone."

"Sorry," she said, realizing how selfish she appeared. "I'm so sorry."

"It's okay. It's going to be a long day."

For the next hour, Luba found herself enveloped in Aunt Veronica-style arms as cousins and their children got reacquainted with her. Where had she been? How was school? Christina began a fresh bout of crying and could not speak as she and Luba swayed together under the tree for a while, with her husband, Ralph, looking on and nodding. Then it was Anatolia's turn. Under her sloppily applied makeup, Anatolia's face was greyer than her dead brother's, but she gave Luba a long, warm embrace. It was strange to be surrounded by family you barely knew.

When the casket was finally in place, the burial ceremony began. Luba did not hear the priest's words—he mumbled at the best of times—and today a blue wind took his words away, floating with the mist over the other gravestones and letting them know there was a new arrival in this underground city of bones. Luba saw no life in all the upright bodies gathered around Orest's new home. Black and grey and brown apparitions, they gazed into the freshly dug hole with blank eyes.

Luba was aware of a suspended sensation, like she was looking down at this scene from some other place. Her hands and feet went numb; it felt as though someone else were controlling her entire body and her thoughts. She wondered what Orest would see, how disappointed he'd be with this morose crowd. He'd say, "What a sick party. Don't these people have better things to do? Why aren't they singing, laughing, playing soulful music? My music. My music is the best! They never figured that out, the morons. Well, screw them all!" She smiled.

Luba felt a sharp jab in her ribs. Volya was glaring at her. Luba had to shift her feet—they were stinging with thousands of pinpricks from standing so still. They must have fallen asleep, like the rest of her body. The priest had finally stopped mumbling because they were all singing "Vichnaya pamyat." Forever remembered. She wondered, just what did they remember?

After the casket was lowered, Aunt Veronica and Uncle Marko tossed handfuls of dirt into the grave. Oddly, there was no sound, as if the dirt was still falling, falling, never landing. Everyone turned away. No one spoke; women sniffled and the wind moaned. Luba hurried to Greg's side and asked in a desperate whisper if there was any room in his car. To her dismay, Volya chose to come, too, and planted herself in the front seat. Her cousin, Nicholas, slid into the back with Luba and Greg. There was no crying now.

"Hey, baby cousin, you're all grown up." Nicholas leaned over and tousled Luba's hair. "Haven't they married you off yet?" He grinned wickedly at her.

"I could ask you the same question, especially since you're so much older. What's your problem?"

Greg chuckled. "I told you she was able to dish it out, Nicky."

Nicholas tilted his head closer to Luba and whispered, "Maybe we should get hitched, you and me. That'd shut 'em up, eh?"

"Greg, he's been in the woods too long."

She lowered her voice and leaned close to him. "Look, Nicky, when I get back to TO I'll send you one of those inflatable dolls. Just don't use any sharp objects near her, or play with her near a campfire." Nicholas smirked. "Or maybe you'd prefer a different kind of doll, hmm?"

He whispered back, "I think you're confusing me with someone else. Send the girl doll, size forty-four. I like 'em big." Luba stifled a chuckle, hoping her bat-eared mother had not overheard them. There was no reaction from the front seat; Volya sat rigid, staring straight ahead.

They were all deposited at the church, and solemnly marched into the basement where a lunch had been prepared. This was the closest thing to a party they were going to get. This was too sad. And dull. Nicky looked too clean-cut to be another Orest, Luba thought, but at least he had a sense of humour, warped as it was. He had pretty much ignored her when he was a teenager, so she was gratified that he joked with her now.

Luba ended up sitting next to her mother, across from Aunt Zenia and Uncle Bohdan. The sisters were not speaking to each other. In fact, they were making exuberant conversation with the ladies next to them. The luncheon was an uncomfortable affair. Several family members got up to make little speeches about the bereaved family, but little was said about Orest. What could they say about a kid who killed himself with drugs? It was obvious this was unbearably painful for Aunt Veronica. Uncle Marko's face was frozen in the stunned mode.

Aunt Veronica insisted that Luba and Volya come back to the house with them. She had prepared more food for the family, although everyone was stuffed from the church luncheon. The others had escaped as Anatolia, Christina, and Zachary were off to visit old school friends for a couple of hours with Greg chauffeuring, and Ralph offered to take the children to a nearby park to let off some kinder energy. Aunt Zenia declined the invitation, saying she had a headache and needed to lie down for a while. Uncle Bohdan dropped Luba and Volya off and promised to come back shortly, then he sped away.

"Please, please sit down in the living room. I made rohaliky, filled with walnuts and honey, the way you like them, Volya." Aunt Veronica waved her guests into the dark room lined with overstuffed chairs and shuffled back into her kitchen. As they settled themselves into the soft chairs, Luba noticed the curtains were drawn. Nicholas snapped on a lamp at one end of the sofa, causing the tassels to wave along the bottom of the green shade. He sat in a wooden rocker on the other side of the lamp, mostly in the shadows.

"Nicola, vodka or beer?" his father shouted at him from the kitchen. "Anyone else for a drink? I have everything here, any kind of drink you like. Luba, some wine? How about you, Volya?"

"You know I don't drink!" Volya shouted back at him.

Uncle Marko grumbled an unintelligible reply. The light from the kitchen was blocked momentarily as Aunt Veronica appeared in the doorway with a tray of Ukrainian pastries. She bent in front of them, perspiring in her navy velvet dress, like a dark rain-heavy cloud. Out of politeness Luba reached out for one of the sugary treats. This ritual of hospitality and graciousness had been drilled into Luba since birth, and declining was not an option right now.

A crash in the kitchen made everyone start. Nicholas jumped to his feet and rushed into the kitchen.

"Now what has he done?" Aunt Veronica asked, her expression weary.

A few minutes later Nicholas walked back in, carefully balancing another tray, this one laden with drinks.

"Here's a tea for you, Aunt Volya. Sugar and milk, right?" He smiled at her sweetly as he handed her the cup and saucer. The cup was white porcelain with a red-and-black geometric design, and rimmed with gold—Aunt Veronica's best Ukrainian china.

"How did you know I like my tea this way?" Volya asked, obviously trying to ignore the mayhem in the kitchen.

Nicholas winked at Luba. "I make it my business to know these things. And a glass of white wine for my little cousin." He handed her the wine she didn't order. Luba took it and sipped a little. Her preference ran to Guinness stout, or dark rum, but she doubted they had either of those in her uncle's otherwise well-stocked home. Nicholas had a bottle of beer for himself: Labatts Blue. The same brand her Toronto friends preferred, and Orest's favourite.

Uncle Marko staggered into the room. He let his large body fall into the chair opposite her without letting go of his drink. Vodka she guessed.

"So how's the wine?" he boomed at her.

Aunt Veronica appeared in the doorway again. "You do not have to shout, Marko. Nobody here is deaf."

"Nicola, anything new to tell us?" Volya turned to face her nephew, seated again in the shadowed rocker. "You must have a girlfriend. When are you getting married?"

Nicholas leaned forward into the light, his blue eyes gleaming.

"I might just have a girlfriend, Auntie," he teased.

Volya took the bait. "Oh? So tell me—what is she like? Who is she?"

"We-ell," he drew out the word before proceeding, "she's shorter than I am, has long black hair, dark brown eyes, just like you Auntie, and she sings in a quartet, the Sweet Adelines. Beautiful voice, alto."

"What does she do?" Volya asked.

"She's a school teacher. Very respectable, I assure you."

"And her name?"

"Sharon Miller."

"Oh, she's English then?" Volya persisted.

"No. She's Jewish."

There was total silence in the room. Nicholas' face was impassive. Was he joking? Luba couldn't tell.

"You will not marry a Jew!" Uncle Marko thumped the arm of his chair.

Nicholas' eyes blazed. "First of all, I never said anything about getting married. And secondly, it's none of your concern if I do."

"Nicola! You know what they are like. I do not have to tell you."

"No, tell me, Tato. What are they like? What is Sharon like?" Nicholas challenged him.

"They are pushy, greedy people. Cannot be trusted."

"Yes, so you keep saying, Tato. So tell me, what happened to the Jews in your village?"

"I never laid a finger on those Jews. I know nothing of what happened to them. I was in Italy during most of the war," he explained and took a deep drink from his glass.

Nicholas leaned so far forward Luba was afraid he'd tip over the rocker. His hands gripped his knees, his jaw was clenched. "The Jews were persecuted in Italy, too, Tato. I remember a photo of you in Italy. Weren't you wearing a German uniform? Didn't the Nazis take boys and men from the Ukrainian villages and send them to Italy? You were a Jew killer like the rest of them."

"Nicola! Marko! That is enough of such talk! Stop this now!" Aunt Veronica's sharp voice startled Luba more than the argument in progress.

"You ignorant boy. Do you not realize we had to go? They were going to hurt our families, kill our parents, mutilate our sisters. We had no choice!"

"Did you help round up the Jews? Did you?" Luba had never seen Nicholas so passionate, so angry.

"I do not have to tell you anything. You just blame, you know nothing. You have no respect, no understanding. Get out of my house, go back to your Jew friends. You, worthless, stupid...." He stopped ranting, his breath ragged. He lowered his head and placed his free hand on his forehead. His chest heaved; a sob broke out. The glass fell out of his other hand, bounced on the carpet, and cracked against the leg of the coffee table. No one said a word.

"Hello? Where is everybody?" Uncle Bohdan had returned.

Without thinking, Luba jumped up, spilling wine on her lap. Volya noticed, but made no comment. She rose also, and practically pushed Luba out of the room. Luba couldn't stand the stricken look on Aunt Veronica's face and gave her a long, hard hug before they left.

The ride home was unusually quiet. Uncle Bohdan parked the car in front of Volya's house, but he did not get out. Volya asked if he was coming inside.

"No, I think I will go back to church for a while. I need a little quiet, to clear my head."

"I cannot blame you, God knows. Supper will be ready at five." Volya took Luba's arm and led her to the house. Her mother looked exhausted.

"Why don't you lie down, or sit for a while, Mama. I can start supper if you like." Luba knew her mother would want to get the next meal going right away. That was how she operated, never resting.

"Oh no, I can peel while I sit. But thank you for offering. You can sit with me if you like."

Luba would have preferred to go for a walk and clear her own head, but it had started to rain. She pulled up a chair and watched her mother expertly twirl potatoes and peel, never missing a spot, never cutting herself like Luba would.

"Bohdan is right. The church is a good place for quiet and peace. I used to go to church a lot more when I was younger. In between masses, when I could."

"There are other places to find quiet."

"Perhaps. But in church you can stop thinking, worrying about your life and the physical things. You can let everything go, let God take over for you."

"You mean let God make your decisions for you? Or his so-called representatives, the priests?"

"I am not talking about priests, Luba," Volya shook her head. "Ah, you young people do not believe in the healing powers of the church. That is because you have never been desperate enough to know you needed God's help."

Luba wanted to interrupt her, to tell her that she had known desperation. Had her mother forgotten what had happened to her? Then she remembered the serenity, the solace of the monastery, and wished she could be beamed over that very moment. Whether it was the music, the chanting monks, or the isolation and distance from the ugly things in her real life, Luba had felt the healing power of a sacred place. So she kept her mouth shut. There had been enough arguing that day.

"I don't understand why those two can't get along. They don't see each other for years at a time, then fight like cats when they get together. I've never heard of anything like it in other families. I don't get it."

"Neither do I, Luba. I once asked my mother if there was some big blow-up just before you guys left. I was living in Vancouver then. Mother doesn't like to talk about what happened, but I think it involved our grandmother. Baba moved in with my parents for a while, but I think she was put in the nursing home not long after you left. One thing's for sure, our mothers have had tough lives, especially your mom." Greg and Luba were hanging out in the rec room downstairs where he had come to say good-bye.

"Yeah, I know. It was hard in the old days, kind of like our pioneers, I suppose. She's told me bits and pieces of life in Ukraine and Germany. It's odd, you know. She gives me the broad facts but that's it. Well, I assume they're facts, the way she tells it. But she never talks about certain details—you know, how she met my father, or any boyfriends she might have had, stuff like that. Nothing truly personal. I can read history books, but I'd rather know my mother, the person. I know her generation isn't comfortable talking about those things, like it's taboo, but sometimes it gets to be ridiculous."

Greg nodded knowingly.

"When I started having my periods, you know what she did?" Greg shook his head and smiled.

"She gave me a little booklet to read, handed me a Kotex pad and this horrible elastic garter thing, and sent me to the bathroom. She let a pamphlet tell me what was happening, while I thought I was bleeding to death! Then one of my friends at school gave me a tampon with no instructions. I looked at this thing, took it out of the cardboard, and figured it would never work by itself. So, I laid it on top of a pad and strapped those babies on. Took another three years before I was brave enough to find out how tampons are supposed to work!"

Greg hooted with laughter. "Well, I didn't have to worry about those bodily functions, but the folks were pretty awkward when it came to discussing the birds and the bees. Anyway, they really messed up with me, didn't they?"

"I think you turned out splendidly."

"Thank you."

"Do you think your mother would talk to me? About what happened between her and my mom?"

"Yeah, maybe. She feels sorry for you, being here with your mother, being raised by only one parent, being an only child. And sometimes I think she feels cheated because she only had sons."

"Greg? Are you downstairs? Come up here for a minute." Volya's voice reached them from upstairs. They obediently marched up to see her.

"You all ready to go? Here, I packed you a sandwich." Her mother handed over a huge brown grocery bag, stuffed with more than just a sandwich.

"Aunt Volya! I told you not to make any food for me. I'll bet you sneaked a coil of kobassa in there, didn't you?" He opened the bag and sniffed. "Uh-huh, just as I thought. Now what am I going to do with all this kobassa? You know I work close up and personal with people all day. I can't have garlic breath!" He tried to look stern, but it was wasted on his aunt.

"You can freeze it. Eat it on the weekends. Fry some thin slices with scrambled eggs—just delicious! You drive safely now, and no speeding."

"You've got my address and phone number, Lube. And next time you're down in TO, you let me know, okay?"

Greg winked at her then gave her a tight hug. She was going to miss his oxygenating presence in her mother's suffocating house.

As the engine rumbled, Volya yelled, "Put the kobassa in the freezer as soon as you get home. And do not leave it at your mother's!"

"Bye!" Greg waved and backed his silver Volvo out of the driveway. It was suddenly very quiet. Luba could not imagine surviving an entire summer with her mother. And now, if the planets aligned and the sunspots didn't flare and her application to Ryerson knocked them flat on their asses, she had somewhere to go, someone to go to.

The Rivalry

Volya shook her head in disgust as she surveyed Luba's room from the door. What had happened to that girl? She used to be so tidy when she was younger, every article of clothing put away before she left for school each morning, her bed nicely made up. Now she tossed her dirty clothes into a basket until she had nothing clean left to wear. And she never made her bed, not properly anyway. She was lazy, that was her problem, thought Volya, but it was more complicated than that. Young people today had too many choices. When Volya was a girl there were no options; you cleaned, you cooked, you obeyed or else.

She thought back to last evening, just after supper, when Luba announced that she planned to return to school. Volya's first reaction of surprise was quickly chased down by feelings of resentment and dismay. Once again, she was probably the last person to know what was going on in her daughter's life.

"And when did you decide this?" she asked.

"Oh, a couple of weeks ago."

"And you never said anything."

"I've been thinking about it for a while, but I wasn't sure. Anyway, I'm just applying, I don't know if I'll even get into the program."

"Surely they will make an allowance for you. You were ill, you had to leave for health reasons. Your grades have always been so good."

Luba cast her eyes down. There was more she wasn't saying, Volya thought.

"I'm not going back to U of T, Mama. I'm applying to Ryerson." She looked up, as if caught taking the last cookie.

"Ryerson? What kind of school is that? Where is it? I never heard of such a school."

"Ryerson Polytechnical Institute. In Toronto. It has an excellent reputation. It's highly competitive. I'll be lucky if they give me an interview."

Volya's head was spinning. She was stuck at the word polytechnical. To her, technical school meant the trades: carpentry, plumbing, electrical, mining. What was her daughter thinking?

Luba held up her hand as if to stop Volya from speaking. "Mama, I know what's going through your mind. I'd like to give interior design a try. I did the research, and it's exactly the kind of thing I love to do. I already have most of the courses I need to get in—if they like my work."

Volya, who had been standing in the kitchen all this time, sank into a chair. "What work?"

"I'm sending them a portfolio of my artwork. Some projects from high school, and that drafting course you thought was so useless."

"Artwork? You want to be an artist now and throw away two years of university education?" Volya rubbed her forehead. It was worse than she first thought. "Did that psychologist put this into your head?"

Luba sighed. "No. Well, sort of. She got me thinking about what I want to do with the rest of my life. I want a career, and I can't live here forever. Interior design isn't just art, Mama. It's design, you know, like interior decorating, only more concrete stuff, like rooms, buildings. Kind of like architecture."

"Architecture?" Volya couldn't picture this at all, her daughter designing houses and skyscrapers.

"Not exactly. I could end up designing theatre sets, and working with architects. I'll need to draw, draft, be able to design, and maybe make furniture. I'll be using math and physics, as well as my art and colour sense."

"Ah, there you go. You and your colours. You can paint all those rooms red and orange now. And you think you can make a living at this, this design work?"

"Interior design, Mama," Luba said slowly. "Yes, if I'm accepted. I want to give it a try. I think I might be good at it."

A picture flashed through Volya's mind then, of a defiant young woman standing up to her family. A woman with dreams of high fashion, of crafting beautiful clothing with her skilful hands. She shrugged the vision away and studied Luba's hopeful, hungry face in front of her. The times had changed and a girl with Luba's abilities could do so many things Volya would never have dreamed of in her youth. Suddenly, she did not have the heart to argue with her daughter. What good would it do, anyway? Luba had stopped hearing her long ago.

Volya supposed it was for the best that Luba was returning to school, even if it was for interior design. And now that she learned her daughter might be staying with Greg, she felt more comfortable with the idea. She hoped Luba would at least write to her when she returned to Toronto. In the two years she was there, she had written only once. Phone calls were better, but the long distance made it too expensive. Still, it was so fast. Like when she got news about Luba in the hospital. If it were not for the phone—she did not even want to think about it.

Volya took a step into Luba's bedroom and looked to the night stand. She was dying to know what her sister had written in the letter Luba had received that morning. Volya did a quick scan of the room without touching anything, but did not find it. She probably took it with her, thinking Volya might read it; sad when a daughter did not trust her own mother. Zenia was plotting something again; she could taste it like a clove of freshly crushed garlic. And that letter was only the beginning.

Volya thought bitterly how Zenia's letters tended to wreak havoc in her life. She remembered the first letter Zenia had ever written, arriving two months after she and Bohdan had left for Germany. Mama carried that letter around in her pocket always, reading it over and over. The stamp was peculiar, and the address as well. Mannheim. The city was so far away, she could not imagine it. Zenia had written that both she and Bohdan had jobs in a uniform factory—Bohdan working in the shipping department while she sewed buttons for nine hours each day. She complained about it, of course, and how cramped they were in their tiny apartment and how she was always exhausted because the trains ran all hours of the night and day, and the walls were so thin she could hear the neighbours peeing in the pot just beyond their bedroom. Volya imagined the neighbours could hear Zenia's high-pitched whining as well. Volya had already decided back then that Bohdan was either a fool for putting up with her sister, or a saint, and it seemed nothing had changed to that day.

After some time Bohdan was promoted and they were able to move into a small house away from the factory. All the time they remained behind in Brinzi, her mother worried about Zenia and Marko, and never about Volya. It aggravated her to think that they were starving to death while Zenia complained about getting meat only once a week. Volya would have given her left arm for a piece of meat, no matter how small. And then her sister had the nerve to write that if the only cow she ever saw again was on her plate, she would be happy. That made Volya furious, thinking about the fate of their poor Kalyna. Zenia was always so thoughtless and selfish, and that had not changed, either.

In spite of the horrific circumstances, with their village in flames as the

Nazis herded them into carts and wagons, Volya was relieved to finally leave Brinzi for Germany. She was sixteen years old when she and her mother left their home for good; it was 1942. They were packed into dingy, rank cattle cars at the back of a long train—her mother, some of the other villagers, and a lot of strangers from other towns. No one made a sound, fearing any attention from the grim soldiers who pushed them around like a flock of hapless turkeys. Even today, Volya shuddered to think of the dark and cold inside those cars, and how they had hardly any food or water for what seemed like days. She could still feel the dryness in her mouth and throat. Later she learned it was only eleven hours, but she had never wanted a drink of water so badly. When they arrived at the train station in Poland, they stood in long lines on the platform, swaying with exhaustion and hunger, waiting to be registered. Mama spoke Polish well enough to answer their curt questions. Volya remembered trembling when she noticed a German official behind the counter staring at her, and she forced herself to look away. The stern Polish clerk taking their information looked like she could have been German herself, her gold hair coiled in a tight braid on top of her head, and her uniform crisp and intimidating. She stamped their piece of paper, handed it to Mama, then they were waved away toward another train. Volya did not exhale until they were safely out of sight.

The train to Germany was no better and took even longer. When they arrived at the Mannheim station, they were directed to a series of barracks nearby, then watched as soldiers splashed what looked like dirty water inside of the buildings.

"What are they doing, Mama?" she asked.

Mama snorted in disgust. "They are delousing the barracks before we go inside. Imagine, they want us to sleep in that!" But they had no choice; the soldiers pushed all of them inside and locked the doors. Volya recalled her panic as she heard the bolts clang into place. By then rumours of concentration camps and atrocities against refugees had made the rounds, so Volya was sure they would be burned alive inside the wooden buildings.

Her mother tried to calm her. "Hush, my child," Sylana warned. "I know it smells like a pigsty in here. Just hold on until morning." They tried to find a clean place to lie down, but all the straw reeked of disinfectant and urine. They huddled together instead, looking around the room at the scared, tired faces of friends, neighbours, and strangers—two hundred or more Ukrainians, Poles, and Lithuanians. In the morning they formed one line in front of the breakfast wagon and as they moved along, their bowls were filled with a steaming greenish liquid.

"What is it, Mama?" Volya asked, wrinkling her nose at the pungent aroma. Mama dipped her spoon in and sipped cautiously.

"Nettle soup," she muttered. "We fed this to our cattle back home."

Shortly after noon, German civilians began to arrive and then leave with certain travellers, perhaps taking them to farms or factory jobs. Mama wanted to be posted in the city so she could be nearer to Zenia. Their turn came late in the day. A German soldier grabbed Mama by the arm and started to lead her away, leaving Volya behind.

"What about my daughter?"

There was some confusion while the Germans waved their arms about and conferred in sharp tones. To Volya's ear, their language had a harsh sound and made her head hurt. Finally, one of the soldiers pointed and waved at her to come forward. Mama reached for her hand.

"They tell me you will be working at the farm next to me." She wiped her eyes and whispered. "Try to look strong, try not to cry."

They were hustled off to a wagon hitched to a large bay horse just outside the train station. Three other Ukrainian refugees already sat in the back, glum and silent, waiting for the ride to their new homes. In the dark, Volya clutched Mama's arm and huddled against her until Volya was beckoned off the wagon. A tall woman came out of a modest, older farmhouse and stared at the shaking girl. The driver mumbled something to her, pointing at Volya and her mother. Mama listened intently. She had only a basic understanding of German, so she strained to make out the words.

The woman looked displeased as she stood with her arms crossed, peering at Volya through thick yellowed glasses. Volya remembered looking up at her, shy and afraid. She noticed the long apron tied around her neck and waist was badly stained.

"Volya," Mama spoke softly. "This is Frau Veber. You will be working for her and her husband. They tell me I will be at the next farm over. Be good and respectful. I will see you tomorrow, I promise." But Mama sounded nervous as she pushed her daughter gently toward the imposing woman.

Frau Veber barked something at her and turned toward the house. Volya stood still for a moment, watching helplessly as the wagon creaked and moved away, Mama a dark shape in the back. Volya had a strong urge to turn around and run after the wagon; it had not gone far. Just then, her new employer threw open the door and lamplight spilled all over her, exposing her hesitation. Under the Frau's glassy glare, Volya felt her stone legs move and carry her into the strange house. At that moment, she realized she would never see her own home again. Nor would she cry again for a very long time.

Crying got you nowhere.

Dismayed by Luba's room, Volya could not help but tidy up. She made the bed and then sorted through her daughter's overfilled basket of laundry. Volya wondered if her daughter would even notice. She could not bear the thought of Luba doing her own washing, knowing how careless and frivolous she was with her clothes. If a sweater shrank in hot water, she would buy a new one without a second thought. Everything had to be instant this, automatic that. Luba just rolled her eyes and laughed when Volya tried to tell her how they had to wash everything by hand long ago, just so she could appreciate the modern electric appliances. Luba's way of life was just so different from what Volya's had been at that age, how would she and Luba ever find some common ground?

She thought back to the tough life she'd had on their small farm in Brinzi. Even that experience did not prepare Volya for the hard work ahead of her at the Veber farm. At first she pretended she was having one very long, bad dream. But each morning, she woke in the same dark, musty-smelling room, the prickly straw of her mattress poking through the worn cotton cover. The very first morning was the most unsettling. Volya was shocked at the filth that surrounded her pallet, obviously a thoroughfare for rats and mice, and shuddered to think they might have been in the room with her that night. She choked on the thick dust created while sweeping out the soot and dried rat pellets; the small window opened only a few centimetres to let in fresh air. The rest of the house was not much better; Frau and Herr Veber seemed content to live in slovenly conditions. Later she learned that even with the thick glasses they wore, they could see only a very short distance ahead.

Though Volya was hired to help with the farm and to keep the house clean, she came to think of herself as a rented-out farm implement. The paltry amount of money she made barely put her above the level of slave. However, there was one task she was not assigned but would have preferred: she wished she could do the cooking. Volya had never known anyone so miserly with their food. Hunger was not new to her, but at the Vebers the pains never left her, especially when she lay exhausted on her pallet each night and smelled the food she had no access to downstairs. She could feel the sharpness of her hip bones as her hands rested on her growling stomach. She was wasting away. On her second day with them, Volya was served a slice of bread with an entire spider baked into it; the fat black body was a centimetre wide and the spiny legs reached right through the slice. Of course she could not eat that piece of bread so she left it sitting on her plate. The Frau snatched it up when Volya left the table and devoured it with a second bowl of thin cabbage soup. They were animals, she thought. Volya nearly vomited on the spot, but held on until she was outside. That night she did not notice how uncomfortable her bed was for the knives churning in her stomach.

She remembered wanting so much to see her mother, but the Frau did not seem to understand her when she asked, so she stopped asking. Volya was sure she would never learn their ugly language. They certainly did not care to learn hers. So each day Volya chopped wood for the stove, hauled water from the well, fed and milked two cows, then shovelled up their manure, fed the chickens, and collected their eggs, watered and hoed the garden, washed all the dishes, and cleaned the house. Luba always thought Volya was exaggerating when she described her daily routine. The first day when she was told to sweep and tidy the upstairs rooms, she counted three regular mattresses piled in a corner of the Vebers' bedroom, including the one that should have been in her room. Volya almost cried at the sight—she had never encountered such mean and hateful people.

On Sunday Volya was finally allowed to visit Mama and found herself standing in the manure-splattered back of the Vebers' truck, wearing her one unsoiled, cotton dress. She did not want to sit in the dirty straw, and tried to keep her shoes and clothes clean as she held desperately to the flimsy railing along one side as the truck lurched over a rutted road. When they stopped in front of another farmhouse about two kilometres from their farm, Frau Veber motioned at her to get off. Volya saw mud all around the truck, so she decided to climb over the railing onto a clump of dead grass. But as she stepped down she felt a tug at her waist and heard a ripping sound; her dress was caught on a wire securing the rail to the platform of the truck. The truck's engine roared.

"Stop!" Volya shouted in Ukrainian. "My dress is caught!" The truck moved away and when she grabbed at her skirt she heard another rip and it came loose. Volya stood there, looking down at her torn dress, her eyes searing, her face hot. This was her only good dress. It was Sunday. What was she going to do?

Then she felt an arm around her shoulders and looked up to see Mama smiling at her. A tall, pale woman with a worried expression stood next to her.

"Volya, come inside, we will mend your dress. Frau Koennig has a modern sewing machine. It will not take long." Mama and the kind Frau led her inside the tidy, simple house. They found her a housecoat to wear, then Mama proudly opened the gleaming wooden sewing machine and selected thread that nearly matched the washed-out blue of her dress.

The Frau said something to Volya in German. Volya looked at Mama in confusion.

"She wants to know if you would like some tea," Mama explained.

"Yes, please."

"We will all have some tea before we go to church," Mama said, threading the machine. Volya watched in fascination as the thread, like a snake gliding though a labyrinth, slipped into various metal holders, disappeared into the machine, then reappeared on the other side.

"Mama, this machine is so complicated."

Mama smiled and nodded. "Frau Koennig showed me how to use it the second day I was here. She saw me sewing by hand and said, "Nein, nein," and that I must learn to use the machine. I did not want to—I was afraid I might break it. But when she learned I was a seamstress, she asked me to do all her sewing. I might even do some sewing for neighbours if we need to trade for goods she cannot find or buy."

The Frau returned with a fancy tray carved from oak bearing three cups of hot tea. Volya still remembered that tray as if it were in front of her now. The cups were decorated with delicate flower patterns in every shade of pink and green, and the rims shone with gilt. There were also sugared biscuits on the tray, and Volya's stomach began to rumble. It had been so long since she had seen sweet treats of any kind, she could hardly believe these were real. The shiny egg-white wash sprinkled with sugar made them appear like ceramic disks encrusted with tiny diamonds. Frau Koennig must have noticed her eyeing them and she smiled encouragement, pointing to a biscuit, then to Volya. Her hand shook as she reached out for the treat. Volya had to swallow before she could take her first bite—saliva had flooded her mouth.

Frau Koennig appeared angry and said something in a sharp, disapproving voice. Volya stopped chewing, the chunk of biscuit lying heavy and dry on her tongue. Mama regarded her daughter sadly, and Volya wondered what she had done wrong.

"Everything is fine, child, eat. She just said that the Vebers probably do not feed you anything at all. They have a bad reputation." Mama's brown eyes drooped and her mouth turned down as she continued. "On Sundays at least you will get some decent food. Frau Koennig is a widow—she does not have much, but she is kind."

She turned back to the machine and began arranging the torn dress under a long metal arm. Volya presented a sorry picture, thin and dull-skinned; Mama probably found it difficult to look at her. "You need to learn German. We will practise a little today."

"But why, Mama?" Volya pleaded, not wanting anything to do with Germans at all.

"Because language is power."

Volya knew not to argue.

"Here it is, done! See, I told you. Put it on, over there; there is no one else in the house today."

Volya looked down at her reconstituted dress. It was a miracle: she could not even see where the tear used to be.

"Can I learn to use the machine, Mama?"

"Of course—after you learn to speak German."

Volya, who had been resisting up to then, became an eager student of the language she hated. Within a few weeks she could understand much of the conversations she listened in on between her mother and the Frau, as well as her employers and their one elderly farm hand. Of course, she did not let on to the Vebers, and continued to pretend she understood only the few commands they had taught her. She often felt like one of those horrid Shepherd dogs everyone kept, except the dogs were fed better. Volya detested her employers and looked forward to Sundays with Mama and the Frau, the peacefulness of church, the warm meals. She learned to sew as easily as she had learned to speak German, and spent her best moments in a welcoming house, where the sounds of women's quiet voices suited her perfectly. Mama had not forgotten about Zenia, of course, and with the help of the Frau she soon learned that Zenia and Bohdan were still in Mannheim, although at a different address from the one on the letter.

After church one day in early June, a friend of the Frau's took Volya and Mama across the city. Volya had been only to the outskirts of the city where the church and farm supply store were located, and the place seemed huge and terrifying to her now. The truck slowed down in front of a row of tiny houses; they appeared to be well-kept and had not been touched by the bombs. There was a fat woman watering flowers in her minuscule yard, and Volya noticed the bright reds of her poppies and the purple and yellow pansies below, and could not help thinking of Brinzi. She had not seen such colours in a very long time.

Mama was out of the truck almost before it had rolled to a stop, and running towards the fat woman with a watering can in her hands. It was Zenia, pregnant. Volya froze, still inside the truck, watching Mama and Zenia as they hugged and cried and laughed. Then Bohdan emerged from the far side of the little house and joined the women. Volya was nudged out the door of the truck, and walked slowly towards her sister.

She heard Mama say, "So when are you due? July maybe?" Zenia nodded her head and began to weep again. Mama tried to console her while Volya looked on, embarrassed and confused. At sixteen, she knew very little about sex or pregnancy since Mama had never talked to her about it, except to hand her rags and washing instructions when she began to menstruate two years before. She felt unsure what to think. Zenia still had not noticed Volya nor acknowledged her, although Bohdan wrapped her in his big arms and called her "little sister."

Wordlessly, she followed the three of them up the short flight of stairs into the house. Volya thought she would be excited to see her sister after all that time, but all she felt were anger and resentment: the same feelings she had always had for Zenia. Her sister looked so healthy—plump with the pregnancy, and glowing. There were nice things in her home—well-made furniture, new unchipped china, framed pictures on the walls, and even a small radio—whereas Volya had nothing. Yet, in spite of all her advantages and wealth, Zenia still managed to lament her lot, making Mama feel sorry for her, too. That, Volya decided, was too much.

The Digging Begins

"Hi Luba! Come on in." Bella Davies stood in her tailored suit with her usual brilliant smile, waving Luba into her tell-all parlour. Luba wondered how she managed to look so cool, so together, as untouchable as the lingerie models in her magazines. And, on top of that, she could get people to confide in her like she was a dear older sister they hadn't seen for years. Luba slipped into her usual place on the couch, and thought only how she desperately wanted to be just like her. Cool. Unflappable. Straight course ahead. Everything Luba was not.

"You sounded anxious on the phone. What's been happening?" Bella asked, sitting across from Luba and calmly resting her hands in her lap.

"I'm not sure what to do next. I need advice," Luba blurted then paused, collecting her thoughts.

"I'll try, but first tell me about the funeral."

"The best I can say is that it's finally over with, thank God."

"And how did it go?"

"Remember I told you that my Aunt Zenia flew in from Toronto and stayed with us?"

Bella nodded.

"Well that was awful. I think she and my mother were civil to each other for half an hour during the entire visit. They never stopped arguing. Now they're all gone, including Greg. My mother is still in a foul mood and only seems to calm down when she's telling me about the old days. Then it's like she goes into a trance or something and the rest of the time she tunes me out."

"How do you feel about that?"

"Sometimes I think I bait her just to see if she'll react."

"So you have been paying attention to me, I see."

Luba smiled. "Yup, and I'm beginning to see how satisfying it can be to get my mother all fired up. It's so easy. Like yesterday, when she started to criticize the way I cut bread, I purposefully told her I was going to write my will, and that I wanted to be cremated. She freaked. I hate that open-casket thing. I don't ever want people gawking at me like they did at my poor cousin, but my mother and her traditions are tighter than the blood bond between us, that's for sure."

"What did she do?" Bella asked gently.

"She hit the ceiling a few times and when she returned to earth she was screaming about Catholic rites and how no daughter of hers would be cremated, and she ordered me not to talk about it any more. So I got really mad because she was telling me how I was going to be buried, and I guess I started to swear, something she never tolerates, so she stormed into her bedroom and slammed the door shut. It was an odd sensation. For once I felt like I was in control."

Bella tilted her head and smiled slowly. "You're getting better." And then, "Does your mother react that way often?"

"No. I'm the one who usually runs to my room and slams doors. I left then and went out to see my Aunt Veronica."

"Do you find it comforting to talk to your aunt?"

"I did before Orest passed away. Now, we don't actually talk much. She usually embroiders or crochets while we watch television together. That's okay. I don't want to add to what she's already been going through, so I don't usually say much about what's happening at home. But she knows. She always knows when I come over like that. I used to do it a lot before I left for Toronto."

"How long have you been going to your aunt's?"

"Since we moved here when I was twelve years old, I guess."

"Did you have anyone to talk to when you lived in Toronto?'

"We lived with my grandmother then. She kind of took care of me while my mother was at work, and when I came home from school. I liked having her around. She cooked for me and sewed clothes for my mother. But she told me stories about life in old Ukraine, scary stories about the war, really nasty stuff."

"How did you feel about that?"

"Well, I remember having nightmares. Especially when she talked about the Nazis bayoneting babies and mutilating people. It was disgusting. I think I was a little scared of her, actually. She'd get this strange look in her eyes and then drift off into these awful stories. Kind of like my mother has been doing lately, now I think of it."

"And does your mother stay in touch with your grandmother?"

"No. Just before we left Toronto, my mother was arguing a lot with my aunt and my grandmother. I'm not sure why."

"It's not so unusual," Bella said, her eyes on Luba.

"You're right. Families are always having squabbles."

"What about your father?"

"My dad was a kind person, really gentle and sweet. That's how I remember him, anyway. Even my mother doesn't criticize him much. I don't remember them ever raising their voices or arguing, but then he wasn't around much. She says now that he worked hard and didn't make much money because he didn't have a good education, but it's not like she's complaining about him, just trying to make a case for me going back to school."

"And do you feel she loved him?"

"I think she was fond of him, but love? She probably married him so she would have someone, some stability in her life. She was twenty-nine years old already. She's not much into love, except for the soap operas she's obsessed with."

Bella laughed. "Again, not so unusual. Maybe she never found the right person."

"Maybe."

"And did you feel loved by her when you were a child?"

"Yeah, I think so. You know, I haven't really thought about it much. I always assumed she did because that's what mothers do. When my father died I remember she seemed more nervous, she kept close tabs on me, to the point of being over-protective. I'd say that's probably when she started to feel more bitter, more cynical. Then things changed again when I turned thirteen, because according to her I was so rotten and never did anything the way she wanted me to. She was quick to put me down, insult me. She could be so mean and then accuse me of being an ungrateful, unloving, cruel daughter because I didn't offer to iron the towels or vacuum the house every other day. I realized then that her love was not unconditional."

"I see. Do you actually believe that her love was dependent on your behaviour?"

"Yes, and there were times I absolutely hated her for it. But, most of the time, I just didn't think about it. Right now I can't figure her out. I felt bad because I failed at school and I know that meant a lot to her, so lately I've been trying to make her happy. I'm trying to get into a really competitive program at Ryerson, but she's sour about the whole idea. I even plan to stay with my cousin, the lawyer. You'd think she'd be pleased."

"So do you think she's disappointed that you're not studying medicine or law?"

"That's part of it."

"And what else?"

"I don't know. Maybe..." Luba stopped. She realized that after seeing Bella this long they had never discussed her overdose of pills, the real reason she was in these sessions. Why it had happened. Every moment was leading to this one, and she didn't want to open that door, not yet. Was it too late to change topics, think of something else, quick? Would Bella notice?

"Maybe what?"

Luba remained silent, trying to think of something else to say.

Bella looked gently into Luba's eyes. "Maybe since your suicide attempt?"

Luba drew in her breath. She'd never actually called it that. To her mother it was a mistake, to her it was an accident. But Bella was probably right, damn her. That night, those pills, how could it have possibly been an accident?

"Luba? I'm sorry if I've upset you, but it's important that we talk about it."

"I know," Luba said in a weak voice.

"Do you think your mother is afraid you'll try again?"

Of course she is, Luba thought. It would certainly account for some of her mother's weird and erratic behaviour lately.

"Maybe."

"But, you're angry because she won't trust you."

Luba finally looked at Bella. "Yeah, I guess. Sometimes I find her staring at me, like I'm a stranger in her house and she doesn't know what to do with me. Like one of her stupid dolls, broken, unfixable, but she won't throw it away, just keeps it dusted and hidden on the shelf behind the others."

Bella sighed. "And this makes you feel..."

"Ashamed, embarrassed."

"Ashamed? Why?"

"Because I should never have let some stupid guy get to me like that."

Bella smiled and sat back. "You, my dear, are getting stronger and stronger by the minute."

"You think so? I feel like such an idiot, so naïve sometimes."

"Well, you're not, and you are making major steps to move forward in your life."

Luba nodded and let out a lungful of air. She felt drained.

"Shall we change topics for now?"

"Please."

"You mentioned that your mother and her sister have a tense relationship. Any ideas about that?"

Luba sat up straighter. "I got a letter from my Aunt Zenia yesterday. I didn't tell my mother about it until this morning, and now she's furious with me because I wouldn't tell her right away what it was about. It's an airline ticket for Toronto, leaving this Saturday. Aunt Zenia wants me to see my grandmother."

"Oh," Bella said, widening her eyes, which reflected her silver-green satin blouse. "What are you going to do?"

"I don't know. If I told her, we'd have another huge scene. But Baba Sylana is getting old and her health is failing and I may not have many more chances to talk to her." Luba pulled at a clump of her hair and twisted it around, glaring at the split ends. "But the more I think about it the guiltier I feel about my mother. Which makes me mad. I don't want to feel guilty about her any more. Not about any of it, the pills, flunking out in school, just being a failure..."

"Luba, listen to yourself. Listen to what you've just said." She paused and looked at Luba intently. Luba looked away. She didn't want to think about what she had just said. She wanted to trade places with Bella at that moment, to be on Bella's side of the room, sitting in her chair, not as a patient on the couch, whining, hating who she was, wishing she belonged.

"You're right. It's my life."

"You are the only one who can decide exactly what will make you feel happy—you're right about that. But you also need to forgive yourself once in a while and give yourself permission to be selfish if you want to call it that. Do you want to go and see your grandmother?"

"To be truthful, I didn't want to at first. But I think I need to go."

"Okay?" Bella sat back with one of her shiny smiles and her hair cascading like a golden waterfall over slippery boulders.

"Okay. I'm going."

"Good. I will look forward to hearing all about it," Bella said, and Luba believed her.

Luba felt more settled than she had in a long while. And excited, though a bit nervous about spending time with Aunt Zenia and Baba Sylana, the women her mother couldn't love.

Luba did not divulge to Bella the other thing she was worried about—flying. She had never been in an airplane before, and now here she was about to land in Toronto, feeling terrified. The first leg to Sudbury on a tiny twelve-seater plane was turbulent the entire way. Going up it felt like she had left her stomach behind and had to grab for the airsick bag almost immediately. A false alarm. Landing was even worse as the plane plunged then rose up again two or three times before touching down, Luba flushing so hot she was soaked with sweat, sure they were going to crash. Now they were on the final approach to the airport.

Ooh, another dip, another stomach flip. She prayed silently, "Please God, if you exist, let me survive this last landing and I will take the bus back up north."

Aunt Zenia had told her not to worry about anything when Luba called to confirm that she was coming. She wanted to give her niece some time to relax, take her shopping, get her some decent clothes before she returned to school. Luba was not totally comfortable with this sudden generosity. She couldn't help but be suspicious that this had nothing to do with her and everything to do with Aunt Zenia and her mother. Then she wondered if she'd she been so poisoned by her mother's cynicism that she also believed everyone was out to take advantage of everyone else. No, Luba had other life experiences with back-stabbing friends to blame for her own budding paranoia.

When the plane finally touched down gently and came to a stop, she couldn't wait to get out of that hellish tin can. Inside the huge main terminal Luba tried to remain calm as she scanned the masses of people for her relatives.

"Luba! Over here!" She turned around and saw Aunt Zenia waving at her, looking very smart in a fitted navy suit with white trim.

"How was the flight? You look pale, did you get sick? I always get sick, so I take Gravol. I should have warned you, poor darling, I didn't even think of it. Look Bohdan, how green she is." Aunt Zenia unwrapped Luba from her arms and turned her niece to face her grinning uncle.

"I'm fine, Auntie, really. I just hated those landings. How do you stand it? I've never flown before." Luba realized what a milestone this was as soon as she spoke the words. Her aunt hooked one of her arms and led her toward the baggage claim area; Uncle Bohdan had already relieved her of her carry-on bag.

"Are you hungry?" Aunt Zenia asked.

"No, I don't think food would stay down anyway."

"Well, I'm not like your mother. I won't force-feed you if you're not hungry. But then again, I can't let you lose weight while you're with us. You are just perfect the way you are. And so pretty. Definitely, the prettiest of all your cousins, prettier than my daughters-in-law. Former and present," she chuckled. "Even with your dark colouring, you look more like our side of the family than your mother's. Don't you think, Bohdan? She could be our daughter."

Luba looked back and forth at her aunt and uncle. That was a big stretch. She had their height, but it ended there.

"Auntie, I'm not sure I look like anyone in our family. Not like my mother or father, either. You know, sometimes I wonder, I wonder, if maybe, I wasn't adopted?"

"Adopted!" Aunt Zenia snorted. "Hah! No way, you are definitely your mother's daughter. You looked so much like her when you were younger, but of course, you've changed now you're all grown. No, Luba, you're not adopted."

They arrived at the baggage claim where Zenia ordered her husband to grab Luba's suitcase.

"It's too heavy for you." She held Luba back while Bohdan heaved the bag off the conveyor. He returned to them, grunting.

"Well, at least let me carry the smaller bag, okay?" She grabbed it back from her uncle. He smiled and patted her head.

"Lubochka. You Tatenko women know your minds. Heaven help us men who try to get in the way. Okay, follow me. The car is just out front." The two women followed his amiable bulk outside then into a cream-coloured Oldsmobile.

"Adopted! What an idea. Are things that bad with your mother these days?" Aunt Zenia turned around to eye her niece in the back seat, a peculiar expression on her face.

"No, things are normal." Luba hoped her aunt wouldn't ask what normal meant.

"And what about Veronica? How is she holding up?"

"She's doing her best. The police ruled Orest's death accidental, so I think she feels better about that."

"How could they possibly know that?"

""It was an accident," Luba said, feeling a little defensive. "The police investigated, there was no foul play."

"But Luba, he took drugs. That is no accident. He chose to take drugs. That's like choosing to die."

"I don't know. It was probably carelessness," she countered.

"Carelessness? Taking drugs is a sickness, not to mention immoral," she asserted, and turned away to face forward again. Luba opened her mouth to protest, but stopped. If her aunt only knew about her own dance with death. She sank back in her seat and wondered if she had travelled all this way for the same environment, the same arguments, the same mother in a different skin. Her uncle was right to beware of "those Tatenko women," but she didn't consider herself one of them. God, she hoped she was not one of them. Maybe her grandmother could at least help her understand what made them tick and whir.

Reawakenings

"Did you sleep well?" Zenia flitted about in her yellow-and-blue kitchen while Luba sat at the counter, squinting at the brightness and stifling a yawn. Her aunt made her think of an efficient little goldfinch gathering food for her hatchlings. As for the kitchen decor, she presumed they had chosen the colours of the Ukrainian flag on purpose. How patriotic. How gaudy. Other than that, and the usual bits of embroidery draped on dressers, tables, and over the crucifixes prominently displayed in each bedroom, Zenia and Bohdan had a huge, modern house compared to their poorer relations in Copper Creek. They had moved up a few notches from the time Luba had lived here ten forever years ago. But then, Aunt Zenia was a successful real estate agent, running her own office, and her uncle owned a construction company. Luba guessed they could well afford to buy her expensive ticket, which she intended to exchange for bus fare for her return trip.

She yawned. "Thanks, I slept really well, Auntie. Don't know why I'm yawning. I slept nine hours. That should be enough." She yawned again.

"You probably need a lot of sleep, like Bohdan and the boys. Of course, they never get enough, workaholics, the whole family!" She threw up her hands, beaming.

"Do you think you're up to visiting Baba this morning? I have the whole day off so we may as well get that over with."

"Sure," Luba said, and picked up a piece of buttered toast. It didn't sound like her aunt was too keen on the visit. After all, Aunt Zenia was the one who had put her grandmother in the nursing home when she decided that Baba had gone senile and needed full-time care. So why had she been so insistent on Luba coming down to see her grandmother?

"Coffee? It's a fresh pot."

"Yes, thanks." Luba smeared peach preserves on her toast, spooned sugar and dribbled cream into her coffee.

"How is Baba doing?" she asked. Since her mother had discouraged Luba from visiting either Aunt Zenia or Baba when she first returned to Toronto to attend university, it had never occurred to Luba to ask more questions or to ignore her admonitions. She had been so anxious to get away from her meddling family, it was easy to pretend these relatives didn't exist, and Toronto was big enough to disappear in. At this point, Luba had no desire to bring up the two last years, or try to explain why she hadn't even tried to see her grandmother, let alone her aunt and uncle.

"Oh, you know," Zenia finally replied when she sat down across the chrome-and-glass table from Luba, "Baba has her good days and her not-so-good days. The last time I visited, just after we got back from the funeral, she was alert and I told her about the trip. I didn't say anything about the funeral. Such a morbid subject, I didn't want to upset her."

Luba noticed that her aunt was dressed in a taupe polyester suit and she wondered if she should change out of her jeans and T-shirt for this visit.

"Is she easily upset? Should I be careful what I say to her?" She had a picture of her grandmother bustling about, packing up lunches, feeding her dumpling-and-potato milk soup after school. Luba couldn't envision her in a fragile state or as an invalid. She had always been so strong, in charge, even fierce to the little girl who Luba used to be.

"It's hard to know. Sometimes you say something simple to her, maybe about the weather, or how the grandchildren and great-grandchildren are doing, and she gets this strange look on her face, and you know she's gone. Can't talk to her after that. She might say something, but it won't mean anything, just nonsense. So, we usually leave if she falls into one of those spells."

Luba didn't want to think of her like that, but being so close she couldn't push Baba out of her mind like she did before. She was scared again, afraid of what horrible story her grandmother might tell her about the war. Luba shook her head. Silly, she was an adult now.

When they entered her room in the nursing home two hours later, Luba saw there was no substance to her fears, but the shell that remained was worse than she had imagined. She had never been inside one of these places. The smell that assaulted her when they began their trek down the beige, linoleum-lined corridors was not of decay, but the sharp, warrior-strength odour of cleaning solvents. Her respiratory centre automatically shut down, and Luba had to force short breaths through her nose. Her stomach was asking her brain if it was appropriate to begin somersaulting again. She tried to breathe normally as they stood at the foot of Baba's bed, watching her sleep.

"Mama," Zenia said in a quiet voice, "are you awake? I brought you a visitor."

The shell stirred a little, but otherwise did not respond.

"Maybe we should come back later," Luba whispered. A tightness behind her eyes made her head pound. The air in the room was poison and she found herself holding her breath again.

"Oh no, she sleeps on and off all day and night. She's just dozing. Mama!" she said in a sharper tone. "Wake up!"

The tired old lids squeezed tight and Baba brushed her forehead with a bony, withered hand. She was a wrinkled old woman with sparse white hair. Just ten years ago, at the age of sixty-seven, her long hair, braided and coiled on her head, was much darker. Luba remembered some wrinkling then, but now the old woman had shrunken further into her skin. Luba fought back tears. When had this happened, where had her Baba gone?

The eyes popped open then, but she did not look at her visitors.

"Mama, look who's here! It's Luba! She's come from Copper Creek just to see you." Aunt Zenia pushed Luba forward so she stood a few inches from her grandmother's face. "Say something, Luba. Maybe she'll recognize your voice."

"Hello, Baba," she managed in a hoarse whisper. If her aunt hadn't been standing right behind her, she would have turned around and bolted.

The old woman did not see Luba. She looked straight ahead into space, her lips moving, maybe forming words, but making no sound.

"Speak up, Mama. We can't hear you!" Aunt Zenia shouted next to Luba's ear, making her jump aside. Luba sidled over to the foot of the bed and stood there while her aunt tried to connect with the old woman, peering into her face, scolding her like she was holding out on purpose. This looked like a spell to Luba, not to be broken with cajoling or bullying.

"Aunt Zenia, why don't we come back another time?"

She looked at Luba, exasperated. "I can't just keep coming back here, I have a job to go to. It'll just take a few minutes for her to come back to reality."

But there was none of their reality for Baba that morning. After another fifteen agonizing minutes of pleas and threats, they left. Luba was shaking as they stepped outside into a warm, spring day. She flushed her lungs with deep breaths of clean air. Her aunt kept a sullen silence as they drove back to her house.

"Auntie?"

"Yes?"

"Is there a bus I can take to the nursing home? I don't mind coming back by myself. I mean, I am here to visit, and I don't mind going down there alone. Really." In fact, she would prefer it.

"The closest bus is two blocks away. And I think you have to transfer downtown to a different bus to get to the west end where the home is. It would probably take you an hour."

"That's okay. I'm used to taking buses and subways in Toronto. That's what I'm here for. Isn't it?" Her aunt didn't reply.

By the time they finished lunch, Zenia was relaxed again and chatted about her life in Toronto and her four grandchildren. Baba had been forgotten. "Now the oldest, Gillian Grace, was three years old when you left and Adam and Susan had just divorced the year before. Adam has been a wonderful father to Gillian, but she's turned her back on him completely. Only when she needs something, then she calls him. I'm sure Susan puts her up to it. Thirteen years old, and such a smart little thing. Beautiful blond girl. Tall, just like her father. She's already done some modelling. I just hope her mother doesn't push her too much. I think she's too thin, but that's how they like models to be. Twigs, like that Twiggy girl.

"Were you here, Luba, when he married Anne? No, you had already left by then. Right. Anne had a boy, Christopher, in 1970, and little Margaret in '72. They are the sweetest two children you'll ever know! Anne isn't Catholic, but she takes them to our church anyway. I don't think Susan has gone to church since she left Adam. That poor Gillian, raised like a heathen. Margaret had her first holy communion this winter. She was adorable! Come into the living room, Luba, I'll show you the pictures."

She took a fat grey photo album from a shelf filled with albums, and opened it to a page of photographs of a young girl wearing a fancy white dress, white socks and shoes, and a white crown and veil. Luba saw herself in that face, a forced smile staring up at them. At Luba's communion, her own expression was more pained. She had just lost a front tooth and her mother wanted her to smile, but not to show her teeth, resulting in a fierce grimace no one was happy with. She recalled the entire day as sheer misery and trauma. Luba felt sorry for this little girl, too. The things their parents made them do for the security of their souls.

"Now, here's Anthony. He was in the same group, same age as Margaret. You don't know Anthony, do you? Bill divorced his first wife, Alice, then remarried in, uh, '71, '72, something like that. Right. To Sylvia Squires. This is their little boy. He's dark, like her. Nice girl, his mother, Sylvia. Anthony is very quiet, like her. A sweet boy, but he has a hard time at school."

Luba remembered something about one of the children being slow to develop. This must be the one. She could sense a sadness in his eyes, not understood by those around him, maybe ridiculed for being "slow"? But he didn't look dull, just left behind. Luba knew that feeling, too.

"We're having a little party over here on Saturday. They will all be here," she announced. "Except for the ex-wives and one granddaughter, Gillian." Luba sat up straighter, more alert. She needed to pay more attention, maybe commit some names to memory so they didn't think she was dull and slow.

"Auntie? Do you have any photos from when you lived in Germany and England?" She wondered if she might be able to fill in some of the details that her mother had been leaving out.

"Oh sure. Here we are. Black-and-white only, in those days." She hauled three huge, wooden, lacquered albums from the top shelf. They were like Volya's—a heavy cloth spine holding two wooden covers decorated with bright Ukrainian designs made of coloured straw. The covers were smooth and shiny, coated with a clear, glossy varnish. Two fine woven ropes of embroidery thread and tassels hung from the top of the spines. Aunt Veronica had several of these photo albums as well. On Luba's last visit, a few days before she left for Toronto, Aunt Veronica had taken one down from a shelf and showed photos of her children, including several of Luba taken by Uncle Marko and Luba's father. Her aunt was sad, but she remained calm and didn't cry. Luba sensed that her presence was a comfort to her aunt and resolved to visit as much as she could when she returned from Toronto.

Zenia opened an album carefully to the first page. A large photo held in place with carefully pasted, gilded corner holders showed Zenia standing in front of a small flower garden, a plain brick building in the background. She was so young, maybe Luba's age, and yet she cradled a baby in her arms while a toddler clung to her skirt, bowed legs emerging from his shorts. Luba perked up right away. This looked like a picture she'd seen before. No, she hadn't seen this particular photograph, but it felt so familiar.

"Here we are in Mannheim, just before the end of the war. That's Adam standing and little Greg as a baby. Bohdan took that photo. Ah, here we all are. Our neighbour took this picture. Now Greg looks just like his father when Bohdan was twenty-four, don't you think?"

Luba nodded. Her uncle certainly was handsome back then. She smiled at his broad, proud grin. That was her good-natured Uncle Bohdan, all right, but too bad he hadn't kept up his trim figure. She glanced at her aunt, the probable cause of his deterioration.

"How long did you live in Mannheim?"

"We arrived late in 1941 and didn't leave until 1947. We were there when the war ended and we all had to move to refugee camps. It was absolutely miserable." She shook her head and carefully turned to a new page of photographs. Luba continued to nod and look at the photos while her aunt described life in the camp. She made it sound much worse than her mother ever did—this was just like being at home. Luba settled in for a long afternoon of listening.

Impotent Angels

Volya returned to her pew in the church and knelt to say her penance after confession. Not much to report to Father Buchkovsky this week. Losing her temper with Luba did not really count, but she mentioned it anyway since her list was so short. The Father was understanding and waved that one away, so only one Hail Mary this week. But Luba tried her patience so, even when she was 360 miles away. Volya had warned her repeatedly: her Baba would not be able to communicate with Luba. Her daughter sounded so disappointed when she called to report on that first visit. What did she expect? Mama was already losing her memory when she and Luba left Toronto; she spoke utter nonsense. Luba was old enough to understand that now, but at the time it was best to keep her away, to leave Toronto altogether. And now her mother lay there, wasting away, not even aware of where she was.

That vision brought to mind another time when her mother lay in a hospital, but as a much younger woman who was keenly aware of her circumstances and her pain. It was 1942 or '43, after one of the bombing raids over Mannheim. How Volya had prayed for her mother's recovery, spending as much time as she could in the church, whenever she could get away from the farm.

The church in Mannheim was grand, larger than anything she had ever seen before. She especially liked to go early, before the church filled up with old women and children. Inside it was quiet, and dark with wood. Light passing through the stained-glass windows turned deep blue and blood red before it bathed the century-old carved pews and plain wooden floors. The first time Volya stepped inside she had gone dizzy from holding her breath. Contrasted with the mud and steel and concrete outside, the interior was a place she never anticipated could exist in that cold, war-scarred city. She could feel God's presence all around her. At first it gave her a chill, but after studying the carvings and paintings and stained-glass pictures, she realized that the church was actually filled with angels. They buffered her from the hardness and immenseness of God—she knew how cruel he could be. But inside the church she felt safe. She remembered wishing she could stay in the church and never have to venture out into the dangerous streets of the city again. Or, even better, she wondered if one of the angels would come home with her, to the horrible place where she toiled and suffered. Volya thought she understood the angels, and she was sure they would look out for her where God might fail. How wrong she was.

Before that bombing raid, each Sunday had been the same. Volya was dropped off at Frau Koennig's farm or she walked the two kilometres there, then she, the Frau, and Mama walked another four kilometres to the church. Her stingy employers drove off in a different direction to their Lutheran church at the north end of the city and never offered to give them a ride. After Mass, the three women walked back to the Koennig farm and had lunch. Volya remained there for the afternoon, learning to sew with Mama, practising her German, and helping with supper preparations. She shared a hot meal with them, then walked back to the Veber farm in the opposite direction from Mannheim. At first Mama accompanied her if she wasn't too tired. The Vebers were cool, and rarely spoke to her. Mama did not enjoy those visits—she could see that Volya was not being treated well, and it pained her. After a month or so, she stopped coming altogether.

One Sunday a month, Frau Koennig's sister dropped her son Karl off for the day. He was a young man about twenty years old, crippled on the left side of his body. Karl could not walk without a crutch. The Frau explained he had the mental capacity of a child, although occasionally he spoke with an adult's voice. Volya mistrusted him as soon as she met him; she did not understand how he could be both a child and an adult at the same time. She hated the way he leered at her. His black, bottomless eyes seemed to penetrate through her clothing, and he continually scanned her, up and down, up and down, like a hyena deciding if there was enough meat on her bones to eat. As she sat in the pew, Volya shuddered just imagining his face. His hair was always greasy, he had an unwashed, bitter smell, and he never spoke to her or Mama. On the Sundays he stayed with his aunt, Volya tried to keep Mama between herself and Karl. On those days she had respite when they went to church, just her and Mama, while Frau Koennig stayed behind to mind her nephew. At the time, neither she nor Mama understood why the Frau could not leave him alone for the two hours, but she insisted that Karl needed to be watched in case he fell and hurt himself. Indeed!

The day Mannheim was bombed, a Friday in late April as she recalled, she had been instructed to purchase a coil of rope from the dry goods store in the city. Since the Vebers had used up their petrol ration through the end of May and their arthritic, elderly labourer had quit, Volya had become their legs and strong back as well as their eyes. Herr Veber suffered from gout and had difficulty walking or standing for longer than an hour at a time, so the bulk of the field work also became Volya's responsibility. The Vebers were on a waiting list for more farm help, as were most of the other farmers in the area.

Volya did not mind walking to Mannheim; she was pleased to get away from the sour-smelling farm house and the muddy fields. Constant physical labour had hardened her body so she was able to walk all day if need be. She was seventeen years old, and an attractive young woman beneath the thinness of her face. She had turned more than one head when she was out in public, most of them older men or teenage boys too young to serve in the war. She still wore her waist-long hair in a single braid down her back. Frau Koennig said her dark colouring and straight, well-defined nose gave her an exotic look. That made Mama smile and Volya wonder. Mama had sewn her a sturdy brassiere to hold her swelled breasts close to her body, and sewn dresses that were loose enough to hide Volya's generous curves. Not the type of figure modern girls cared for, she thought. Volya supposed Mama feared that she might suffer the same assault that Zenia had, though by then her eldest daughter had a beautiful, blond son and was pregnant again. But there was no Ukrainian husband waiting in the wings to save Volya from disgrace.

On that warm spring day Volya was in a light, almost carefree mood as she marched the six kilometres into Mannheim. The new green all around her and the gay chirping of birds uplifted her spirits to a degree that surprised her, and for a while let her forget about all the work awaiting her return to the farm. She found the dry goods store a few blocks from the west end of town, and joined other customers inside. Volya wandered slowly among all the barrels, peering into shelves, reading labels on cans of mouth-watering fruits, rubbing soft, colourful yarns between her fingers, caressing bolts of satin and linen, and admiring the display of dress patterns. She picked up one of the pattern packages and studied the drawings on the front and back. Perhaps she could memorize the shape of the cut pieces and they could try to sew one of the latest fashions on Frau Koennig's machine. Volya tarried as long as she dared before settling on the rope she had come to buy. She was about to request help from the clerk, a tall woman with blond braids coiled high on her head, when they heard the sirens. The dreamy, cozy store atmosphere erupted into explosive shouting, people running, doors slamming.

"Back here, hurry!" someone yelled. The clerk grabbed Volya's arm and pulled her toward the back of the store, behind the counter, pushing her through a door. She saw others ahead of her in the dimness, clattering down steep, narrow stairs into a cellar. Volya was swept along into the darkness below as the woman shouted, "I'm closing the door!" Volya stumbled in the pitch black and bumped into a wall. The many excited voices made it seem like there were hundreds of people in a vast cavern, until someone lit a match and Volya counted eight people huddled together in a cold, damp storage room. She shivered and did not say a word, and gradually they all stopped talking. One man laughed nervously and was told to shut up. After that there was absolute silence as they waited for the first bombs to fall.

The first hits seemed far away, three or four dull thuds, then nothing. The all-clear sirens did not sound, so they continued to wait in heavy darkness. Volya had never been this close to falling bombs and began to tremble, wondering where Mama, Zenia, Bohdan, and the baby were at that very moment. She felt a few more far-off tremors, then a loud crash and a scream as someone fell against her and knocked her down. Volya lay on the ground, terrified, feeling the earth below her pulse and shudder. The door at the top of the stairs swung open and light spilled onto the group hiding below, showing them sprawled all over the floor and scrambling to stand up. The shaking ceased and a woman began to cry in a low moan. Volya pressed herself against a wall and sat still, expecting they would all be crushed at any moment. Instead, after another minute or two, the all-clear siren rang out. Unbelieving, one of the men moved toward the cellar stairs and tested the lower steps. The entire staircase suddenly fell free from the door sill and collapsed in a heap of cracking, splintering wood amidst screams from the women, followed by a stunned silence.

Eventually, a couple of men were able to scramble back up into the store and lower down a ladder to help the rest of the group climb out. Volya noticed that most of the goods had tumbled off their shelves, and even a few shelves had toppled. There were nails everywhere. Volya crawled over the jumble of cans and boxes to exit the store, having forgotten completely about the rope and canvas she had come to buy. Outside, people were still running back and forth. She heard police and ambulance sirens all around her, and saw smoke rising from a street behind the one she was on. All she could think of was getting back to Mama. She wondered briefly if she should check on Zenia and the baby, but decided it was too hectic and crazy in the city and would be dangerous.

When she arrived, breathless, at Frau Koennig's, no one was home. Volya looked all around the house calling their names, then ran to search the barn and fields for any signs of people. She heard groaning from behind the milking shed and ran around to see a cow lying on her side, covered in blood, slowly waving her legs. Volya remembered standing there, as if paralysed, watching the dying animal. She forced herself to look away, and then noticed the debris lying all about. A bomb. A bomb had fallen here. So close to Mama. Where was Mama? She finally turned and ran back to the house and walked into the kitchen, more calmly this time. She looked down at the floor. Blood. There was blood on the pale grey stone tiles in the porch and in the kitchen. Though she could not know for certain, she was sure it was Mama's blood.

Dazed, she left the house and stood on the road outside. Volya had no idea how to find Mama. There were too many hospitals in the city, and she would have to wait until the Frau returned. She waited another long hour before she returned to the Veber farm. Frau Veber cuffed her across the back of the head when she stepped inside, before Volya could even explain where she had been. She hardly felt the sting. Instead, she launched herself into work so she did not have time to think about what might have happened to Mama.

The next morning, after milking and breakfast chores, Volya announced to the Vebers that she had to see Mama at the hospital, even though she had no idea if she was in one or not. In spite of their protests and curses, Volya left and ran all the way to Frau Koennig's home. The Frau was there, and confirmed her fears. Mama had been milking the cow when a shell exploded less than a hundred yards from the shed. The cow received most of the shrapnel— she had died during the night. Though the cow had saved Mama's life, some of the shrapnel had lodged in her legs as well. Yes, there was a lot of bleeding from the many cuts, Frau Koennig explained to Volya who stood there, knees knocking together, lips quivering. But no vital organs or arteries had been hit, so Mama would be fine, she promised.

The Frau was kind to Volya. Together they walked to a neighbour's home where they were able to telephone Zenia and Bohdan to tell them the news, and to find out if they had been spared. Bohdan told her that they were fine, but part of his factory was damaged. Zenia could not speak to her; Volya heard her crying in the background. Another of the Frau's neighbours agreed to drive them to the hospital where Mama was being treated.

The hospital was overflowing with bomb raid casualties. They walked past rows of bleeding, wailing, bandaged patients lined up along the hospital corridors, most of them refugees and non-German nationalities. Mama was one of those patients. All the regular wards held soldiers recovering from injuries inflicted at the front.

Mama was not pleased to see her. Volya remembered feeling hurt, but she could see that Mama was in a great deal of pain; there were not enough drugs available for everyone. In fact, they soon learned that pain killers were available, but used sparingly, and only for the Germans or the loudest, most injured patients. Mama did not qualify. She lay in agony, but did not utter a sound, unless a nurse or doctor tried to move her legs. Later, after she was discharged, she told them that one of the German doctors had raised her leg to look at it, then let it fall hard back on the cot. He had laughed at her cry of pain.

Volya tried to see Mama as often as she could over the next three weeks. It was difficult to get away from the Vebers who had grown dependent on her for nearly everything. Frau Veber was essentially blind, and Herr Veber was nearly crippled with gout. Volya was certain she would go out of her mind between their constant demands and criticisms and whining. Often their requests were in conflict and instead of arguing with each other, they shouted abuses and obscenities at Volya.

The next Sunday she went as usual to Frau Koennig's, although she had considered not going at all since Mama was still in the hospital. Plus she knew Karl would be there. But Volya was desperate to get away from her brutal employers for even a short time. The Vebers kept her longer than usual and she arrived out of breath from her run. Frau Koennig was pleased to see her because she had been asked to attend a special service at the hospital for all the injured guest labourers, and as Mama's employer she felt she could not refuse.

"So Volya, if you do not mind, child, please stay here with Karl. Don't look so sad. There is another service this evening if you want to go then," she said, trying to placate the girl.

"Oh, I cannot stay that long, Frau Koennig. The Vebers want me back to make their supper tonight." She lied but preferred the tyranny of the Vebers to the care of this monster child. She wished she had stayed at home then, and forever regretted that she had not. But she did not dare argue with the Frau who had been so good to her and Mama.

"Please pass my best wishes on to my mother. Tell her I will try to see her on Tuesday," was all she said.

"Ah, she may be able to come home by Wednesday," the Frau announced. "Let us pray for that. And Karl," she said, giving her nephew a stern look, "do not give Volya any trouble." With that she strode off in her thin, worn wool coat and brown felt hat with one bedraggled, striped feather wanly waving good-bye.

"I am tired," Karl whined from his chair by the kitchen table. Volya started in surprise; he had never spoken to her directly before.

"Do you want to take a nap?" she asked.

"Yes. Help me upstairs," he commanded. Volya stood next to him, but she had no idea how to help him upstairs.

"Here," he growled at her, "take my arm." He nodded sharply toward his useless left arm. She reached out gingerly for the appendage.

"It does not bite!" He stood up and moved ahead a step, helped by the crutch under his right arm.

Volya put her right arm under his left and together they shuffled toward the stairs. She found herself breathing through her mouth being that close to him; his body odour nearly overwhelmed her. As they struggled up the steep stairs, she remembered thinking that his smell reminded her of improperly cured, mouldy old sauerkraut.

With his crutch Karl pushed open the second door on the right and they had to move through sideways so they could both fit through. The bed was just a few feet from the door.

"But this is Frau Koennig's room. Are you allowed to sleep here?" she asked, not sure if she should have helped him inside. She knew there was another bedroom on the second floor, once occupied by the Frau's daughter who had grown up and left home.

"This is where we always sleep," he snarled at her, then turned slightly and deftly pushed the door closed with his crutch. It banged shut and made her jump. Volya was staring into his blazing black eyes, just inches away from her face, and started for the door. But before she could take a second step, he had grabbed her right arm, twisted it behind her back and pushed her forward on the bed. As she landed on her chest, the full weight of his body on her back crushed the air out of her lungs.

"Let me go!" she gasped. "What are you doing?"

"What do you think, you slut! Spread your legs! Let's make this easy, you filthy Slavic bitch!"

He shoved up her skirt, and she felt a claw ripping at her underpants. His right arm still held hers firm against her back. Volya's shoulder burned with pain, but she was more concerned about his left arm, the one she thought was useless. She could feel him trying to slip his hand between her legs, scratching her tender skin with his long, curved nails. Her legs clamped shut in spite of the pain.

"Your aunt will kill you!" she yelled at him. "Let me go!"

"My aunt! Hah! She would not care. Don't you know what that whore and I do on this bed on Sundays? Open your legs, damn you! I know you want it, just like her! Open them or I will kill you, do you hear me? I'm not crippled, you stupid bitch," he gasped. "I can strangle you and throw you out the window, and they will think it was an accident." He kept scraping at her thighs and buttocks until she wanted to scream. He twisted harder on her arm.

"Stop!" she moaned. "Ah, please, not my arm. I'll do it, I'll do it." She had to stall somehow, to figure out how to get away. "I'll do it, only, I don't want to be facing down like a dog. I want to lie on my back. Like normal people. Please... I'll co-operate if you let me lie on my back."

"You're just a bitch. You don't deserve to look at my face while I honour you, slut. What makes you think you have the same rights as real people?" She heard him breathing with exertion and knew he was considering her request. He was tired. Without saying a word, he eased off her back and rolled her over. He leaned over her then pushed himself up so he stood over her, still grasping her arm, balancing himself on his right leg. Volya noticed his left arm hanging at his side.

"No tricks," he warned her and released her arm. "Now take your underpants off and lie down. Hurry up!"

Volya sat up slowly and rubbed her shoulder. She leaned over and tugged at her underpants, torn and bloody, blinking back tears. She could not let him see how frightened she was. His feet were directly in front of her as he stood on one good leg, the left leg dangling, barely touching the ground for balance. She thought, how could this man, this semi-cripple, have overpowered her? Then she felt the anger seeping into her, and with that, strength. Volya pulled the panties over her shoes and flung them away with her sore right arm, past Karl. As her hand let go of the panties, she opened her palm and with all her might pushed and kicked at his right leg then rolled to her left on the bed. Karl lost his balance and toppled over, grabbing for her with his flailing right arm. But Volya was out of reach, at the bottom of the bed, and off the end. She ran around him to the door, yanked it open, and rushed out, hearing him howl in rage as she raced down the stairs. Outside she kept running, running, down the street toward the city, sobbing and running. After a kilometre or so, Volya finally slowed to a walk, her chest heaving, tears streaming down her face.

At first she did not know where she was going. She could not go to the hospital because the Frau was there, and she could not face Zenia. Volya walked briskly, by then feeling the sting of scratches on her buttocks and thighs, her right shoulder throbbing. Her breath had returned to normal, and the tears dried to salt on her cheeks and chin by the time she found herself standing in front of the great wooden church doors. From inside, the sounds of singing voices floated through the cracks. She moved like a zombie up the church stairs, opened the heavy carved doors, and slipped inside the warm, stuffy darkness. She remained standing in the back, with all the others who worshipped in the packed room. The music soothed her; the wafting incense put her mind at ease. She was safe there, inside the holy walls, surrounded by the angels. No harm would come to her in this place. But outside, she was on her own; they all were.

Back at home, Volya made herself some tea and sat at the kitchen table. She had not thought about that incident for years, and now Luba was stirring up all those awful memories, the indignities she had suffered. And Mama, too, poor woman. She had tried to protect Volya as best she could, but, in the end, she was only human. And now Volya believed she had failed to keep her own daughter from harm. She supposed Luba judged her as harshly as she judged her own mother back then. Someday Luba would be a mother and would learn it was impossible to protect your children, even when they were with you. Volya remembered how desperately alone she felt after the incident with Karl. Mama was still in the hospital and she had no one to tell, no one to confide in. She did not want to return to Frau Koennig's. How would she explain why she had left Karl alone after she had promised to look after him?

A week after Mama came home from the hospital, Volya finally found the courage to visit. She was sure the Frau greeted her with coolness. Volya mumbled a greeting, but her face burned red when she remembered that her underwear had been left behind, bloody and torn. What had Karl told her? Perhaps he had said nothing, perhaps he had thrown the evidence away. But Volya was certain the Frau knew something had happened. After all, she never asked why Volya had left Karl alone—poor helpless Karl. Was it true after all, what Karl had said about his aunt? She shuddered to think about the two of them in that bedroom upstairs. Surely not. Then why had she not chided her for leaving him alone? And what about all those whispered stories about girls alone with the big German shepherd dogs? The thought still nauseated her after all those years. Wars turned normal people into desperate, depraved beings.

She remembered spending a long, miserable afternoon at the Frau's home since Mama was unable to walk to church. As Volya left later that evening, Mama accompanied her outside and limped a few steps down the road with her, a long skirt and socks covering all the wounds, by then ugly purple scars under flaking scabs. She still bore the scars thirty-five years later. Mama took her by the arm when they stopped.

"Listen," she said, a worried expression on her face. "Frau Koennig asked me to tell you it would be best that you not stop in on the Sundays when Karl is visiting. She said you upset him and he does not wish to see you. The Frau is not angry with you, but her nephew is a very sensitive boy and it does not take much to hurt his feelings." Volya gasped slightly, then looked down at her shoes. Mama paused, but only for a moment.

"This does not mean you have to miss Mass on those Sundays. I can meet you at church, and maybe we can have a lunch outside. There is a nice spot next to the graveyard. We see other people eating there sometimes. It will not be so bad."

Volya nodded her head but remained silent. "I still do not have much strength, so I will go back now." She squeezed Volya's hand. "Be strong, my daughter," she whispered, and turned away from her.

Volya stumbled forward into the shadows of the evening, tears threatening to burst out. Why did Mama not ask what had happened? She had wanted so much to tell her everything—everything Mama did not want to know. At that moment, Volya had never felt so desperately alone in all her life. While walking home that day, she decided that she was truly on her own now— fatherless, brotherless, sisterless, and motherless. She thought that this must be what it was like to be an orphan. She tried to take deep breaths, but found herself choking, felt a stabbing pain over her heart. Was it breaking? This new fear of being completely alone and on her own almost swallowed her whole being. That night she slept in the Vebers' barn loft. Volya could not bear the thought of sharing the roof with those mean people—with any people.

And here she was again, alone under her own roof this time. And it was her daughter who did not wish to share it with her.

You Can't Choose Your Family

Luba paced her aunt's living room, reciting all the names of the Toronto clan under her breath. In between rounds, she chewed on her thumbnail since she couldn't find her hanky. Would she recognize the faces and be able to match the names? She hated these kinds of gatherings but was trying her best to be positive, since Aunt Zenia had been so patient about taking her through the albums and going out of her way to make her feel at home. In her own way, Luba supposed, her aunt was trying to reach out to her. Though she rarely mentioned Greg when she spoke about her children, she beamed when listing the grandkids and all their talents. Grandchildren seemed to give her greater status, another thing she could lord over Luba's mother. It followed that Luba, and especially Greg, had let their mothers down thus far by not providing heirs. Luba had no intention of ever having children. Did that make her selfish, she wondered? No, she was not supposed to use that word in a negative way; Bella would slap her on the wrist for even thinking like that. Doing things for herself, living life her own way was okay; she just hadn't figured out what her way was yet.

The doorbell rang—cousin Bill, the dentist, and his family had arrived.

"Luba! Don't you look great? Sylvia, Tony, this is my cousin, Luba."

"Hi Sylvia, nice to meet you. And Tony. Hi Tony, how are you?" The little boy looked down at the floor. Oh yes, the "slow one." Luba wondered how a normal-speed six-year-old acted and wasn't sure she'd recognize one.

"So, Luba, it's nice to finally meet you. Bill says you used to live here, what, ten years ago?" Sylvia had a high reedy voice, and Luba had to strain to hear her.

"Uh, yeah." There was no point in mentioning her last two years in Toronto.

"Zenia says you went to see your grandmother. How is she?" Sylvia scrunched her forehead and looked concerned. She was a slender, dark-haired woman, pleasant and somewhat mousy.

"It's hard to tell. She wasn't talking when we visited, so I'm going back to see her tomorrow."

"Ah, that's too bad. What's that, honey?" She bent down to listen to her son, tugging on her sleeve. "Sure, go and ask your grandma. I don't think she'll mind. No? Oh, excuse me, Luba, we need to see Grandma about something." She took little Tony's hand and he led her away. Bill, who had already developed a paunch and was starting to go bald like his dad, looked exactly like what she thought a dentist should look like, bland and non-threatening.

"Wasn't it awful what happened to Orest?" he said, eyeing the plate of fancy bite-size sandwiches on the coffee table. "I hear you were the last of the family to see him alive. What do you think happened?" he asked, then popped an entire sandwich into his mouth.

Before Luba could answer, the doorbell rang again and Adam and his family poured into the house. Luba was ready for them: Anne was the wife, and Christopher was eight and Margaret was six. Hello, hello, hello.

"We were just talking about Orest," Bill said, once introductions concluded and Anne had run after her two children who had heard their cousin Tony in the next room.

"Yeah, what was going on with Orest?" Adam asked Luba.

"I'm not sure I can tell you more than you already know. What did you hear about Orest?"

"Mom said he died of an overdose, but it was probably suicide. What do you think?" Adam cocked his head and looked at Luba intently. His piercing blue eyes and white-blond hair reminded her of someone else, perhaps one of the psychiatrists who had grilled her at the hospital. She decided his occupation also suited him perfectly: a city building inspector.

"Yeah, he used drugs, it was part of his lifestyle, but I don't think he was depressed. I think it was just an accidental overdose." It had to be, she thought. She'd never seen Orest really down. Then again, she didn't know what the drugs might have done to his brain.

"Luba, I hear you quit school. Is that true?" Adam asked with a bluntness that surprised her, though she had been expecting this question.

"I'm just changing programs, that's all. Thought I might try for interior design."

"Interior design!" Bill reacted as if Luba had just contracted an incurable disease. "That's a radical change from pre-med. How did you decide on that?"

Luba was reprieved by the bell—Greg had arrived, dressed in a dark green turtle-neck sweater and casual cotton chinos, his longish fair hair combed back. The resemblance to his father at the same age was remarkable. His two brothers, wearing conservative suit jackets, but without ties, were dull light bulbs next to Greg. He swooped down on Luba, eyes sparkling, and gave her a brotherly hug and peck on her cheek. Then he held her hands and peered into her face until she blushed.

"Little Lubomyra, all grown up. See what a handsome woman she's become! Welcome to Sawchuk Land!"

She laughed. No one ever spoke her formal Ukrainian name. What a ham, putting on a show for his brothers.

"Handsome?" Bill said, laughing. "Really, Greg, you can do better than that. Lovely, beautiful, gorgeous—"

"Stop!" she said, still laughing, "you're all embarrassing me."

"Yes, stop picking on her. We are all beautiful people here," Greg said, then whispered to her, "But some are more handsome than others, like you and me," and winked at her.

"Okay," she whispered back, now feeling more relaxed and at home in the midst of these straight-up virtual strangers.

"Greg," Bill said. "Did you hear that Luba has given up on science and is taking up interior design? And here we thought you were the only artsy-fartsy oddball in the family."

"Oh no, you've got it all backwards. Luba and I are normal. The rest of you are strange. Don't mind them, Luba, they are rigid thinkers." Greg grinned at her.

"So you're an artsy lawyer?"

"Indeed. You probably don't know that I also write and paint. Multi-talented, and my brothers are insanely jealous. You're obviously gifted as well if you could hack a science program as long as you have and still come out smelling like a rose. Oh well, you're embarking on the right path now, that's what counts."

"I'm glad you approve." She grinned back at him. His levity was perfect; he knew just how close she had come to not hacking it. But she did not think of herself as a rose. Perhaps more of a red cabbage, a nice Ukrainian kapusta.

"Dinner's ready!" Aunt Zenia shouted over the hubbub of voices. "Luba, you come and sit here next to your uncle."

"Mama, do you mind if I also sit next to my cousin, seeing as neither of us has an escort?" Greg asked and bowed to Luba.

"Sit wherever you like," she said curtly before she turned back to the kitchen.

Greg was a pariah, like Luba, and maybe her aunt was afraid he'd be a bad influence. Luba found herself smiling at the thought. As long as he was nearby, she would be okay.

Luba glanced at her watch as she walked up the steps to Green Hills Home—only forty-five minutes from Aunt Zenia's by bus, not so bad. The smells and colours were familiar now, but she was glad she had written down the room number, since all the corridors were identical, a warren of linoleum tunnels. When she found Baba's room, the door was nearly closed, so she tapped on it timidly. She thought she heard a grunt, so she pushed it open a little more and slipped inside.

Baba was sitting up, apparently wide awake this time and looking towards Luba.

"Who is that?" she barked in the familiar Ukrainian, squinting her watery red-brown eyes, trying to focus.

"It's Luba, Baba. Your granddaughter from Copper Creek," she said, her voice shaking a little.

"Come here, I cannot see or hear you properly," she ordered, lisping, staring hard at her visitor. Luba approached slowly, not sure how close she needed to be.

"Closer!" She crept forward until her face was only a foot away from her grandmother's.

"Dear God, help me!" Baba shouted and crossed herself, muttering words Luba couldn't make out. Her shocked reaction sent Luba back a step.

"Baba? Are you all right?"

"Why have you come here now? Where have you been? I thought you were dead! Why do you torture me this way?" She waved her hands in front of her face, as if defending herself.

"Baba!" Luba said more loudly. "It is me, Luba. Lubomyra. Your granddaughter." Was this another spell?

She stopped fussing and mumbling, then blinked a few times. "Luba? My little girl, Luba?" Her mouth trembled and Luba froze. Luba felt her own lower lip quivering.

"Luba, is that you?"

She approached again, remembering how intimidated she used to be around her grandmother. Baba reached out for her face, peering at her, then smiled. It was a toothless smile, and Luba remembered that she had false teeth, and how disgusted she used to be when Baba left them on the bathroom sink in a glass of water, or at the side of the tub.

"It is you! Darling little girl, how long has it been? Come sit here." She patted the side of the bed, and Luba sat.

"Oh, wait, my teeth." She twisted herself awkwardly toward the bedside table and fished out the dentures from a glass of water, then wedged them into her caved-in mouth.

"Now I can talk so you will understand me. How have you been, little dove? How long has it been? Tell me everything!" She clasped both of Luba's hands in her bird-like claws.

Luba looked into her grandmother's deep, dark eyes. In spite of the heavy wrinkles and the red rims, she recognized the soul staring out, the same spirit she knew as a child. She paused before she began, considering what to tell her, what to leave out. "It's been ten years, Baba, since Mama and I left Toronto. We live in Copper Creek now, way up north, where Marko and Veronica live."

"And how are they? Does Marko still work in the mine? Such a hard job." Baba looked worried.

"Yes, he still works in the mine, but he is a supervisor now, so it's not so bad."

"And their children? Are they all grown-up like you?"

"Yes, Baba, all grown-up and most of them are married. Did you know you have ten great-grandchildren already?"

"Ten? Oh my." She smiled and squeezed Luba's hands. "And what about you? Are you married also? You are such a beautiful girl, the boys must be crazy about you."

"No, Baba, not married. I'm going to start school here in Toronto this fall, at the university." She winced inside as she said this. Just then she wanted to see her Baba keep smiling, because in an hour or so their entire conversation would probably evaporate like a fog under the hot sun.

"Oh, how wonderful, Lubochka! You were always such a smart little girl. I know you will do well. I only wish my own children had more education, like your poor mother, working so hard. How is she?"

Her face suddenly looked stricken, and Luba tried to reassure her that Volya was well and happy. She changed the focus to Aunt Zenia and her family, how successful they all were, how she had seen Baba's great-grandchildren recently, and all the details she had memorized about them. She kept talking until she noticed Baba's lids flutter just before she yawned.

"Baba, you are tired. I should go now, but I will come back, okay?" The only answer was a moan since Baba had fallen back on her pillow and her eyes had shut. Luba didn't know if she was sleeping or taking a spell, the change was so quick. She tiptoed away from the bed and backed out of the room.

On her way to the bus she wondered who Baba had been thinking of when she first saw Luba. And why did she react that way? Luba had a lot of questions to ask when she saw her again but it could take several visits. She was beginning to understand why her mother and aunt thought Baba was losing her mind, or had already lost it. But Luba had seen that Baba was still in there; she was not completely lost, not yet.

Now this was the way to live. Stretched out on a lawn chair in her aunt and uncle's back yard, being catered to by her uncle, fending off the third burger. It was an unusually warm evening for late May, even in Toronto. She loved it. No screaming little kids around, or trying to make trite conversation with dull people she didn't know and didn't care to know. There was no question about which two were her favourite relatives there. Uncle Bohdan and Greg were both cheerful and outgoing, but not in an aggravating, nauseating way. They made her smile from the inside out; even when they took her seriously they could make her laugh at herself. And they were so unlike the others. They didn't seem to be related to the Tatenko family at all—of course, Uncle Bohdan wasn't related by blood, and Greg had inherited most of his father's characteristics and none of his mother's that she could discern. If she could prove that she really was adopted, or was switched at birth, then she wouldn't be related to Greg, either. Which would suit her just fine. Luba found herself attracted to him, and not feeling guilty enough for having those feelings. She had to be adopted! If not, then she was having incestuous thoughts. Anyway, he was gay, or so he said—maybe it was just a ploy to keep his mother from pressuring him about marrying and having kids. Or maybe he enjoyed aggravating her the way she liked to irk her mother. Anyway, he seemed to genuinely like his nieces and nephews. Nah, he would do just fine as an older brother, and she'd always wanted one.

"Luba, one more!"

"No, please, Uncle, I can't. I'm gonna explode, please."

Her aunt gave Luba a reproving look. "You've hardly touched your salad. When you were little you loved potato salad more than anything, even more than ice cream, so I made a big batch just for you."

Oh, God, not the guilt loading again, thought Luba. It was true, she'd hardly eaten any of her aunt's salad. But it was full of marshmallows and whipped cream and it was sweet. Yuck! She loved her mother's more traditional savory salad, with diced dill pickles, green onions, and boiled eggs.

"Sorry, Auntie, I'm not as big a potato salad eater as I used to be."

"Maybe you don't like my potato salad? You can tell me, I won't be offended," she said making a sad face.

Like hell, Luba thought. She knew that look. It was so Volya. "Auntie, really, I'm into protein these days. And pasta. But please don't make anything special for me, I'll eat just about anything. Truthfully!"

"Except for my potato salad," she said, leaning back in her lawn chair and picking up her drink. She seemed particularly glum that evening, and Luba noticed she was on her third rye and ginger.

"I remember feeling hungry all the time when I was young, until I was just a little older than you are now, Luba. Some of us went crazy when we came to Canada, with all the food available. Look at your Aunt Veronica, and even your own mother. They should watch their diets more; it isn't good for the heart, you know, to be so heavy. But when I finally had all this food in front of me, I was afraid to eat it, I don't know why."

"I know why," Uncle Bohdan said, settling his big frame on a groaning lawn chair. "Don't you remember how sick you were with baby Bill? I thought we were going to lose you. For nine months you hardly ate a thing."

Aunt Zenia nodded her head and stared into the amber drink she swirled under her nose.

"Oh, yes, it was dreadful. But worse than that was crossing the ocean when he was still a baby. I still remember how I wanted to die, I was so ill. Nauseous for eight days straight. I don't think I left my bed except to retch."

"She's not exaggerating, Luba." Uncle Bohdan wore a wicked grin.

"Were you even sick at all?" Zenia asked, her tone almost accusing.

"Of course I was. But I got over it, and so did Sylana, most days. The boys didn't stop running. They could go anywhere on the ship. It was good to be outside on the deck, in the fresh air. But we couldn't convince your aunt to come up with us, Luba. She really had us worried."

Aunt Zenia drained her glass. "Poor baby Bill. Just four months old and my milk dried up because I couldn't eat. He was so bloated from that reconstituted milk, he wailed and wailed, nobody slept. But once we reached Halifax he was fine. We stayed in the infirmary for a few days before we caught our train to Winnipeg. By then I was eating again, but I still felt bad. These days they call it postpartum depression, but back then you were labelled a bad mother. I had wanted to go to Canada so badly, and here I was and I didn't care about anything, not myself, or my children, nothing. Mama said the same thing happened to her after Marko and I were born, but she came out of it. And so did I, eventually."

Uncle Bohdan chuckled. "She certainly did. I remember that day very well. I think it was the shock. You see, Luba, after we reached Winnipeg, we all climbed aboard a pontoon plane to fly up to a small community about a hundred miles north. That's where Marko and Veronica had settled, and he made all the arrangements for us. Your Baba refused to even board the plane at first. But after the rest of us were sitting inside, she decided to join us. She said she would rather die in a fiery crash than be left all alone in this strange, frigid country. I think it was late fall and very, very cold. Adam and Greg were the only ones who actually enjoyed the flight—they didn't know enough to be frightened. It was one great adventure for them. Sylana, your Baba, didn't stop praying the whole time. I just concentrated on trying to understand what the other passengers were saying. Of course, I didn't understand a word—it was in French. I had only learned a little English by that time. Zenia, do you remember how the boys screamed with delight when we dropped down to land on the water? I thought for sure we would hit the shore, we seemed to be diving too fast."

Uncle Bohdan paused and looked over at his niece. "Luba, some ice cream?"

"Maybe later. I'm still digesting those cow haunches you fed me."

He chuckled and helped himself to a large bowl, resuming his story between mouthfuls.

"I must admit I was so relieved to see Marko at the dock to greet us, that I had tears in my eyes. Yes I did, Luba. Marko kissed his mother first, of course, then he gave Zenia a big hug. But she didn't respond at all, not even when he started tossing the two boys in the air. Usually that would make her upset, but she didn't seem to notice. A big Frenchman, I think Guillaume was his name, he came with Marko and took us all back in his truck. We had so little with us, we didn't take up much room. While we drove to Marko's cabin, over a very bumpy road I must say, he told us what to expect so we would not be surprised or disappointed. They only had a small cabin themselves, but he said it would take very little time to put one up for us. Everyone in the community pitched in to help. He explained that the community was mostly French, with some Polish immigrants and Canadian Indians. Most newcomers worked in the mines, some in the woods.

"When we got there, Baba was so shaken up she could not say a word, just kept crossing herself. Zenia did not seem to notice in the least how rough the ride had been. We walked into Marko's cabin where Veronica was preparing a huge meal for us. A typical Ukrainian meal, even in the middle of nowhere. So we walked into the cabin, and there was a table just loaded with delicious hot food and by then we were all starving, of course. But Zenia wrinkles her pretty nose and whispers to me that she needs to go back outside. 'Now!' she says. I had not heard that voice in months."

Aunt Zenia's head snapped up at that point. Luba couldn't tell if she had drifted off to sleep or was just bored with the story.

"That's right," she said. "I finally woke up. It was the smell. It was horrible and made me feel nauseous all over again. I had never smelled anything like it and I had to go back outside before I threw up. Bohdan tried to explain to Marko that I was very sensitive and had been ill, but being Marko he was offended that I smelled something nasty in his cabin. Then Veronica came outside to ask what was happening and when she heard what the problem was, oh my, did she ever get mad. Not at me—at her husband. I'll never forget it. I always thought she was so timid, but she really gave Marko a piece of her mind."

"So, what was it? What was the smell?" Luba asked.

"Let me think, how did it go?" Zenia put down her glass and pressed her two hands to the sides of her head as if she was squeezing out the memories. "Veronica said something like, 'There, did I not tell you? Oh no, you had to do it your own way. You and that half-wit, Alphonse. This is the last time I let you try such a stupid trick!' And Marko just stared at her, stunned, for once short on words.

"Then he said, 'I suppose you had a better way to catch that skunk? Did I hear any brilliant plans from you at the time? How were we supposed to know it would get out of the can?'

"'You should have put a lid on it!' she said."

At that Bohdan roared, and Luba couldn't help but laugh as well, seeing tears streaming over his red cheeks.

Zenia continued, "Marko said, 'You cannot start a fire and put the lid on right away. The fire would go out, you foolish woman!' Veronica told us the men had trapped this skunk in an empty oil can, tried to light it on fire, right next to the house. So of course the poor terrified animal sprayed for its life, tipped the can over and ran back under the house! Thank goodness for Veronica's good sense and good nature. We moved the table and benches outside and ate there in the fresh air. She assured us we'd have our own cabin in no time and then suggested we might build an extra big cabin in case she and the children needed to move in with us. Oh, she was still mad at Marko. That was so funny," she laughed.

"And then we learned about their fierce mosquitoes. Even worse than the ones in the Copper Creek bush, believe me. Between the skunk odour and the cramped space in that cabin, and the mosquitoes outside, I urged Bohdan to hurry and build our own cabin as soon as possible."

Bohdan jumped in, "I was so happy to see Zenia back to herself that I began the building project before I started my job at the gold mine. I think we were in our own cabin by early November. Four rooms, remember that, Zenia?"

"Yes, and I also remember the snow we had by then, but better than those incessant and vicious mosquitoes in the warmer weather. It was so cold. No matter how much we tried to stuff all the cracks, the wind always seemed to find a way inside."

"How long did you work in the mine, Uncle Bohdan?"

"Too long for my liking. Ah, that was a hard and dirty job. And dangerous. They wouldn't let you get away with those deadly conditions today. Not in Canada. I hated being underground for so many hours. There was no other work, so I stayed with it a couple of years. But I realized there was also a need for better housing. No one was happy with their leaky little log cabins. So by the next summer I had started my first construction business. Very small, so I had to stay at the mine another year before I could quit that job. I had to learn English and French in a short time to be able to earn the respect of the locals and to do business. It is amazing what you can do when the need is there."

Aunt Zenia snorted. "I also found out that knowing the local language is crucial to surviving. One day that first spring I walked to the trading post in the small village nearby to buy some food. There was another customer ahead of me, a recently immigrated Polish woman, about Baba's age at the time. I understood that she wanted to buy eggs, but the storekeeper did not. The woman tried to draw the picture of an egg on her open palm. The storekeeper shook his head. She looked at me in desperation but I couldn't remember the word myself. Finally, the woman began prancing around the store, making clucking sounds, lifting her skirt slightly, squatting and pointing at her behind. I felt so embarrassed for her, but the storekeeper finally nodded his head and laughed, and brought out a flat of eggs. The poor woman. By then the sweat was dripping from her brow beneath her black head scarf. She picked out five eggs, paid for them, and left the store. I saw tears in her eyes as she passed by, and the storekeeper was still chuckling and clucking behind the counter. I was so upset I had forgotten what I had come to buy, and left the store myself, afraid to even open my mouth.

"We decided that I could help Bohdan with his orders and accounting, but I needed to learn English better before I could keep the books. So we hired

Guillaume's son, Marcel, a sixteen-year-old boy to tutor us both for the rest of the summer. He was home from the Catholic academy in Winnipeg. When he returned to school in the fall, a young woman, Malvina Wilkinson, came to the community to teach the children. Bohdan convinced her to come to our home two evenings each week and every other Saturday afternoon, and paid her to continue our English lessons. We became good friends, Malvina and I, being about the same age. There were very few others for Malvina to socialize with, and although she was not married, there were no unattached men of her age, either. It was a tough life for everyone out there in the bush.

"You know, I learned much more from our casual conversations than I did during the formal class sessions. I tried to convince Veronica to take lessons with us, but she was embarrassed about going back to school. Anyway, she hated to leave her babies for any length of time. She was such a dedicated mother, even though Mama was always willing to babysit. Having your Baba with us certainly made my life much easier. And we bought her a sewing machine so she was happy and busy. You can't believe how hard we all worked just to stay alive. But it paid off. Here we are," she said, raising her empty glass and waving it in the air to encompass the cushy surroundings.

Uncle Bohdan was snoring softly in his chair. Aunt Zenia rolled her eyes at Luba, then got up and went into the kitchen.

Luba supposed that Zenia considered her sister a failure, being a lowly cleaning woman, though her mother had worked hard all her life, and had a tougher time of it than Aunt Zenia ever did. Luba wondered what her aunt thought of the cleaning woman's daughter. She still wondered what her aunt wanted with her, if she was planning to use Luba against her mother. She hated the way Aunt Zenia treated Greg, and though it wasn't quite the same as the relationship she had with her own mother, it made her think that the two sisters weren't all that different. Whatever her aunt thought of her, she decided it didn't matter. Successful or not, she and her Aunt Zenia did not share the same values, and she would not have chosen to be related to her. If, indeed, she was.

The Cruelty of Angels

Volya switched off the TV and sat back down in her chair, under the lamp. She picked up the pillow case she had been embroidering and studied it. She was nearly out of black thread and it was too late to call Veronica to see if she had any to spare. She would have to buy more next time she was in town. Volya stared at the phone sitting quietly on the side table next to her couch. Only one call from Luba so far and even then she was surprised to hear from her so soon after she had arrived in Toronto. Maybe she felt guilty for leaving like she did, hardly saying anything, no explanations. And now that she was probably having such a grand time in Zenia's fancy house, eating out at restaurants, no doubt, sleeping away half the day, she would forget to call again.

She wondered if Luba had gone back to see Mama already. If the old lady spoke at all, it would be garbled nonsense, garbage, like the last time she spoke with her mother—all that craziness about Gypsies back in Ukraine. She must have been confusing reality with some folk tale she heard as a child. The deterioration of the aging mind, old memories dredged up as well as conversations heard or read, fantasy and reality all mixed up in a soup and dished out, a spoonful here, a bowlful there. Volya had seen this herself when old Mrs. Clark, the elderly mother of one of her clients, was still living with her son's family, before they put her in the Home. No, Luba would not learn anything useful from the old woman; her mind was gone and that was that.

Volya was not convinced that Luba was ready to fly off on her own yet. In fact, she wished Luba would remain in Copper Creek a while longer where Volya could keep an eye on her. But the girl was determined to leave, and Volya could not hold her back. If she got into her program at that trade school she could at least stay with Greg for a while. Then again, perhaps she wouldn't be accepted, and for a moment Volya felt hopeful. Still, she knew her daughter would eventually have to learn to rely on herself more.

Sometimes you did not know how to stand on your own two feet until you had to. Though Volya still attended church regularly, Luba was right about one thing—no one should wait for God to help them or to make things happen. Volya had learned this self-reliance the hard way, and at an early age during the war. After the old hired man left and her workload nearly doubled, she continued to hope and pray for a while longer. One of her prayers was finally answered, and she remembered thanking the angels for sending Yanos to help her with the farm labour.

Ah, Yanos, dear Yanos, her hapless young Latvian prisoner of war. Even without a photo she could still picture him as he stood before her on that first day; thin, light-boned and not very tall. Everything about him seemed washed out—his pale, nearly translucent skin, his watery slate-blue eyes set deep in his oval face, and fine, limp hair capping his head like a dirty bedraggled mushroom. Yanos walked with a slight limp, but he never talked of pain. In fact, he did not speak much, nor look anyone in the eye during his first few weeks on the farm. Herr Veber tried to instruct him, but eventually Volya finished that job and took charge of their new "slave." He did not seem to care who ordered him about—he performed his tasks without complaint or enthusiasm.

After Yanos arrived, everything changed for Volya. In the beginning she pitied the young man, who seemed more dead than alive, and worried that he would not be strong enough to work in the field, planting and weeding the tobacco, potatoes, onions, and other vegetables, or digging and pulling out stumps for new fields. But he never faltered, and Volya began to forget her own complaints. She knew he must have been hungry as she always was, eating the same food, meatless and scanty. He made no mention of hunger; he ate everything put before him. Since Volya had finally been asked to help in the kitchen, she sometimes tried to spice the food to make it interesting, but she soon stopped being inventive. For one thing, no one seemed to notice. And she found that if the food had any flavour, she felt even hungrier than when it was tasteless and flat.

Things changed again, midway through one searing hot August afternoon after Volya and Yanos had finished hoeing the last section of the tobacco field. There was a willow hedgerow that bordered a small stream on the edge of the Veber property, so they decided to take a rest in the shade of the trees. They drank from a bottle of water she had brought along, the two of them soaked with sweat.

"You know, I think I take a swim," Yanos announced in his halting German. She loved the way he pronounced the words. "Do you swim?" he asked her.

"No, I never learned how. I have a great fear of deep water."

"I think the water not so deep. Here," he pointed to the stream behind them. "I go. And you?" Yanos stood up and waited to see what she would do.

She said that she would just watch, so they pushed through a curtain of hanging branches to the stream which was swift and wide, more like a small river, she thought. Volya had rarely ventured anywhere near the fast-moving water. She recalled the shocking sight of a puffed-up blue body of a three-year-old boy near Brinzi. He was found floating in a large eddy of the river, surrounded by upturned fish where they soaked and softened hemp for rope. The adults often told frightening stories about small children slipping into the river and being swept away, but no one ever believed them until that day. For the longest time after, she did not even want to look at the river.

Volya found a large flat rock a few feet from the water's edge and tested its solidity with her palms. She sat on it, turning slightly away from Yanos who had plunged his arms into the water. She did not know if he planned to remove any clothing, and she did not wish to embarrass them both by watching. A splash made her turn her head back to where Yanos had been standing, but he was nowhere to be seen. She jumped up, alarmed.

"Yanos?" she called out.

"Yah, here I am, behind you!" She turned and there he was, in the middle of the stream. He laughed and ducked his head underwater. She could see bubbles come up where he had disappeared.

"Yanos!" He popped up again and spat out a mouthful of water.

"You be careful. That water is deep and I cannot save you if you drown." Volya felt foolish as she said this. He was a fish in that water, freer than anything she had seen of him on solid ground.

"This is no problem if I drown," he laughed again, a pleasant tinkling sound, and swam toward her where she sat.

"It most certainly would be a problem. Who will help me work this farm if you drown?"

"Ah, they find another prisoner. I am not so special." He slapped his hand on the water and sprayed her with a shower of cold drops.

"Hey! Stop that! Do you know how long I had to pray to get you?" She spoke without thinking and was horribly embarrassed.

Yanos laughed even louder. "This is very good. I always want to be answer to prayers of beautiful girl. Come in this water. Not deep here. Cool, fresh, very nice. Come," he beckoned her with a smile that changed his entire face. A water nymph, he stood waist high, his pale naked chest with smooth muscles rippling over the fine bones, almost feminine, fairy-like. He glowed as he stood there, his arm extended toward her.

Volya could not resist, as afraid as she was. She removed her shoes and socks, then slipped off the back of the rock. She touched her toe to the water. It was cool and felt so inviting in the stifling heat. She heard dripping water and looked up to see Yanos standing a few feet away, still holding his hand out to her. She blushed to see him in his undershorts, and a jagged, red scar on his right thigh. She looked down at the water and gingerly stepped in, felt his cold hand take hers as she walked in, a tiny step at a time, until she was up to her knees.

"No farther. I am afraid of the deep water," she said and tried to free her hand. He did not let go.

"Is not deep. Look, this is deep to here." He let her hand go and stepped backwards to the middle of the stream. Suddenly, he disappeared straight down and she screamed. Yanos re-emerged immediately and stood up in the middle, the water only up to his waist.

"See," he said, smiling. Then he stopped smiling and said, "I play joke. You no believe?"

Volya had to compose herself; she did not appreciate water jokes.

"You come?" he asked again. "I hold you. You no fall. I no let beautiful girl drown." Yanos shook his head and held out his hand again, moving closer to her.

Once again, unbelievably, she let him take her hand and lead her further into the water. She gasped at the coldness as it climbed up her body. Her skirt swirled around her and she began to feel so free and light and shivery cold, she started to giggle.

"You see. Feel good, yes?" Yanos grinned at her and lowered himself into the water so only his head showed. Volya held her breath and folded her knees, totally immersing her body. The coldness around her head made her suck in some water as she exploded to the surface again, sputtering and coughing.

"You no breathe!" Yanos laughed at her, and, this time, Volya laughed with him. He seemed about to let hand go of her hand.

"No!" she yelled. "Do not let go, not yet!" Yanos' wide smile exposed his strong, even teeth. This was a totally different person from the dryland version she had felt sorry for and had tried to mother. He reached for her other hand and they stood still for a few moments, the water washing and massaging their weary, salty bodies.

Finally, Volya let his hands go and turned back to the shore. This was enough for her first dip. She dripped out of the stream and pulled herself back on the rock. She continued to watch the transformed young man playing merman in the water, until she called to him that it was probably time to dry out so they could return. She had supper preparations to think of and he had to milk the cow.

"Ah, no drying for me. See, I take off pants and have dry clothes waiting. You are wet!"

Volya averted her gaze, but not before Yanos had pulled off his shorts to expose his nakedness. She did not feel the repulsion she had expected. The incident with Karl was buried deep, but it surfaced for a moment, and just as quickly she shoved it back down. Instead, she remembered feeling a sensation in her groin that was pleasant and disturbing.

As they walked back together, she also sensed that Yanos had been looking at her body in a hungry way that unnerved her. He did not leer, but sent her soft, admiring, wistful glances as they walked close to each other, not quite touching, silent again. At the farmhouse Volya snuck in through the back door, through the kitchen and into her room where she changed into a clean dry dress. She had only the one brassiere, and decided to let it dry. As she looked down at herself, she realized that her nipples showed through the worn fabric of her spare dress. The Vebers were so blind they would not notice, but Yanos might.

By the time they all sat down to supper, Volya had decided she would not repeat the brassiereless experiment again. Each time Yanos looked up from his plate, his eyes caressed her breasts before they landed on her face. She hunched over her plate, and crossed her arms over her chest whenever she could. On his way to bed, Yanos passed behind her as she washed dishes at the sink and whispered, "You are beautiful." Volya did not know whether to hit him with the dish cloth or be pleased, so she pretended not to hear, but thought he could probably feel the heat from her deep blush.

Volya counted that summer as one of the best she had ever known, in spite of living in constant fear of bombs, and in spite of her hateful employers and the hard work. It went by too fast, even so. That October, Zenia gave birth to her second child, Gregory. She had not worked since Adam was born and then found herself totally occupied with the two babies. Anxious about having only her husband's income to live on, she constantly fretted about how much money they did not have. At first Volya had enjoyed her Sunday visits to Zenia's home to play with the babies, to hold them and feed them. But her sister's whining was intolerable and Volya finally suggested that after church she would babysit the boys while Zenia and Bohdan had a few hours to themselves to go out and do whatever they wished. At first they protested, saying that they wanted to spend time with her as well, but they finally agreed. Although she enjoyed playing with and caring for her nephews, Volya soon realized that she was looking forward to returning to the Veber farm on Sunday evenings. Yanos had made himself useful in the kitchen, so she did not have to rush back, and yet she did want to hurry home.

After daily chores were done, Yanos and Volya often took long walks down the main road, and along smaller country lanes. During the fall and winter, there was less field work to do, and even though darkness fell earlier, they both preferred to escape the dank, oppressive farm house for the freedom of the outdoors. They spoke of their lives in their home countries, of their families, of the horrors of the war, of the dreams they had once they left that life of slavery. Volya was being paid a small sum of money for her work, insignificant as it was considering the long, hard hours she put in each day. She worried about Yanos' fate as a prisoner of war, although he told her he was unconcerned. He did brood, however, about his parents and young sisters back home, and wondered if they were even alive.

Over time, Yanos confided many things to her. He eventually told Volya how a German soldier had bayoneted his leg after he had been captured and that a German doctor told him he would probably walk with a limp for the rest of his life. When he admitted that he did not believe in God after the atrocities he had seen during the war, she was not shocked and did not even care. Volya understood how easy it was to lose faith. She was on the edge herself, and had not totally decided for or against. As far as she was concerned, God was on trial. But when Yanos told her he had a sweetheart back home in Latvia, she remembered feeling such a wrenching in her gut, she thought she would vomit. All that time she thought he was sweet on her, so the stabbing pain of her disappointment surprised and distressed her. How stupid she had been!

"We must go home," she said, afraid she might cry.

"But we just start our walk," he protested. "Volya, you have boy, no? From home?"

She had already turned her back on him and began to walk away. "No," she muttered.

He grabbed her arm to stop her.

"Leave me be!" she barked at him.

"I thought you had boy at home. You so beautiful, must have special friend. I only say I have girl, but not true." He drew her close, his arms encircling her and whispered into her hair, "I love you, beautiful Cossack girl. Only you."

She pushed him away; he had to be lying. "Why did you say you had a girlfriend then?"

"Volya, I apologize. I say because I not want you to think I am alone, no-body loves me. Maybe true. Nobody loves me," he said, his face dropping and greying in the evening shadows. He let go of her arms, and stood looking down at the ground. He was pathetic. Volya wrapped her arms around his miserable form, and he revived immediately. She remembered that embrace, so long and hard they could barely breathe.

"Do you love me, Volya?" he asked in a small, hopeful voice.

She could only nod as tears ran down her face. Yanos leaned down and licked her cheeks. She laughed. He leaned down further and touched his lips to hers. She tried not to gasp as jolts of electricity coursed through her body and her pelvis pulsed. Yanos pressed harder, lips to lips, torso to torso. His arms massaged her back, then he moved his mouth to her forehead, kissed her there, finally resting his cheek on her hair. She snuggled in under his chin, hardly breathing, wondering at what had just happened. She was floating with him, her feet no longer connected to her body. Heaven.

"They will never let us be together," he said, breaking the spell. "No one must see us like this." Her stomach twisted again, because she knew this was true. He was a prisoner of war. She was employed by the German government, a refugee at their mercy; they both lived at the whim of a monster. So they walked on, arms around each other, trembling, joyous, terrified. Whenever they saw the lights of a car or other people walking, they broke apart and did not touch again until they were certain no one would see them.

That winter of 1943 was long and cold and tense. There were several more bombing raids on Mannheim, but few bombs fell in the country. Most raids happened during the night, when Volya felt most vulnerable and ached to have the comfort of Yanos who slept in a room down the hall. But they could not go to each other—the Vebers slept in a room between them, and the floorboards would have given any wanderer away. They were nearly blind, but the Vebers' hearing was as sharp as the bats that swooped above them in the attic. She and Yanos were two would-be lovers who had to steal every moment they could spend together, walking down quiet lanes in the dark, holding hands, kissing but not daring to go any further. She did not even want to imagine what Mama would have said if she learned that a Latvian prisoner of war was her sweetheart. No matter that he was born a Catholic, he was not one of their people. But he was not a hateful, accursed Jew, and he was not a despised German or Russian. Volya's heart belonged to him completely, as she knew his belonged to her. They yearned for the day they would both be free to give their bodies to each other as well, though they never spoke of marriage. To do so in that time of slavery and war was to force the hands of fate, something they both believed and were resigned to live with.

By the spring of 1944 they were back in the fields, bending over thousands of plants and seeds, raking, turning up the soil, planting, watering, and weeding. Their passion for each other had turned to the hundreds of tasks they laboured at every day, day after day, week after week. After a long, dusty day of hoeing weeds, Yanos hankered for a swim to cool off and wash. He often took a dip on his own while Volya worked elsewhere. Then came that one hot June day they both went again to the stream. She would never forget that day as long as she lived, even after her mind had gone to mush like Mama's. The water was still cool enough that Volya preferred just to watch the human fish from her dry perch. Yanos climbed out and stood behind her, dripping onto her head and shoulders.

"Go away, you are drenching me! Go on, get dressed. Time to get back," she laughed. Volya felt his arms slip in front of her, his hands clasped over her chest. He kissed the back of her head then she felt his cold cheek slide up against her warm one.

"I do not have clothes on," he teased her. His hands unclasped and he held her breasts. She turned her head, her mouth open, and he quickly kissed her lips. She kissed him back, her heart pounding, her body burning. He sat down on the rock facing her and put his arms around her.

"I love you, dear sweet one. Will you marry me?" She just gasped and stared at him. Before she could answer, they heard snapping branches and sounds of scrambling on the other side of the stream and when they turned to look they saw someone disappearing into the thickets just across from where they sat.

"Oh no," Volya groaned.

Yanos grabbed her shoulders. "I am done, you know that! Volya, listen to me. We make love before I go! I find you again, we will marry. Will you make love to me?" Yanos stared at her desperately, his eyes wide and full of fire.

Volya was trembling, crying. "I cannot, Yanos. I am afraid. What if I get pregnant? What then? You will not be here. What will I do without you?" She stood up but could see nothing, she was crying so hard.

"Volya," Yanos said softly, his voice breaking. "Remember me."

Volya did not remember how she got back to the house, she was so terrified, certain someone would report them. What would happen then? She did not want to consider the consequences. Why had he said anything? Had he betrayed them like that? No, she thought, it was just bad luck. Everything would be fine. Back in the kitchen, she peeled potatoes furiously but kept listening for Yanos' return. Where was he?

The potatoes were boiling on the stove when Volya heard a car drive into the yard and stop. She found herself praying while she continued to set dishes on the table with shaking hands. Herr Veber was outside on the porch, and she heard him speaking to another man. The other person was loud and demanding; Herr Veber sounded defensive.

Frau Veber clattered down the stairs, awakened from her nap. "What is happening here?" she asked her husband as he walked into the front hall. He stomped into the kitchen, his limp barely noticeable, the Frau following.

"Our neighbour caught the two of them naked at the stream!" Herr Veber pointed a wavering finger at Volya. "Guess what they were doing?" he shouted at her.

"That is not true!" she said.

"Do not lie, you whore!" he yelled back at her. "Because of you, we lost our labourer! They should take you away, too, you useless whore!"

Volya suddenly felt light-headed and dropped the knife she was holding. "They have taken him?"

"They have probably been stealing from us, too. I should report her as a Gypsy. She probably lied about her nationality," the Herr continued, while his wife stood there in shock, speechless for once.

By then, Volya was shaking violently, but not for fear of being turned in. She knew they could not afford to lose her as well as Yanos. Someone was shouting outside. She jumped up and ran to the front window to see two German policemen with Yanos between them, his hands fastened behind his back. They jerked him around like a thin piece of paper, and folded him into the back of the police car. He looked straight ahead the entire time, no emotion on his face. He was already dead to the world, sealed off. A third officer slammed the door shut and the car roared out of the driveway onto the road toward Mannheim. As the engine vibrations died in the air, Volya's heartbeats were thudding so loud in her ears she could hear nothing else. She crouched down, put her hands on the cold stone tiles, and drew in all her breath. All her life, her passion, drained out through her feet and hands into the floor beneath, sucked up by the thirsty earth. Her angels had deserted her once and for all.

Inside Jonah's

Luba looked around the dark, smoky pub and wondered how Greg had found this place, his favourite after-work hangout, and not far from the Lawyers' Row district. Greg was up at the bar getting them a couple of beers. The tiny dance floor next to their table was empty at 5:30 in the afternoon, and the air ricocheted with loud voices, music, and the sound of cue sticks striking pool balls in the back. But at that moment it was the smell of fries pushing through cigarette smoke that had Luba's senses at full throttle.

"Here we are! A Guinness stout for you, a pale ale for me. Do you suppose this reveals something about our basic natures? I mean, here I am, a blond drinking blond, and there's you, a brunette drinking brunette."

"At least you didn't say I was a stout drinking stout."

"Luba, my dear, I would never say such a thing. That's where any analogies fall apart, little cousin. You're svelte, not stout. And I've never heard of svelte beer, but maybe there should be one." He winked and raised his mug toward her. "Dai Boje!" he toasted with the reverent Ukrainian expression.

"Dai Boje!" She raised her own mug and tapped his.

"A couple of friends should be joining us by and by. Leo, my housemate as you know, and Don. He's a lawyer at the firm next to hers. Our house is practically around the corner from here, very convenient for work, I must say."

"So, does that provide a juicy source of gossip for certain people? An unmarried couple sharing a house?" Luba wondered why her mother never brought it up, unless her mother didn't know about Greg's female roommate.

"Sure, but more palatable gossip for relatives and others likewise unenlightened than having them accuse us of being who we really are. Did I mention that Leo is Ukrainian, too?"

Luba nodded. She was curious about Leo, and a little nervous as well. She knew a few gays and lesbians, but had never met a bisexual before, that she was aware of, and wasn't sure what to expect.

"Leonida Krawchuk. Sawchuk and Krawchuk. Has a nice cadence to it, doesn't it? We should start up our own law firm," he smirked and sipped. Suddenly he looked up, smiling broadly.

"Don, there you are!"

A tall, striking young man in a pale blue suit walked up to their table, a big grin on his smooth face. Greg stood up and the two clasped each other. Greg planted a quick kiss on Don's left cheek and Luba smiled and stared. She had never seen her cousin with one of his gay friends before.

"Don, this is my little cousin Luba from the hamlet of Copper Creek in the far true north," he said, leaning over to put an arm around her shoulders.

"Luba, enchanté!" Don gave her a firm handshake and sat down across from her, next to Greg. "So I can see you are the other variety of Ukrainian, the far eastern look, isn't it, Gregorovich? You two don't look related at all!"

Don himself was dark-haired, but with fair skin and blue eyes rimmed with thick black lashes, a masculine version of Elizabeth Taylor, Luba thought. The two of them, the best-looking guys around, and obviously gay. Figured.

"Luba is unique, no doubt about it. She has those exotic, high cheekbones and olive skin."

"You mean the Mongolian/Tartar influence?" she suggested.

"Not with those legs! Luba is the true artist in our family. She's off to Ryerson this year." Greg lifted his glass to her.

"If I get in."

"You will. Don, can I get you a brew?"

"No, can't stay long. Have to get back to an evening meeting, so I'm just grabbing a burger to take back with me."

"They're keeping you after hours again? That's unconscionable! The Blair case, I suppose?"

"You know I can't tell you, but that's a pretty good guess. Ah, here's the lady! Leo! Haven't seen you in a bitch's age! Where have you been hiding?"

He stood up to greet a woman who was a little shorter than Luba, and stocky without appearing to be overweight. She was built like Luba's mother was in her youth—large-breasted but slim through the hips. Her shiny brown hair was straight, and cut bluntly just below her ears, longer on one side than the other, and her face was round, her eyes almond-shaped. But what Luba couldn't get over were her deep dimples, exclamation marks at either end of a full-lipped, easy smile. A thin gold hoop dangled from her exposed ear, and a smart burgundy suede jacket and skirt embraced her curves. So that was what women lawyers wore under those black robes.

Leo stood on her tiptoes as Don leaned down so they could kiss each other's cheeks.

"Don, I should ask you the same. What did they do—truss and tie you to your office chair? You haven't stopped by for over a week."

Without waiting for an answer, she turned abruptly and said, "And you must be Luba, so nice to meet you!" She leaned over to give Luba a strong, energetic handshake, still smiling and dimpling.

"Hi Leo. Nice to meet you."

"Is that Guinness you're drinking?"

Luba nodded.

"Aha, another Ukrainian woman with good taste. Can I get you another, since I'm going up for one myself?"

"Not just yet, thanks, I still have a ways to go." Leo strode up to the bar where she and the bartender immediately began to chat and laugh together.

"Luba, how long are you in town for?" Don asked.

"I don't know yet. My ticket is open, but I'm hoping to come back for summer school, if I get in to the program. And that starts in three-and-a-half weeks, I think."

"Summer in T.O.? Ugh! It's hot and humid, but otherwise a great place to live. Do you like live theatre?"

"I do, but it's a little expensive on a student income, which in my case is zero."

"Oh, don't I remember those days! Jeez, I'm glad to be out of school. I loved law school, don't get me wrong, but this cut-throat world is where I thrive. Don't know about you, Greg, but I detest the weather here. I'm a west coast boy, myself, thinking about heading back to Vancouver sometime."

"Don, you're such a butterfly. Can't settle on anything for long, can you?" Greg laughed at him.

"That depends," he replied, raising his eyebrows at Greg and tapping the table with his long fingers. Greg merely smiled and drained his mug.

"Well, must go. Are you going to that banquet next Saturday, Greg?"

"Haven't decided yet. I'll give you a buzz if I plan to go."

"Please do. Later!" He waved his arm and disappeared into the crowd.

As Leo returned from the bar, her beer mug already half-empty, Greg said, "Here's our other social butterfly. How's dear Drew?"

"Recovering pretty well, I'd say." Leo sat next to Luba and leaned closer to speak over the background din. "Drew broke up with his partner two weeks ago. They'd been together... how long was it?"

"Three years, I think," Greg said, "and he took it pretty hard."

"Yup, Sam just up and left without any warning. Then he finds out Sam has been seeing another guy on the sly for quite a while. What a slime! He could have been more honest with Drew."

Luba tried to digest all this. Drew was the bartender and Sam was his girlfriend. Or was it his boyfriend? She'd have to concentrate more to keep everyone straight.

Greg was shaking his head. "I'm beginning to think long-term attachments are unnatural. How many people end up staying together? Both of my brothers are now on their second wives, and your brother has been divorced twice, hasn't he, Leo?"

"Yup. And he's dating again. Actually I really like both of his exes. He's the one who messes up." She turned to Luba with a serious look. Her eyes were dark brown and fringed with heavy black lashes, although she didn't seem to be wearing any make-up. "My parents separated when we were kids, which is a big deal since they're both Catholic. My dad lives with a woman who is younger than I am, while my mother lives alone and is very bitter. It wasn't the happiest family to grow up in. And there's just me and my brother, thank God."

"Oh, I see."

"I hear you've been to see your Baba. She's a doll. I've just gotten to know your grandmother this last year. How is she?"

"Well, on the first visit Baba was out of it, didn't recognize us at all. The second time I went alone, and she was alert and talked to me a little. Mostly I talked, caught her up on the last ten years. She seemed quite startled and upset when she first saw me, thought I was someone else, I guess. I was afraid she'd have an attack or something."

"Her sight is failing her," Greg said, "and she does get confused sometimes."

"Maybe. I feel badly that I didn't go to see her when I was here for over a year. I shouldn't have listened to my mother—I usually don't. I just didn't feel like reconnecting with any family, having them keep track of me, reporting on me. It was the first time I was on my own. A new life." Luba stopped, thinking how she had screwed up her new life, but Greg and Leo were both nodding with sympathy.

"I'd like to talk to Baba, get to know her again, if that's still possible," she said.

"I think it's wonderful that you have a grandmother alive. My grandparents all died in Ukraine before I was born, so I adopted your Baba. Anyway, I think it's great that you're here to see her. Family is very important." She stopped short and picked up her beer.

"Are you guys hungry?" Greg asked.

"Yeah," they both answered and laughed, relieved to change the topic.

"Are we ordering food here or eating at home?"

"Here," Leo decided. "There's nothing much in the fridge, and I'm starved. We're not being very good hosts to Luba, here. Let me get you another and I'll bring a menu." She stood, scooped up their mugs, and left the table in one fluid motion.

"That woman has so much energy, she makes me dizzy," Greg said. Then he leaned over. "You and I and Leo all have something in common, I believe."

"Which is?"

"Our mothers. I don't know if the stories I hear about yours are all true, but, if so, prepare yourself for something much worse—the original wicked witch of the west, herself. Do you know that Leo's mother moved to Toronto from Edmonton to be near the daughter she doesn't get along with? The Tatenko sisters are angels in comparison."

Now this would be good, Luba thought, swapping mothers-from-hell stories. Leo returned and plunked a frosted mug of beer in front of Luba, and handed her a menu.

"I must complain to Drew about the favouritism he shows you. I never get a frosted mug." Greg pretended to pout.

"He goes overboard for women just to show what a good sport he is. All you have to do is ask. Now, decide what you want to order. Luba is fading away in front of us."

Luba's stout quickly evaporated and a third one appeared in front of her.

"Okay, Luba, now I want you to tell Leo your version of the funeral. Did my mother behave?" Greg gave her a lopsided grin.

"No!" she said, her voice indignant, then burst into giggles.

"See, Leo, what did I tell you? Mother went up to stir up trouble and succeeded. Anyway, they only stayed as long as they needed and Mommie dearest hasn't said much about it since they returned. Not that she confides in me."

Luba turned to Leo. "I don't know why our mothers are feuding. I think mine's jealous."

"Over what? The big house and fancy cars?" Greg smirked.

"And how brilliant and successful her sons are. And here's poor me, a dropout, a failure—"

"Whoa! Who said that?" Greg's face was serious.

"That's what my mother thinks."

"Now, I find that hard to believe. I used to hear your mother bragging about you to my mother when you two lived here, for hours on end. It really irked good old mater. I mean, she didn't want to say anything bad about her niece who was only ten or something, but she couldn't let your mother have the last word, either. I always thought she was disappointed she never had a daughter, and held that against your mother. And took it out on us, too."

"Huh? You think she wanted a daughter? Well, my mom was pretty mad when I accepted your mom's invitation to come out here. Mama's afraid I won't love her any more." Luba took another sip. "Did you ever hear any arguments between them before you left Toronto?"

"Oh, I suppose I heard them quarrelling over the phone from time to time, and my mother bitched about yours occasionally. Back then I was so self-absorbed, I didn't pay much attention to the content. Anyway, we had our own blow-ups to deal with. I tried to have open, rational discussions with her, you know, about paternalism in the church, civil rights, outdated social and legal codes that deal with things like racism, sexism, abortion rights, but she turned my arguments into ammunition before I could finish a sentence. I keep telling her she should have studied law—she'd either be disbarred by now or sitting on the Supreme Court of Canada. At least with a realtor's licence she can't get into too much trouble."

Leo swirled a French fry in a small pool of ketchup. "I'm thirty-two years old, and my mother and I have never been able to have a quiet, reasonable, unemotional discussion about what happened to her and dad, or my lifestyle, or even the weather! I just don't talk to her any more, unless I absolutely have to."

"What's it like living in the same city? Do you ever see her?" Luba asked.

"Nah, I rarely visit. Maybe call her on her birthday or Mother's Day. Anyway, this city is big enough so I don't run into her. We don't move in the same circles, nor will we."

"She's probably disappointed that you're not married and haven't provided her with a load of grandchildren. I know that's how my mother would feel."

"No, actually, my mother doesn't want grandchildren. She's so bitter she won't go to weddings, not since Dad left her. And she avoids children. I've suggested countless times that she should go to see a therapist, but you can imagine what kind of reaction I get for that. So I've stopped trying. And I think I have finally, after all these years, finally forgiven her for how nasty she was to me when I lived at home. But I wouldn't have been able to do it without going into therapy myself." She looked at Luba and smiled. "Most of us end up going at some point or another. Helps us to get on with life. We don't think we're wacky, do we, Greg?" Leo crossed her eyes and stuck out her tongue.

Greg picked up his mug. "A toast to Marvin! The best alternative lifestyle therapist around! Why, I'll bet at least half the people in this room have been clients of his, or still are. What do you think, Leo?"

Leo swung her head around and Luba followed her gaze. She saw groups of people you'd see in any regular bar, but now she also noticed, through a beery veil, that most of the couples were the same sex—men with men, women with women. She looked back at Leo, who met her eyes and chuckled.

"Greg, you didn't tell her?"

"Tell her what?"

"That Jonah's is a gay and lesbian bar?" Leo continued to hold Luba's gaze. "Luba, you gonna be all right?"

"Sure, I'm fine," she said, and raised her mug. "To alternative lifestyles!" All three tapped mugs in mid-air and laughed. This was not what she had been expecting—it was much more fascinating.

She stumbled, trying to run up a steep hill, exhausted from the climb but anxious to escape her pursuers. Ahead of her, perched at the very top, stood a crumbling old castle. She thought she could hide inside and willed her heavy legs to move faster. By the time she arrived at the top, she was so tired she could not walk—she crawled the last few feet on hands and knees. She knew they were close behind, whoever they were. She managed to get inside and heard a heavy metal door clang shut behind her. Was she finally safe, or trapped inside? A shadowy figure began to form in front of her and she tried to move away, but her body would not respond. Why couldn't she move her arms, her legs? A middle-aged woman in a shapeless, brown tunic with a military helmet stood in front of her and held out her hand.

"Give it to me!" the woman commanded. Luba trembled as she lay on the ground, paralyzed. "Give it to me now!" She bent forward and removed an egg that Luba had been hiding. She held it high in the air, cackled wildly, then dashed it to the ground. It exploded into hundreds of tiny fragments. Luba screamed.

"You cannot leave until you have confessed. Confess or rot in this prison!" she laughed hysterically and disappeared into the shadows again. Luba heard pounding behind her. Was someone trying to get in, to help her escape? Or to hurt her?

"Luba? Are you awake? I have to go or I'll be late for work."

Luba opened her eyes and saw her aunt's head poking inside the bedroom door.

"Uh-huh, I'm awake," she croaked.

"Good. I've made some coffee for you. You know where all the food is."

"Yes, Auntie, don't worry about me. I'll be fine," Luba said, yawning, not being able to quite focus on her.

"If you'd been up earlier I could have made you some breakfast, but I didn't want to wake you. You must have come in pretty late last night. How did you get home?"

"Uh, Greg drove me." Luba scooted up a little since it seemed her aunt was in a mood to chat, though she claimed to be running late. "I tried to be quiet when I came in."

"Well I did notice it was nearly one a.m. I'm not used to having anyone but us in the house any more."

"Oh, I'm sorry. I didn't mean to wake you."

"Oh, it's no problem. As long as you're all right."

"Yeah, fine. Just a bit tired."

"So what did you do all evening?"

Luba suddenly felt very awake, and annoyed. Her aunt had wedged herself in the door and had no intention of leaving until she had a full confession. It was just like home, but she decided to play along.

"We ate supper at the pub near Greg's place. Just hung out, you know. Met some of Greg's friends."

"Oh, which friends?" Her voice took on a sharp, familiar tone, like that horrible woman in her dream, like that other meddlesome woman back in Copper Creek.

"Um, let's see. There was Leo, and a bunch of other people. You know, I'm not good with names, especially not before coffee. Wait, there was Drew, the bartender, nice guy."

"Not here a week and you're already at the bars. What is your mother going to think?"

"So who's going to tell her?"

"Well, I'm not."

"Good. Neither am I. Auntie, I'm an adult now. We had a couple of beers and a burger. That's what adults do. No big deal." Luba wished her aunt would go to work.

"I know. I just want to make sure you'll be all right. I don't know if it's such a good idea to spend a lot of time with Greg and his friends. I know your mother wouldn't approve. I'll have Anne give you a call. You should get to know her, she's—"

"Auntie! Don't worry about me, okay? I'm going to see Baba today, and maybe check out the library. Anyway, little kids make me nervous, so I'd rather not visit with Anne and the kiddies."

"Oh!" She pressed her lips together, then looked down at her watch. "I have to go. I'll see you when I get home, okay?"

"Uh -huh."

She closed the door and Luba heard her heels clicking on the porcelain tiles down the hall. A door banged shut, then total silence. Luba slumped back on her pillow, still tired but so irritated she couldn't have gone back to sleep had she wanted to. Aunt Zenia obviously knew her son was gay, and she preferred Luba didn't see him—as if she could control where Luba went or who she spent time with.

She thought about that nasty dream woman in the castle. Well, she was not a prisoner in her aunt's castle. But what was with the egg? It crossed her mind to write down some of this stuff, and talk to Bella about her weird dreams when she got home. She missed Bella, she suddenly realized, and wished she could just waltz into her office for a session that day. She'd have to be patient, wait until she was back in Copper Creek. Greg was nearby. He was a great listener—she could talk to him. But could she really spill her guts to him?

Last night something odd seemed to be happening. Maybe it was just the atmosphere at the pub, maybe it was the way Leo was looking at her. She wondered if Leo was attracted to her in a sexual way. What a weird feeling, that a woman might be lusting after her body. She wondered what Bella would say if Luba told her? She knew the answer—Bella would ask Luba how she felt about that. And, well, she felt, well, titillated. Yeah, that was the word. Oh my God, she thought, surely she was not so inclined? How would she know? How did one find out that they were gay or lesbian, or bisexual? She had never even considered it. Until last night. Until now.

Shower, coffee, breakfast first. She didn't want to think those thoughts right then. She would just forget about it and start her day over. Go see her sweet old Granny. She couldn't imagine that Baba had ever had an impure thought in her life. The poor woman would never have had time to daydream if all those stories of hardship in the old country were true. Luba wondered, though. They always held back, the old folks, never telling her any of the juicy details of their lives. She'd probably never know, but then, they'd never know her stories, either.

Baba was much more alert than the last time Luba had visited. Of course, as soon as she walked in the room, Luba spoke and reintroduced herself. It took her grandmother a moment or two to orient, then she waved Luba over.

"Ah, my little Lubomyra. Did you know we named you after your uncle, Lubomyr? He would have been such a good boy, if he had lived. He was your mother's pet." Her eyes misted over and she seemed to go inside herself for a few minutes. Luba figured she had drifted off again and wondered if she should leave for a while. Then, just as suddenly, her watery red eyes sharpened and she peered at Luba with an intensity that made her shift where she sat on the edge of Baba's bed.

"Baba?"

"Yes, Luba?" She was back.

"Do you think Mama wanted a boy and got me instead?" Luba was thinking about what Greg had said last night, that his mother had wanted a girl, and got three boys. Maybe her mother wanted the opposite. She always spoke so lovingly about her baby brother, Lubomyr.

"Hah!" Baba tossed her head back and exposed her wrinkled neck and protruding collarbones. She shook her head and smiled. "No, no, your Mama was happy when you were born. Everyone loved you. Zenia made the biggest fuss over you when you came to live in Toronto. Your Mama argued that she was spoiling you, and Zenia accused her of not taking proper care of you. They were both wrong." She smiled and clasped her hands together on the cover over her knobby knees.

"Do you think you could help me up and take me outside for a while? I feel like some fresh air today, and it looks warm and sunny outside." They both turned to look out her small window. The sky was blue and the grounds were green, far more advanced than chilly Copper Creek. It was warm outside, so it seemed a reasonable request to Luba if they could wrap her up adequately. Baba showed her where the extra blankets were and Luba helped her into a worn, rose-coloured chenille housecoat. The lace around the collar was tattered and Luba felt embarrassed as she tied the belt around her thin form. There was hardly anything to her grandmother. She helped her out of the bed, a large, floppy doll in Luba's arms, and carefully arranged her in the wheelchair. Her ankles peeked out from below the long gown, simply bones coated with brown skin which held all the hundreds of fragments together, and shaped into gnarled feet that fit into fluffy pastel blue slippers.

"Ready? You tell me where to go, okay, Baba?"

The old woman smiled, raised the heavy arm of her housecoat, and pointed. Luba followed her finger. She had seen that finger, that arm before, probably in a late-night movie, and she shivered: the grim reaper in shedding pink rags.

Outside, she wheeled the chair down smooth asphalted walks that wound amongst lawns and trees, pushing their new life into the warm, carbon-rich air. Baba sighed deeply, and Luba inhaled the clean, living green atmosphere. How many springs had her grandmother lived through? Did Aunt Zenia say she'd be seventy-seven that year? And Luba was a mere twenty-two springs old. Oh, the things Baba must have seen in all those years. She wondered how many more there would be for her, and shook her head to fling those thoughts from her brain.

"So, Baba, do you think Aunt Zenia was disappointed to have three boys and no girls?"

Baba snorted, but Luba couldn't see her expression as she was still behind the wheelchair, pushing. "Here," she said, pointing to a place near a bench. "You can sit down so I do not wear you out."

"Oh, Baba, you won't wear me out. I don't mind going further."

"Well, we have gone as far as we can. There is not much of a lawn for all the people they pack into that warehouse. Stop here so you can sit and I can look at you."

Luba parked her chair at a ninety-degree angle to a long bench. There were two other people sitting at the other end: an ancient gentleman and a middle-aged woman with short, grey hair. They were speaking quietly in a language she didn't understand. Was it German, or maybe Dutch?

Baba settled back in her chair and squinted at her surroundings. Luba wondered exactly what she did see through those weak eyes. "Are you warm enough, Baba?"

"Oh, yes. Wrapped up like a baby, I am. This is what happens to us as we go around the circle of life. Back to a helpless infant." They sat quietly for a while, hearing the strange sounds from the couple next to them, and an occasional bird whistling or chirping in the trees.

"Ah, babies," Baba murmured. "Zenia decided three was enough. I think she wanted to have a girl, but in some ways she was never suited as a mother. Not enough patience. So three was more than she ever wanted. And, anyway, she has granddaughters now, and that is even better."

"Did you know me when I was a baby?"

"No, you lived in Vancouver when you were a baby, until your father died. I used to make little dresses for you. Your Mama did not have to tell me the size, I just knew, and they fit you perfectly. She sent me photographs. The day you arrived in Toronto, and you came by train, do you remember it?"

"Sort of." Luba had only a hazy memory of the train ride. It happened shortly after her father's funeral.

"Well, we all went to the train station to meet you and your mother. And you were wearing a bright pink dress that I had made for your birthday that year. The only thing wrong was that it was too short. I had no idea how tall you had grown and I thought you would be shorter like your parents. And look at how tall you are now, a beautiful girl. Tall like your grandfather and like Zenia's boys."

"You mean Grandfather Boryslav?" Luba asked. She had no idea what her father's parents looked like; there were no photographs of them. Her father had said that his family lost everything when the Nazis invaded and burned down his village. His parents had died after he left Ukraine, and only a few cousins were left behind.

Baba became silent. She seemed to be staring down at a spot in front of her feet.

"Baba, you okay?" Nothing. "Do you want me to take you back now?" Luba stepped in front of her, peered into her face. She was gone again. Luba moved behind the wheelchair and started to push it back. Still her grandmother said nothing.

What had done it this time? Talking about the past, Grandfather Boryslav? He had been a horrible man. Maybe that had triggered some long forgotten memory, a trauma, something Baba didn't want to face. Luba wished she knew what was going on in the old woman's brain. Now she was beginning to wonder if it would be such a good idea to bring up the antagonism between her daughters. Maybe she'd never get to the bottom of their quarrel. Maybe it didn't matter.

And, yet, she knew it did matter, felt strongly that her mother and Aunt Zenia's dispute had something to do with her. Perhaps it reached further back and involved Baba as well. Luba wished she could let it all go, like Leo seemed to have done with her family. It bewildered and dismayed her that she could not control this compulsion to dig up her family's history at the same time she wanted to bury her own. She'd simply have to get past the cranky bears waking from hibernation and find a way into the dens they protected.

In Limbo

Volya was surprised at how much she missed having Luba at home, now that she was gone again. Over the past two years she'd become accustomed to living alone, but the silence that now filled her home was oppressive. What made her loneliness more acute was the thought that Luba was spending time with her sister rather than with her. If Zenia expected to influence Luba by showering her with gifts and spoiling her, she'd be disappointed. There was no telling that girl anything—she knew it all. She was headstrong and stubborn, her mind filled with nonsense and many mysteries.

Volya sighed, sitting back in her comfortable living-room recliner, the television buzzing unheeded in the background. She should stop in to visit Veronica tomorrow, she thought. At least Luba had spent time with her grieving aunt, which had taken some pressure off Volya. Poor woman, there was nothing they could do to make her feel better. Veronica had been so kind and understanding with Luba's troubles and had never said a word to anyone about what had happened, not even to Marko. Volya was grateful to her sister-in-law. But where her daughter had survived, her nephew Orest was not so lucky. Volya felt guilty when she was with Veronica. Two days ago, during her most recent visit, her sister-in-law sat at her kitchen table, hunched over the photo album of her babies. Volya sat with her as she flipped each page, fingering the photos, caressing them like one would a favourite pet, talking about Orest. He was not a bad boy. A lot of energy, yes, mischievous like boys could be, but not bad, not then.

When she finished with that album, Veronica picked up an older one, from the years she lived in a refugee camp. They were all in Germany back then, after the war. The album cover reminded Volya that she had made those very same cover decorations in a different camp while waiting for news of her relocation. The younger girls cut and dyed straw while the older ones created Ukrainian designs by gluing the straw to wooden book covers which had been cut, sanded, and polished by the young men. The albums were sold to bring in a little money for their upkeep in the camps.

Volya felt fortunate to be able to attend school while she lived at the camp. After leaving the Veber farm she was sent to one of the abandoned military barracks where they housed all the single girls. At first, the eastern Europeans were all tossed together like a basket of odd fruits, vegetables, pastries, and sausages. But eventually they sorted themselves out according to nationality—Ukrainians, Poles, Latvians, Lithuanians, Czechs, Slovaks, and Russians. Zenia, Bohdan, the two boys, and Mama got to stay in what used to be officer's quarters. Not very large, but at least they had some privacy.

They were also fortunate because, unlike Zenia, Bohdan was able to keep his job at the clothing factory. Zenia would never let her family forget that Bohdan had an important position, being manager of the shipping unit. There was no question of letting him go with his experience and skill at handling people, traits that were indispensable with all the postwar labour re-entering the work force. Women went back to their homes to care for their families while young men returning from the front replaced them at the factories and offices. Some women were relieved they no longer had to work outside the home, while others were resentful. Zenia was definitely one of the latter.

While Zenia stayed with Mama and the two children, Volya was able to attend a business and trades college with other young women and girls. During one of her evening visits with the family, she told them about the knitting projects they had started. She said, "I am going to make myself a white sweater with blue trim. We got some patterns from England. Look, here is the one I am going to make. Mrs. Vesny said I could take it home to work on once I have learned the proper stitches." She showed Mama and Zenia the sketch of a slim model wearing the sweater with a rather short skirt and high-heeled shoes. They sat around the small round table commenting on the sketch and examining the pattern, when a small, pudgy hand appeared over the edge and grasped the corner of the tissue paper.

"Adam, no!" Zenia tapped his hand but he did not release his grip. Mama put her brown, weathered hand over his pale fist, and, with the other, tickled him under his arm. Little Adam squealed from under the table, and his hand disappeared, leaving the pattern behind, crumpled but intact.

"Will they allow you to have that much yarn?" Zenia asked, puckering her brow, always the naysayer.

"Of course. We can keep our first practice sweater. Eventually we will sell them to the Americans. They are crazy about these imported sweaters over there. Mrs. Vesny told us so. They even provide us with the wool, but most of it is white or cream. So I want to make sure I do a good job, because I intend to wear it a lot."

Zenia turned from the table to follow Adam, who decided to torment his younger brother by stealing his wooden train. She scooped up the older boy, kicking in protest. "Knitting is easy, I could have taught you that. No need to go to school to learn knitting," she snorted.

"We are learning other things, too," Volya told her, and described the book covers. "We will be making lots of money selling those as well as the sweaters," she added, knowing exactly how to aggravate her sister.

"Hah! Lots of money! Who is going to pay lots of money for cheap handmade crafts? You do not understand how the market works, little sister. Large-scale manufacturing, that is where you make money. I have all sorts of ideas about that. I cannot wait to get out of this hell. I am going to start my own business, you wait and see, and then we can talk about lots of money. I might even offer you a job," she taunted.

"All big talk," Volya countered, but she was not pleased. Zenia had a way of belittling all her younger sister's accomplishments and dreams.

Mama looked sad. "This is not so bad here. We have food to eat without breaking our backs. We do not worry about bombs falling on our heads every other minute. You should stop complaining and thank God we survived the war. As soon as we hear from Marko, all my prayers will be answered."

"Those are your prayers Mama," Zenia said pouting. "Oh, do not look so shocked. Of course I will be happy when we know Marko is alive. But I have other dreams—dreams about life in the real world, maybe England, maybe the United States. This is a make-believe city, Mama. Look around you. How long do you think they will keep us here, feeding us, housing us? We still have to go to the country to get fresh eggs and meat, and trade with anything we can get our hands on. I am hungrier now than I ever was during the war. They are going to run out of money, you wait and see. We will be lucky if they do not send us back to the Russians!" As if sensing her agitation, Adam began to cry.

She continued, "I know you two had a hard life on those farms, so of course you think this is heaven, living in a camp. You cannot begin to appreciate what a loss I have suffered moving here from the city apartment. You have no idea how hard it has been for me!" She stood with her hands on her hips, a pained, indignant expression on her face.

Volya was aghast at her sister's nerve. Zenia was the one who had no idea, none at all, of what she and Mama had lived through on those farms, of her own suffering. Trembling with fury, Volya stood up without meeting their eyes or saying a word, picked up the pattern, folded it, and walked to the door.

"Are you leaving?" Zenia asked in surprise. "Where are you...?" Volya heard no more as she closed the door on her sister. She held her breath until she was outside, then took in deep gulps of air. She remembered the day she stood alone on the road in front of Frau Koennig's house, her mother retreating inside, not wanting to know what had happened with Karl. The feeling that she was being accused of assaulting him. They never spoke of it again. And later, she believed Mama divined her huge loss when Yanos was taken away, although Volya had never admitted her feelings for him. Mama never brought it up, never asked Volya. There were times Volya wished she could talk to Mama about him, and other times she was glad to keep his memory her own. She certainly never wished to share any details with Zenia, who had no empathy at all.

No, Volya had new friends amongst the girls who shared the barracks, whom she went to school with. Some of them became very close over the months that stretched into a year, then two, while they awaited relocation. A number of her friends found boyfriends amongst the other refugees and two even got married while they lived at the camp. Volya was happy for them, but the weddings were miserable occasions for her. She tried to pretend she was delighted—she danced, she sang, but usually she left early, exhausted after all the preparations. And through it all she noticed Mama watching her, a concerned expression on her face. Mama knew she was unhappy, and Volya could see it made her sad. She was only twenty, but already acting like an old world-weary woman.

In June, Mama's prayers and greatest hopes were answered when she finally received a letter from Marko. All that time, he and Veronica had been living in a German refugee camp about one hundred kilometres north of Mannheim. They had married the previous year and it turned out that Veronica Stachevich was originally from a village only fifty-five kilometres east of their home in Brinzi. They had a brand-new baby girl, Christina. Marko wrote that they had managed to buy passage on a ship sailing to Canada, and there was a job waiting for him in a strange-sounding place called Manitoba. They would be sailing in late July, so there was time to visit them at the Mannheim camp before he and his young family left for the new world. At the end of his letter, he made one request. He did not wish to discuss what had happened during the war. All those things were in the past, he wrote, and he had no desire to relive the pain of what he had seen. They all agreed, of course, but wondered what horrors he had witnessed and what it had done to him. Now,

Volya thought, it had been nearly thirty years, and he had never spoken of it, and she had never asked.

As they flipped through the photos, Volya asked Veronica if she remembered the day they met at the Mannheim train station.

"How could I forget?" she said. "I was so nervous to meet Marko's family." Indeed, she was. Volya remembered holding a huge bouquet of flowers, trembling with anticipation. Zenia held a bouquet as well, and was shaking worse than her sister. As the train chugged in to the station billowing clouds of steam, Mama began to cry. Volya had not seen her shed a drop since the end of the war and now the dam was breaking. Finally, after years of worry and upheaval, her entire family would be together again.

Marko leapt out as soon as he spotted them. Veronica stepped down carefully behind him, clasping her bundle close, like a fragile glass sculpture that might shatter. First he hugged Mama and kissed her wet cheeks; then he embraced his two sisters and hugged Bohdan. By then Veronica had kissed her mother-in-law and allowed her to take the baby from her arms. She seemed afraid to take her eyes off the babe, but Zenia led her away and introduced her to the two nephews. They chatted all the way back to the barracks, where a small party had been organized at the mess hall.

Veronica's anxiety under the scrutiny of the Tatenko clan was obvious. She was a thin, big-boned woman of medium height, with hazel eyes and warm brown hair worn in braids wrapped around her head. She was only nineteen years old and said that her mother and sister Daria lived in northern Germany, and her father had disappeared in Ukraine during the war. She had met Marko at the camp, like many young displaced people. They had fallen in love and decided to marry within a very short period of time.

Veronica blushed and looked down while Marko spoke. "I knew she was the one when I first saw her. Is she not beautiful? And a wonderful cook and housekeeper. I knew you would approve, Mama."

"Of course, why should I not approve? Welcome to the family, Veronica. We are so glad to have you. I hope Marko has been treating you well?"

"Oh yes. He has been wonderful. And so good with the baby," she answered, gazing at the child sleeping peacefully in her arms again.

"She is a natural mother, this one!" Marko boasted, and slapped his wife lightly on the back. Even Zenia winced at that comment, and looked at her mother, who rolled her eyes with a subtlety only her daughters would notice. "So, Volya, you are not married yet? Be careful, you do not want to be an old maid. Nobody to suit you here? Ha, ha!"

Her oaf of a brother had apparently not matured much. "No, Marko," she said. "I have been waiting for someone just as smart and handsome as you, but no one can quite match up to your fine qualities."

"Be careful now. You have to watch you do not set your standards so high or you will never get married. Not every girl can be as lucky as Veronica here."

Zenia snorted at that. "Lucky girl? Poor girl, she deserves our sympathies for your swollen head and pride. You are the lucky one to find someone so tolerant. You have not changed a bit, Marko Tatenko!"

"Ah, you girls do not know what you are talking about. I will have another glass of that good beer, Bohdan, there is a good man. Now I have been around and I know what is what. If you do not marry before twenty-one, you are likely to become an old maid," he said, wagging his finger at Volya.

"How would you know? You are only twenty-one yourself," Zenia said.

"It does not matter if I marry or not. There is nothing wrong with being a maid all my life. I would not have to cater to the likes of you!" Volya made such a face at him that even Veronica laughed at his surprised expression.

"Some respect here, please. I just got here and you are already insulting me?" he complained.

"So do not be giving us unwanted advice, little brother. We are happy to see you. Just keep your mouth shut and drink up." Zenia lifted her glass of beer in the air. "Here is to joyous reunions, and to our Lord!" Zenia was indeed pleased to have Marko there, and especially to learn how he planned to escape to the new world.

Volya was pleased that Veronica remembered that day just the way she did, and for a few moments at least she was relieved of her burden of grief and Volya of her guilt.

When she returned to her dark, empty house, Volya found herself feeling more alone than usual. All those memories stirred up, the what-ifs of her past life. What if she and Yanos could have remained together, where would they be now? But then there would be no Yarko, no Luba. Why was there so much pain paired with love? Evil, the shadow side of light and good, what the priests loved to dwell on in their sermons. They were right, at least about that.

After putting the kettle on for tea, she walked into her living room and reached for the stack of photo albums on the bottom shelf. Aha, there was the same photo she had just seen in Veronica's album. Neither of them could remember who took it—one of her girlfriends at camp perhaps? Volya still marvelled at how thin Veronica was back then, though with the dark shadows beneath her eyes, she did not look healthy. Bizarre, the resemblance to Orest in the casket. She shuddered at the horrible thought. They were all thin while they lived at the camps, even though they had more food than during the war, except perhaps for Zenia in her city home. A good thing there were so few photos from that time—they were all nearly unrecognizable. Like those poor Auschwitz victims, she thought, shaking her head.

At least they were able to get away soon, Marko and Veronica and baby Christina. By December that year, Marko, good as his word, had started to send them money to help pay for the trip to Canada. That was about the time Zenia learned she was pregnant again, but she did not tell Bohdan until February. He was ecstatic and told Volya about it on his way to work as she was walking to school that day. After classes, she rushed to see Zenia to offer congratulations.

"I will thank you not to congratulate me!" Zenia scowled. "The timing could not be worse."

Her bitterness hit Volya like a slap in the face. She felt herself shrivel beneath her sister's wrath and sank into a chair next to Mama at the table.

"It is not as easy as you think, not getting pregnant. You are not married, so you do not have to worry about such things. This totally ruins my plans to leave this place by spring. Now we will have to wait until after the baby is born."

Mama shook her head but did not look up from her sewing. She was embroidering a small shirt for Greg. "You would not be able to leave before June, anyway," Mama said. "At the rate Marko is sending money, and what we are able to save with Bohdan's wages, we will not have enough until September, anyway. Unless you planned to leave me behind, then you could leave in July."

"You know we would not leave you behind, Mama," Zenia said, then started to cry. Volya sat quietly and decided to say nothing about a rumour she had heard that day, about a possibility that all the girls in her barrack and the next one would be offered passage to England in April.

Zenia was not the only one who wanted desperately to leave. In the few months before, life at the camp had revealed terrors they believed had been left behind with the war. First, word came in August that the Russians and Americans had struck a deal. The Russians had offered to transport all the Ukrainians, Poles, Byelorussians, and Lithuanians back to their home countries to help out the Americans with their repatriation efforts. When the refugees learned of this deal, several poor souls climbed the clock tower in the middle of the camp and threw themselves off, dying in crunched broken heaps at the base. The American staff running the camp immediately called a meeting of refugee representatives. When they learned what deep mistrust and fear they all had of the so-called "friendly Russians," they cancelled all transport plans with their allies.

What followed was a miniature replay of the Stalin years. The Russian government, still an ally of the Americans, had access to the German camps, and refugees began to disappear, one here, one there. Occasionally their bodies were found, most often outside the camp. Men and boys were stabbed, hung, and shot, and all made to look like suicides. Then a day that was burned into Volya's memory for all eternity—a day when a few of the girls noticed a commotion near the mess hall on their way to classes. They ran over to investigate and watched a man trying to resuscitate a pale, wet body that a few boys had just pulled out of a cistern. Laid out on the ground, they could all see it was a Latvian boy named Titus, only sixteen years old. As he lay limp and wet, water pooling around him, Volya pictured the face of Yanos beneath the blue skin and started to wobble on her feet. Her friends pulled her away, all of them sobbing with new fear and sorrow. This was the first victim they had known personally, but for Volya the loss was even more heart-wrenching.

As the days stretched into weeks and months, the refugees were increasingly anxious and desperate to get away from the camp and Germany. Any opportunity that arose was snatched up. Volya did not say anything about going to England until two weeks before, when final arrangements were being made. She told only Mama, and asked her to keep it to herself since she did not want to incur Zenia's mad jealousy and wrath for any longer than necessary. Bohdan heard about it a week before she was due to go. He also chose not to tell his wife, knowing how eager she was to leave, and how miserable her pregnancy had made her. She had become nearly impossible for all of them to live with, and even the children began to avoid her.

The night before Volya's departure, she finally found the courage to see Zenia and say good-bye. "Zenia, I am leaving tomorrow. For England," she announced abruptly, before losing her nerve, but was not able to look her sister in the eyes. She heard Mama sigh deeply behind her and she steeled herself. Bohdan had taken the two boys out for a walk just after supper, knowing that she was coming to talk to Zenia. He hoped to spare the children from a hysterical scene.

"England? Tomorrow?" Zenia was stunned, but did not look angry, not yet.

"Yes. There are twenty-five of us going. We take the early train up north, then—"

"Oh, never mind, I do not need to hear details," she said wearily, but calmly. After a pause, "What will you do up there?"

"They have different factory jobs lined up for us. Mostly in a cotton mill, I think. I will send the address to Mama once I know where I will be staying. I want to come to Canada with all of you, eventually, but this way you will have enough money sooner for your own trip. I can join you all later, once I have saved enough money."

Volya found herself unexpectedly close to tears, now that the prospect of being severed from her family loomed again. A huge black hole of loneliness threatened to swallow her up. She breathed in deeply, pushing away the old feelings she had tried to leave behind. She was not alone, she reminded herself. She had new friends, wonderful, close friends who would be travelling with her, making a new home with her.

Zenia rose and embraced her, but only briefly, lightly. There were no tears in her eyes, no anger, no relief in her expression. "You will find yourself a nice young man to marry, maybe a rich Englishman," she predicted in a dull tone. "You will have to learn the language first. They do not like us DPs if we cannot talk their fancy language. So, good luck. May God be with you." She turned away from Volya and sat down, picking up the mending she had been doing. "Have you packed?"

Volya nodded, then, biting her lower lip, shook her head. "No, I have not finished yet. Mama, will you come with me for a few minutes?"

Mama accompanied her outside. There they saw Bohdan returning with the two boys. He looked at them with an anxious expression.

Mama shrugged her shoulders. "She is all right. She may like some company, though. I will be back soon."

Mama was not at all worried about Volya. She fully expected the next few months would be miserable for herself, Bohdan, and the boys, but Volya knew Mama was most concerned about her dispirited daughter who did not want to have that baby. A very bad thing, she must have thought, for a child to come into the world unwanted. And in the end Volya supposed it was a good thing Mama was around, considering how ill Zenia was after little Bill was born. She had always felt sorry for all three of the boys, but Bill had it the worst when he was a baby. As things turned out, Volya was not in the most positive frame of mind either when she was first pregnant with Luba. But life had a way of making sharp turns when you least expected them. It was just as well they could not see their futures. Would she have gone to England if she had known what was waiting for her? Probably not. Mama should have been worried about her youngest daughter, not her oldest one. But now she would never know.

Girls Just Wanna Have Fun

"Luba! Telephone for you!" Zenia called from the living room.

"I'll get it down here, okay?" Luba wondered if it was her mother as she picked up the receiver in the downstairs rec room. She'd been rather lax about her promise to call with updates. She listened for a moment, but there was no telltale click of her aunt hanging up.

"Hello?"

"Hey Luba, it's Leo."

"Oh, hi!" Her heart raced and her cheeks burned.

"Are you bored to tears yet?"

"Uh no, not really. I'm okay. Went card shopping today. I missed Mother's Day so I'm in deep shit for that, and her birthday is coming up soon..."

"Right, you wouldn't want to miss two in a row, God forbid. What about Christmas cards? And we can't forget Easter."

"Are we being a little sarcastic? And no, I don't do Easter."

"Well, that's okay, then. Say, you interested in a little soirée some friends are having tomorrow night? You may not be wasting away over there, but I detect a note of ultra politeness which means your relatives are in earshot, right?"

"Uh, well..."

"Say no more. So what about it? I can pick you up if you want to come along; I know where you live. Just a few friends, some food, good music, nice crowd. Even a graphic designer or two in the group if you want to talk art."

"Sure, I guess, sounds good."

"Great! I'll be there around eight then, okay?"

"Okay."

"Bye now. Be good."

"Like I could be anything but. Bye." Luba held on to the receiver after she heard the dial tone, then a soft click which followed confirmed her suspicion. Damn that woman, she'd been listening. Her aunt was worse than the Dragon Lady.

Luba snorted and circled the room like a trapped, wild filly. She stopped at the foot of the stairs and tapped her foot, imagined herself storming up to confront her aunt. But she was not brave enough—she had seen Aunt Zenia with the claws out, and knew she was no match, not yet. Luba was taking notes, though. After a few short weeks with her mother, her self-defence skills were sharpening up again.

"Luba!" The shout from upstairs made her jump.

"Yeah?" she shouted back, wondering if Aunt Zenia could pick up the irritation in her voice.

"Why don't you come on up here for a minute?" Her voice sounded normal. Luba started up the stairs, compelled to do her bidding as the guest and darling niece.

She found her aunt and uncle in the living room, watching television, sitting on their comfortable couches, feet up on ottomans. Her aunt's left hand gripped her usual drink which rested on a brass, glass-topped end table. She raised up her whiskey and swirled the ice cubes, making them clink against the smoke-coloured tumbler. Zenia patted the cushion next to her. Luba wondered if this was an aunt thing since Aunt Veronica liked to do the same. She was beginning to feel like a reluctant pup being trained to do tricks.

"Come and sit with us for a while. You've come all this way to visit, so let's visit. Bohdan, turn the TV down," she commanded and plunked her drink down hard, splattering some on the table. "Oh, look what a mess I've made."

"I'll get a towel, Auntie." Luba turned back into the kitchen and grabbed a couple of paper-towel sheets.

"Thanks, Luba, you're such a sweet girl. Here, sit down." Luba did as she was told and stretched out her own feet to rest on a footstool that matched the richly flowered brocade of the couch.

"So, what's new?" her aunt asked oh-so-casually, and took another sip. By her mannerisms Luba guessed this was her fourth drink.

"Oh, not much. I had a nice talk with Baba today, which I already told you about. I bought a card for Mama, which I showed you. Not much new since then." Luba didn't intend to make this easy. She ran her buffed nails over the pad of her thumb, then spread her fingers out in a fan and placed them on her thighs.

"Who was that on the telephone?" She looked straight at Luba, daring her to lie.

"Leo. I'm going out with her tomorrow, if you don't mind. To a house party."

Luba stared straight back. Her aunt turned away and cleared her throat.

"Well, actually, I do mind. I don't think you should be going out with her or her friends."

The long, contorted face she made was remarkably like Volya's, but in a different colour scheme: one red and one purple dragon in the Tatenko family. How nice, thought Luba.

"It's an unhealthy group to hang around with. I think your mother and I would agree on that."

"What do you mean, unhealthy? Are they sick?"

"Yes, they're sick. Mentally deranged. You are young and impressionable. They could easily influence you." Her voice rose, and her hand trembled as she took a noisy gulp of her drink.

Luba felt heat rising through her tensed body. She couldn't help herself. "Auntie, is that how you feel about your own son?"

"Greg was fine until they brainwashed him! You don't understand how dangerous these people can be. Anyway, he's not really like that, once he can get away from them. I just don't want you to get involved with those, those... perverts."

"Zenia!" Bohdan interrupted, his voice sharp. "They are not perverts. Luba is an adult—she's a sensible girl. She can decide for herself who's safe and who isn't—"

"What do you know? Where were you when Greg needed a man's guidance? 'Oh, just leave him be, Zenia,' you said. 'He's a sensible, smart boy, he knows what he's doing.' Well just look at him now! You know what people say about him. I am so ashamed. I can't even go to the Bazaar any more to face that Mrs. Halach." She began to sob and covered her face with shaking hands.

"That's the whole problem, Zenia," Bohdan said, more softly this time. "You are ashamed for yourself. What Greg feels is not important, just what he looks like to your world. I tell you he can't help it. There is all kinds of scientific proof for it. You can't force him to be something he isn't, just accept that. And don't jump all over poor Luba here, she gets enough of that back home." He looked at his niece apologetically before he spoke again.

"Never mind, Luba, you go out and have a good time. Leo is a nice girl. Not everybody in this world is cut out to marry and raise children. She's had a hard life with her parents splitting up and not giving her the care she should have had." He shook his head.

"But we gave Greg every opportunity his brothers had," Aunt Zenia recovered enough to rejoin. "And why did he turn out so different? It's those friends of his, I tell you! He was not born that way!"

Uncle Bohdan acted as if he hadn't heard her. He continued speaking to Luba. "I just read about a study in England where they looked at the family living situations of homosexual men born during the Second World War. They found that there is a much higher percentage of homosexuals born to families who lived through the bombing raids in London. They say that fetuses at certain stages are very sensitive to the mother's—what do they call those chemicals that come from the mother's glands? When they are pregnant? You know biology, Luba. What do they call it?"

"Hormones?"

"Yes, hormones. Anyway, they think these hormones, certain ones, go up or down and can affect the way a boy will act later in life. You know..." He trailed off, embarrassed.

"Affecting sexual orientation," Luba finished for him. She hadn't heard this theory before, but it made sense. She had learned enough in biochemistry to know that the sex hormones and stress hormones were related chemically, and one type could form and influence the other.

"Theory, shmeory," Aunt Zenia pitched in again. "Bill was born during the war, too. And he is normal."

"There were no bombing raids while you carried him, in case you have forgotten. You were pregnant with Greg when Sylana ended up in the hospital with shrapnel in her legs. Well, I remember, if you do not."

"So that makes it my fault he turned out the way he did? My hormones caused him to be abnormal? Thank you very much! Always the mother's fault. Such an easy excuse for you." She stood up, wobbled slightly, and left the room, her head raised.

Uncle Bohdan sighed. "Luba, I apologize."

"Never mind, Uncle, it's okay. I am curious, though, about that study. Did it say anything about homosexual women? You know, lesbians?"

"I don't remember. I'm not sure if they studied women, only men that I read about. Anyway, don't you worry about this. I try not to bring the subject up. You can see how she is about the whole thing."

"I'm sorry I started it all," Luba said, feeling rotten about putting her uncle through the wringer. It was obvious he had trod this path many times already.

"No, you did not start it. She did. Anyway, you go out tomorrow and have a good time. Leo and Greg have some very well-educated, smart friends. Not all of them are, well, you know..."

"Sure. I know." Considering his age and background, her uncle was a liberal thinker. Thank God there was at least one of them in that generation of her family.

"Who brought the potato salad?"

"Leo."

"I thought so. It has Ukie written all over it!"

"Who's been writing on my salad?" Leo shouted from the end of the table where she was leaning over the baked beans. There were people crowded around the long table, hungrily piling food onto their floppy paper plates.

"Say, did you hear the one about the message written in yellow snow at the White House?"

"Yeah, yeah, 'Kissinger was here.' But whose hand-writing was it?"

"Hey, you're ruining my joke!"

"Everyone knows the joke!"

"You don't even know whose hand-writing it was!"

After more laughter, someone yelled, "Patricia Nixon wrote it, you ignoramus. I thought you were a political junkie." Then another person remembered a better 'yellow snow' joke.

Luba was glad someone provided the punch line; she had never heard the joke, either. Nonetheless, she was beginning to feel at home in this place. Here she was bumping elbows with people who seemed like old friends. They were welcoming, warm, and not at all stiff or snobby. The day had started off badly with Aunt Zenia's cold shoulder treatment that morning. Uncle Bohdan was already gone when Luba woke up, so he wasn't around to provide a buffer. Then she started to get nervous about the "smart, well-educated" friends of Leo's. Who was she to mingle with them? Most of them would be older than she was, professionals like doctors, professors, lawyers, and established artists probably. What if they were heavy-duty intellectuals that she couldn't talk to? What if she embarrassed Leo? Luba began thinking of excuses not to go, but then she couldn't have faced Aunt Zenia's smugness, her sense of victory. That would have been much worse.

Her aunt was working late that day, so Luba poured herself a rye-and-ginger half an hour before Leo showed up. "Here's to Boryslav and all the other Tatenko drunks!" she toasted her relatives, living and dead, before chugging the calming potion.

"Leo, do you think my aunt is an alcoholic?" Luba asked as they sat on the floor of the blue rec room, heaped plates balanced on their laps.

Leo snorted. "Is the Pope Catholic?" She bit into a drumstick, holding the end while she chewed. She pointed it at Luba. "Bill and Adam drink a lot, too. Don't know for sure, but I think Bill is an alcoholic. Adam may be into other stuff. They keep it pretty well disguised, though. Don't look so shocked, everybody has a vice, or a deep, dark secret. What's yours?" She grinned at Luba then shovelled a forkful of jellied carrot salad into her wide mouth. Luba couldn't get over her dimples, imbedded into her bulging cheeks. At that moment Leo reminded her of an elf who hadn't eaten for a week.

"Great potato salad, Leo. You're a credit to the race." Luba raised her loaded fork in salute. A large cube of creamy potato slid off and plopped into her drink, splashing both of them.

"Hey!" Leo and Luba looked at each other, then burst out laughing.

"Food fight!" someone behind them shouted.

"Nah, Luba's just a slob. What do you expect from peasant stock? Hey, watch that fork!"

Luba made a mock jab at her, then speared an olive from her plate.

"Oh, a thief, too! You'd think you were raised an orphan. Or a Gypsy!" She grabbed a radish from Luba's plate.

"Why, thank you, Leo. I've always fancied myself a Gypsy. My mother calls me that when she's disgusted with me, like I've just contracted a contagious skin disease. Tsiganka! So naturally I consider it a compliment."

The music had just switched from blues to rock. "Roxanne" by the Police. Luba was surprised to hear it in this older crowd, a song that had just hit the charts. A couple jumped up and began to dance to much clapping and hooting. Another couple joined them. Three women and one guy, so far. She noticed that the couples at this party consisted of all possible combinations of men and women. It was an anything-goes kind of party, not unlike parties she had gone to with her musician friends.

Steve, the party host, scooped up their empty plates and cutlery, chanting, "Rock on, baby, rock on." Leo followed him into the kitchen with their drink glasses, and Luba decided to stand up as well since her legs were starting to cramp. She nodded her head in time to the music and stamped her legs to loosen the muscles.

"Here's a foxy lady who's ready to boogie." Steve reappeared next to Luba and took her arm, pulling her toward the group of about eight people gyrating to the music on the plush blue carpet. She still felt self-conscious but didn't resist. She loved that song and found her arms beginning to wave and rise, then the rest of her body followed the rhythm. She had always danced, as long as she could remember. When Luba was very young, she danced in her parents' little home to the scratchy folk tunes they played on their ancient record player. Soon she was part of the local Ukrainian dance troupe, whirling around the stage, bright ribbons streaming from her headdress. She loved the scarlet costume, layers of skirts, embroidered blouse, and especially when she graduated to the knee-high red boots with real heels and pointy toes. As a teenager she became shy—she didn't want to stand out from her school friends so she stopped dancing altogether for a long time. Luba rediscovered the joy of moving to music at her high school prom. In Toronto the clubs and bars with dance floors became her favourite hangouts on weekends. The night she met Tom, they had danced to Fleetwood Mac's "Riannon" during a band break. She had to be careful—dancing did funny things to her brain, sometimes more so than alcohol. It was a drug to her, putting her into a state of emotional vulnerability perhaps. If she had decided to carry on with a career in medicine, she figured she'd want to study a field like neurochemistry or psychiatry. Learning how the brain worked appealed to Luba much more than caring for sick people.

"Go, Luba! Hey!" she heard someone shout above the music. A male voice. She looked around but didn't see the person attached to it. When the song ended she stood panting and sweating next to a beaming, admiring Steve.

"You Ukes are a wild bunch."

"Thanks, Carl. You throw a great party." He bowed politely.

"Another?" he asked as the music started up again. "Dancing Queen" by Abba this time.

"Think I'll get something to drink first, if you don't mind. But I'll be back," she said, and headed for the kitchen. Steve was already dancing, one of the throbbing bodies on the crushed carpet. Luba noticed for the first time that even the lamps were blue, throwing a pastel light over the entire room.

"Aha, here's our Gypsy girl." Leo handed her a fresh drink with lots of ice as Luba stepped into the kitchen. Now she could see who shouted. Greg was talking to a couple of women at the other end of the huge, bright kitchen. This room was done in yellow and orange, from floor to ceiling.

"That's me, the party girl. Guess I couldn't hide it from you forever," she said and gulped thirstily.

"Leo, introduce me to your friend." A muscular, dark-skinned young man appeared next to Leo as she mixed another drink. He had the blackest, shiniest hair Luba had ever seen. Reflecting orange from the walls, it didn't look at all natural.

"George, Luba. Luba, George," Leo said without ceremony and winked at Luba. "Luba is Greg's little cousin from up north."

George ran his eyes up and down in appraisal, and Luba looked down at herself, wondering what he was taking in. She didn't notice anything alarming. Her tunic top was loose and modest, even with the low scooped neck; her jeans were well-fitted and snug, flaring at the bottom. The platform sandals gave her added height, so she was nearly as tall as George. His eyes finally parked on her chest.

"Not so little, I'd say." He seemed satisfied with the inspection.

"Are you a horse-trader or what?" Luba snapped.

Leo shrieked with delight.

"My, we're quick-witted and sharp-tongued, aren't we? I like that in a woman. Doesn't put me off one bit." He smiled at her.

Leo put her arm in front of Luba and leaned against the wall. "Nothing puts you off, George."

"Well, excuse me, I didn't know she was taken. The only fresh property on the place, and claimed already. Wouldn't you know it." He turned away.

Leo turned back to Luba and shrugged. "He's a creep, one of Steve's buddies. And a lonely heart."

"And he will be for a long time with his winning ways."

"Luba! How did you get away from my mother's clutches?" Greg was now standing next to them.

"Your dad vouched for my good behaviour. So here I am."

"Uh-huh," he said and gave her a knowing look. "Well, if dad had seen you dancing in there, he'd know you were a full-blooded Ukrainian gal. I remember how you used to dance at all the concerts. Such a little show-off!"

"I was not!"

"Were too. Mother used to glow and tell us about what a good little model child you were. Dancing in your little costume, all those colourful flowers and flying ribbons, the sweet little red slippers—"

"Oh, stop!"

"No, you listen. We had to suffer, so it's payback time. It didn't actually bother me too much. I was off doing my own thing. But Billy, oh Billy hated you. 'Why don't you join the dance group, Billy? Why don't you sing in the choir, Billy? Why don't you want to be an altar boy like Michael and Petro?' She nagged and nagged. I swear he was ready to kill you." Greg had a deadly serious look on his face.

"Get out of here," Luba said, not believing a word.

"It's true, Luba," Leo said.

"How do you know?"

"Bill told me. That's when we were on speaking terms, when Greg and I were first hanging together. So I couldn't wait to meet this perfect little cousin of theirs. Sounded like a snotty little kid, all right. The kind we all hate."

"Me, too. But I wasn't that kid. I've never been a model child. Ask my mother!"

"No, ask my mother," Greg said. "She knows about model children because she didn't have any. Sorry, Luba, you take the goody-two-shoes prize in our family. Your reputation is unblemished." Greg crossed his arms and looked down at her with a smug expression. He was teasing, wasn't he?

"Well, you're wrong there. I don't have a spotless reputation."

"What awful thing have you done—rob a bank?" Leo snickered.

"No. Not a bank," Luba said reflectively, wondering if she should say more.

"Well, what then? Greg, I think she's going to confess a crime. What did you rob? Or did you try to murder someone? Your mother? You can tell us, we won't breathe a word, honest," she chuckled.

They really didn't believe she could have been stupid, done something awful. Luba opened her mouth but couldn't say the words she had prepared in her mind. She found herself wanting to shock them, show them that she wasn't so perfect or innocent. Of course, Greg already knew she had messed up. But what would Leo think of her? She'd probably think she was an idiot, that's what. Luba felt tears oozing out and their faces blurred.

"Luba! What's the matter? What did we say? Oh, Luba, I'm sorry." Leo's sympathy unleashed the flood and Luba felt arms around her, felt her murmuring and soothing and patting her head. Leo led her out of the kitchen, her strong arm firm around Luba's shoulders. They entered a dark room and sat on a soft couch. Leo leaned away for a moment to switch on a lamp. They appeared to be in a small, dark green study. She moved the hair away from Luba's face and peered at her closely. Luba continued to blubber, unable to stop.

"Luba, I apologize. We shouldn't have been teasing you like that." Her dark eyes were questioning. She looked at Luba, steady and unwavering, her arm around Luba's shoulders, her hand gently rubbing her arm.

Finally, when Luba was able to breathe normally again, she said, "No, it's okay. I'm sorry for breaking down like that. I was about to tell you something, but couldn't—"

"You don't have to tell me anything. We weren't really serious you know."

"I know, but I wanted to tell you. About what happened to me a few months ago. It's the liquor. I mean, I'm not usually so weepy, but booze will do that to me... and dancing..."

"Hey, me, too. Don't apologize. I understand."

"No, I want to tell you about it. I tried to kill myself. I took an overdose of pills. Didn't work, though," Luba laughed hoarsely.

"Oh honey, I'm so sorry." Leo put both arms around Luba and hugged her tightly. It felt good. Luba lay her cheek on Leo's shoulder. As Leo massaged Luba's head, she began to cry again, softly. Leo rocked her, made her feel safe and loved. For the first in a long time, she knew this was someone who understood the pain she had suffered, someone who wouldn't judge her. And maybe Leo knew what she needed, what she was looking for. Luba wasn't sure she knew herself. At that moment, she wanted Leo to hold her forever.

Greg slipped into the room and sat on the other side of Luba. They talked, the three of them, about everything and nothing until the dawn. By the time Greg drove Luba home, the house was empty, his parents both gone to work.

"Guess they'll chew me out when they catch up to me," Luba said as she walked in the door, not really caring.

"Will you be okay?" Greg patted her shoulder.

"No problem. Think I'll hide out with Baba once I've had a little nap—if I can fall asleep."

"Tell Baba I'll see her on the weekend." He cupped her cheeks and kissed the top of her head. "Ciao, bella Luba, and sweet dreams."

A Peek into the Closet

Luba did sleep after crawling into bed that morning, but not deeply. When she finally awoke, groggy, her head throbbing, she could not remember any of her dreams. Just as well, she thought, given how disturbing they'd been lately. After showering and eating a cup of leftover soup, she took the buses to the nursing home. Once again, Baba was in another world and could not be reached.

Luba found herself back on the steps at the entrance, looking out at the lawns. She couldn't bear the thought of returning to the house so soon and decided to walk the grounds for a while. In spite of the low clouds and threatening drizzle, the dull tree trunks appeared to be exploding bright green leaves into the sky. The grass below them was vibrant with life, a lush carpet beneath her feet. She walked among the trees, reflecting on what had happened last night, trying to sort it out. Was that really her? It felt like someone else had inhabited her body for several hours. Not a total stranger, more like a close relative, someone she'd been trying to reach who remained just beyond her grasp and comprehension. Or had this person been trying to seek her out?

Luba pictured Leo's face close to her own, the concerned, bottomless, ageless eyes. She wished Leo could be with her now, walking alongside, talking to her, convincing Luba that she was sane. The way she felt after talking to Bella, like she'd let someone take a peek at her soul, then was relieved and grateful that they didn't scold her or think less of her. Luba wondered if she was attracted to Leo. She liked her a lot, but in that way? And now, after pouring her heart out, proving what an idiot she'd been, she worried that Leo thought less of her, in spite of her assurances to Luba. She wished she could talk to Bella. Maybe she would call her later. But from where?

"Hello! Hello there!" Luba looked up to see one of the nursing attendants waving in her direction. Luba looked behind but saw no one there. She pointed to herself.

"Yes, you. You're Mrs. Tatenko's granddaughter, aren't you?"

She nodded her head. "Yeah."

"I saw you in her room earlier. She's back with us, if you know what I mean. If you'd like to visit with her now."

"Oh, sure. Thanks."

Baba was just finishing a snack when Luba entered her room. She looked up, smacking her lips, then stopped, her mouth open, juice dribbling from the corner. Her thin eyebrows shot up in surprise, the same look she had given Luba when she first saw her.

"Lazlo!" she croaked, and her hands flew up to her face.

"Baba, it's me, Luba." In spite of the reassurance, the old woman did not seem to recognize her granddaughter. Luba approached her slowly. Her grandmother was muttering so she couldn't make out her words.

"Baba," she said quietly but firmly. "It's Luba. Lubomyra, Volya's daughter. You know, your daughter—"

"I know who my daughter is," she cut Luba off, still looking at her with a worried expression. "You remind me of someone." Her hands had fallen to her sides as she studied Luba, squinting.

Luba sidled up to the edge of the bed and sat on it. Baba had calmed down and the ghosts had cleared out of her eyes.

"Who do I remind you of, Baba?"

Baba looked down at her hands; her lips tightened before she answered. "A man who used to live in our village. A Gypsy named Lazlo."

Luba felt her ears prick forward and her heart wings flap. "You knew a Gypsy? I didn't know there were Gypsies in your village. Mama never told me about them. I thought they travelled around and didn't live anywhere in particular." Luba leaned toward her, questioning.

"That is true, they did travel. This Gypsy was only in the village for a short time. I used to care for his little son, Nestor. I knew them better than anyone else in Brinzi." Her eyes misted over.

"Baba," Luba said quickly so she didn't lose her again. "Tell me about the Gypsies."

She looked straight past Luba and a shadow fell over her face. Luba shivered.

"I promised I would take their story to the grave with me," she nodded. She noticed Luba's disappointment. "I broke that promise once when I tried to tell your mother. I do not want you to be angry with me, too."

"Is that why she left Toronto?" Luba asked, already suspecting the answer. Baba nodded, her eyes cast down.

"Baba, I am not like my mother. I won't be angry with you, I promise."

Baba shook her head. "People are so strange. They come in here and talk to me like I am stupid. They ask me things they do not really want to know about. I answer them, they get angry. Or they laugh when I am serious. They give me pills that do nothing. The whole world is going crazy. So I am crazy, too, and you cannot believe anything I say."

"Baba, I believe you. Why shouldn't I? I'm not one of them!"

"Hah! They think I am going crazy and they are right. You should not listen to an old woman. All lies." She lay back and turned her head away from Luba.

"Oh, Baba, that's not true. I do believe you. I know what it's like when people don't take you seriously. You can tell me anything, I won't judge you." She did not respond, so Luba waited another minute, then began to get off the bed. Baba turned her head back to her.

"You really want to hear a story?"

Luba thought she could see a twinkle in her dark eyes. "Yes, of course I do!"

"When your mother was a little girl, she complained every time I cut her hair, especially her bangs. She wanted long hair like the older girls and was impatient to have braids. Then one day when she was playing at the far end of the village with the other children, she saw one of the boys up on a roof. He threatened to pull down his pants and pee on them. Your mother always was such a serious and prim child, she could not stand by and let this happen. She climbed up onto the neighbour's roof and tried to jump across to stop the boy, but she lost her balance and fell head-first into a well between the two houses!"

Luba listened to the story she had heard countless times, how her mother had split the skin on her forehead, and her bangs had covered up the mess. She smiled and nodded at her Baba. She had also heard Volya's version, the fear that her father might discover what she had done and give her a beating for it. Saved by the hated bangs. What Luba hoped was that this story would lead to another one, the one about the village Gypsy. But, like the previous visit, Baba suddenly ran out of steam and fell asleep. No further talk of Gypsies or the story that had upset her mother and driven her away. Damn. So close. Luba resolved to return as many times as necessary until she convinced Baba to trust her, to believe that she would not react the way her mother had. She was not her mother.

"Hello, I'd like to speak to Bella Davies."

"This is Bella." The voice immediately painted the picture Luba needed to see. A calm, shimmering island, rock solid, surrounded by a soft, warm, sandy beach. The receiver trembled against her cheek.

"Hi. It's Luba. Can we talk now?" Her voice wavered, though she had made this appointment the day before.

"Yes, Luba. I shouldn't have any interruptions. How about you? Are you in a place where you're free to talk?"

"Yeah, I'm at my cousin Greg's place. There's no one here. No one to eaves-drop, either." Luba's hand still shook as she leaned back on the sofa and closed her eyes. She imagined herself sitting on the green couch across from Bella. She took a deep breath.

"You sounded pretty upset when you called yesterday. What's been hap-pening?"

"A lot. You know I'm staying with my aunt and uncle. He's a real sweetie, she's a witch. It's nearly as bad as home, and in some ways worse."

"How do you mean?"

"Uncle Bohdan stands up for me, and Greg, he's super. But Aunt Zenia is so like my mother, except she drinks. She doesn't seem to lose control when she's drinking, but she's mean and critical and bossy. It started out okay, but since I've been hanging out with Greg and his gay and lesbian friends, she's changed completely."

"Oh. Has she not accepted Greg's lifestyle?"

"Yeah, you could say that. She wants me to stay away from them, which doesn't surprise me, I guess. But it gets more complicated. You see, I really like Leo. She's Greg's house mate and I kind of think she likes me, you know, more than a friend. She's a lesbian, well, technically a bisexual." Luba paused again, waiting for Bella's inevitable question.

"And how does that make you feel?"

Luba strained into the phone, trying to pick up any subtle intonations, to imagine Bella's facial expression. Were her eyebrows arched, had her green eyes narrowed to cat slits, or were they wide open in surprise? But no picture came. She was on her own.

"I'm not really sure, I'm all over the place. You see, Leo had a rough child-hood, her folks split up, and like me she doesn't get along with her mother. Well anyway, she's so understanding, I feel I can tell her anything. I have, I've told her everything. And I feel like we're connected. I feel safe with her, I guess, like I can trust her with my life. It's so weird, I've never felt like that about anyone before. And so quickly."

"Women can relate to each other on many levels. Would you describe your feelings toward her as what you might feel towards a close sister?" Luba could not detect censure in Bella's voice, but surely she must have been alarmed.

"I don't know, I've never had a sister. It's nothing like my relationships to my female cousins, if that's what you mean. Much, much closer."

"More intimate?"

"Yeah, I think so."

"Has she indicated that she might want to be more physically intimate with you? By touching or kissing?" Now she sounded clinical.

"We-ell, that's hard to say. She has touched me, but just the way two regular friends might. Or sisters."

"If you didn't already know she was a lesbian, would you suspect she might be interested in you in a sexual way?"

"I, I can't say for sure." For some reason Luba felt disappointed, close to tears.

"Would you want her to be interested in you that way?"

"I, I don't know. Maybe. Isn't that weird?"

"No, not at all, Luba. Those are perfectly normal feelings."

"They are?"

"Sure. It's a wonderful feeling when you think someone understands you. It's even better when you can trust a person with your innermost thoughts and feelings. You haven't had that person in your life until now. You're just starting to reach out, and you're finding people who understand and care and don't judge. It's natural that you should feel strongly about them. As for physical attraction, that happens within the same sex more than people realize."

"It does?" Now Luba was surprised. Here she thought it was taboo to even think that way, but perhaps she was not so unique after all. She couldn't tell if she was let down or relieved.

"Many women go through a phase, or even several phases, of wondering if they are lesbian."

"So how do you find out?"

"Most of us have to experiment to know for sure. But it's a tough step to take. I'm sure you know that gay and lesbian lifestyles are still not well-accepted."

"But you don't think it's abnormal?" Luba needed reassurance.

There was a pause. "Based on what we know today, it is within the normal range of human behaviour. We can't explain why some people have homosexual preferences and others, the majority, are heterosexual. And there's much more overlap than people know. Women in particular tend to be more flexible in their sexual preferences. You needn't feel guilty having homosexual thoughts."

"Well, I guess that's a relief."

"Good. Anything else you want to talk about?"

"Well, no, not really. I'm a little ticked about my grandmother. She started to tell me about the big blow-up when my mother left Toronto, then clammed up. But I'll go back and see if I can sweet-talk her into it anyway."

"Is it sensitive family history?"

"Seems to be. I tried to ask my aunt last night, but she was mad at me for staying out all the night before. Anyway, she thinks my grandmother can't keep her stories straight any more, that she's gone senile. I think she's still sharp, but she often drifts off. Anyway, I'd better sign off. Greg told me to go ahead and talk on his phone, but it's his long-distance bill and I don't want to run it up too high."

"All right, then. But please do call if you need to talk, and feel free to reverse the charges."

"Okay."

"And Luba, please give me a call when you get back to Copper Creek. I know you plan to leave for Toronto eventually, but I'd like to have at least one more session with you. Maybe just a wrap-up session if you like, but I think it might be helpful to you."

"Sure. And thanks."

"No problem."

Luba sat back and heaved a sigh. She still felt unsettled, though Bella had been reassuring. A wrap-up session? For some reason she thought she'd be seeing Bella at least through August. Bella must have thought she was doing well to even suggest an end to the counselling. Luba should have felt pleased in Bella's confidence, but instead she felt annoyed and let down. Was she doing better? Luba wasn't so certain. Or perhaps she'd become too dependent on Bella and it was time to end that relationship. Anyway, she had Greg to talk to now, and Leo. Maybe she didn't need professional counselling any more.

"Now who would be calling in the middle of supper hour? People are so thoughtless!" Zenia complained, pushing her chair back from the table.

"So let it ring," her husband advised. "They will call back if it is important." But she was already on her way to the phone. Luba was glad for the respite.

Up until then their dinner had been an uncomfortable affair. Her aunt was barely speaking to her, and Uncle Bohdan's attempts at conversation were cut off by his wife's cryptic remarks. Even he shut down under her barrage. Luba began to understand how her mother and aunt could go for years without speaking to each other. And she had to come all this way just to learn that.

"Luba! It's for you. Your mother." Aunt Zenia sat back in her chair to resume her meal.

Luba felt her heart pounding as she picked up the phone. "Hello."

"So where were you all day? I tried to call earlier," she asked as if Luba was supposed to anticipate her infrequent phone calls.

"We were all out," she answered calmly, but was irritated at her mother's rude, demanding tone, like an echo from her aunt's dining room.

"Well, I hope you are having a nice visit and not causing any problems," she continued her pre-programmed comments.

"Yes, I'm having a lovely visit. And how are you?"

"My right knee is acting up again. I cleaned for nine hours yesterday! What a mess they left in the Union Hall."

"You shouldn't work such long hours. You shouldn't be doing such heavy labour."

"That is easy for you to say. Where else am I going to work? Who is going to hire an old lady?"

"Mama, you are not that old. What about restaurant work?"

"On my feet all day? No way! I put my years in when I lived in England. That is much harder on the body, believe me. You kids do not know about hard labour."

"You're right, Mama. So anything else new?" Luba was wondering why her mother had called. She knew it wasn't to discuss her health, although that topic was invariably raised. Her mother never called for idle chat, especially long distance.

"I have a letter here for you. You told me to call if there was a letter from Toronto."

"Who's it from?"

"How would I know? I do not read your mail."

"I told you, you could open it if it was from Ryerson. It should say on the envelope. The return address, Mama."

"Just a minute, let me get my glasses." There was a pause. She heard paper rattling. "Ryer-son, Poly—"

"Okay, okay. You can open the letter and read what it says." Luba heard the sounds of paper being mangled and realized that her brow prickled with sweat. Just like the Academy Awards, "And the winner is... and the loser..."

She listened while her mother read in halting English. She could hardly believe what she was hearing—she had been accepted to the Interior Design program, and they had registered her for summer school. Still more amazing, they were offering the scholarship she had applied for! Just like that. Bang, bang, bang, she was in. Luba had a ticket out of Copper Creek, a second chance. They bought all that hyperbole on the forms she'd filled out, about her vision, her potential, her future dreams. They must have liked her work. They believed in her. Luba began to sweat even harder. Now she had to go. Oh, God, was this what she really wanted?

The Gypsy

"Baba! We've come to visit. Luba and I. How are you today?" Greg cheerfully marched up to the old matriarch seated in a wheelchair next to her bed. He leaned down and kissed her dried plum cheek. She smiled and chirped.

It was Saturday. Luba had booked her return flight to Copper Creek for Wednesday so she didn't have much time left to spend with her grandmother. As anxious as she was to get away from Aunt Zenia, she was worried she'd miss something important if she left Baba now. Or worse, what if her grandmother died before she could return to see her again? Luba knew these thoughts weren't rational, but she couldn't push them out of her head.

Greg had agreed to help her out with the memory mining. He claimed to have influence with the old lady, that he was her favourite grandson. He was the only grandson who visited her regularly. The other two said it was too frightening to expose their impressionable children to a senile woman who might blurt out almost anything. But that was exactly why Greg and Luba thought she was so wonderful.

"I brought you some fresh chamomile tea," Greg told Baba. "You said you'd run out. Do you want me to make you some?" He was kneeling down next to her and she grabbed his large, smooth hand with her wrinkled claws.

"Not right now, I am ready to go out. Look at me, I am all dressed up for you!" She beamed at him. Luba wished she had a camera to capture the two of them together.

"Luba, you, too," she commanded. "We need to get out of this stuffy, smelly old place. Bunch of dying, crumbling old bodies here. I need fresh air!"

"Watch out! Clear the path for us, Luba, we're coming through. Race you to the exit!"

Luba watched the nurses stand back, shaking their heads as Greg whizzed by. Elderly patrons shuffling down the hall looked alarmed. Baba laughed and cheered.

They walked a few rounds of the grounds before parking themselves at a bench next to a thick hedgerow of holly. The birds on this late May morning were loud. Were they scolding the trio for being too close to the nests they were trying to build? Or were their eggs in the nests already? Baba cocked her head and smiled, apparently enjoying the brouhaha.

"How about a drive to the lake later?" Greg asked her.

"Maybe," she said. "I might fall asleep on you. I am not very good company any more."

"Nonsense, Baba! Look, Luba came all the way from Copper Creek to see you. I know she enjoys her visits with you."

"Yes, Baba, I'm so glad to be able to see you after all these years. And I'm really sorry I didn't come sooner." She reached over and patted her Baba's hand who covered hers and gave it a squeeze.

"Oh, I know. It is not easy to travel. This country is so big! Too big when you cannot be near your family. I am glad you came. But you are leaving soon, are you not?" How did she know?

"Yes, on Wednesday, in three days. But I'm coming back. I'll be going to school here in Toronto, Baba," she choked out the last words. She could hardly believe it still. Luba was on a speeding train and she couldn't get off.

"Good. You are a smart girl. You finish your education before you think about getting married. But, you do not have to get married," she added. "Marriage is not meant for everyone. Still, I think you will have beautiful, intelligent children if you do." She nodded her head, then looked up into the trees where there seemed to be a battle of birds. Loud shrieks, branches rustling, then three birds flew out, two small grey ones chasing a large black crow. They all watched their aerial tumbling until the birds disappeared into the oak trees at the edge of the grounds.

"So, Baba," Greg started up again. "I hear you've been telling Luba about your life in the old country. My feelings are a little hurt, you know. I thought I was your favourite grandchild, and here you are telling Luba stories you never told me before."

"Because girls are more interested in family stories. But if you want to hear them, perhaps you can write them down. Record them. You told me before you like to write stories." She stared up at Greg.

"Uh, sure, I hadn't thought about it before, Baba. If you want me to."

"I think someone should record our history. But maybe not all of the stories. Some are too personal, maybe even shocking."

"Shocking, Baba? Like what?" Greg leaned close to her, wearing his serious, lawyerly expression.

"I cannot tell you," she said.

"Why not? If it's family history, shouldn't we know?" Greg pushed.

"Not really," she dismissed him as if he were a small child.

Luba couldn't stand it. "Oh, Baba, please! I've come all this way to see you, and learn about what happened. I need to know. It wouldn't do any harm, would it? We wouldn't tell anyone else if you didn't want us to."

"It might be harmful."

"Who would it harm, Baba?" Greg asked gently.

She sat quietly and contemplated for a few moments. She turned to Luba, looking sad and injured. "Perhaps my granddaughter will think less of me. My daughter did."

Luba looked Baba straight in the eyes. "I am not your daughter. Mama and I are very different people and we certainly don't think alike. Anyway, she didn't ask to hear your story. I am the one asking. I want to know." Baba did not look convinced.

Luba tried again. "Baba, didn't you say I remind you of someone else?"

"Yes, but if I tell you, you may not believe me. No one believes me, especially not your mother." She closed her eyes and furrowed her brows. "Actually, I think she did believe me but did not want to."

"Is that why she was so angry?"

Baba nodded her head.

The three of them remained quiet for a long time. Luba despaired that she would never hear the story after all. It would go to her Baba's grave with her just as she had promised. Luba let out a long, deep sigh and put her head in her hands as she leaned on her knees.

A loud clap made her sit up. Her grandmother was grinning so widely that her eyes had disappeared into her ancient elfish face. "You are a determined girl, I must say. That you have in common with your mother. Very well, I will tell you the story of our village Gypsy. It was so long ago, but I remember it better than what I had for breakfast this morning. The Gypsy came to our village in the fall of 1925. His name was Lazlo Lazorovich, and he came with his two-year-old son Nestor, but no wife. He was probably tired of travelling alone with the little boy, so he set up a camp just off the road leading into Brinzi, in a clearing surrounded by beech, oak, and myrtle trees, close to a brook. His home was a horse-pulled covered wagon made of beautifully decorated wood, canvas, and iron. His kitchen was the tripod standing over a firepit in the middle of his encampment. When he was not cooking, the fire was used for warmth and working metal. Lazlo was a Kalderash Gypsy, from a tribe of highly regarded coppersmiths who travelled through Poland and the western provinces of Ukraine.

"At first the villagers were suspicious of a Gypsy travelling alone in his wagon, without a wife or any family members other than his young son. Gypsies have strong ties to their clans and families, often choosing to intermarry rather than leave. So everyone wondered if he had been cast out due to a serious dispute, possibly involving murder. We heard many stories of how evil and clever Gypsies could be, that they were not to be trusted." Baba paused for a moment and stared up into the branches of the tree above.

Luba realized she had been holding her breath again and released it before she passed out. Oh God, she hoped her grandmother wasn't drifting off again. "Baba, what did this Gypsy look like?"

The old woman looked straight ahead at nothing, and smiled. "He was tall, olive-skinned, smooth-faced, with the typical wavy black hair. His eyes were dark and sombre, almost black under his heavy brows. He was quiet, he kept to himself, working at his portable smithy just outside of town. When people sought him out to repair metal goods or make new parts for their ploughs and other farm implements, he was courteous, greeting everyone with a quick smile that transformed his face for a moment.

"But his eyes, his eyes… when you looked into his eyes they were filled with deep sorrow. No one asked directly about his past and when they hinted at it, he only spoke vaguely of his clan. He did tell one of the village elders that his wife had died in childbirth, which accounted for the motherless son. But he revealed nothing else of his personal history. Of course, that only made everyone all the more suspicious of him. But he never did anything to cast doubt on his integrity.

"In fact, Lazlo's metal work was of such high quality that he attracted customers from neighbouring villages, even those that had resident blacksmiths. He was soon able to be more particular about the jobs he accepted, preferring to work with copper when he could. Eventually he was invited to set up his bellows and shop in the village, inside an old stable that was no longer in use. This offer came at a good time. It was early winter, and the winds sweeping down the eastern slopes of the Carpathian Mountains had frozen our muddy roads and fields. Nothing was paved in those days. Children used to entertain themselves by jumping from frozen ridge to ridge, occasionally falling into the tracks left by wagons and cracking the ice in the deepest ruts.

"I suppose Lazlo was happy to be sheltered from the wind as he worked the bellows and fed his fire. The front door of the stable remained open, so passers-by could always look in and see him at work. More often than not, someone would be standing outside, speaking to him, stamping their feet to keep warm. Lazlo himself was never cold when he worked. His fire was so hot he often removed his shirt while he was working the metal, and the young women made excuses to wander by and have a peek inside. But they would not talk to him; it would not have been proper.

"My husband came to know Lazlo quite well and occasionally helped him in the smithy. He knew a little about blacksmithing from his own father. It was Boryslav who suggested that I take care of Nestor, since I was already at home caring for our two young children. Zenia was Nestor's age, and Marko was just a few months old at the time. At first I was annoyed that I was expected to care for a third child as well as everything else I had to do. But I found Nestor a good-natured boy, and he got along so well with Zenia that it actually freed up some time for me when the two-year-olds occupied each other. Unlike most other favours that Boryslav did for the villagers, this one was repaid. Lazlo made sure that there was extra food available to feed his son. In fact, he provided more food for all of us.

"Lazlo rarely stepped inside our home. Although he was often invited, he did not go into any of the village homes. Do you know why?" she asked.

Greg and Luba shook their heads.

"Gypsies considered the homes of gadje, non-Gypsies, somehow unclean, and they preferred to remain outside or in their own shelters. Their tents or huts or wagons were subject to special cleaning rituals, which they did not expect the gadje to understand or adhere to. Lazlo did, however, join the men in a drink at their informal outdoor tavern after work each day. He had one drink with them, occasionally two, and then headed for his home camp. He stopped at our house to pick up Nestor on his way, and perhaps to drop off whatever food or goods he thought we could use.

"At first we said very little to each other. Sometimes I reported on any incidents with Nestor, but there were few. Lazlo was polite, but never made conversation except to thank me for caring for his son. One afternoon in early December, I overheard the two children singing. I listened for a while before realizing they were mimicking one of the songs I often sang while I worked about the house. But this was their own version. I asked them to sing it again, and they did, over and over. It was delightful. So when Lazlo came to pick up Nestor that evening, I asked if he would like to hear the children singing.

"'Why, of course!' he said. 'My people love to sing, it is in our blood. Let us hear the baby choir!' He was so enthusiastic, I could hardly believe the transformation in his face and posture. He seemed to glow. He had grown taller. He stepped inside out of the cold, and the two children sang their little hearts out for him. Lazlo scooped his tiny son up into his arms and tossed him into the air.

"'Ah, the voice of an angel! This must come from his mother. My singing is so poor it frightens the birds of the forest,' he said. I noticed a shadow flutter over his face, then it disappeared. Then he said, 'You know, I can play the Russian guitar. Perhaps I will bring it sometime so the children can sing to proper music. And maybe even dance.' That day I heard him laugh for the first time.

"'Thank you, Mrs. Tatenko. You have helped bring joy into a lonely man's life,' he told me before he left.

"I was so worried that Nestor and Lazlo might be too cold that winter. He assured me that they kept quite warm, bundled up in their blankets, a roaring fire nearby. Some of the older children occasionally snuck up to his wagon after nightfall, to see if he practised any type of magic. They reported, with disappointment, I must say, that the only magic they heard was the music from his guitar. Once they thought they saw him dancing, but then they argued about whether the fire had played tricks on their eyes.

"Oh, those villagers liked to gossip and speculate about him, but I felt he was an honest man. I also believed that he still grieved over his wife's death. Every time he mentioned her, that same shadow crossed his face. I myself had a bad marriage, so sometimes I was almost jealous of the feelings he still had for her. It seemed unfair, to him and to me.

"One day in March I was outside hanging up laundry, and Boryslav came home, staggering drunk. This was not unusual. He ordered me to get him some food right away, and went inside the house. I was about to follow him, but first I had to bring in Zenia and Nestor who were playing in the yard.

"When I got inside, he just exploded with anger because I was too slow. He hit me hard across the face and back before he collapsed and passed out on the floor. I was bleeding, so I washed myself, then took the two older children, still screaming in fear, to our neighbour. Mrs. Kulak was, unfortunately, accustomed to such emergencies and always worried about the safety of the children.

"Later her husband came over to help me put Boryslav into bed. Otherwise he would have been in a foul mood if he woke up on the cold floor. Still, it always shamed me when other people saw what was happening in our home. It is still difficult to speak of it," Baba whispered, her head bent.

"He was a brutal man, Baba. You didn't deserve to be treated like that," Greg said, patting her hand.

"Sadly there were many like him. So, where were we? Oh yes, Boryslav was still unconscious when Lazlo came by to pick up Nestor. By then the children were back and asleep, including baby Marko.

"When Lazlo saw me, he was shocked. 'Good Lord, woman! What happened to you?' were his first words. 'Is Nestor all right? The children?'

"I told him they were all fine, but I was so embarrassed when he saw me in that state, my face swollen, a gash over my eye. He asked if Boryslav had done this to me and I told him it did not matter, that the children were fine, he did not touch them, he never did. He said he would speak to Boryslav the next day, but I asked him not to, that it would only shame Boryslav and make him angrier with me.

"After that day I felt that Lazlo regarded me differently. He never referred to that incident, I healed as I always did, and life went on. By the middle of June, after all the crops had been planted and some early hay was harvested, the village council decided to have a celebration. They invited Lazlo to bring his seven-string guitar and play for us, preferring that he play music rather than dance, as they still feared for the hearts of their daughters. It did not take much coaxing. Lazlo was delighted to provide our music.

"The entire village was there: women, children, men. We really knew how to party back then. We had lively circle dances around a large fire in the centre, while Lazlo strummed out all the tunes he was asked for. I remember a boy from a neighbouring village had been invited to play his violin, and, even without rehearsals, the guitar and violin blended perfectly. After each number there was enthusiastic clapping and cheering. We danced for hours.

"The moon was on its way back down by the time we took ourselves and the children back to our beds. I offered to keep Nestor overnight, but Lazlo said he would be by later to pick him up. He always insisted that the boy sleep in his own bed. I was asleep when Lazlo showed up, a little bit drunk.

"I said, 'Mr. Lazorovich, are you sure you are fit to carry your son home? You can hardly stand up straight.' He assured me that he could carry both the boy and the guitar, then he asked me to please call him Lazlo. I knew then that he was drunk. He finally accepted my offer to carry Nestor for him when I convinced him that it would be best for the boy not to be dropped. I felt certain that the children would be fine for that short time and that Boryslav would not be home until the next day at least, given his condition at the party. I knew he would be sleeping under the stars that night.

"It was a clear, moonlit night, as I recall. Not quite a full moon, but it seemed brighter than usual as it hovered just over the tops of the trees. It was on its way to nest for the day—that was how my own grandmother described it, which meant it was halfway between midnight and dawn.

"A couple of times Lazlo tripped, but he managed to right himself before he fell. 'Good thing you have the boy,' he said several times. 'His mother would never forgive me should any harm come to him.' He paused a few moments, then said, 'She was a beautiful girl, Eugenia. I loved her dearly. The Lord took her away too soon, too soon.'

"I thought I could hear him crying softly, but said nothing. What could I say? Perhaps it was good for him to talk about her, to finish grieving.

"'How old was she?' I asked him.

"'Only seventeen when she died. It was my fault. We were so much in love. She was sixteen when we married. She suffered so much when Nestor was born. We heard her screams from the birthing hut. I could not stand still, listening to that agony. I had not heard such screams from any of the other women—it was unnatural.' By then we had arrived at his camp.

"Lazlo took the sleeping boy from my arms and climbed inside his wagon. I waited outside, feeling so out of place, wondering if I should say goodnight before I left. I should have left right then and there, but something made me hesitate. Then Lazlo reappeared and said, 'Please, I am such a poor host. I will make a fire, we will have some tea. I must repay you for all your kindness. You do not need to go yet.'

"I was torn. I needed to return to my children. Yet something about him made me want to stay. So I said, 'Boryslav may worry...'

"And he burst out with anger, 'Ah, he is not worrying about you, that scum!' which quite startled me. He said, 'He is out, cold and dark as the bottom of the Black Sea. He will be lucky to wake with tomorrow's roosters, the amount he drank. No, no, you will be safe here. I will just make some tea, it will not take long.' He moved off behind the wagon and returned with an armload of wood which he automatically arranged inside the fire pit.

"'I am such a poor host. Please, sit here,' he said, and pointed to a spot shaped almost like a chair where a large gnarled root protruded from the base of a stout tree. He laid a sheepskin across the root and up the side of the trunk. So I sat on this guest chair and watched him relight the fire, which had not completely burned down in his absence. He set up the metal tripod, disappeared for a few minutes, then returned holding a kettle dripping with water.

"'It is nice to have this stream so close. A perfect Gypsy encampment,' he said. He hung the kettle over the fire and brought out a small tray holding two glasses and a small pot. He set the tray next to the fire, then sat on the ground, not far from me.

"I suppose I was a little afraid of him and wanted him to keep talking, so I said to him, 'You never speak much of your people.'

"'It is painful to speak of them,' he said, staring into the fire, then stood up to fetch his guitar. He still had a slight wobble to his step. He strummed quietly for a few moments then asked if I wanted to hear about his people. Of course I did. I told him that I wondered why it was he lived alone with his son, whom he loved so dearly. What had happened to his tribe?

"So he said, 'I will tell you. You are the only person in the village I would trust to tell my story.' He strummed a while longer before he continued. It was obviously very hard for him.

"'Men are not allowed to go to the birthing hut during the birth of a child. Only women may do such work. To do so marks a man as magerdó—you know, dirty, polluted. It is a grave offense. But I was a foolish young man, and this was my wife crying in agony. I thought they were killing her. I ran to the hut. I pushed inside. Ayyy!' he cried out in real pain, then, his hand falling against the strings so the guitar screeched to a stop. I felt horrible that I was forcing this poor man to relive that awful time in his life. Then I heard him sob and his hand returned to the guitar and slowly, gently, he resumed a sad tune.

"'There was blood everywhere, the women were soaked in blood. I thought they must have killed her. I hardly remember what I did. They told me later that I grabbed all the women and shoved them outside. I held my poor dying wife in my arms. The other women finally came back inside and separated us. She was dead. I killed her in my thoughtlessness. I interfered, I broke the laws.'

"I could not speak. I wanted to comfort him, to assure him that blood is a normal accompaniment to childbirth, that not all women survive the process. He did not cause her death—it would have happened anyway. But I remembered what my mother had told me about some of the Gypsy customs and ways. Men and women were not allowed to use the same wash water or containers when cleaning themselves or their laundry. Women were considered unclean, especially during their bleeding cycles and childbirth. When such blood touched a man, it was a grave sin, indeed. They were polluted, marked, outcast.

"Lazlo continued his story. 'The Kris, our council of elders, met and told me I must burn all of Eugenia's things, burn the wagon, my soiled clothing, and marry her cousin if I wished to remain with my clan. I tried. I did burn our clothing—everything that was hers. But I knew I could not marry her cousin, who looked so much like Eugenia. I was only nineteen years old. I could not get beyond my pain. I lived apart from them, just outside the community. No one would speak to me. I was totally isolated. Not even other Gypsies from different clans. That is our way. When Nestor was just over a year old and able to eat solid food, I took him from the nursemaid and left. I kept the wagon to live in. Perhaps I should have burned it. But then we would have no way to travel and live. This is my story.'

"By then I was in tears. And he said, 'I have distressed you, I am so very sorry. You are such a kind person, now I have caused you sorrow. So I must make up to you now by playing a happy song,' and immediately he began to play a lively tune. When he finished, Lazlo jumped up and grabbed my hand.

"'Come,' he said, 'I did not have a chance to dance tonight, so please do not refuse me!' What could I do? Suddenly I found myself dancing a polka around the fire. Lazlo was bouncing around like a crazy man but he was able to guide me safely around the flames. Then he showed me a Gypsy dance. I had never seen anything like it. His arms curved gracefully over his head, he thrust out his chest, and he stamped his feet as he snapped his fingers and twirled in place. I could feel his energy radiate from his body as he danced around the flames.

"Before I knew it, I was spinning around with him, twisting this way and that way, arms in the air. Yes, me! I must have been enchanted. Sometimes I wonder if he had cast a spell on me. I stayed with him for, oh, I do not know how long. I came home just before dawn. That morning Lazlo did not arrive with Nestor at his usual time. I waited all morning, wondering what I would say to him when he came. What do you say to a near stranger who has just stolen your heart and mind and body? Finally I took the children into the village to walk by the smithy. There was no fire, no Lazlo. Neither were there any signs of Boryslav. Someone told me they saw Boryslav walking in the direction of Pavlo's farm earlier that morning. At least, I thought, he did not come home to find me gone. But where was Lazlo? I did not dare ask about him or go to his camp that day, coward that I was.

"That night Boryslav returned and seemed in reasonably good humour. The next morning when Lazlo failed to appear again, I mentioned that I was concerned that something might have happened to Nestor. Perhaps he was ill. Boryslav offered to go to the camp to see if they were all right. He returned with bad news. They had disappeared, not a sign of them anywhere, just the firepit, and the coals were cold. Boryslav wondered if Lazlo had stolen something and then decided to leave in a hurry. Or perhaps it was something worse.

"I was so upset. I felt responsible for having driven him off. If only I had not succumbed to his charms. For a while I had even considered asking him to take me and the children away, away from Boryslav and my hateful life with him. But then I realized such an act, even if he agreed, would have put him and Nestor in danger. It was selfish of me to even consider such a thing. The next while was a terrible time for me. I worried about Lazlo and Nestor. I never saw either of them again."

"Oh my God," Luba whispered. "That is tragic. And did you ever learn what happened to them?"

"No. There were all sorts of rumours, of course. No one found anything stolen. Parents were wondering if he had taken advantage of any of the daughters who used to swoon over him, but they were all accounted for that night. Still, they were certain that Lazlo was guilty of something.

"No one paid much attention when two of us married women had babies about nine months later. I was thankful that Boryslav was away working in a nearby town the two weeks during and after Volya was born. She was so unlike Zenia and Marko, with her black, wavy hair and deep blue eyes. Even her skin was noticeably darker than the others. Eventually her baby hair was the same colour as mine, and her eyes turned brown. Not as dark as Lazlo, but she had his strong nose and full lips."

Luba gasped. Of course. She had been looking at those differences all along and not seeing them.

Baba sighed deeply. "Boryslav may have been a drunk, but he was not stupid. He would never admit to anyone that he knew exactly what Lazlo had stolen. And he made us both pay for it, Volya and me. So of course your mother is angry with me. I may have given her life, but it was a life of pain."

They were all silent for a few minutes after Baba had finished her story. Luba looked across the grounds at the trees, so thick you could not see the road on the other side. She thought about that Gypsy camp, the magic there. She did not want to think about the brutality her mother and Baba suffered through all those years with Boryslav. One night, one act, that's all it took. Luba knew a little about that. But her miseries seemed so trivial in comparison. No one had ever hurt her physically, except for occasional spankings. She was relieved when Greg finally spoke.

"Do you have any idea what might have happened to Lazlo, Baba?"

"No. He disappeared like he came, from nowhere into nowhere. I am sure he did not survive the Nazi round-up of Gypsies. All of them were exterminated in western Ukraine, or sent to Auschwitz, or other camps. We learned this much later, of course, after the war was over."

"All the Gypsies were killed? I'm sure there are some left in Ukraine. Old Kavitsky was visiting his village last year, and he told us there were still Gypsies travelling through, like the old days."

"Well, perhaps not every one of them died. I do not know." The old woman was looking at Luba, her eyes red and tired in their deep sockets. Luba reached over to hold her hand.

"Thanks for telling us, Baba," she said in a small voice.

"I know some of the Gypsies emigrated," Greg continued.

"Oh sure, I have seen the name Lazorovich here in Canada. It is not uncommon. You remember old Hanya Moroz? No, probably not. She used to live in Edmonton until she came to live here with her daughter. She told me about a family with that name just outside of the city, dark like Gypsies. She said one or two of the children were excellent dancers, and came to Edmonton for lessons. And we know Lazoroviches in Toronto, of course, but they are Ukrainian, not Gypsies. And who knows where Lazlo's name came from."

"Baba, aren't you curious to find out if they might be related?" Luba asked.

"No! What would I say to them? What is past is past, it is no longer important. Anyway, like I said, it is a common name, and they misspelled a lot of our names when we came to Canada," she said with irritation. "I am tired now. Take me back to my room," she ordered, closing her eyes—and the subject.

Her grandchildren did not protest, but rolled her back up the walk and into her room, then tucked her into bed. She lay on her side, her back to them, but Luba leaned over and kissed her cheek before they left. There was no response. She felt her chest tighten as Greg put his arm around her shoulder and led her out of the room.

Kiss and Tell

Luba sat in a pew between her aunt and uncle, staring at the perky pink hat of an elderly woman in front of her, wondering if it was the source of the faint mothball smell. She had decided to go to church with them this one last time, especially since it seemed to keep Aunt Zenia on a happy plane. Anyway, it was a good place to think and plan. She was still digesting Baba's story from yesterday, so much so she could hardly eat any breakfast that morning. Her stomach twisted in place, like the poor hanky she wrung out during anxious moments. Luba couldn't understand why this new revelation bothered her so much. She was delighted to learn that the brutish Boryslav had been re-placed by a Kalderash coppersmith in her pedigree. It helped to explain why she felt different from her family, why she was tall and her parents were short, why she had a darker complexion and her hair was nearly black like Mama's used to be, but not at all like the others. She was different, and now her hered-ity proved why—she had Gypsy genes. And yet, it felt as if the ground beneath her was shaking and crumbling, turning to quicksand.

Was this the reason her mother had left Toronto in such a huff when she learned about her real father? Of course Mama didn't want to believe Baba's story. Maybe that's why she insisted, over and over, that Baba was senile, and that you shouldn't believe anything the old woman said. Although they had left Toronto ten years ago, Luba's recollection of Baba was as a vibrant wom-an with a sharp mind and memory. No doubt the ordeal of having one daugh-ter reject her and the other toss her into a nursing home took a heavy toll on her mental health. The poor old woman had suffered enough already.

If Mama had thought, even for an instant, that Baba's story was true, she must have been livid with anger. For one thing, her mother didn't think much of Gypsies. Whenever she was really disgusted with Luba's behaviour, she called her a dirty tsiganka. Was Mama upset because her pure ethnic Ukrainian identity might be soiled? Or was she mad at Baba because Boryslav, suspecting that Volya wasn't his daughter, had been so cruel to her? All of these injuries made worse by being conceived in sin. Yes, Luba could picture Mama in a fury, uprooting the two of them to run from the mother who betrayed her and from the sister she apparently hated.

Luba now had a taste of what it was like to put up with Aunt Zenia, and she could understand why her mother wouldn't need much of an excuse to put some distance between them. Luba couldn't wait to leave her aunt, either. It was worse than home because she felt she couldn't speak plainly or protest when her aunt was being unfair or too critical. She didn't want to argue with Aunt Zenia, and she surely didn't want to hurt Uncle Bohdan's feelings. No matter what, he was always sweet and kind to her.

Finally, the service was over. Luba could not understand what kept people coming back every Sunday. Up and down on those kneeling benches, stand up, sit down, an hour that lasted forever. As they filed out she noticed that none of her cousins was at mass that morning. She could have brought it up, but Aunt Zenia would certainly have had good excuses for them. Adam was probably off golfing. Greg was godless, everyone knew that. And what was Bill up to? None of the wives were Ukrainian, so maybe they had gone to their wives' churches. Hah, not likely. Anne was Jewish, for one thing. Somehow this Catholic family had accepted her, but not a chance they'd allow any grandchildren to be raised as Jews.

Luba vaguely recalled the controversy just after they had moved to Copper Creek. Mama had a nasty fit when she heard Adam was marrying a Jewish girl. At the age of twelve, Luba had decided that when she was ready to marry, she would look for a black Jewish husband just to pay Mama back for being so prejudiced against different races and cultures. Or better yet, she thought now, what about a woman? She'd have to ask Greg if gay guys ever got married and how they did it. Now that would stir things up. She thought she would give him a call after lunch, and wondered if Leo might be home today. Luba wanted to see her again, but Leo hadn't called her, even to ask how she was. Luba had probably scared her off with that emotional display at the party. Anyway, why would Leo want to see her? She was just Greg's screwed-up kid cousin. Why had she ever opened her big mouth?

The ride home was quiet, uncomfortably so. Once back in her kitchen, however, Aunt Zenia banged around with unusual energy as she organized their lunch. It seemed she had every pot out on the counter, as if she were getting ready to clean them all, something her mother sometimes did when she was irritated and had no one to pick on.

"Can I help you fix lunch, Aunt Zenia?" Luba figured she might as well be as polite as possible for the time she had left with them.

"No, it's nearly ready. Bohdan, can you get the phone? There we go again, you can count on people calling just as you're ready to eat." She bustled around her kitchen, an efficient, well-oiled machine wearing a white apron edged with red-and-yellow embroidery over her navy satin Sunday dress. Luba stood back, out of the way as requested.

"Zenia! It's for you," Uncle Bohdan called from the living room. Aunt Zenia wiped her wet hands on her apron and left the kitchen shaking her head.

Uncle Bohdan began to set the table.

"I can do that," Luba offered.

"No, no, you are still our guest. You sit. What would you like to drink?"

"Water is fine, Uncle."

"That's Anne on the phone. She was asking about dinner tonight, but those decisions are Zenia's department. No matter what answer I gave her, it would probably be the wrong one. Always best to let the boss decide," he said, winking at his niece and chuckling.

"I suppose so," Luba agreed, feeling her stomach tense. Her aunt was probably planning their entire day at that very moment, and Luba had no intention of spending another minute in her company. She had to think of an excuse, fast. "I, uh, was planning on going to Greg's for the rest of the day," she said. Oh how she hated lying to her uncle, but she had to escape.

"That's fine with me. If we go out to Anne and Adam's you don't need to come along. We like to see the grandchildren and Sunday is about the only day everyone is free."

"That was Anne," Aunt Zenia announced, and opened the fridge door to take out a bowl of salad. "She invited us over for the afternoon and for supper. I told her we'd be along in about an hour or so."

Luba said nothing as she sat in her chair at the table. She looked at her uncle and he smiled at her, understanding the silent request. "Luba has other plans, I believe. I'm sure Anne won't mind if she doesn't come along."

"Since when does Luba have other plans? She never told me about any plans. And yes, Anne would mind. She specifically asked that Luba come along, and I said she would. We're all going." She plunked the bowl of salad down hard on the table.

"I'm sorry, Aunt Zenia. I didn't have a chance to tell you earlier," she said in a level, calm voice.

Aunt Zenia pulled a steaming roast out of the oven. "It doesn't matter. You can cancel your other plans."

"No, I don't think I can cancel my other plans. I don't want to cancel my plans. Anyway, you should have asked me first before you told them I was coming."

Her aunt hoisted the roast out of the hot pan onto a wooden cutting board, then plunged a two-pronged fork into the centre of the roast. Luba watched the juices running down into the lip around the board. Aunt Zenia raised the knife above the roast, speared one end of it then began to saw through the quivering mass.

Uncle Bohdan was sweating again; his big hands gripped the edges of the delicate white china plate. He tapped it on the table, and Luba watched in fascination, expecting it to shatter any moment. Oblivious to her husband, her aunt continued to talk while she worked on the roast.

"We have been trying to be good, hospitable hosts to you, Luba. All we ask is for some respect and consideration. You haven't spent much time with us, and no time with your two cousins and their families. Think how they must feel. You come all this way and ignore them. I know you weren't raised to be inconsiderate, but you seem to have forgotten your Ukrainian heritage and good upbringing. I just don't understand young people any more." She jerked the roast violently back and forth as she sawed, shredding it into a mound of slivers on the cutting board.

"Well maybe it's because I'm not pure Ukrainian," Luba shot back. "So I don't act like one all the time. Maybe I have a mind and style of my own."

The effect of her words was electric. Aunt Zenia froze in place, her left hand clutching the fork, her right grasping the knife. She turned to face Luba with an indescribable look on her face. Not angry, not worried, not curious. What was it? Even Uncle Bohdan had stopped tapping his plate.

"Did Baba say something to you? About your family?" she finally asked.

Luba was not sure how to answer. Did Aunt Zenia know about Lazlo? Baba didn't say anything about not telling her aunt. Maybe Mama told Zenia—even if she didn't believe it, or want to believe it.

"Yes, she said something," Luba answered carefully.

"Oh," she responded in a muted voice, and turned back to her shredding. "I didn't think she'd say anything about your father. I keep telling everyone she's senile, the things she blurts out."

"My father?" Luba said, confused, and watched her aunt freeze again.

She regarded Luba once more, this time with her inquisitor's face. "Yes, did Baba say anything to you about your father?"

"Like what?" What the hell was she talking about? Not Lazlo? Was there something about Luba's father?

"What did Baba say to you? She's going crazy, you can't believe the stories she tells. It's all nonsense." She returned to the pulverized roast.

"Wait a minute. What about my father? Is there something I should know about him?" Another new door had just been cracked open, then quickly slammed shut in her face.

"No, Luba, whatever Baba said, it means nothing. Forget it. She's just filled your head with garbage." She scooped up the dark brown shreds of meat into a serving dish and brought it to the table. Uncle Bohdan had set a bowl of boiled potatoes down as well. He was helping himself to the food, acting as if nothing unusual was happening.

"How about my grandfather? Do you know about him?" Luba challenged her aunt who was helping herself to salad. Luba's plate remained empty in front of her.

"Your grandfather? Which one? Your father's father or my father?" She forked a potato onto her plate. "You'd better eat or the food will get cold," she said calmly. Too calmly. Luba was convinced she was trying to cover something up.

"My grandfather Lazlo!" There, she'd finally said it, spilled the beans. She waited for reactions.

"Who? You don't have a grandfather Lazlo. There was Boryslav and... what was Yarko's father's name?"

"Volodimyr, I believe," Uncle Bohdan filled in for her. He seemed to be totally engrossed by his food, but Luba knew he was paying attention to come up with her grandfather's name so promptly.

"No, Boryslav is not my grandfather."

"Yes he is. I told you, I don't know what Baba has been filling your head with, but it's foolishness. Just forget it. Eat your lunch. You didn't eat breakfast."

Was she going mad? Maybe they didn't know about Lazlo. But why had Aunt Zenia mentioned Luba's father?

"What do you know about my father?" Luba asked again, her hands in fists on either side of her cold, empty plate.

"You are one stubborn child, Luba. I never knew your father, I never met him. If you want to know about your father, ask your mother!" She threw down her fork and stood up. Without another word, she left the kitchen and stomped off to her bedroom, banging the door behind her.

Luba implored her uncle with her eyes, but he simply shrugged and shook his head. Whatever it was about her father, he didn't seem to know, or wouldn't say. But Aunt Zenia knew. And with a reaction like that, it had to be something scandalous.

Luba heard the rumble of Leo's Corvette before she saw it. When the red convertible turned into the driveway, Luba leapt off the front steps where she had been waiting. She slid into the leather passenger seat and admired Leo's stylish tight jeans and embroidered jean jacket. Must be nice to have your own money and lots of it, she thought. Leo was obviously doing well in her practice. She'd been on Luba's mind a lot since her meltdown at the party. Sitting on the steps, Luba realized she knew very little about Leo, her unhappy family life, how she decided to go into law, and just how she became who she was now. Of course, Luba had few opportunities to ask her, and wasn't sure Leo would even want to talk about herself.

"Thanks for coming to the rescue," Luba said as she shut the door. "You must have been in warp drive."

Leo gave her a warm smile and patted her arm. "I thought we'd go to Hyde Park. Is that okay?"

"Sure, anywhere. Just get me away from that madwoman!"

Leo laughed, stepped on the gas, and the convertible catapulted into the street and down a hill.

The day was gloriously warm and green as they walked along a gravel path between newly planted fir trees, but Luba's mind was not on the natural elements of the park.

"I'm surprised you didn't call earlier. I know your aunt well, remember. Let me guess, you said something about Baba's amazing story—Greg told me the whole thing. I hope that's all right. He didn't think Baba would mind if I knew."

"Oh no, I'd have told you myself. You're practically family, anyway."

Leo had been watching her intently. She put her arm around Luba's shoulders and gave her a squeeze. "Yeah, I feel like I've been adopted—by some of your family. Your Baba is terrific. You know for an old lady brought up in such a misogynistic and rigid culture, she's pretty open-minded about a lot of stuff. More than her daughters for sure." Her arm slipped down to Luba's waist. It felt comfortable there. Shyly, Luba put her arm around Leo's shoulders. Like sisters, maybe. They continued to stroll, attached this way, beneath the green canopies of the park.

Luba recounted the bizarre conversation she had with her aunt at lunch. "I am so frustrated. I'm trying to learn the truth, and I keep running into these blocked secret passages. Do you think Baba is crazy? Or senile? I know she gets confused sometimes. Maybe the story she told is about my father, not my grandfather. But that wouldn't make any sense."

"Yes, your Baba gets confused at times, but since I've known her, she's been lucid more often than not. And I believe her story, and Greg believes it. He said the details were so real, so vivid. And let me tell you, in our line of work we deal with a lot of liars and deluded people, and of course the truly mentally ill. Your Baba is not one of those. She tells the truth, even when she is a little lost in the time lines."

"So why would Aunt Zenia mention my father? Do you think she's keeping another story from me?"

Leo sighed then looked up into the trees above them where a squirrel chattered loudly. "You know, Luba, there are a lot of stories out there. The challenge is to discern which ones are mostly true and which ones are mostly false." She sighed again then dropped her hand from Luba's waist and turned to face her. "When we were kids, my brother and I had a babysitter, Deana, a teenage girl who lived in the neighbourhood. She had an older sister, Carmen, who lived away from home and liked to hang out at the bars with her girlfriends. Carmen told Deana, who told us, that they often saw our dad at the same bars and he was cozy with the local floozies. He'd buy them drinks, then when they were so drunk they could barely walk, he'd leave with them."

"That's an awful thing to tell children. How old were you?"

"Oh, around six to eight, I guess. That was bad enough, but we found out later, when we were teenagers, that he'd been having sex with Carmen and Deana, and Deana was only fourteen at the time! Jesus, if it wasn't for the statutes, we could have nailed him. If we could have convinced one of those under-aged girls into pressing charges. It still makes me ill when I think of what he got away with, and what he did to those girls."

"When did your mother find out? I assume she did."

"Hard to say. I think she suspected for a long time, but didn't want to create a fuss because she was afraid to be on her own, with two deadweight children to deal with. She was a housewife who never graduated from high school. She either figured she couldn't support us, or she didn't want to."

"I suppose she thought it was a big sacrifice on her part?"

"Oh yeah. So much so, she hasn't forgiven us yet. Sure she's still bitter about my dad, but she blamed us for his infidelity. In fact, she started to punish us right around the time Deana started telling us those stories, long before my dad left of his own accord. Mom didn't allow any of our friends to come over, and she didn't let us go out anywhere, either, and not because she was trying to protect us. As soon as we came home from school she made us stay inside, in our rooms whenever possible so she didn't have to look at us. It was hell. We learned how to escape through our windows, until she caught on and had bars put up."

Luba gasped.

"Yup, we lived in a prison. So we started going to our friends' homes after school, until their mothers got tired of us hanging around. Probably thought we were a bad influence on their children, that we didn't appreciate our poor abandoned mother. None of the adults believed we were prisoners in our own home until we were much older. By then I had left home, found work to support myself and save for university."

"God, how did you manage to do that?" Luba's complaints about life with her own dragon lady seemed like mosquito bites next to a shark attack.

"I took menial jobs, like cleaning houses, serving in fast-food restaurants, that kind of thing. I ran into girls working the streets, and, oh man, it was tempting as much as it revolted me. For a while I actually considered it, even had a couple of pimps proposition me. I thought the revenge would be so sweet. I'd show up at my mother's dressed for work, caked with make-up, hair dyed orange, short skirt, stilettos, and tell her how successful and rich I'd become thanks to her. But I was never desperate enough to go that far. I always found work of some kind. Plus, I didn't want to work for one of those pimps. And violent, my God. One of the hookers in my seedy apartment told her pimp she was quitting, and next thing you know, she OD'd on heroine. But she was one of the clean girls, she didn't do drugs. Everyone knew her pimp had murdered her. Apparently it wasn't the first time he got rid of an uppity girl."

"Jesus, did he get caught?"

"Nah, but I heard he was killed in a knife fight with one of the dealers a couple of years later. Anyway, I moved out of that area as soon as I could afford to. And by then I found out I could apply for scholarships, and between those and my part-time jobs, I scraped through." She grinned at Luba's sympathetic expression. "I've made up for it since then. Like my car, for instance, and nice clothes. Now I'm saving for my own house. How conventional, eh?"

"Geez, you've done a lot in a short time, I'd say. What's your law specialty, anyway?"

"Oh, mostly contract and patent work, some corporate law. I wanted to stay away from general practice, family law like our socially conscious, compassionate Saint Gregory. I don't think I could handle all the sad stories, divorces, and selfish, stupid people. I get enough of that as it is. My compensation is a decent paycheque, so now I can live on my own terms."

They had settled on a wood and iron bench overlooking a large manmade lake. Neither spoke for a few moments as they watched ducks paddling by, followed by strings of fuzzy golden ducklings.

"Wow," Luba started up again, shaking her head. "What your mother did is criminal, unforgiveable. She makes mine look and smell like a rose. But your dad—do you think the awful things he did is just old history, that it doesn't matter any more? I mean, you're doing so well, you're independent, have a great career and all. You seem well-balanced and rational to me. Do you think those historical details make any difference in the end?" Luba's head spun. Why was she getting so worked up because she didn't know everything about the past? So what if her dad may have had an affair? It didn't impact her—he was always good to her, loving and kind. He and Mama seemed to get along well, they rarely argued, and never raised their voices that she recalled. If he did have an affair, maybe her mother didn't know about it. Or maybe she found out after he died, and, like Leo's mother, she blamed Luba for her father's sins.

Leo sighed. "In my particular case, the details are important. There were so many lies and deceptions that in the end I didn't believe anyone. When you lose trust at an early age, it's damned hard to recover it. You start questioning everyone's motives; you analyze everything they do and say. It may be an asset in my work world, but it's hell on relationships. Maybe I'm overreacting, but I value honesty above everything else. For instance, when a couple makes a commitment to each other, they should try hard to make it work. And that means they should be honest with each other at the very least."

"Honesty at any price?" Luba asked her. "What about Baba, was she wrong to do what she did?"

"Yes and no," she said. "I can't blame your Baba. I would have done the same with an abusive husband like Boryslav. But she had no idea what the repercussions would be. It's not always black and white, good or bad. Honesty in a relationship is an ideal, something to strive for. A standard. I didn't have it in my childhood—my parents lied circles around us. But now I'm an adult, it's precious to me. I guess the bottom line is that I don't trust anyone. Not completely, anyway. That's why I don't ever expect to get married."

"Not to man or woman?" Luba asked.

Leo laughed, her face breaking into dimples, her almond eyes sparkling. "I won't say never! But I'd have to be able to trust a person completely, absolutely. I just hate to be vulnerable, you know? Anyway, I definitely won't ever have children. Too easy to screw them up. I couldn't handle that type of responsibility. So for now I'm happy to be unattached and unencumbered."

"So you're not dating at all right now?" Luba wondered if she was stepping into sensitive territory.

Leo laughed. "I'm not that traumatized, but I'm not looking for a long-term relationship, either. Only good times, with fun people."

Luba's face flushed and her heart raced. "I'm probably not much fun to be with, obsessing about old family secrets which may or may not exist, feeling sorry for myself, all that crap."

Leo threw her arm around Luba's slumped shoulders and shook her. "You are a nut case, you know that? I love hearing about your crazy family, silly Lubochka!" she said, and pinched Luba's cheek.

"Hey!" Luba laughed and grabbed Leo's hand.

"We're family, we have to put up with each other. Anyway, I think we share a lot of life history. The details may be a little different, but we're cut from the same cloth. You're a sensitive soul, dear little Luba, you're smart, sassy, and fun to be with."

Their hands were still locked together, as if in a dance, Leo's other arm still around Luba's shoulders. Leo leaned over, lips puckered, and planted a kiss on Luba's nose, then another on her cheek.

Before Luba could react, they heard the alarmed chitter of a squirrel overhead, followed by high-pitched voices up the path. Then a child's shriek and a deep male voice. They broke apart and sat back on the bench, watching as several children appeared on the path, then raced past them. Two adult chaperones came along shortly, nodded at Luba and Leo and disappeared after the children.

In the silence after their passing, Luba's stomach grumbled loudly.

"When was the last time you ate, Luba?"

"Uh, yesterday?" Luba had not realized how ravenous she was. Her heart was still racing after Leo's affectionate pecks, drowning out all the gurgles below.

Leo popped up from the bench and put out her hand. "Let's go, little duckling, time to get you fed."

"Okay, momma bird. My butt's got to be rippled by now, these slats are murder."

"Yeah, they don't encourage loitering in the park."

Luba had not realized how ravenous she was. As soon as they arrived at Greg's house, Leo put her to work slicing vegetables for a salad while she boiled water for spaghetti. Luba heard a cork pop behind her, then wine being poured. She was handed a large glass of red wine, which she raised into the air to meet Leo's.

"To trust, and lasting friendships!" Leo toasted.

"Amen!" Luba said, then laughed. "It is Sunday." They sipped the wine, their eyes meeting over the rims. Luba blushed and turned back to the cutting board. She could see how easy it would be to fall for the lovely, seductive Leo, and imagined all sorts of men and women being attracted to her.

"I did have one very serious relationship back in Calgary," Leo said, as if reading Luba's mind. "A girlfriend, a lover—the love of my life, I thought." She shoved a handful of stiff noodles into the roiling water, then turned to Luba, a thoughtful look on her face. "It turns out she was seeing at least two other women at the same time, but claimed I was her one and only. I believed her for the longest time—two, no, almost three years. I mean, I have no problem with people having several lovers, but I expect them to be open about it. It took me a long time to get over the shock when I found her out. Maybe I'm still not over it. I'm over her, but I'm afraid to get that involved again. Like I said, I only date casually now."

They sat down to their spaghetti supper, complete with candlelight. As they lifted their refilled wine glasses for another toast, they heard a key in the door. Greg walked in wearing a Kelly-green jogging suit, a small towel draped around his neck. He huffed and leaned against the doorway, wiping sweat from his brow and ruffling his longish blond hair. He made for a very handsome male specimen, Luba thought.

"Greg, just in time for supper. We made lots. Help yourself." Leo waved at him with her wine glass.

"Oh! Hello, Luba. Thanks for the offer, Leo, but I'm having dinner with Don tonight. So how are things at Tatenko Towers, Luba?"

"You know, the usual. We had a scene over lunch and your mother slammed her door."

"Oh?" He looked at her, eyebrows up. "I think there's a story behind this, but unfortunately I've got to shower, change, and run. You will tell me later, won't you?"

"Sure, cuz. I still have to get through two more days over there. I'm sure there'll be more stories to tell before I go."

"Look, you're welcome to spend the night here if you don't want to go back. Or the rest of your time for that matter. Isn't that right, Leo?"

"Sure! I won't even yell at her or slam doors."

"Actually, I won't be coming home tonight, so use my room if you like. Well, gotta run. See you later, girls!"

"Hmm, going out with Don. Won't be home tonight." Leo grinned at Luba.

"You met Don? Sure you did, at the pub. What a honey, eh? Lots of women would love to wrap their legs around that hunk, but he's for boys only." She laughed and twirled more spaghetti around her fork.

After Greg left, they cleared the table and Luba stacked dishes in the sink.

"Luba, don't bother with the dishes. I'll do them later," Leo said.

"It won't take long. Anyway, I feel like such a mooch. I'd like to do the dishes, okay? It will make me feel better. I was at church today and I've got Catholic guilt build-up. This is how I purge." She opened the hot water tap too quickly and splattered herself.

"Fine," Leo said, and reached into a cupboard for liqueur glasses. "I'm getting out of here before you purge me, too. Do you like Tia Maria? Or brandy?"

"Tia Maria sounds good. I'd like it on ice, please, if you have any."

"TM on ice, coming up." Leo removed an ice tray from the freezer, and Luba scrubbed dishes. She made herself slow down, realizing the wine had made her as frothy-headed as the soap suds. It wouldn't do to break Leo's nice dishes. Or were they Greg's? Luba was used to her mother's non-breakable Corelle ware and her third-hand student ware. Here, the new kitchen appliances were a trendy olive green. She also liked their choice of wallpaper, a dark green vine pattern over a cream background, with gold-and-green trim along the ceiling. No garish colours in this house. Whoever made the decorating decisions understood how the colours worked together, and how they complemented the function of each room. She had taken note of the Robert Bateman prints and original watercolour paintings, probably by local artists. Most were nature scenes, wild animals, wild forests, but there were also a few black-and-white photos, cityscapes by night, stark portraits of semi-nude men and women. She'd have to ask about their artwork—which ones belonged to Greg and which to Leo. When she had passed by Leo's open bedroom door, she caught a glimpse of a giant, erotic red poppy, one of her favourite Georgia O'Keeffes. She felt comfortable in this milieu. It was a house she could live in.

Dishes done, Luba tottered into the living room where Leo had put on the Moody Blues. "Knights in White Satin" floated through the air, a good fit with the dark, quiet atmosphere. A purple-green lava lamp had started to glow and bubble in one corner. Leo slouched on the black leather couch, her drink in front of her on a low, ebony table. Luba's drink, with ice, was waiting next to hers.

She lowered herself carefully into the sofa in front of her drink. They both reached for their liqueurs at the same time, and gently clinked them together.

"To our wonderful futures, whatever they may be," Leo offered.

"Yes, to our futures," Luba agreed, and sipped the sweet, thick liqueur. It dribbled slowly along her tongue, her throat, leaving a cold, burning trail all the way down.

"So, how do you feel about going back to school?" Leo asked, setting her drink down and linking her hands around one knee.

Luba swallowed and swirled her drink. "I've got mixed feelings. Excited to begin a new program, a whole new chapter in my life, I guess. And kind of worried about all the details. Worried that I may not like it, may not be good at it, might even bomb out."

"Sounds normal to have all those responses. Greg said you might stay here while you're looking for a place."

"Yeah, if you don't mind."

"Not at all. Do you have any other friends here you plan to look up when you get back?"

"Oh, a couple I suppose. They both have steady boyfriends and one of them is engaged. I don't think I'd feel comfortable with them any more, not since what happened to me. I'm having second thoughts about who I am and what I want. I mean, from a relationship." Luba felt her heart race and her face heat up.

"How do you mean?" Leo asked.

"Well, I've been wondering if maybe I'm well, I don't know..." She swallowed and almost choked. "Attracted to women, maybe?" There, she'd said it. Her cheeks burned, so she brought the drink up to her face and rolled the iced glass against her hot skin.

"Oh." Leo seemed surprised.

"I talked to my therapist a few days ago. She told me it was normal to feel this way, to have questions about my sexuality. And to experiment if I wanted to know for sure." She stopped, feeling foolish. Why was she telling this to Leo? She felt like a timid child needing reassurance. What did she want from Leo? What if Leo told her she was crazy? Silly little Luba. But she couldn't stop herself, couldn't stop searching Leo's eyes, Leo's beautiful face.

Leo shifted herself slightly then reached for her drink. "Are you attracted to anyone in particular?" she asked in a level voice.

"Yeah, I guess. To you, I think."

"I'm flattered. Am I the first woman you've thought of that way?"

"I think so," Luba said. She blinked hard, felt the pressure of tears.

"Do you think it's because you know I'm bisexual?"

"I don't know. Maybe. I mean, what attracts people to each other? I can't figure it out. You're so nice, you're cool, confident, but you're also sensitive, you understand me and you care. And..." Luba swallowed. This was so hard, as if she was doing a strip tease in front of Leo, removing layer after layer of skin until she burned with both embarrassment and arousal. "I think you're gorgeous, you're smart and sexy. I don't understand it, I just know how I feel, not why."

"I'm sorry to grill you like this, Luba, but I think a lot of you. I really like you. And you're Greg's little cousin, you're so innocent—"

"Innocent? I don't think so!"

"No, I mean innocent about loving other women, about lesbians, bisexuals. Am I right?"

"Yeah."

"A lot of young women are curious about that, about making love to another woman. And sometimes it seems so, I don't know, romantic, against the grain, cool. Some are probably more attracted to the idea of homosexual love than to the person they think they want to make love to. For others it's more an act of rebellion than following their true nature. Do you understand what I'm saying?"

"Yeah, I guess so."

"What I see in you is a confused young woman trying to figure out where she fits in, who she is, where she's going. And carrying a load of anger. I don't blame you, I was there myself. Sometimes I'm still there, trying to make sense of my life and my direction. Being a lesbian is a difficult path to follow in our society, even if it is your true nature. I mean, I'm not totally committed myself. That's why I'm bi."

"But how does a person find out? I mean, without experimenting? How will I ever know?"

"I guess you do have to experiment." She paused. "Is that what you'd like to do, Luba?" She reached out and touched her hand lightly. Luba set down her drink and placed her free hand over Leo's.

She whispered, "Yes."

"You're sure?"

"I'm sure." But she wasn't. She shivered, afraid and excited.

Leo leaned closer to Luba and kissed her cheek. Luba didn't know how to respond or what was expected. Leo said, "If you're uncomfortable at any point, you just tell me so. We'll stop, okay?" Luba nodded her head. She could hardly hear her for the roaring of blood in her ears.

Leo put her hands on either side of Luba's face and kissed her lips. So gentle. So soft. Luba gasped and, for an instant, was frightened. Then there was only warmth, the radiance of Leo's face, her body, and Luba put her arms around Leo and kissed her back. It was an unsettling feeling, and yet so exquisite, so exhilarating. Leo returned the kiss with more pressure until Luba opened her mouth. She felt Leo's tongue slip inside. She gasped again.

Leo knew exactly what to do. Her hands slipped under Luba's shirt and up to her breasts. Luba found her own hands on Leo's breasts, then unbuttoning her blouse. Leo moaned. "To bed?" she whispered. Luba nodded.

Leo led Luba by the hand to her bedroom. She closed the door behind them and pushed Luba up against it, kissing her all over her face, her neck. Luba stood unresisting while Leo undressed her, slowly, expertly, then Leo guided Luba's hands to her shirt and Luba undressed her until they were both naked, and Leo pulled her onto the bed, and began kissing her again. She felt Leo's soft lips at her collar bone, then her breasts, her nipples. The body that was responding to Leo's touch did not seem to belong to Luba any more, and every sensation had an intensity she did not know she was capable of. Leo knew exactly what to do to arouse Luba to a peak. When the dam burst she heard herself shouting, then laughing at the noise she had made. Leo laughed, too, and kissed Luba's lips again. Luba laid her head on Leo's shoulder, light-headed, joyful, and relieved.

In the morning they took a shower together. Luba was more self-conscious than she had been the night before, and more sober, but Leo was so natural that she relaxed again.

"Go ahead, you can touch them," Leo told Luba who had been admiring her breasts while they towelled dry. "The girls are rather magnificent, aren't they? I raised them myself."

Luba laughed nervously, but cupped Leo's breasts in her hands. She then leaned over and kissed her nipples.

"Mmm. That's nice," she said, stroking Luba's wet hair.

"Shall I continue?" Luba asked, looking up at Leo's blissful face.

"Only if you want to. I don't have to rush off yet."

Luba smiled. She wanted to make Leo feel as good as she had felt last night, but was not sure she had the skill. It was more than repaying a favour. She loved Leo's soft, voluptuous breasts, and she tingled whenever she touched them. She knew now this was what was missing when making love with a man. That and the sweet cuddling after sex, and a woman knowing instinctively how to please her, and taking time, and just being in tune with her body and mind.

After a second, briefer shower, Luba borrowed one of Leo's shirts when she noticed the wine stain on hers, not remembering when that had happened. They were both laughing about it when they left Leo's bedroom and saw Greg sitting at the kitchen table, reading a paper and drinking coffee. He looked up, startled.

"Luba! You're here. I thought you'd gone—" He stopped, confused, then furrowed his brow.

"When did you get in?" Leo asked, taking two mugs down from the cupboard.

"Oh, about half an hour ago." He stared at the paper in front of him. "Well, gotta go. I'm meeting a client at nine." He left the table and picked up his briefcase from the counter.

"Any big plans for the day, Luba?"

She poured cream into her coffee, afraid to meet his eyes. "Back to see Baba again. Maybe straighten out a few details. About my dad."

"Your dad?"

"I'll fill you in later, Greg," Leo said.

"Sure, I'll be all ears." He gave Leo a long look. "Later!" And he disappeared.

Luba sat at the kitchen table while Leo sliced two bagels. "Do you think he disapproves?" she asked.

"I think we surprised him. Don't worry, I'll have a chat with him."

"What are you going to tell him?"

"The truth. Is that all right?"

"Yeah, sure."

"It bothers you, doesn't it?" Leo sat across the table and met her eyes.

"A little."

"Okay, here's how it will probably play out. Greg has become quite protective of you. You're like his little sister, and he's very fond of you. Here I am, also like a sister to him, an older sister perhaps. He was expecting me to take you under my wing and perhaps be your confidante, help you get through a rough patch, maybe provide a role model as a survivor of parental abuse, help you rebuild your confidence, maybe encourage you academically. All this, but not take sexual advantage of a vulnerable, emotionally traumatized, inexperienced young woman, his own kin. That's crossing the line."

"You didn't take advantage of me! It was my idea, I started it."

"That irrelevant, Luba. I'm the mature, world-wise adult, and Greg entrusted you to my care. That's how he'll look at it. Remember what field he's in. He has the brains of a lawyer but the heart of a social worker. So, yeah, he'll be upset, and I'm sure he's stewing about it this very minute. Perhaps I was a little rash, moved too fast."

"No!" Luba sat back, surprised at her own outburst. "No, you weren't rash, and I was ready." She paused and looked up at Leo, worried. "Are you regretting what we did?"

"No Luba, honey," she said and reached out to hold Luba's hand across the table. "I loved every wonderful minute of it. And you, your silken touch, you may be new at this, but you, my dear, are a gifted lover. I'm more concerned that I may have hurt Greg, betrayed his trust in me. I think, in this case, Greg the open-minded egalitarian, is somewhat biased. He'll be looking at you as an injured fledgling who should have been given more time to heal before being seduced by an older woman."

"But—"

"Let's change the genders for a moment and look at the situation from Greg's perspective. I'm his house mate, a thirty-two-year old male, single, jaded, looking only for casual sex, and Greg has left his young cousin, recovering from a horrible relationship, nearly dying as a result of it, in my care. And he comes home to find that we had sex, in his supposedly safe-haven home. The fact that it was consensual and between adults will not change his view."

Luba sat silent, lips pressed together.

"To Greg, the fact that we're both women is not the main issue. But consider what you'd be facing. It is, in case you don't know it, a homophobic world out there. I'm sure Greg's thinking about it also. He'll know all the angles and permutations. The situation between the three of us is complicated, and that's what it's like out there, but much, much worse. This lifestyle is no lark. I'm telling you now because I like you and don't want to see you get hurt. And I don't want you to blame me or be angry with me for keeping the truth from you. It's damn hard to live this way. Every time you make a choice, there are consequences. That's the way it is in this big, ugly old world." She got up and hit the lever on the toaster. The bagels dropped inside with a clang.

"More coffee?"

Luba held up her cup. "Fill 'er up. I'll need it to stay sharp." She had a lot to digest. Her magical night and morning with Leo, her worry that she may have ruined Greg and Leo's relationship, her sexual awakening and what it might mean to her. All this and only two days left before she returned to Copper Creek. Luba had her work cut out for her in that short time, dealing with a disoriented grandmother and a disgruntled aunt as she pressed on, digging for truth. And she still had to figure out what she was going to use for a shovel.

Careful What You Wish For

"Hello, Baba! How are you today?" Luba had decided to use Greg's approach. Baba was sitting up in bed, looking alert.

For a moment she squinted at Luba in confusion. Then the fog cleared away and she grinned. "Luba! You are all grown up. You look wonderful."

Luba continued to smile and wondered which of Baba's time zones they were in at that moment. "Where is your Mama?" Baba asked.

"Oh, Mama's back home. In Copper Creek. That's where we live now." Luba studied her eyes for clues about what she might remember today.

"Yes, yes, you moved there, I know that. I just wondered if your Mama was with you, but I suppose she did not come. How is she?"

"She's fine, but she works too hard. Still cleaning houses and some of the big halls. I was just home not long ago. You know I'm going to school in Toronto now?"

"Yes, you are a smart girl. What are you studying?"

"Biology," Luba lied.

"That is good. Are you studying to be a doctor?"

"Maybe. I'm not sure what I'll do yet. Anyway, Baba, I was just home, and looking at some of the old photo albums. Did you ever meet my father?" She peered into Baba's eyes. The old woman furrowed her brow and became unfocussed for a moment.

"Your father? No, no I never met him. They came from England, your Mama and Tato, and they moved to Vancouver. But he died, your poor Tato. I never saw him."

"Aunt Zenia told me something different about my Tato, Baba. It's okay, I know the truth. You don't have to try to protect me." She hoped this tactic would work, but Baba only looked more lost.

"I do not know what you mean."

Now what? How else would she tease out this information? Maybe Baba really didn't know anything about Luba's father.

"Do you remember when Aunt Zenia and Mama were arguing, just before we left? It's about that." This was a wild gamble, but Luba was floundering.

Her eyes clouded over, then she looked around the room. "No, no," she muttered.

"Baba, I want to know why they were arguing. I want them to get over these bad feelings they have about each other. I need to know."

"No, it happened so long ago, it does not matter."

"But Baba, they are still mad at each other. It's been ten years!"

"What happened to Zenia was not her fault. It is her own business anyway. No one needs to know. And maybe the same happened to your mother. I do not know! They should not be so cruel to each other." Her grandmother grabbed a handful of bedcovers in her trembling hands and brought them up to her mouth.

"Maybe it is my fault. I did treat Volya differently, I tried to protect the poor child from him, but I could not. I failed her." She lowered her head and began to cry. Tears ran into the crevasses of her face until her cheeks turned dark red and wet.

Luba was disgusted with herself. "Baba, Baba, I'm sorry I brought it up. Please don't cry. I'm sorry," she said and put her arms around her grandmother. "It wasn't your fault Grandfather Boryslav was so mean. And didn't he die young anyway? Mama wasn't very old."

"No, she was not. She tried to do what she could to please him, but he was impossible, especially when he drank. What happened to him was not her fault—it was meant to be. But she felt guilty anyway. And then the war, Germany, that awful cripple. I do not know what happened then, either, but something dreadful, I am sure. Oh, your poor Mama, so many disappointments in her life."

No, this was not what Luba had intended to do. She wanted only information for her selfish self and she managed to bring back some horrible memories for her dear old granny. It was probably best that Baba didn't know everything—what she did remember was painful enough.

Luba was determined to write down this new dream and show it to Bella. She had been to hell and back. Truly. She remembered looking into a mirror, and smearing black greasy paint across her face, neck, shoulders, and chest. She couldn't see what else she was wearing, if anything. When she was ready, she walked down stairs into a deep, dark cavern, down, down, down. At the bottom of the stairs, He greeted her—not exactly what she thought the Devil would look like. He wore a silvery outfit—odd-shaped pieces of cloth glued to each other so it almost appeared that he was dressed in rags. He was pleased to see Luba. He led her to his office and gave her an assignment.

"My mother is a beggar in Vancouver, on the east-side docks," He told her. "I want you to find her and bring her back to me. She belongs here. Go!" He pointed to the stairs and Luba left immediately. She decided to take the elevator back up—it was a long climb.

Back at the top, outside in the fresh air and vibrant greenery, she decided she didn't want to look for the Devil's mother, but she was afraid to disobey him. What would he do to her if she didn't carry out his command? She felt that she owed him something and she had to do as he had asked. But what was the favour the Devil had done for her? Had she struck a deal with him?

While fretting about what to do next, she woke up from her afternoon nap on the couch with a pounding headache.

Luba sat up and grabbed her head. She felt horrible. The last few days had been so full of revelations, denials, emotional crests and troughs, she didn't know what was real any more. Did Baba make up the story about Lazlo? Why wouldn't anyone say anything about her father? She had just made love to a woman but felt the same as before. No, not exactly the same, something had changed, but she couldn't figure out what. Was she just infatuated with Leo, like she could be infatuated with a new guy, like she thought she might have been with Greg? Was she sick? What was wrong with her? Maybe she needed to call Bella. No. No, she could figure this out on her own.

Who was the Devil in her dream? Why did he want his mother in Hell? To suffer with him? Maybe Luba was the Devil, dragging all sorts of people down with her.

Damn, why did she feel so out of sorts? There was a gargantuan lump at the bottom of her stomach, a bucket of ashes from hell. Was it guilt? Yeah, she'd been a total jerk with Baba. Luba knew her questions might disturb Baba, but she was not prepared for how much they had upset her. All three of them, the two sisters and their mother, must have been deeply shaken by something just before the exit to Copper Creek. Uncle Bohdan had to know something about it. He was the only sane, straight-shooter of the older bunch, but even he would try to hide the truth if he thought it would distress her or Aunt Zenia. Damn! Why couldn't people just be honest?

Honesty. Trust. Leo's pet peeves. Luba never thought of them as such unattainable ideals. Tom wasn't honest with her, but Pete probably was, damn him! Aunt Zenia hadn't been honest with her and her own mother probably hadn't been either. And Luba had not been honest with Baba, which she rationalized was okay because she was simply searching for the truth—by trick-ing it out of her. Oh my, she had become such a fine student of deceit. When did that happen? And yet, she understood that withholding the truth, or even lying, was preferable to causing great pain to the people you loved. There was nothing else Baba could have done in her situation. But who was Aunt Zenia trying to protect? Her sister, Volya, or Luba, or herself?

She heard a car door slam.

"Hello, Luba! How are you today?" Uncle Bohdan clomped into the hall with his heavy boots and leaned over to take them off.

"Hi Uncle. I'm well," she lied again and winced, rubbing her forehead. "I visited Baba this afternoon."

"Oh, good. How was she today?"

"A little confused about the time. I mean the year. I guess she forgot I've been here nearly two weeks already."

He walked into the kitchen and to the fridge. "Want a beer?"

"No thanks."

"Let's go outside while it is still nice out."

Luba followed him to the patio. They sat on the lawn chairs and basked in the late afternoon sun.

"I have a confession to make, Uncle," she said unhappily.

"Oh, what is that?" He sipped his beer and seemed unconcerned.

"I asked Baba about the big blow-up just before Mama and I left Toronto. I was trying to learn more about my father. But it upset her. Made me feel pretty bad, too."

"If it makes you feel better, she probably forgot all about it in a few minutes. She cannot concentrate on anything for very long. I think they call that a poor short-term memory."

"I hope so. But I can't believe she made up the story about my real grand-father. The detail—she was reliving the whole thing, it wasn't something she dreamed up, you could see it on her face, in her eyes. She says I look like him. It makes sense—Aunt Zenia and Uncle Marko don't look anything like my mother. Baba said she tried to tell my mother the truth about her real father, Lazlo, but Mama didn't want to believe it, got mad, and left Toronto. But there was something else that happened. Aunt Zenia and Mama had a big fight, too, didn't they?" She watched him like a hawk for any break in his composure. All she saw was a tired face.

"Your mother and her sister always fight. They have been squabbling as long as I've known them. There may have been a disagreement just before you left, but nothing special that I can remember."

"What about my father?"

"Luba, I never met your father. He was a good man from what I heard about him. Very gentle and kind."

"That's what everybody says. That's what I remember."

"So, is that not good enough?"

"I suppose. I guess I'd like to know more about him, exactly what he was like. I know he worked on the ships, and sometimes on the docks, and there was a bad accident. Do you remember when he died, what happened exactly? Mama doesn't like to talk about it."

"Yes, it was terribly tragic. A ship from Chile was being unloaded, and one of the boxes hadn't been properly fastened. It fell, and the crane swung loose and caught him on the back of the head, over a hundred pounds of metal moving at fifty miles an hour. Crushed his head. He died instantly, at least. Awful." He shook his head.

They heard the garage door opening—Aunt Zenia was home. Uncle Bohdan excused himself and went inside.

Luba was no further ahead with Uncle Bohdan. She'd have to lie in wait for the big catch. She had been studying the two sisters, taking lessons from the pros. She figured she was ready for Aunt Zenia, but she had to be patient, take her time, look for the opening.

Luba ate supper with them and talked very little, except to tell Aunt Zenia that she had visited with Baba that day. After dinner, she went to her room to read for a while, but had trouble concentrating. She knew Aunt Zenia was out there, feet up, watching sitcoms, downing the rye-and-gingers. At ten Uncle Bohdan wished her a good night as he passed by her open door. She waited a few minutes, then came out.

Her aunt was in her spot in the living room, still drinking, watching TV, a newspaper spread out beside her on the couch. Luba sat in Uncle Bohdan's chair and put her feet up. Zenia ignored her.

"I had a nice visit with Baba today."

"So you said." Her words slushed a little.

Good, thought Luba. At least four drinks, maybe five or six.

"You know, I don't think she's crazy or all that senile. She and Mama tell the same stories. Unless you think Mama is senile."

Aunt Zenia gave her a sour look. "Are you back on this grandfather fantasy?"

"No. My father. Baba told me what happened. I don't understand why you won't admit it. I just want to know one thing, how did you find out? Because

I don't think Mama told you, did she? You're the brains in the family, how did you figure it out?"

Aunt Zenia was looking at Luba totally stupefied, her jaw dangling. Her hand automatically reached for her drink which she tipped into her gaping mouth. She set it down and continued to stare at her niece, who didn't flinch.

Aunt Zenia pushed herself up from her slouched position, grabbed her empty glass, and clasped it with both of her hands as she leaned over. "The very first thing that made me suspicious is that she didn't want us to meet him. I mean, they come all this way from Halifax and won't stop over in Toronto. I even offered to put them up, pay any extra fare. I figured she was hiding something. They stopped in Copper Creek, not here, to have you christened, then straight to Vancouver. So when Yarko died, we invited her to move here and she finally agreed. She sent her things ahead by moving van, and the two of you came on the train. I was unpacking a few boxes when I found some photo albums and things. So I looked inside. It wasn't marked private or anything, I wasn't really snooping." She stared with irritation at her empty glass still clutched in her hands .

"I found your birth certificate. You were listed as Luba Tatenko, not Kassim, born in Victoria General Hospital in Halifax. Fine. Sometimes they make clerical mistakes at the hospital. Especially back then, and your mother's accent can be difficult to understand. But I thought it was odd that in all these official papers, immigration and so on, there was no marriage certificate. All the papers were in your mother's maiden name. And there were also a few papers in your father's— well actually your stepfather's name."

Luba felt the blood leave her face, but willed herself to look normal, breathe normal. Aunt Zenia had said stepfather. Luba nodded her head, like she'd heard all this before, but didn't dare meet her aunt's eyes.

"But the clincher came when you were in the hospital to have your tonsils out. I was there with you when you were admitted and all the paperwork was being signed. They tested your blood. It was O type. Not that it mattered, you didn't need a transfusion or anything like that. Bill was studying biology then so I asked him about blood types. I remembered when I'd seen Yarko's papers that he was listed as having AB blood. That's the rarest type of blood. And Bill said that if one parent was AB, the child would have A or B or AB blood, but not O. Your blood type. Of course I didn't say anything to him about why I was asking. Even Bohdan doesn't know." She set her glass down on the table beside her.

Luba swallowed and composed her voice. "So, do you know my real dad, then?"

"No, I do not. Volya up and left after we had that argument, the one about your father. She would never admit to my face that I was right, but she knew I knew, and she couldn't stand that. We've never spoken about it since."

Aunt Zenia looked wistful. Did she regret the argument, the damaging words they must have exchanged?

"And now, if you tell her you found out, she will think I told you. We were never sure if Baba knew. I'm surprised Baba remembered that argument. Your mother will never believe it was Baba who told you that Yarko wasn't your real father. Are you going to tell her?"

"I don't know," Luba said truthfully.

She sighed deeply. "Don't be too hard on her if you ask about your real father. Who knows, maybe something horrible happened to her. A lot of girls were... taken advantage of during the war, and afterwards. It was a hard life for everyone, families split up, losing everything and starting over. Maybe you shouldn't ask. Imagine what she'd feel like."

Aunt Zenia was worried about her sister's feelings? Or was she worried about revenge?

"I'll think about it carefully, Aunt Zenia," Luba promised. Her aunt stood up slowly and turned to leave the room.

"Good night," she said in a weary voice, not looking at Luba, and shuffling off to bed. Her door clicked shut softly.

Luba remained cemented to the chair, too heavy to move. Her held-in breath was expelled in shaky bursts, a volcano letting out steam. The deception worked: it netted the truth. And the truth was a stranger.

Aunt Zenia and Uncle Bohdan were clomping around the house, getting ready for work like every weekday morning since Luba had arrived. And she ignored them, as usual. She hadn't slept well and hoped to drift back into dreamland after they'd gone. But the machines of her mind would not quit grinding and whirling. She found herself meandering on a quiet path, then the scene shifted and she was racing down a busy super-highway. Her dreams ended with a faceless person, someone dangerous chasing her through a forest. No roads, no other people, nothing to help her escape her pursuer. In desperation she ran into a black cave, which closed in and suffocated her until she woke with a jolt, breathless, wrapped in and fighting with the comforter. Why was it called comforter when it could smother you?

Luba didn't want to get up. Nothing to do today except pack, get ready to leave. No point in visiting Baba. She couldn't face her grandmother after the way she had jerked her around, even if Baba had forgotten by now. And she didn't want to see Leo or Greg. She had heard nothing since she left their house, nothing about any fallout from Leo's talk with Greg to discuss the night she slept over. In this case, she was certain that no news was bad news. Otherwise, why hadn't Leo called to reassure her that all was well? And maybe Leo now regretted their one-night stand, and wanted nothing more to do with her. Luba groaned and pulled the covers over her head. For such a short visit, she'd managed to create colossal mayhem in her family. And now she was too cowardly to say good-bye to two people she had come to care about. Not only that, she didn't want to divulge to them what she had learned last night. Why? Was she embarrassed? Disappointed? Like a clumsy little girl, she had been reaching for a precious glass sculpture on the top of a shelf, and just as she touched it, the object wobbled and fell, smashing into a thousand shards.

It was okay when she had discovered her grandfather Lazlo. Someone exotic, exciting, kind, not like that brute Boryslav. But it wasn't okay that she had lost her father. She didn't know who to replace him with. She wanted to ask Mama, but she was afraid to. Afraid to learn who he was? Yeah. Is that how Mama felt when Baba told her about Lazlo? Mama knew Boryslav, nasty as he was, and perhaps she didn't want to make room for another father, even if he was a nicer man. Maybe Luba's own father was someone horrible. Maybe he raped her mother. Or he may have been a very ordinary man. Was he Ukrainian? Somehow, she thought not. She was probably a mongrel.

Luba used to scorn the idea of being something so pedestrian, so common as a Ukrainian. Now she realized that she'd always felt special, having a pure eastern European pedigree to keep her a shade away from the ordinary, from all her Anglo or French-Canadian friends. And now she was not so special. She still had Lazlo the Gypsy in her pedigree. But what was her other half? Would she feel more complete if she knew? Would she know herself better and how to avoid crashing in the future? Would it make her happy?

If she told Mama that she knew Yarko Kassim wasn't her real father, her mother would be furious with Aunt Zenia. What would she do? Maybe Mama knew something about her sister, something awful. Baba said what had happened to Zenia wasn't Zenia's fault and that maybe the same thing happened to Luba's mother? What was that all about? Luba hated living with all these secrets that affected her and her family. But what would happen if she told her mother what she knew, if Luba continued to break the chain of secrets? Would anything change?

"Hello! Anybody home?" Aunt Zenia was home early.

"Yeah, I'm in my room," Luba shouted through her open bedroom door.

"Oh, there you are. Packing?" She stated the obvious as she stopped in the doorway. Luba looked up. Aunt Zenia had a pleasant smile on her face. Oh-oh.

"Yeah, getting organized. My plane leaves pretty early so I thought I'd better get it all done tonight." She kept stuffing clothes into her suitcase.

"Yes, I know. I won't be able to go to the airport with you tomorrow but Bohdan will take you. I thought maybe we could go out to dinner tonight, since it's your last night. Do you have any plans?"

"No I don't. But you don't need to take me out—"

"Yes, we do. I've had a tough day and didn't have time to plan supper. So it works out better for me anyway." She was still smiling.

"Okay."

Aunt Zenia continued to stand in the doorway while Luba put her extra shoes in a plastic bag.

"I have the perfect shoe bag for you. Wait a minute." She disappeared and returned with a blue vinyl bag. "See, you just draw the string at the top, and the shoes won't fall out. Here, you can keep it, I have plenty of others. I go through a lot of shoes in my business."

"On your feet a lot, huh?"

"Oh yes. Walking, driving around, showing properties to clients. I need lots of dress shoes, and, believe me, I wear them out." Her aunt kicked off her shoes at that point and picked them up. "Your mother hates it when I come clomping onto her clean floors with my high-heeled shoes. But I detest those knitted slippers of hers. Last time I brought my own slippers, and she still thought they were street shoes because of the small heel. Remember?"

"Yeah, I remember." Luba smiled at the thought of her mother scolding Aunt Zenia and trying to make her wear the god-awful turquoise-and-green nylon knitted slippers. On her mother's polished floors, those slippers were dangerous—no grip, all slip.

Luba fished out a pair of slippers, yellow with orange stripes, from the back corner of her suitcase. "She tucked these into my suitcase before I left."

"Did you even put them on your feet?" she laughed.

"No." Luba giggled with her. She stuffed the offensive footwear back into her suitcase, and zipped it up partway. She turned back to her aunt, who was still chuckling and holding her shoes.

"Aunt Zenia, you remember what we talked about last night?" Luba hated to bring this up, but it had been bugging her all day.

"Mm-hmm."

"Well, I still don't know what I'm going to do. I mean about asking Mama about Tato. I just wondered, well, if I do, she'll probably think you told me, no matter what I say. She'll get mad at you."

"She's always mad at me. Anyway, it doesn't matter. If you talk to her, you tell her there are no secrets here. I mean, there are no secrets between Bohdan and me, and perhaps we should all just leave well enough alone. Will you tell her that?" She regarded Luba earnestly.

"Yeah, sure. If I decide to say anything at all. Anyway, Baba told me about my dad, not you. " Luba stared down at her toes as she continued the lie. She was beginning to hate herself.

"Well, I should have kept my mouth shut. Anyway, she'll pry it out of you. I know your mother. She's a master in the art of interrogation."

"Uh-huh," Luba agreed. She couldn't believe that Aunt Zenia hadn't tripped her up yet.

"Is Italian okay?"

"Sure, Aunt Zenia."

"Good. I'll make a reservation for six-thirty."

"Do you have your boarding pass?" Luba showed the pass to Uncle Bohdan.

"Here's the gate. I guess we're a little early. Let me buy you a coffee." He hovered over his niece as she fell into a lounge chair.

"No, thanks, Uncle. I'll get breakfast on the plane. I couldn't stomach a coffee this early." It was nearly seven a.m. and her body was still not awake.

"I've always been an early riser," Uncle Bohdan told her as he sat in the seat next to her. "Which is a good thing in my business. If I get to work before the crew, it gives me some time to clear my head and make plans for the day. I get the first pot of coffee going for the guys. Afterwards the office staff takes over."

"Am I making you late for work?" Luba yawned.

"I'm never late for work—I run the show. Ah, it is nice to be your own boss. But sometimes it's a headache when you have too many people working for you. You listen to me. Get yourself into a line of work where you can call the shots, but don't have so many people working for you that you can't remember their names, their wives' and kids' names, and where they live and what they do for hobbies. That is my advice." He gave her a wide cheerful grin.

How could this man be so chipper, so early in the morning, day after day? Luba gave him the best smile she could muster after another nearly sleepless night. She was determined to find a job that started at noon. She wondered if designers could work from noon til eight p.m. or later to fit into her night owl biorhythm.

"Please give my best to your mother, and your aunt and uncle, when you see them."

"Yes, Uncle."

"And Luba." He paused and took one of her cold hands into his big warm paws. "I want to thank you for coming and putting up with us. You may not believe this, but Zenia is much better off, we both are, since you've come and—how shall I say this—stirred things up? Actually, Zenia did most of the stirring, but you didn't let her push you around. That is what she needs—someone to stand up to her. I don't know what happened the night before last, but all I can say is that Zenia is a much more relaxed person. I know it is hard to imagine. But she cleared some things up, some misunderstandings you might call them, from long, long ago. Zenia decided it was time to unburden herself, which has brought her much relief. So, thank you, little Luba, for bringing her some peace of mind." He leaned over and gave her a smacking kiss on her cheek. Luba stared back at him, astonished. She had no idea what he was talking about. No doubt another secret, one Zenia had been keeping from her husband for many years.

"You tell your mother that all is well between us. Volya has had a hard life, too. I know she can be tough on you, but just keep that in mind when you can. You will understand more, like how to forgive, when you get to be my age. God gave us this one life and we each need to make the best of it for ourselves and our loved ones. Ah! Is that the boarding announcement? Well, you're off, then."

When they stood up, Luba threw her arms around him and hugged him hard so he didn't see the tears that had welled up in her eyes.

"Thank you, Uncle Bohdan, for being so understanding and loving and wise. And when I get back to Toronto, I'll be visiting you once in a while, if you don't mind."

"Are you kidding? You can visit as often as you like, and if you ever need a place to stay—"

"Thank you for the offer, but I think I've got that covered."

He chuckled. "Good-bye, little one."

Luba slung her bag over a shoulder, waved, and turned for the gate, ticket clutched tightly in her right hand. Just before she entered the corridor, she looked back to see him smiling and waving. What a wonderful man. They were all lucky to have him in their family.

Tortured Souls

"Luba? You awake?"

"No," she mumbled from beneath the covers. Just when Luba had found a safe spot on a warm island beach, her mother wanted to drag her back to ugly old Copper Creek. Let me sleep, for God's sake, she thought. She grasped for the sand, but it had slipped away. Damn!

"Do you want me to make you some breakfast before I go to work?"

"No. No, thank you."

"Okay. I will be back at two."

Luba fell asleep again. Her warm sunny beach had changed to a steep, rocky coast under a brooding grey sky. Huge frothing waves crashed on the shoreline. Inside a beach house, she felt secure and started to get ready for bed. The room was too bright, so she looked for blinds to close, drapes to draw, but couldn't find any. The ocean continued to roar outside and rain began to pelt down on the tin roof. The walls of the little beach house shuddered from the assault of wind and waves. Another crash and one wall caved in, then was washed away in the deluge, leaving Luba exposed, cold, wet.

She woke up, shivering and soaked with cooled perspiration. The extra sleep left her feeling awful, not refreshed as she'd hoped. A shower and a coffee later, her brain began to churn again. She had to think about packing and how she planned to get back down to Toronto. She'd left most of her things behind with a former schoolmate, so there wouldn't be much to take down besides her clothes. The plane trip back to Copper Creek had been smooth, and now the thought of long bus rides made her feel queasy.

Luba reread the letter from Ryerson explaining how to register for summer school. There was supposed to be another form in her small pile of mail. What was this? An envelope addressed to her with a return address she didn't recognize. She ripped it open. Inside was a note and business card from Bella with a new address in Richmond Hill. Luba stared at the note, surprised and dismayed. Bella would be gone in two weeks, and regretted she could not take any new appointments. She provided the names of three psychologists who would be taking over her case load. Though Luba had decided earlier that she wouldn't need to see Bella again, she had changed her mind en route to Copper Creek. Like Aunt Zenia, she needed to unburden, and there was no one else she could confide in. So much to tell, to sort out; her lesbian experience, how she found her real grandfather then lost her father, and whether or not to tell her mother that she knew Volya Kassim's deep, dark secret. And part of that secret was that her mother's name was actually Volya Tatenko. Luba carried the last name of a man who had never married her mother and probably never legally adopted her. In fact, Volya wasn't even a Tatenko—she was a Lazorovich.

Oh, for God's sake, Luba thought, shaking her head. She was an adult, she'd left a mess behind her, but she should be able to deal with it. Sure, she felt like Bella had let her down by not saying anything when they spoke only a few days ago. Bella must have known she was leaving Copper Creek, unless she suddenly quit. But no, the card had the address of a clinic in Richmond Hill, so she already had a new job lined up. A mailed notification, even courteous and professional like this one, seemed so cold and impersonal. But Bella had included a written note as well, inviting Luba to give her a call anytime once she was back in Toronto.

Luba was on her own. Perhaps there was some way to learn the truth about her father without a direct confrontation. Like Aunt Zenia, what if she accidentally came upon some information already in the house? She could ask a few critical questions, and force the truth out that way. It had worked with Aunt Zenia. Her mother was probably too clever and too much in denial to fall for such tactics, but it was worth a try. Yeah, that would be the best way, but where to look? She'd already been through the photo albums. There was no other man in the photos who could be her father besides Yarko Kassim. He was pictured with her and Mama at every stage, starting with her christening ceremony. But no photos before that. What happened in Halifax? What about her hospital records from Vancouver?

The guilty gremlin rode on Luba's shoulder as she marched into her mother's bedroom. She yanked open the top dresser drawer, trying to shake the tenacious beast. "I have to know, it's my right to know," she muttered, and began by removing everything carefully and replacing each item where she found it. Nothing but clothing and some cheap costume jewellery.

At the back of the lowest drawer in her bedroom, Luba found an ornately carved wooden box. It was made in Ukraine. No painting, just two bears standing on their hind legs facing each other, as if in a boxing match. She didn't remember ever seeing that box before. It was locked! Luba felt her heart racing. Was this the place Mama had stashed the evidence? She searched the drawer for a key, but came up empty. Wait a minute. She had seen a key in the jewellery box on Volya's dresser. She removed the key and slipped it into the lock of the mystery box. It fit perfectly. She twisted the key and the lid clicked open.

Luba lifted the lid with a shaking hand. The lining was a dull red felt, and inside there was more jewellery as well as paper. She scooped out the baubles and lifted the first piece of paper. A newspaper article about painting Easter eggs. Her mother's faded face, young and smiling, appeared at the top with three eager-looking children just below her, wearing traditional embroidered blouses. Luba was one of those children. She didn't remember this photo being taken. The Toronto Star, March 7, 1965. She was nine years old then.

Luba looked further. More articles about the Ukrainian Women's League, the church, a bazaar. No personal papers, no medical records. She threw herself back on the bed where she'd been sitting, the box still in her lap, and groaned. She noticed the necklace she had tossed aside earlier, and picked it up. She remembered this one, a mother's day gift from eons ago. It had cost $5.00, a lot of money for a ten-year-old kid back then. The necklace was ugly as sin, yellowed rhinestones glittering on a cheap, tarnished-grey metal chain. Why would she keep this junk? And the metallic pink broach in the shape of a flower? Luba's tastes in accessories had changed a bit since then and she was glad her mother never wore those pieces in public. She had no idea Mama was such a pack rat.

After replacing the box and key and smoothing down the bed, Luba left the bedroom and began searching the basement. Three hours of scouring produced a lot more junk, some of it hers from years gone by. She got lost in the scrapbooks and artwork of a young girl, remembering the dreams she'd had. A tossed salad of emotions tumbled through her—sadness at how those dreams had evaporated, anger at how stupid she'd been to let that happen, frustration at how long it took and a serious crash to rekindle them, and now anxiety mixed with excitement about the new path she had started down.

Luba's new bravado crumbled at the thought of confronting her mother. But there was someone she could talk to, and maybe Aunt Veronica would know about her real father, or at least she might provide a few useful clues.

In spite of the long distance across town, being outside and walking briskly in the warm June air made her feel much better. She thought again about calling Bella, but decided against it. Luba didn't see how Bella could help her on this one.

Her aunt's house was a modest stucco, a lot like her mother's but larger, with one-and-a half storeys. The roof needed some work, but Uncle Marko just couldn't seem to get round to it. When he wasn't at work in the mines, he was lounging about drunk or off fishing or hunting. Now that she had spent time with Aunt Zenia, she saw how very similar she and her brother were. Aunt Zenia was a quieter alcoholic, and though she worked around the house, she also had a house-cleaner come over twice a month. No wonder the two of them looked down on her mother, the teetotaler charwoman. She understood more clearly why Mama might resent Aunt Zenia so much.

"Aunt Veronica? Anybody home?" Luba stuck her head inside the unlocked door. There was no answer, so she stepped inside.

"Hello!" she shouted louder. Luba walked to the darkened living room and saw the blue TV lights dancing on the opposite wall. When her eyes adjusted to the dimness, she could make out Aunt Veronica slumped on the sofa across from the TV, a pile of white embroidery cloth and thread in her lap. She snored softly.

Luba sat in a chair and watched her aunt for a few moments, not wanting to disturb her. Her gold-rimmed glasses had slipped down her nose at a wild angle, one lens indenting her soft cheek, the other flattening a nostril. The other, unobstructed nostril fluttered as she struggled to breathe in through one side of her nose. Luba wished her aunt would lose some weight. She was always huffing when she walked. It couldn't be good for her heart. Why couldn't she be slim like Aunt Zenia? But when Luba thought about Aunt Zenia's heart, she pictured it a compact, efficient machine encased in teflon and buried deep in her core, compared to the big juicy heart pumping near the surface of her corpulent aunt who snoozed peacefully in her cave of a home. The snoozer snorted loudly and her head jerked up.

"Luba? When did you get here? Are you okay?" she asked with a worried, startled look.

Luba got up to give her a hug while Aunt Veronica patted her niece's back.

"I'm fine, Aunt Veronica. Didn't Mama tell you I was home?"

"Oh, yes, she told me. I just forgot exactly when."

"I got in last night, late. And I slept in. I'm packing to go to school in Toronto, to Ryerson."

"Yes, your mother told me. And she said you would be staying with Greg for a while. No matter what she says, I think that is a good idea. I was always worried when you lived by yourself. Toronto is such a big, dangerous city, it is not safe for young women on their own." Her aunt reached over to turn on the lamp next to her and Luba flashed back to the last time she was there and Nicholas sat near that lamp, glaring at his father.

"So tell me how your visit went? How is Baba? Did she recognize you?" she asked, and peered at her threaded needle, which soon disappeared into a fold of cloth.

"Baba didn't recognize me at first. She sometimes forgets what year it is, and she confused me with someone else for a while. Someone she used to know very, very well." Luba paused to see if Aunt Veronica might comment.

"Oh? Who did she confuse you with? She gets confused a lot, Zenia says." She glanced up briefly from her embroidery, but only a slightly curious look registered on her face.

"My grandfather, Lazlo."

"Lazlo? I don't remember that name. Are you sure it was Lazlo?"

"She told me that Boryslav was not Mama's father. It was a Gypsy named Lazlo Lazorovich. Greg was there when she told us. She said she tried to tell Mama one time, but Mama wouldn't listen, and that's when we left Toronto."

Aunt Veronica put down her sewing and stared at Luba. "That is crazy talk! I can see why your mother did not want to listen to such nonsense. You do not believe it, do you?"

"I think she was telling the truth. Why would she lie to us?"

"I do not think Baba was lying. She must have been confused, got it mixed up with another story she heard from someone. Zenia told me she is losing her memory and she gets things mixed up all the time now. That happens to older people. It is very sad, but you should not believe everything your Baba says." Aunt Veronica shook her head and picked up the needle once again.

Now Luba was annoyed. "So you don't think it could possibly be true?"

"No. Not your grandmother. It would have been impossible to sneak around behind Boryslav's back in that small village. If he thought she had betrayed him he would have killed her. Marko tells me some terrible stories about his father. No, I cannot imagine Sylana doing anything like that."

"But look at Mama. She is so different from Aunt Zenia and Uncle Marko. And me, look at me! Baba said I reminded her of Lazlo. No one else has this dark, wavy hair, or my skin colour. And look at my nose. Where did that come from?"

"Your uncle Lubomyr had dark hair, too, just like your mother. You can see it in the old photos. And who knows what your father's parents looked like. You might look like them."

"That's another thing. My father. I mean Yarko, I learned something about him, too." Aunt Veronica dropped her embroidery again; the needle was stopped in mid-air. Luba finally had her entire attention. She did know something.

"Did Baba say something about your father, too?" Her expression was guarded.

"Not a whole lot, but Aunt Zenia filled in the details. I know that Yarko isn't my real father, but Auntie says she doesn't know who that is. Do you know?" Luba drummed her fingers nervously on the taut, over-stuffed cushion in her lap.

"Your real father?" she said slowly, dully. "Well, I thought your father was Yarko. Who else could it be?"

"Aunt Veronica, I know he isn't my biological father. Our blood types don't match. And when I came home from the hospital, my last name was still Tatenko. And, have you ever seen any wedding pictures with Mama and... and... this man she says is my father? Who I thought was my father? How about a marriage certificate?"

Veronica's mouth was open and she struggled to speak. "Who told you this?" she finally said with a weak voice.

"Aunt Zenia. Baba said something about what happened to Zenia may also have happened to Mama. And whatever happened to Zenia wasn't Zenia's fault. Aunt Zenia found out that Mama's husband wasn't my father, and maybe they weren't even married. Do you know what happened?"

Aunt Veronica shook her head and looked down. "Your aunt was raped by a German soldier. It was the war, those things happened. She and Bohdan got married and left for Germany right away. I do not know what happened to your mother. She never told us much about your father, about Yarko. She knew him in England and they came to Canada together. They stopped here in Copper Creek on their way to Vancouver where he had a job waiting for him. That was the first and last time we ever saw poor Yarko. He seemed like such a nice man. Very gentle, very kind, considerate."

Luba popped up out of her chair and paced to the end of the room, then back to the sofa. "Yeah, the same story. A kind and gentle man....who isn't my father."

"Luba!"

"I'm sorry, Aunt Veronica. You see, I'm not his daughter. I'm not nice and gentle and kind like him. And if he isn't my father, maybe Boryslav isn't my grandfather either. Who knows!" Her hands flew up and she fell back into the sofa. The cushion bounced onto the floor and rested at her aunt's feet.

"Have you talked to your mother about this?" She looked at Luba, her brow furrowed.

"No. Not yet, because I don't know what to say. I want to know who my real father is. Don't I have a right to know?"

"Luba, your world is so black-and-white sometimes. Maybe Baba is right. Maybe something terrible happened to your mother in England, or in Canada. She was alone. If she has not told you, it may be something very painful and embarrassing. She never told us. Sometimes these things are better left unsaid."

"Secrets," Luba muttered. Yes, secrets. Now she finally understood what Uncle Bohdan meant about her stirring things up, that there were now no secrets between him and Zenia. Her aunt must have told him about the rape. And perhaps also that Adam wasn't his son. Why did she tell him now? Of course, Luba's mother. Aunt Zenia was afraid Volya would spill the beans because she'd think Aunt Zenia told Luba about her real father. Tit for tat.

Secrets. Luba thought about Nicholas and Uncle Marko, arguing about the fate of the Italian Jews in that room not so long ago.

"Auntie, did Uncle Marko ever tell you what happened to him during the war?" She wondered if this was also taboo territory, but she believed her aunt would tell her the truth, if she knew it.

Aunt Veronica continued to embroider, not looking up. "No. He made it very clear he did not want to discuss it. Not ever. So we never talk about it. You young people can never understand how frightened we all were for our lives, for our families, our friends. The Nazis were much worse than the Russians. Every day we woke up wondering if there would be food to eat, a place to sleep, who would be the next one taken away and shot in the woods, left to rot. It was a terrible time, Luba. People did what they had to do to survive." She took the red thread between her teeth and sawed at it until it broke. When she looked up her lips were quivering.

"I'm sorry, Aunt Veronica, I didn't mean to upset you. It's just that after learning about some of the stuff that happened to Mama and Aunt Zenia, I can understand more about why they say and do the things they do. Why they can be so irrational sometimes. It's hard, but I know I should be more patient with them."

"You are right, Luba. It is hard to be patient. You know your Uncle Marko drinks too much. Everybody knows it. It was difficult for me in the beginning, to make sense of him and his drinking. I only learned a few years ago what did happen to him during the war, from an old friend who served in his unit under the Germans. Marko, being the good host, was pouring the vodka like it was water. They sat right here in this room, catching up on their lives since they left Europe and came to Canada. Roman lives in Winnipeg now. He can hold his liquor better than Marko, who fell asleep before they finished the first bottle. But Roman was not done reminiscing, so he told me the story, the whole thing. I have not told a soul, not even Marko, what I heard that night. I know how your mother feels about Marko and his drinking, and perhaps you feel the same way. But if you only knew...." Her aunt covered her face for a moment then sat up straighter, blinking back tears as she stared into Luba's eyes.

Luba sat frozen in her seat. "Auntie, I'm terribly sorry. You're right, there is so much I don't know, and I'm sure it was awful during the war. But there are all these secrets in my family, and I'm frustrated when they affect me and people expect me to be patient and understanding, but they won't tell me why they act the way they do."

"Sometimes they do not even know themselves why they behave in certain ways, Luba. And I know you are trying, God knows as well. It has been hard not to have a father to help raise you, and your mother with her own problems." She put her two hands together as if in prayer, paused a moment, and smiled sadly at Luba.

"Very well, Luba, I will tell you Marko's story, but you must never, never let him know. He is a proud man and he has done the best he could with his family. He loves all of us, I want you to know that."

"Of course, I know that, Auntie. I promise, not a word to anyone."

Aunt Veronica breathed in deeply and closed her eyes for a moment. "When Marko and three of his friends left their village—I think it was in 1942—they were just a few of the hundreds of young boys and men transported by the Nazis into Italy. They could have remained behind in hiding and fought for the resistance. We know now that most of those who did died. Or they could fight with the Nazis against the Russians. At first they were afraid. They had no idea what to expect, but they soon found that life as military cadets was not so bad, especially after being starved half to death back in Ukraine. And they looked forward to returning to their homeland to drive the hated Russian oppressors further north, back to the Baltic Sea and beyond. That's what they were promised. First, the Germans wanted to train the youngsters, give them free schooling and teach them trades. With the war raging all around them, Italy was a haven for these boys so the Ukrainian recruits counted their blessings. They were even able to attend church on Sundays, and more often if they wished.

"Marko and the other boys had more food and comfortable clothing than they ever had in their villages back in Ukraine. They shared rooms in the army barracks at the outskirts of the small town of Este, not far from Padua. Still, they all felt the occasional pangs of guilt, wondering if their mothers and sisters were still in the villages, or if they had been forced to emigrate to Germany, or worse."

"Yes, I know, Mama told me all those stories of the awful train trip to Germany, the people all packed together, the filth. And the conditions on the farms." Luba shuddered, remembering the details.

"My experiences were very similar to your Mama's. Marko and Roman and their friends heard many unsettling stories about what was happening outside of Italy, but they never knew the entire truth. That was kept from them as much as possible. Roman said they occasionally managed to find a local newspaper, and with their new Italian reading skills, they were able to piece together some of the war news. It was disturbing, of course. They could not believe that Jews were being rounded up and placed in camps all over Germany, Poland, and Ukraine. There were even rumours that these Jews were being exterminated as the camps filled up. Even Marko, who has no love for the Jews, thought that was going too far, and it couldn't possibly be true.

"About a year later, Roman said, there was a call for volunteers to help with a special building project about a hundred kilometres south of their unit. Marko, Roman, and Danylo decided they had learned enough algebra to last them a lifetime, and were eager for action. They drove down with a group of twenty young men to join others assigned to build a bridge across the Montone River. The work was not nearly as glamorous as the boys thought it might be. They toiled as labourers, hauling heavy rocks and beams, often in pouring rain and mud. They had been on the job only two weeks when the officer in charge of their work unit announced that he needed three men for duty in a nearby town. Without asking for volunteers, he selected the three boys from Brinzi. They packed up and were transported to Rimini, a lovely little town on the Adriatic coast. The boys were naturally delighted with their good fortune. After a brief training orientation they began their duties as sentries with occasional clerical work. The Germans were constructing a large military base just at the western outskirts of Rimini, complete with a huge administration building, mess hall, and barracks, Roman said.

"The boys were all encouraged to meet and socialize with the local Italians. That is the best way to learn a new language, for sure. At one of the market bistros, Roman said that Marko met a beautiful young woman, Carmella, who was equally attracted to him." Aunt Veronica paused, smiling at Luba's raised eyebrows.

"Do not worry, Luba. This was a while before he met me. He was still a teenager then. Roman said she was petite, with fair hair and blue eyes, unlike most of the Italians they had seen so far. Carmella explained that her family came from the south of Italy, where fair complexions are much more common. After a few months of seeing each other in the company of his and Carmella's friends, she suggested he meet her family so he could ask her out on a proper, unchaperoned date. Marko borrowed a civilian suit from Roman after Carmella told him the military uniform would not be appropriate. He was welcomed warmly by her mother, also an attractive blond, and even shorter than her daughter. Carmella's father, Lorenzo, greeted him with a stern expression and firm handshake. They all sat down to dinner after Marko was introduced to Carmella's two younger brothers.

"Marko apparently found that his appetite had shrunk to nothing as he sat with the family. Carmella's father was a tall imposing man who glared at Marko from across the table. After saying a brief prayer of thanks, Lorenzo began his questions.

"'Tell me, young man, what exactly do you do for the Germans? Carmella tells me you are from Ukraine.'

"Marko was very nervous, of course, but he tried to be truthful. He said, 'I do some sentry work in the evenings. From time to time I help with accounting. You know, I take money to the bank for deposit. Sometimes I run errands for the chief accountant.'

"'So, you like working with money?' Lorenzo challenged him.

"'I do what they ask me to do. I suppose they trust me to handle the accounts.' He was hoping that this was the correct answer.

"'Have they asked you to look for Jews?' At this point, Marko told Roman that Lorenzo's stare was so cold that he had to grip the edge of the table to steady himself.

"'No,' he said, quite honestly. 'Why would they ask for something like that?'

"Lorenzo's mouth showed the slightest hint of a smile. 'Are you really so naive? Believe me, they will ask you. I am telling you, there are Jews everywhere. They are just like us, hard-working, good people. Carmella's best friend is Jewish. How old are you?'

"'I am eighteen, sir.'

"'Hah! So young. Do you know you have a good Italian name, Marco? You could be one of us,' he chuckled and passed the polenta to Marko.

"'Carmella tells us you are Catholic.' Her mother smiled at him. She was a very gentle woman, Roman told me, and a loving mother. And they welcomed Marko as if he was one of their own after that.

"Two months later Marko was ordered to the commandant's office. He and Roman were nervous—Danylo had been gone for two days and no one knew what had happened to him. Their friend had been ordered to the commandant's office just before he disappeared. Marko saluted his superior and was told to sit down facing him across a huge black lacquered desk. He noticed that the office was decorated with enormous Italian oil paintings which covered most of the walls. The Germans always took the best artwork everywhere they went.

"The commandant took Marko's personal information, then said, 'You probably notice your compatriot, Danylo Horiy, is no longer with your unit. We had some disciplinary problems with him. He is in detention. I expect we will post him to the front eventually. He is young, but he will learn. Now, I want to know how willing you are to learn a new job. Military work is not always pleasant, as I am sure you know, but it is essential to keep peace and order. I am afraid that a certain group of people is causing unrest among our generous and patient Italian hosts, and we simply cannot allow this to continue. You have been here long enough to know who these people are. Your new assignment will be to find these trouble-makers and bring them to our new facility here. It is comfortable; they will have food and all necessities. We will hold them here for their own safety. It is quite possible, no probable, that the Italians will take matters into their own hands if we do not separate them soon. We certainly do not want to see such violence in this peaceful, prosperous little town.'

"'Your assignment will be to bring in all the Jews. I know this can be difficult. You may even consider some of them your friends. But, believe me, they will turn on you in a moment, as soon as they are not getting their way. I see by your face, young Tatenko, that this may be very difficult for you. But you have no choice. Danylo told us about your family, your mother, Sylana, your sisters, Zenia and Volya. We know exactly where they are in Germany, in Mannheim to be specific. I am certain you would not want any harm to come to them. Is that not right, Tatenko?' He smiled icily at Marko, who sat trembling in his chair. In spite of Marko's fear, Roman said he reported every word to him later.

"'In fact,' the commandant continued, 'let us go see your friend Danylo, just to convince you how serious we are.' The commandant pulled on a thick, red, braided cord hanging behind his chair. He stood up and motioned Marko to do the same. Two sergeants marched in and took Marko's elbows to steer him out of the room. They walked briskly to the back of the building, through corridors Marko had never seen before. At this point, he admitted he did not recall how he managed to walk through that maze, or how he found his way back to the barracks afterwards. At the far end of the corridors, Danylo lay on a cot in a darkened cell. One of the officers turned on a lamp which swung overhead. Marko could not recognize his friend—his face was puffed up to twice its size, blue with streaks of red, his eyes mere slits. With horror he saw that where his right ear used to be there was only a dark red, pulpy mess of tissue. The streams of blood had dried onto his face and clothing.

"'Is he alive?' he asked.

"'Sure,' one of the sergeants said. 'He will make it. A strong boy, but not very bright. I think you are a lot smarter than him. Is that not so, Tatenko?'

"It was Danylo's face that accompanied Marko through the end of the war. Every time he walked into their homes, he did not hear their protests, he did not meet their pleading eyes. He only saw Danylo. He tried to be angry with Danylo for betraying him and Roman. But he knew how strong and loyal Danylo had been, how much it would have taken to break him. Do you know, Marko even risked his life to try to warn Carmella's friend that her family was next on the list? But he and the others were watched carefully by then. They were no longer allowed on any social visits with the locals. He was caught leaving the barracks unescorted, and came up with an excuse they believed, luckily for him. The next day, he could not look at Carmella's dearest friend as he escorted her and her family to the truck awaiting them. It broke his heart. Neither Roman nor Marko ever saw Carmella again, or Danylo. Marko told Roman he barely remembered anything from the next two years of his life. Those were the things these reluctant soldiers had to do to survive all the horrors they lived through. It is not for us to judge them." Aunt Veronica wiped her cheeks with the back of her hand, then she resumed her sewing.

After a few minutes of absolute silence she said, "What will you do, Luba?"

"I don't know yet. Probably nothing."

"That would be the best. Leave it alone. Your mother has suffered enough."

Alone in a Crowd

"Do you have to go tomorrow?" Volya huffed, scrubbing the stove top, her back to Luba. "You can't wait another day?"

Luba had not budged from the table, but sat, as if studying the patterns in the tablecloth. She had not offered to help with supper or clean-up, but Volya did not dare say a word to upset her. She could tell Luba was on edge. Not a word about the visit, either. No doubt Zenia must have said something, done something to her, but Volya was not going to ask.

"My first class is on Monday, Mama. That doesn't give me much time. I still have to register for classes, figure out where I'm going. And on top of that I'll have a nasty, long bus trip to recover from."

"So Zenia did not offer to pay for another plane trip to Toronto?" She heard Luba snort behind her. Volya could just imagine the look on her face but she did not turn around. She could not understand why Luba tried to aggravate her all the time.

"I'd say she was pretty generous paying for a round trip to Toronto, already. There's no reason for her to spend any more money on me. She's also paying a lot to keep Baba in the nursing home. It's not cheap, you know."

"If she was a decent human being she would not have Baba in a nursing home. She should take care of her in that big, fancy house of hers. She could afford to have a nurse come in, she just cannot be bothered. All that matters is that she has money; family is nothing to her!"

"Mama, that's not fair. Maybe Baba is happier in the nursing home. How would you know? You haven't talked to her in ten years. You call that a decent way for a daughter to treat her own mother? What has she ever done to deserve that kind of treatment?"

"That is between me and her, and none of your business," Volya said, turning around to face her daughter.

"That's not entirely true. The way you two treat each other affects me, too, you know. I'm tired of all these family secrets. I know about my grandfather Lazlo. Why don't you just accept it and get over these stupid, stubborn feuds?"

"That is pure garbage. Baba is crazy and now she has filled your head with those insane stories!"

"If it's garbage, how come you're so mad at her? Why should the ravings of a senile old woman make you so mad if it wasn't the truth? Why can't you be honest with each other?"

"I can ask you the same thing. Have you been entirely honest with me? Have you told me everything you have ever done?"

"Well, not every little detail—"

"Why not?"

"Because. You'd worry too much, and there really isn't much to worry about—"

"You almost died, and you expect me not to worry? Orest did die! He did not tell his mother the truth, did he? And look what happened to him."

"Mama, that's different. I'm not a drug addict. You can't compare me to Orest—"

"So do not compare me to Zenia, either. You could not possibly understand what happened." Volya whipped off her apron and started to leave the kitchen.

"But I want to try to understand. Why won't you tell me?"

"There is nothing to tell." Volya stomped off to the living room and turned on the TV, cranking up the volume. She knew Luba would not try to continue the conversation while the TV was playing. There was no point in telling Luba anything. She would only blame, blame, blame. Luba never told Volya about her private life; she did not have to tell Luba about hers. There it was: stalemate.

It was unusually quiet in the house, especially with Luba in it. Her silence, her anger, made the air hard to breathe. Volya lay in her bed exhausted; already one in the morning, and still she could not sleep. That girl could be so frustrating. Volya had always thought that Luba's teenage years would be the worst, but it seemed she had not finished tormenting her mother. What had happened to her? First she tried to kill herself and would not say why, and now Luba was hounding her with all these questions about Volya's past. Maybe she wanted to blame Volya for her own state of mind. All this talk of genetics and inheritance. Phooey!

And this Lazlo thing again. It made little difference who Volya's father really was when it was Boryslav she'd had to deal with. Of course he liked her least of all the children. She was not as pretty as the others or as cheerful or co-operative. No, it was not that, either. He may not have cared for Volya's attitude, but there was something else as well. He was a bully, he needed to pick on someone—Volya was it. There was also the long string of unsympathetic relatives and poorly chosen companions. She had no choice with the relations, but why was she always so unlucky when it came to the people she met? Running into Karl in Germany, then poor Yanos. After the war, Volya was ready to make a clean break from all of her memories, and that included her family.

The opportunity to travel to England without them was a gift. At least, that was what she told herself at the time. It was a hopeful trip. It was April and warm and the countries she passed through were already green and lush. Still, it was a long journey by train through Germany and France, then by steamship across the channel, followed by another train to Manchester. It was long, but far more comfortable than her first train ride, packed in a filthy cattle car. At least they all had their own seats, and even money to buy food en route. Not much, but enough for most of them. Several of the girls had already picked up enough English to get by. Volya's best friend, Zora, was the most fluent. She heard from a fellow traveler, a middle-aged woman from England, that they had better get used to "fish-and-chips." When she finished describing the dish, and Zora had translated, they all nodded their heads—some with excitement, others wrinkling their noses. Fish with fried potatoes. That did not sound so bad. Nothing could ever be as bad as going hungry for days, weeks on end.

At the train station in Manchester, they were greeted by a tall unsmiling woman in her fifties. She led the weary young women to the back of a covered lorry with benches lining both sides. It reminded Volya of all the drab military vehicles they had just left in Mannheim, and after they obediently climbed in, a couple of the girls began to cry quietly. They wondered how much further they still had to go. The Englishwoman announced something in a brisk voice. She gave them a brief salute and walked away as the tailpipe spewed black smoke and the lorry lurched forward. The girls were wedged in so tightly with their luggage, they could hardly move.

"Where are we going now?" someone asked.

"We will be staying at a hostel in Bury. That is what the lady said," Zora explained.

"Where is Bury?"

"She said just a little north of Manchester, maybe eleven kilometres. We can walk to the factory from there."

"And how far will that be? Another ten kilometres?" a sarcastic voice piped up.

There was silence after that. None of them had slept properly since they left the camp in Germany. Volya began to dread what they would find at the end of this little adventure. More barracks, perhaps.

The hostel turned out to be a reasonable place to live. There were four girls to a room and eight such rooms in the building, a dull red brick rectangle surrounded by many other similar structures. It was on a busy street in the middle of town. They chose their bunks and roommates and, by early evening, most of them were asleep.

Volya was assigned work in the cotton factory. Her job was to watch a thread of cotton unroll from one spool, drop into a vat of water, and end up re-spooling at the other end. She was responsible for stopping the machines at this point if the thread broke or became knotted. She had a set of special scissors that could cut and retie the thread in seconds. Then she would restart the machines and the thread continued to unwind and rewind. Yard after yard after yard. Day after day after day.

Volya recalled that it took most of them a full year to earn enough at their various factory jobs to repay the British government for their passage, while still paying for their room and board. Rationing was still in effect—tea, coffee, eggs, butter, meat, and sugar were scarce. Only pork was relatively abundant, but facing those dry, mealy, shriveled pork chops on their plates three times a week put off even the girls with the least discriminating tastes and biggest appetites. And they could not understand why their tea was so sweet when sugar was being rationed, until one evening when Ludmilla, the tiniest of the group, was "volunteered" to stay in the mess hall after dinner to spy on the cooks. Sure enough, she watched them taking all the sugar packets from the ration boxes, stuffing them into their overcoat pockets, then filling the sugar bowls from a small yellow box they kept in the spice cupboard. After they turned out the lights and locked the doors, Ludmilla crept out from beneath the corner table where she had been crouching nearly breathless for two hours. She opened the cupboard, grabbed the box, and ran back to the dorm rooms.

"Saccharin. That explains why our tea is so sweet."

"And have you noticed how bad their teeth are? Rotting right out of their sweet, thieving mouths, the old hags."

"That is our sugar they have been stealing."

"And I thought they only did this to you in Germany," Volya muttered. She had eventually figured out that the Vebers had taken her youth ration card to improve the quality and quantity of supplies they could get for themselves. None ever made it to Volya, of course. She supposed that happened to a lot of others as well.

"We will go on strike. That is what we need to do," Zora announced.

"What, are you crazy?"

"We will refuse to eat any of their food until they give us our sugar, in the ration packets. Sugar that belongs to us!"

After heated discussion, they agreed. Everyone in the hostel, regardless of national origin, united in this effort. By the end of the next day, the cooks relented. The girls were amazed at their success. Instead of using their sugar rations, most of the girls stashed the treasured packets in their rooms, in carefully concealed nooks. One never knew when they might come in handy, to barter with, for instance.

Zora, Volya, and another Ukrainian girl, Irina, decided to look for an apartment together during the second year. They now felt comfortable in their adopted English city and had saved enough money among them to afford better, more private housing. They had also grown tired of the hostility between certain ethnic groups in the hostel—in particular, the English-speaking tenants who looked down on the girls from eastern Europe. Even the Irish girls considered themselves a better class than the uneducated peasants or DPs, which was what they called displaced persons. Volya thought they would be more sympathetic. Many came from poverty similar to what she had endured in her own childhood, perhaps even worse.

It was not much better at the factory. A few months after they had arrived, the English workers, all women, complained to the supervisors that they should be getting more money than the foreigners. Volya was astounded when the management gave in to their requests and increased the wages of the English women. Volya wondered if they should stage a strike like they had at the hostel, but her foreigner friends squashed that idea immediately. They still felt like invited visitors who could be evicted over the most trivial dispute. Better to keep your mouth shut, they counselled her. You have a job, you can feed yourself, what more could you want? The horrors of the war were still fresh in their memories.

Meanwhile, Zenia and Mama and the rest of the family had emigrated to Canada by the time Volya was settled in her new job and life. As happy as they were to leave Germany far behind, they reported some difficulties settling into their adopted country. Marko wrote that the insects in northern Manitoba were so huge they practically carried off his little Christina. Volya remembered how horrified she was at the thought. For a while she really believed they had flies the size of fat rats. They had added two more children by 1948: Anatolia and Zachary. But Marko made good money at the gold mine, and Veronica never complained—at least not in the few lines she added to Marko's letters. Volya always wondered about it at the time, but once she got to know Veronica, she admired the woman's stoic nature and big heart.

Zenia, on the other hand, never stopped whining about life in the bush, as she called it. Not long after they arrived, Zenia was already planning her family's escape from Manitoba. Bohdan had started up a small construction company in the same town where Marko and Veronica lived. They seemed to have enough money, according to Marko, but Zenia hated living there. When she wrote to Volya, Zenia complained of cold and insects and being stuck inside with three small boys. And she had the nerve to say she was lonely! Marko resented the fact that Mama spent more time at Zenia's helping her with the children than she did at his home. But he never said that it bothered Veronica.

Of course, Volya did not want to portray her life as anything but satisfactory. Although her work was a daily misery, she did not wish to abandon it for the physical discomforts Zenia described in the wilderness of Canada. Let Zenia think she was having the time of her life, she thought, making pots of money, meeting all sorts of eligible English bachelors. Volya did not need to lie; she just made things sound, well, rosy.

She did meet a good number of young men of different nationalities. There were even a few Ukrainian men from refugee camps in Europe. Volya was certain that Zora would marry one of the Englishmen who were so attracted to her vivacious, generous nature. She was a pretty girl, with curly blond hair, deep blue eyes, and a wide, sincere smile. But Zora knew that fate had meant for her to meet Zenon, a tall thin boy from her neighbouring village in Ukraine, so in April 1949, two years after they arrived in England, they were engaged to be married.

They had all been saving their ration coupons for quite a time and had enough for a September wedding that year. Finding material for bridesmaids' dresses was another matter. There were eight maids and eight ushers in the wedding party. It seemed like madness when Volya remembered it now, all that excess when they had so little. They never had weddings like that any more. As maid of honour, Volya made the wedding the focus of her entire life for the next few months. She even sewed all the dresses since she had such a flair for dressmaking. It absorbed all her time for many evenings and all her days off. When Volya was sewing, she could disappear to another place where there was little thought, as if she was floating above herself. Perhaps it was what some people called meditation. She remembered the feeling of splitting in two: one body stayed below, sewing, and the other watched her and commented on her technique, critical and helpful in turn.

Zora kept hinting that there would be a number of handsome unattached men in the wedding party, such as Zenon's brother who came by train all the way from Germany where he had settled. What was his name—she had already forgotten it. Volya shrugged off Zora's encouragement and suggestions. She found them irritating. Every day she fought a great loneliness, knowing that it would not make that much difference to her life when Zora left—as much as she adored her friend. She was convinced there would never be anyone for her, that she had already lost her intended. There was no point in even looking.

But she wrote to Zenia and Mama that her life was wonderful, that she was having great fun at all the weddings of her friends, that she was always meeting new people. It was true that her skills as a seamstress were constantly in demand. She had a steady job, she could support herself. There was no reason on earth why she should leave England for Canada. Life could not have been better.

Dancing Genes

"Hey Luba? You home?" Greg shouted as he walked in the front door.

"Yeah!" Luba shouted back from the living room. "I'm not deaf, you know."

A few moments later she heard a muffled laugh from his bedroom, then Greg rushed into the room where Luba sat on the couch, reading her mail. He stood ramrod straight in front of her, waving an envelope in the air, and grinning as if he'd just won the lottery.

As he continued to say nothing, she said, "Congratulations. You have mail. So do I. You'll never guess who wrote me."

Greg dropped his envelope on the coffee table in front of her. "Okay, you try to guess what's in my envelope, and I'll try to guess who wrote to you. The one who gets the right answer first gets dinner cooked by the other one the rest of the week!"

"Uh-huh, sure." Luba's culinary skills left much to be desired, so she didn't believe Greg would last that long on her simple cuisine if she lost the bet. He, on the other hand, was the gourmet cook in the house, and loved to create fabulous meals that Luba loved to eat. But maybe he wanted to take a break. Or he planned to teach her to cook properly—something he'd been hinting at for the last few weeks.

Luba glanced down at his envelope which had only a return address. She held it up. "The O'Keefe Centre. Tickets?"

"Yeah, that's the only clue you get."

"I don't think I like the odds here. It could be anything. A rock band?"

"Nope," he crowed with delight. "You won't guess. Just give up and start cooking dinner, Gypsy-girl."

Luba rolled her eyes. He was right, she would never guess. God, he was bubbly today. Which was good, she supposed, when there were so many days he came home from work drained and depressed, something she learned only after living in the same house for a few weeks. At the time she wondered why he stayed in that type of practice, providing legal aid for relatively little compensation and so much aggravation. But helping people was number one for Greg. Sometimes his selflessness made Luba feel guilty, but not today. Today he was full of beans.

"May I ask who these tickets are for?"

"For us, darling cousin. Paula bought them months ago, but now she can't go. Her mother's sick so she's going home for a week to be with her, and Phil didn't really want to go to the ballet to begin with—oops!" He put his hand to his mouth and collapsed on the couch next to her.

"Which ballet?" Luba didn't know whether she was all that keen on ballet, herself.

"Oh, guess!"

"No."

"You're such a killjoy sometimes, Luba. The Royal Winnipeg Ballet, Canada's best! This weekend. What do you think?"

"I dunno. Friday or Saturday?"

"Why, do you have plans for this weekend?"

"No, but maybe I don't want to go to the ballet." She stuck out her bottom lip.

Greg pinched her cheek.

"Ouch!"

"Oh, good, you still have some feelings. Listen, chiquita, you need to get out more. This is Toronto, a cultural Mecca. I saw the Royal Winnipeg three years ago, they're marvelous, and I promise, you'll love them."

"I will?"

"Have you ever seen a professional ballet performance?"

"No."

"Then give it a try. You can't study all the time. It's not healthy. I'll call your mother and tell on you."

"Okay, okay, you win. But I'm not cooking dinner every night. You know I have some late classes."

Greg pushed himself up from the couch. "You always find a way to wiggle out. So who's the letter from?"

Luba studied her cousin standing squarely in front of her, hands on his hips. She didn't think of Greg as male any more, or as any sex at all. They shopped together, and he helped her pick out her clothes—she trusted his fashion taste as much if not more than her own. It helped that he was more sophisticated and hung out with style mavens, and had some money. Since she'd been sharing the house with him for five months, they had become very close and squabbled daily, but only in a lighthearted, sibling sort of way. Greg was like an older sister. He didn't hold back on offering his opinions and advice, but it was rarely offensive. Nothing like her mother's interference. Greg knew how to nudge Luba and challenge her without pissing her off. And he was never angry with her, or disappointed. All in all, he was pretty easy to live with.

"Come on, cuz, guess who it's from," she said.

"Okay. Your dear mother, my Aunt Volya."

"Nope."

"Our saintly Aunt Veronica."

"Nope."

"Cousin Zachary?"

"Double nope!"

"Tricky Nicky."

"Nope."

"An old boyfriend."

"No, but you're getting warmer."

"Okay, I give up. Who?"

"It's from Leo."

"Ah, Leonida, how is she? How come she never writes to me? She's hurting my feelings," he said, pouting. "So what does she write?"

Greg spoke with levity now, but for a good while Luba fretted that he and Leo would never regain their close friendship. Upon returning to Toronto for summer school, Luba's fear was realized. Greg reacted just as Leo had predicted when she explained what had happened between herself and Luba. Even after Leo assured him that henceforth her relationship with his little cousin would be strictly sisterly, the tension in the house had been unbearable when Luba first arrived. Greg became a suspicious papa bear, lurking and listening, ready to strike down the lustful stalker sniffing around his girl-cub. Luba acknowledged that Leo's decision was reasonable. After all, their liaison was an experiment, a test for Luba, not just any two attracted people beginning a relationship. And though she was somewhat relieved, she also felt keenly disappointed, as if Leo had chosen Greg over her. Which, in fact, she had. And for a while Luba resented Greg for making Leo choose. But Luba was the interloper, after all, and the last thing she wanted was war between two people she adored.

"Well, first, she asked about you, of course—out of politeness, I expect. No, really she wanted to know if you took up Gamble's job offer, so you'd better write her about that. I know you'll enjoy embellishing all the sordid office politics. She'll get a kick out of it. And she was wondering how I've been managing, how school is going, stuff like that. She told me about one of her friends here who just broke up with her girlfriend, wondered if I'd like to meet her. You don't suppose she's trying to set me up?"

"Oh," Greg started, a serious, almost anxious look on his handsome face. "She probably feels a bit guilty and would like to see you make new friends."

"She has nothing to feel guilty about. She was ready to move on when she saw that job posting—it was perfect for her. Anyway, it's old news, Greg, we all know she wasn't ready for a relationship back then. She was still getting over her old flame, even if she wouldn't admit it. And my heart was not broken because I wasn't ready either. I'm still not ready. Besides, I don't have time to be making all sorts of new friends." In truth, Luba was crushed when Leo decided to move away, hating to lose her so soon, and feeling dreadfully guilty that she was the reason Leo wanted to leave. Luba realized then that she still held a hope of eventually rekindling their intimacy, a desire that was apparently not shared by Leo. And that also smarted.

Greg sat back down on the couch. "Have you kept up with any of your old friends?" he asked.

"You know I haven't."

"Okay, you don't need to get your back up. I just don't see you spending much time with anyone, not even at Ryerson. We all need friends, Luba."

"Give me time. I want to finish this program, not screw up like I did before. I don't have time to socialize when I have all these projects to do, papers to write." Luba suddenly pictured herself sprawled on a floor, the hazy room spinning around her, a dull pounding of music in her ears. The end of another drunken soar and dive party with people who had lost their bearings. She had chosen to be with them, those losers, to help her fail. In her previous life.

"But you never go out, Luba. Once in a while wouldn't hurt. You know you're always welcome to join me and my friends—"

"Yeah, I know, even if they find me odd, which they do. Look, I'm fine. Don't worry about me. I'm not one of your cases."

"I know, Luba, that's not what I meant." He furrowed his brow. "Okay, so who's doing dinner tonight?"

"Your turn. I did the burgers last night. Jeez, you older people forget things so fast, it's scary."

Greg stood up and headed for the kitchen, holding his head. "Oy! Trying to fill your mother's shoes is giving me a headache and destroying the few brain cells I have left."

Luba picked up the letter again and reread the last paragraph, the news she didn't share with Greg. She simply could not trust her reaction if she spoke the words out loud. Leo wrote that she had found someone shortly after her arrival in Vancouver, but she didn't want to say anything at the time. She assumed this would be another casual affair, that she was lonely and looking only for companionship. Now, she announced with some trepidation, she believed she had found her soul mate. A woman slightly less damaged than she was, who shared Leo's values, who understood the risks and joys of commitment and was ready to take them on. She was Asian, thirty-four years old, and she managed a travel agency on the same street as Leo's firm. They met at the counter of a neighbourhood Starbucks over a discussion of the best scones. Her name was Leia. Leo and Leia—isn't that a hoot, she wrote, obviously delighted.

Luba swallowed, and her hand trembled. Leo had moved on and Luba was happy for her friend. But Leo was the first person she had connected to so deeply, so completely with heart and body. Luba didn't feel she had the energy, nor did she trust herself to make new friends yet. Anyway, she didn't know who she was any more; she needed to sort that out first. Man or woman, who did she want to be with? Maybe both. Maybe she just wanted to be left alone—no relationships, no complications. Yeah, that was it. She just wanted to live a simple life—that was all. Just a simple, uncomplicated life.

Where did Greg find that black wool cape with the royal purple lining? He seemed to enjoy swirling it around as he made sharp turns through the crowd. Luba didn't recognize anyone in the mass of people at the O'Keefe Centre, so it didn't matter who saw them together. Oh well, she thought, it was only a ballet, and there were a few other flamboyant dressers at the theatre that night. The arts community could be so colourful, or so black, which was her choice for the evening.

"Look, Luba. I'll bet these three, no, four dancers are Ukrainian. See?" He pointed to names on the program after they had settled into their seats. An excellent view of the stage, close and smack in the centre. Luba peered over at the names.

"Chestna, Valiuk, Lazorovich, Voloshyn. They've got to be Ukrainian, Luba. Lots of Ukes in Winnipeg, so it shouldn't be surprising."

"Except they get their dancers from all across Canada, don't they? They should be proportionate to the percentage of Ukrainians in the Canadian population."

"Maybe Ukrainians are better dancers than the average Canadian. You were pretty nimble on your little feet when you were a tadpole."

"I don't think you can go by some simple folk dancing," she objected. "And tadpoles don't have feet."

Greg crossed his eyes at her. "Don't sell our folk dancing short. Most of my Anglo friends couldn't do it."

"They didn't get a chance to learn the *hupavka* at the tender age of two."

"I see you're in one of your curmudgeon moods tonight. Shush. The lights are dimming."

Over the next hour, Luba lost herself in the drama on stage, the whirling bodies, twisting, unwinding, floating. She marveled at the power and plasticity of the dancers, at their artistry in transporting her into their world. Her toes flexed and pointed, her feet arched as the dancers flowed across the stage. She thought with dismay at how weak and flaccid her own muscles had become, and recalled the posters she had seen on campus, advertising jazz dance classes. Perhaps that was what she needed. She'd been sitting still far too long.

Luba glanced at the program in Greg's lap—one more piece before intermission. It began with a darkened stage. A dancer leapt from the back right corner into the centre spotlight, and Luba's mouth fell open. Who was that woman? As if in a waking dream, Luba watched herself dancing on the stage. This dream version of herself was a tall, lithe goddess with wavy waist-length ebony hair. Luba blinked hard and continued to stare. When she turned to Greg, he wore the same expression he had all evening—a small, gentle smile, eyes half-closed and rapturous. Surely he must have seen the similarity. Luba followed her leaps and falls across the full stage. She was writhing on the ground. A male dancer grabbed her arm and jerked her up, then across his back. He was spinning impossibly fast. Watch out, you'll drop her. Don't drop her!

It was over. The curtain dropped, the lights went on too fast.

"Greg!" She clamped onto her cousin's arm, her eyes squinting and watering in the harsh brightness. "Show me that program."

"Here you are. Wasn't that wonderful? What gorgeous bodies. But the women are a bit too thin, don't you think?"

"I knew it. I knew it." She stabbed her finger at the program. "Look. Ena Lazorovich. I bet that's her. The dancer in the last piece, that's got to be her."

"What are you talking about, Luba? Who is her?"

"Didn't you notice the resemblance between us? Between me and her, I mean? And her name—it's got to be her!"

"Luba, you aren't making any sense. Who are you talking about?"

Luba took a deep breath and tried to speak slowly. "The dancer in the last piece. The woman with the long, black hair. The main dancer. Didn't she look a little like me?"

"Oh, her. I suppose so. Not striking, though. Maybe a little. Same nose?"

"Yes, and same hair, except hers is blacker. And her name. I'll bet it's Ena Lazorovich. My grandfather's last name was Lazorovich. The Gypsy, you remember. He had a son named Nestor. Anyway, even if this Ena isn't from the same family, she may be related to the same Lazoroviches. I'll bet you. I'll bet you a month of dinners."

Greg studied Luba for a few seconds. "You seem awfully sure of yourself. How about a week of dinners?"

"Okay, a week. Shake?" They shook hands, then stood up to stretch their legs. Most of the theatre had emptied for the intermission. Luba found it hard to stay still; she felt herself vibrating with impatience. Greg shook his head at her.

"I'm not sure I want to be seen with you in this state. I think you've flipped. I know Baba's story seemed credible at the time, but she may not have got all the details straight. You really believe this Gypsy grandfather might be connected to this ballerina?"

"I know it, I can feel it," she stated flatly and hopped up and down like a besotted fan about to meet a rock star hero. "We'll go backstage after the performance and introduce ourselves. I'll bet anything that dancer is Ena."

"Mm-hmm, sure."

For Luba, the last half of the performance seemed to drag on forever. Ena came back in two of the dances in minor roles. At first Luba hardly recognized her—her hair was up and twisted into a top knot. Maybe she didn't look that much like Luba after all. Maybe she was getting carried away because she wanted to believe this woman was related to her, wanted to make Baba's story come true. But she was determined to pursue this, no matter what she learned.

As the curtain dropped for the final time, Luba shot up out of her chair. Why couldn't those people move any faster? Luba grabbed Greg's arm and pointed to a door at the right end of the stage.

"What are you doing?" he asked.

"We're going backstage to find out about Ena," she said, tugging at him.

"You are serious about this, aren't you?"

"If you don't want to come along, that's fine. I have to find out. Coming or not?"

"Okay, okay. But you're acting like a fanatic. They won't let you see anyone back there in your state."

Luba gave him an exasperated look, but he remained perfectly calm. She was reaching for the doorknob when she heard a cough behind her and a sharp, "Excuse me, miss!" A frosty-haired gentleman in a dark suit suddenly inserted himself between Luba and the door.

"Can I help you?"

"Uh, yes. We'd like to speak to Ena Lazorovich, if we can."

"And you are?" he asked bowing slightly.

"Friends of hers. Old, old friends. From Edmonton," she added and winced, wondering if that detail was such a good idea.

"I'll see if she is available. Please wait here." He disappeared backstage, shutting the door behind him.

They waited, not saying anything, but Greg had raised his eyebrows and gave Luba a questioning look when she'd lied to the usher. She had surprised herself at how easily and quickly those words had been spoken, but thought it more likely Ena would see them if she was from the Edmonton Lazorovich family. Of course, if Lazlo had settled in Canada, it could have been anywhere, even Toronto.

The door finally opened and the older gentleman stepped out, followed by the black-haired beauty. She was not as tall as Luba had expected, though taller than Luba by an inch or so.

"Here they are," he said, bowing, and returned backstage, much to Luba's relief.

Ena tilted her head and regarded them with curiosity.

"I'm sorry, I don't remember your names," she said tactfully. Her voice was as silken as her hair, now flowing loosely around her thin shoulders. For a moment Luba was mesmerized and tongue-tied, until she realized they were standing in the shadows. She stepped out into the dimmed lights of the great hall and offered her hand to the dancer who took it and gave it a firm squeeze.

"My name is Luba Kassim. This is my cousin Greg Sawchuk. We loved your performance, by the way. I just wondered, if you didn't mind my asking, if— well, if you were related to a man named Lazlo Lazorovich?" At the mention of his name, Ena drew back slightly and let go of Luba's hand.

"That's my grandfather's name," she said quietly.

Luba took another deep breath. "And your father?" She felt her throat go dry. "Was his name Nestor?"

Ena clasped both of her hands to her chin. "Yes," she whispered. Then louder, "Did you know them?"

Luba shook her head, unable to speak. It was true after all, her grandmother's story had to be true.

"Ena," Greg's level voice broke in. "Would you have time to join us for a coffee? Or a drink?"

Ena continued to stare at Luba. Then she lifted her head and said in a cool voice, "Sure, I'd like that. Maybe a drink. A tall, strong one. There's a nice lounge just around the corner."

"Yes, I know the place. You'll probably need a coat. It's a chilly November night." Greg put his arm around Luba's trembling shoulders.

"I'll be right back," she said, and disappeared to fetch her wrap.

They settled around a low, polished table in the back of a quiet bar. The soft notes of a piano could just be heard over the murmur of conversations. Luba noticed that several others from the ballet troupe had discovered the same place. Without their make-up and transforming costumes, down off the stage and out of the lights, the elite dancers blended in with everyone else. Almost blended in, Luba thought, as she watched one of them glide from her table to another group. Like an alien being, she appeared to be walking on an invisible cushion, every movement fluid, seamless.

The three of them said very little on their way over, except for the usual comparisons between Toronto and Winnipeg weather. Once they had ordered, Luba waited nervously for her drink. Ena sat rigidly in an overstuffed arm-chair, the fur-trimmed wool cloak draped over her shoulders. Luba sensed her shivering underneath the garment, and her own hands shook so badly she kept them clasped in her lap. Greg, on the other hand, was his invariably calm, social self, pumping Ena with questions about the ballet company and her life as a performer.

"The winter weather rarely bothers me. We're practising or performing or travelling so many days of the year, we don't get to be outside much. But I do find Toronto so damp!"

"Maybe you should have ordered a Spanish coffee, or rum toddy," Greg suggested, and popped a few peanuts into his mouth.

"No, I don't drink anything with caffeine. I'm a natural night owl anyway, and when I get into bed I have to sleep soundly or it will affect my perfor-mance the next day. Good, here are the drinks." The waiter handed her the double scotch, which she started to drink immediately.

Luba took a long sip from her Southern Comfort. Her throat was parched, her lips were dry, and the liquor burned as it slipped down. She reached into her purse for a Chapstick and smeared the fragrant wax over her lips.

"I go through dozens of those every winter," Ena said, pointing at the stick as Luba tucked it back into her purse.

Luba found her voice again. "You're right, Toronto is quite humid, summer and winter. I hear Edmonton is supposed to be dry."

"Oh? I thought you were from Edmonton." She looked at them with a question in her dark eyes.

Luba gulped her second long sip. "My grandmother said she thought there were dancing Lazoroviches in or near Edmonton. She's the one who told us about your grandfather. And father."

Ena leaned forward slightly and set her glass down on the table. "Yes, I'd like to hear how and what you know about my grandfather and father." With her eyes riveted upon Luba, Ena's face showed no emotion, and Luba had no idea what she was thinking.

She gave Greg a quick glance. He seemed to be enjoying himself immensely. His eyebrows shot up momentarily then he flashed his cousin a warm, encouraging smile.

"I'm not sure where to start," she began. Luba decided to tell Ena the story her Baba had told them. From the way Ena had looked at her, had recognized her, Luba was sure she would accept the story as fact. Perhaps she already knew the story, or a version of it.

By the time she had finished, Ena and Luba were well into their second drink. Greg had switched to coffee, settled back in his chair, and remained silent.

Ena was also quiet for a long, reflective moment. Then her body seemed to relax. She threw open her wool cocoon and rested her head on the back of her chair. "Well," she finally breathed out. "I guess we're cousins then. I didn't think I had any cousins on my father's side. He was an only child, or so I thought."

"So, you do believe my Baba's story?" Luba was amazed that Ena had accepted it without a challenge.

"Luba, look at us. You recognized me as soon as you saw me on stage. Greg, you look at us. Don't you see a resemblance?" Ena leaned over and put her face close to Luba's.

Greg regarded the two faces. "Oh, I suppose. Especially if I don't have to compare the bodies. Yes, you two could be sisters. You're a lot alike," he laughed. "Did you know that Luba used to be a pretty good dancer until she decided to be a scientist and now an interior designer. It must be in the genes."

Luba leaned over to slap his wrist, but Greg lurched away, nearly spilling his coffee.

"Cousin abuse," he accused. "Watch out, Ena. She's a tiger under that sweet exterior. Luba is very hard on cousins."

Ena laughed. "That's okay, I'm no pussycat. Ask my brothers, or my co-workers."

Luba wanted to know everything about Ena. Her family, where she grew up, what her life was like, what it was like now. But first, she wanted to know what happened to Lazlo and Nestor.

Ena looked down into her drink and swirled it slowly. "I don't know what happened to my grandfather. My father was raised by a Ukrainian family near Lviv. I guess they adopted him when he was about five years old. They found him at the edge of an orchard, crying. Not far away were the remains of a burned wagon. There were some clothes in a basket, and some smithy tools. That's how they learned his name, and his father's name. Lazlo Lazorovich was engraved on the tools. The farm family was kind, generous, and fairly well off for those times, and they tried to find his parents. But no one had seen any Gypsies in that area, so they finally gave up. They raised my father, Nestor, and gave him their family name, Dubovich. They didn't tell him until after the war that he had been born with a different name, that he was probably the son of a Gypsy.

"He said he knew all along that he didn't quite fit in. So, in 1946, when he was twenty-one, he emigrated to Canada. He changed his name back to Lazorovich, then settled in the area that became Vegreville, married a Ukrainian girl, my mother, who was already a third-generation Ukrainian."

"And you and your brothers were folk-dancers in Edmonton?" Luba suggested.

"Yes, we were. How did you know?"

"Baba told us there was a family of Lazoroviches in Vegreville, that some of the children danced. I'll bet she kept track of you. Maybe she even knew about your father, but was afraid to make contact. She felt so guilty about what happened, like she was responsible for Lazlo leaving the village and maybe being killed by Nazis."

"I don't know if he was killed by the Nazis, or what happened to him. My dad tried to find out, but by the time he started looking for clues, the records of the area had been removed or destroyed by the Russians first, then more by the Nazis later. He was pretty frustrated. He also started feeling guilty toward the end of his life that he had left behind his adoptive family. After all, they had saved him from probable death or destitution, had raised him like a son. So many Gypsies had been exterminated by the Nazis. It was so sad..." Ena's voice trailed off and she lowered her head. Luba looked to Greg for help. He reached into his pocket and offered a tissue to Ena.

Ena blew her nose. "My dad wrote to Ukraine to see if he could find his Lviv family, see how they were doing. That was a year ago. He died three months ago, a week before the letter came back. So he never knew. They were so happy to hear from him. They are still there, doing okay, I guess. As well as they can do, anyhow. I'm going to try to visit them someday. So that's my story." She looked up again, and smiled sadly.

Luba leaned over to touch her arm. "Ena, I am so sorry. I've been finding and losing family members for the last six months." She felt dangerously close to spilling over herself. Ena gripped her hand.

"So today you found a new cousin. And I found a new cousin! Are there any more?" she asked eagerly.

"No, I'm an only child. But I hope I can meet your brothers sometime. And I'm happy to share Greg over there with you." She nodded at her cousin yawning in his chair. He came to attention and tried to poke her.

"He's not much of a dancer, but his beef stroganoff is excellent. Do you have time for a visit while you're in town?"

Ena shook her head. "No, unfortunately, and I can't eat rich stuff like that until I retire. But I'll let you know as soon as I do."

"The way you dance, I hope it won't be for a long time." Luba smiled at her, feeling proud and in awe of this accomplished stranger—her cousin, a dancer with the Royal Winnipeg Ballet. Incredible.

So now she had living proof of Baba's crazy story. Lazlo and Nestor existed, and here was Nestor's daughter, sitting next to her. Her mother might deny that Lazlo was her father, and there was no way to prove that part of the story. But the remarkable resemblance between Luba and Ena was irrefutable. The great, divisive secret was out. Who's the tsiganka now, Mama? Ha!

Starting Over

"Mama, I'm going to send you a photo of a young woman Greg and I met here in Toronto. She's from Winnipeg, a beautiful ballet dancer. She used to live in Vegreville, near Edmonton—"

"I know where Vegreville is. What are you doing with a belly dancer? You are supposed to be studying."

"Not a belly dancer, a ballet dancer," Luba enunciated slowly, tapping her toe on the floor with impatience. "She's with the Royal Winnipeg Ballet Company. I want you to see the picture Greg took of the two of us together. We look a lot alike. I think she's my cousin—well, my half-cousin." There was a pause at the other end and Luba prepared herself for an explosion.

"What kind of crazy talk is this? You do not have any half-cousins. Why in the world would you say something like this? Why are you dreaming up relatives that do not exist? You are getting stranger and stranger all the time, Luba. What is wrong with you? I thought living with Greg would settle you down."

Luba waited patiently for her mother to finish the tirade. She had steeled herself for the accusations and abuse which now slid off her shoulders and formed a murky pool at her feet. Standing in the kitchen and leaning on the wall by the phone, Luba shifted back and forth from foot to foot. She considered the colours in that room, thinking back to her first impressions a few months ago. What was tasteful then now tired her eyes, and needed more life. Maybe she'd offer to repaint the cupboards next spring, perhaps a soft lemon to complement the olive appliances.

There was silence on the line, and she took a breath. "Listen, Mama, you may not be interested in this girl, but you should be. Her father was Nestor, a little boy that Baba used to babysit. And Nestor's father was Lazlo Lazorovich, a man who used to live in Baba's village, and who she told me was your father—"

"I told you not to talk about that. Your Baba is crazy, and now you are act-ing crazy. How can you believe in such nonsense?" she shouted.

Luba held the phone away from her ear, but her mother had paused so she jumped in again. "The reason I believe it, and Greg believes it, too, is because of this girl we just met. Ena Lazorovich. She has the same story as we have. Or at least parts of it. She is Lazlo's granddaughter, and I am Lazlo's grand-daughter, and we could be sisters, we look that much alike." Luba's voice had risen an octave, so she took another deep breath. She didn't want to be angry, but her mother knew just how to push those buttons. Volya did not respond, but she had not hung up the phone, either.

"That's why I want to send you this picture. So you can see for yourself."

"I do not want to see your photo, so do not bother sending it. This is all foolishness. Your Baba has told you a fairy tale, and you believe it."

"And Greg believes it. And everyone will believe it except you. Why is it so hard to accept that someone else besides Boryslav could be your father?" Now she was exasperated and angry for losing her temper.

"Stupid lies, that is what this is. No one will believe such an insane story. Do not call me again if you are going to talk crazy. I will not listen to this garbage!" The jarring click in her ear made Luba jump.

She listened to the dial tone for a moment before she hung up the phone, her eyes squeezed tight to keep the tears back. She picked up the photo of Ena and herself, taken just before her cousin climbed on the bus for Montreal, the site of their next engagement. They both wore silly grins, their foreheads nearly touching. There was no mistaking the resemblance, more in the photo than in real life, perhaps. Luba was certain her mother would be shocked if she would only look at it. Even Volya could not deny the similarities, but of course she would excuse it as coincidence. Luba knew in her bones that she and Ena were related. Closely related.

Luba whirled away from the phone and imagined herself wearing Ena's costumes. She pirouetted into the living room, still holding the photo in front of her. She landed breathless on the couch and plastered the photo to her chest. She would not let her mother diminish the excitement of finding an exotic new cousin. But if she wouldn't admit to this change in Luba's pedi-gree, how would she ever admit that Luba's father was someone other than the man her mother had claimed it was all these years?

That was it, the connection—their fathers. If her mother accepted that her own father could be someone else, she would open the door to Luba's discovery of a "new" father as well. Maybe she would send the photo to Aunt Veronica, who could then talk to her mother. Maybe get her to at least have a look. Luba shook her head. No, she didn't want to put her aunt in the middle of this mess. This was between her and Mama.

Luba wondered if this rendezvous was such a good idea. She had forgotten how busy and packed the stores could be just before Christmas. Luba was sure she'd recognize her in any crowd, but would Bella recognize Luba with her new haircut? She'd had five inches chopped off since they last saw each other in the spring. Otherwise, Luba didn't feel like she had changed all that much—at least not to look at.

There she was. Bella looked exactly the same, yet different. It was probably the elegant long wool coat, deep forest green, just as she had described it. Her hair was the way Luba remembered it, burnished gold spilling over her shoulders. Luba waved and caught her eye. She waved back and headed straight for Luba, beaming.

"Luba, it is so good to see you again." She pressed Luba's hands warmly in her own. "You look fabulous. I think Toronto agrees with you. How is school going?" They automatically sat at the table where Luba had been waiting.

"I'm doing pretty well. It's been hectic with exams and projects due, but exciting. I love the program. How about you? How's the new job?"

"Oh, it's great. Did you plan to have lunch or just coffee? I'm starving. They have terrific sandwiches here," she said, picking up a menu.

"That sounds good to me, too. Any recommendations?" Luba picked up a menu and noticed it was a long list.

"The pastrami on rye is a winner, the clubhouse is good. I think I'll have the French dip. I haven't had that in a while."

A waitress appeared just then, and Luba ordered the clubhouse sandwich and a coffee.

"So?" Bella began.

"So," she said. "First I want to thank you for meeting me like this. I didn't know who else to talk to. My cousin is great, but he's family, and, I don't know, we keep going over the same turf. Besides, you already know my history."

"It's no problem. I meant what I wrote in my note, to call me anytime. Anyway, I come into the city to shop every few weeks, and sometimes for a show. I'm just glad that you're feeling so well. It's a pleasure to meet you as a friend this time." Her smile was genuine.

Luba breathed out, realizing how tense she must have been, anticipating this meeting.

"I'm just dreading my trip back to Copper Creek for Christmas. I feel like I'm being forced to go."

"Why is that?"

"Aunt Veronica told us that my mother has been really depressed this fall. I tried to find out if it had to do with the last phone call when I tried to tell her about my newly discovered cousin and she got really mad at me again. But my aunt's been vague about the whole thing. Now I'm starting to feel guilty, like I'm the cause of it all. But I don't know how to be any different."

"Why do you need to be different, Luba?"

"Because I make my mother unhappy being the way I am." As Luba said this, she realized how lame it sounded.

"Could you be happy living up to your mother's expectations?" Bella asked, sipping her coffee.

"I doubt it. Anyway, I don't want to. But I suppose that's being selfish."

"No, absolutely not. It's when you try to be something you're not that you get into trouble, emotionally, physically. It sounds like your mother is suffering, but I think she's the one who's trying to be someone she isn't. Didn't you say that she won't talk to you about your grandfather?"

"That's right. She refuses to believe my grandmother's story. The proof is pretty strong, but she won't even consider it. Actually, I think it's the truth about my real father that's eating her up. I've opened up a Pandora's box and ruined all the illusions she created for me."

"And for herself," Bella added. "Oh, great, here are the sandwiches."

Luba found herself smiling at Bella. Even though the counsellor had come out, she was getting a glimpse of the personal side that she hadn't known before. For the first time in a long while Luba realized that she was hungry for a friend, a confidante who wasn't a relative. She watched Bella dip the thick French bread and roast beef sandwich into a large cup of golden-coloured liquid. Somehow she managed to fit her mouth around the whole end. She looked up at Luba and lifted her eyebrows, pointing at Luba's equally huge club sandwich, neatly cut into quarters, adorned with slabs of pickles. Luba picked up one of the quarters, removed the long toothpick, and studied it.

"It's a work of art," Bella mumbled. "If I can do it, so can you," she challenged Luba, and dipped her sandwich again.

For a few minutes they bit, chewed, giggled. As Luba finished the third piece, she remembered why she had asked Bella to meet with her. "So how do I get my mother to open up, to tell me the truth? I've tried the direct approach. That didn't work."

"I don't know, Luba. You know your own mother best. What usually gets her talking?"

"She gets nostalgic sometimes and spontaneously starts telling me about the good old days. Other times I ask her about a particular time or person, and then the stories start coming. I guess I could ask her more questions about my dad—the one she says is my dad but who really isn't. Maybe I can trip her up."

"You don't think she'd be too smart for that?"

"Oh, probably. Maybe I could just ask her to fill in more details about what happened after she left Germany and before she came to Canada. She was in England several years before she came over. But if she won't tell me, she won't tell me." Luba threw up her hands.

Bella tilted her head and gave her a sympathetic look. "It's really important to you, isn't it?"

"Yeah, I guess. It's like I'm trying to do a painting of Luba Kassim. When I learned about my Gypsy grandfather, I found all this colour and texture I had suspected was there, but didn't know exactly where it fit in. But there's still a huge patch of the canvas that's blank, totally white. I'm trying to understand who I am. I need the rest of the information. And the only person who can help me complete this painting, this portrait, is my mother, and she won't co-operate. She won't tell me what the colours are."

"You probably won't like this suggestion, but have you tried putting yourself in her shoes? What if you had a secret for twenty-some years, and your whole life was built on that secret? Wouldn't you be terrified that everything you had built would come crashing down if that secret was revealed?"

"But she already knows that I'm suspicious, even if I haven't asked her point blank. I just want to find out who my real father was, what he was like."

"Perhaps he isn't a person she wants you to know. Maybe she's ashamed of him. Are you willing to tell your mother things you might be ashamed of?"

"I don't have anything like that to tell her," Luba protested.

"You don't?" she asked gently.

Did she? What about Leo? She could never tell her mother about her, about what they had done together. Or what she had gone through before she tried to kill herself.

"You think I need to tell her my darkest secrets so she'll tell me hers?"

"Not necessarily. But maybe there are things you could offer to explain about yourself that will allow her to trust you more. It does work both ways, although children seldom think it does. She needs to know you won't judge her harshly for what she has done. Maybe, by showing her some of your vulnerability, she'll feel she can show you hers."

"I'll think about that, but I don't know. I definitely won't tell her about my lesbian experience." She glanced up at Bella to see how she would react to this statement. She hadn't spoken to her since she first had those feelings about Leo. She was not sure why she told her now, but Luba trusted Bella not to disapprove or think less of her. Bella was right about the trust, it did loosen tongues.

Bella didn't say anything for a moment. She took another sip of coffee and made a face.

"Cold?" Luba asked.

She nodded, then put both hands on the table. Her nails were so perfectly manicured, Luba wondered if they were real. She admired the opalescent nail polish and thought she should get some to cover her own stubby nails, which she kept hidden in her lap.

"I never told you what happened in Copper Creek, why I left."

Luba shook her head. She just knew something unusual must have happened.

"You see, Luba, I'm a lesbian."

Luba stifled a gasp. This was not what she had expected.

"One of my co-workers found out. A real homophobe. Word got out quickly, and I became a pariah at the office. Only one of the other counsellors was sympathetic and the rest hardly ever talked to me. It was a miserable place to work after that. Then I started hearing rumours that they were trying to figure out how to can me. They felt I would be a bad influence on the impressionable teenagers I counselled. I knew that as soon as any parents heard these rumours there would be pressure to get rid of me. I had only good evaluations, but that didn't matter, so I started looking for a new job. I found one down here and put in my resignation. And here I am," she said cheerfully. She looked away and motioned to their waitress. "Excuse me. Could we have refills?"

Luba found her voice. "Wow, I had no idea. So that won't be a problem here? I mean, if they find out."

"Not so far. The crew I work with is much more open-minded. It's also a private practice, unlike the provincial clinic in Copper Creek. So far, so good. I like the people I work with, I like the area, I like most of my clients."

The waitress topped up their coffee cups, and Luba poured a packet of sugar into hers and started stirring.

"If you stir much longer it'll get cold. I'm sorry if I've made you uncomfortable, Luba."

"Oh, no. I guess I'm just surprised. I had no idea. Wow. I don't know what to say," she sputtered.

"It's okay. You've got a lot to deal with right now. A lot of new emotions, new relatives, old relatives. And you're pleased with your school program?"

"Yeah, I love it. One of the best decisions I've made so far, it's such a good fit for me. Then moving in with my cousin, Greg, the nearly perfect housemate. He helps ground me when I need it, and gives me space when I need to be alone. Most of the time. I mean, he is a relative and can be a bit overprotective. Yeah, I do have a lot to think about, but I'm so impatient—I want to finish that painting."

"A little advice, Luba—take your time. Some people don't figure things out until they're in their fifties and sixties. We're always learning about ourselves and others. It's a lifelong project for most of us, so try to enjoy where you are, moment by moment, as much as you can. Let's face it, you've packed in a lot of life experiences into the last year. You might try to practise some positive thinking while you're heading back up north—buoy yourself up for the dreaded visit." Her smile was infectious and Luba grinned back at her.

"Okay, counsellor, let's do some math," she said, holding up her fingers and exposing the chewed nails. "This year I got rid of a demoralizing boyfriend, I dropped out of a program I never wanted to be in, I got to really know and appreciate my grandmother and a neat cousin, and the sweetest uncle ever. Then I discovered that my real grandfather was a wonderful, artistic man, not that alcoholic brute, and I found a fascinating, brand-new cousin. What else? I learned a little more about my feelings and that I may not be straight, and I chose to start a new career. And now I have a great new friend who actually understands me, and sees me." She looked at Bella shyly and hoped she was not being too bold.

Bella reached across the table and held both of Luba's hands in her warm ones. Luba felt her hands trembling, and realized that her fingers were ice cold.

"Yes, you have a friend in me, Luba. Please call me anytime. I mean that." She let Luba's hands slip out of hers and they both reached for their coffee cups.

"I won't be bugging you so much for advice, I promise. I'll get this thing with my mother settled one way or another over Christmas. And I'll think about what you said. Maybe next time we can talk about your mother."

"Only if we can do something fun at the same time. My family history is boring compared to yours, Luba. What kind of music do you like?"

"Mostly rock, sometimes classical. David Bowie is coming in February, but Greg will be out of town then."

"David Bowie? I didn't know he was coming to Toronto. I'd love to see him."

"We can check at the box office right now if you'd like. But if it's sold out, we can see what else is coming up." Luba stood up and started to pull on her coat. The waitress appeared on cue and left a bill. Bella snatched it up.

"My treat. Merry Christmas, Luba, don't argue. C'mon, let's see what's happening at the box office."

"Luba, you're finally home. Thank God." Greg rushed at Luba as she walked in the door. She was nearly blinded by the brightness in the front hall. He must have turned on every single light in the house. His eyes were wild, his hands flapping by his sides.

"What's going on? Were we robbed or something?" She dropped her backpack on a chair just inside the kitchen.

"No, nothing like that. Aunt Veronica called, your mother's in the hospital. She had surgery today—a hysterectomy!"

Luba was not sure how to respond to this news. She had never considered hysterectomies as life-threatening—just something that a lot of older women had when they went through the "change of life."

"Is she okay?"

"I guess so. She had the surgery this morning. Aunt Veronica tried to reach us earlier, but didn't get through until I came home at six. I didn't know where to find you."

"I was finishing a paper at the library. I told you I'd be late." She looked at her watch. It was eleven-thirty. Luba walked to the fridge and pulled out the juice jug.

"You seem awfully calm. Aren't you the least bit worried about her?" Greg stood at the entry to the kitchen. His hands were on his hips and his legs spread, just like her mother during an inquisition. Luba took a gulp of juice, trying not to smile at him.

"What's to worry about? You just said she was okay." She took another sip.

Greg shook his head. "Your mother just had emergency surgery, and you're drinking juice like nothing special has happened. You are amazing. Don't you care about her, even a little?"

"Yeah, I care, but what can I do? She's already had the surgery. She's recovering, right? I didn't know it was an emergency. So what happened, did Auntie say?" Luba sat at the table, exhausted from a gruelling long day. Her hand quivered as she raised the glass to her lips.

Greg sat down across from her and put his hands on the table. "Apparently she'd been seeing a gynecologist for a while now. About hemorrhaging. Didn't she tell you?"

"No. She doesn't like to discuss women's problems with me. She's private about those things, especially anything to do with reproductive organs. Remember I told you how she accused me once of reading the medical book she had stashed in the back of her closet, just because I figured out how babies came out? I was ten years old, or eleven, at the time. She's always been over-protective and secretive about anything to do with sex and reproduction. So, no, she never mentioned she was having those kinds of problems. But I figured she's been going through menopause. She's been more moody than usual, if that's possible. Aunt Veronica told you all this?"

Luba was surprised her aunt would discuss such matters with Greg, but then, he was so easy to talk to. She remembered her mother chatting with Aunt Veronica and Christina just after Orest's funeral. When she first overheard snatches of the conversation, she thought they were discussing the best way to prepare and cook a pork roast, and was taken aback when she realized they were discussing the status of their uteri. All the while they nibbled dainty sandwiches and sipped tea.

Greg strummed his fingers on the table. "Yeah, we had a good long chat. I think Aunt Veronica needed to talk. She said your mother has been more depressed and irritable this year. We figured it was because of, well, Orest, and you. Your mother has been worried about you."

"But she shouldn't be now. I'm in good hands, aren't I? I'm at school. Why should she be worried about me now?"

"I don't know. Maybe she's worried because she thinks you'll end up an unemployed, starving artist. She used to boast about your high grades, how she figured you'd be a doctor someday and take care of her in her dotage."

"So you don't think she's happy with my change in career plans?" She gave Greg a wry smile. They both knew the answer to this.

"I can't figure your mother out. And sometimes I can't figure you out."

"So what do you think I should do, oh Wise One?"

"Now, you're not being sarcastic, are you, little cousin?"

"I'm not. I'm seeking your advice. I've got bus tickets for the day after tomorrow. You think I should leave immediately? You know how long it takes to get up there. And so close to Christmas, I don't know if I could get an earlier ticket."

Greg jumped up and opened the cupboard under the phone, removing the Toronto Yellow Pages book.

"What are you doing?"

"I'm going to find out if you can get up to Copper Creek tomorrow." He flipped pages and reached for the phone on the wall.

"Wait a minute. I have a paper due tomorrow. I haven't finished my Christmas shopping."

"So shop in Copper Creek."

Luba groaned at the thought.

"I'll hand in your paper. It's finished, isn't it?"

"Yeah, but I still have to type the cover page—"

"Get cracking then. Oh, hello. Yes, I wondered if there were any seats available on the bus to North Bay tomorrow, connecting to Copper Creek? Sure, I'll wait." He looked down at Luba with her mouth gaping, and waved his hand to shoo her away.

"Hello? Yes? You do? That's great. Can I trade in a ticket for Thursday? Oh, perfect!"

Luba heaved up her pack and left the kitchen. Greg was so efficient. If she ever had a secretary, she wanted her or him to be just like her cousin. Luba rubbed her eyes and headed for the typewriter. A fine way to wrap up her first term at Ryerson. On the bright side, there was one less day to anticipate the dreaded bus ride to hell.

Out of the Well

Luba could not sleep. She'd had one too many cups of coffee that day, trying to finish her final paper. She could hear the soft rumbles of Greg's snores one room over. Oh, for God's sake, she thought, why was she so restless? Sure, she had to get up early to catch the bus, and the news about her mother didn't help. She was probably okay. Aunt Veronica would have let them know if her mother was in any danger—wouldn't she? Like maybe she wasn't recovering well, or they discovered something else during the surgery... like cancer. Shit. That was her mother's job, to worry incessantly, not hers.

She wondered if she should get up and have a drink to take the edge off. So tempting. But she knew it wouldn't really help; it usually made her more restless at night. Luba opened her eyes wide and stared at the ceiling of her dark room. At this very moment, her mother was lying in a narrow bed in a sterile room where it never got dark at night. Alone, or maybe she shared a room. The constant noises in the hallway, other people moaning, snoring nearby. Luba could almost smell the disinfectant; she was back in that room. Was it only eight months ago? It seemed as if a lifetime had passed, as if it had happened to someone else, someone she used to know. How did she get there, anyway? She closed her eyes.

It had started with the note from Tom. No, it had started long before the note, but that was the day her life finally cracked open and everything rotten inside spilled out. She remembered the fury she felt. She had started drinking. First the rum with Coke, which probably got her even more agitated. There wasn't much in that bottle, so she switched to rye even though there wasn't anything left to mix it with. Lots of ice, then no ice at all. Then the vodka. No, wait, she took a break, a rampage through her apartment. Everything Tom had to go: photos ripped up, into the trash; his albums snapped into pieces, into the trash; a toothbrush, a razor, trash; his shirts. What did she do with his shirts? No room in the trash bin by then. She vaguely recollected throwing something out a window. She was wasted by then, before she even got into the vodka.

She remembered the music that night; she played her favourite sad records. Thelma Houston's "Don't Leave Me This Way," the Bee Gees' "Stayin' Alive," and the Harbour Rocks' only recording, "You're Killing Me Baby":

Don't do this to me
You're killin' me baby
Just tryin' to make it
Hangin' on, hangin' on,
I'm gone.

Then she picked up Rod Stewart's "Tonight's the Night," their song. Like hell. That one she smashed and stomped into the carpet.

She remembered the phone call, parts of it. She dialled a couple of numbers before she found him. He was at Pete's, of course. She cursed him, called him a coward, a dip-shit, a dickhead, a lot of things she couldn't remember now. But she did remember his last words, and her own.

"You know what Luba? You're shit-faced drunk. Wanna talk to Orest? He's right here," Tom said.

"No. Fuck the lot of you, dope-heads! You're going to pay for this, asshole!" And she hurled the phone onto the floor.

She remembered hugging the rim of the toilet. At least she didn't throw up in the sink like the last time she binged. She'd never been so low, so miserable. She was supposed to be a bright star, and now she was nothing, a black hole, her life was worthless, everything down the toilet. She couldn't face them, her family, her mother. The shame. She thought about taking the pills. She thought about it; she didn't remember doing it.

Her next recollection was the sound of mourning doves cooing. "Loo-bah, Loo-bah, Loo-bah."

No, not doves. She recalled thinking someone was calling her outside to play, but her mother wouldn't let her. Evil Volya made her iron all the sheets and towels and do her homework before she could go out. But she would never finish in time, it was already dark outside and Mama sent her to bed. Still in a stupor, she drifted off to sleep again. When she was truly aware of her surroundings, she realized she was in the hospital.

But there was something else. Something she just remembered now, lying in her own darkened room, sweating under her heavy bed covers. She threw them off, felt her heart racing, her face flushing. That nurse, the one who was always smiling and had a velvety voice. In between interrogations by the psychiatrist and other doctors, Luba had spoken to her. She asked the nurse if she knew who had found her the night she was admitted. The nurse said she'd try to find out; she tracked down the paramedics who rode in the ambulance with Luba.

"I'm sorry, dear," she said. "All they know is that it was a young man who called for the ambulance. He didn't give his name. He just said he was a friend checking up on you."

"Did they say what he looked like?" Luba asked. She didn't really know the neighbours in her apartment; everyone minded their own business and they weren't particularly friendly.

"Yes, they said he was medium height, very thin, pale, and had long dark hair. Tied in a pony tail, I think. Does that help, dear?"

At the time, Luba was so confused, she didn't remember what she replied. But the words now formed the picture she had not recognized in her disoriented state. Orest. It was Orest who had saved her. Holy shit. Poor Orest had found her like that. And a few weeks later he was gone, no one to care enough to save him in time.

Just tryin' to make it
Hangin' on, hangin' on,
I'm gone.
And then, finally, she cried for him.

Reunion

"Mama, why didn't you tell me you were having problems?"

"I did not want to interrupt your studies. You are always too busy to call me."

Before Luba could object, Volya waved at her tray.

"I am thirsty. Pass me the cup." Luba held the cup up to her mother's chin and manoeuvred the bent straw to her lips. Volya sipped twice then spit out the straw.

She grimaced. "So sour."

"It's grapefruit, it's usually sour. Want some apple juice instead?"

"No, I wanted grapefruit, but this is terrible. I think it must be spoiled. They are trying to poison me. Want to keep me longer, make more money, those greedy doctors."

This was the most her mother had spoken in the two hours Luba had been there.

"And you wanted me to be a doctor, just like those sharks?" Luba put the juice back on her tray by the bed.

Volya turned her head toward her daughter and gave her a look as acidic as the rejected juice. "No need to be sarcastic. I want you to do something worthwhile, something you can be proud of."

"Me? Don't you mean you?"

"I mean all of us, your family. You, me, your aunts, uncles, cousins."

"What about choosing a profession that suits me, that I can be happy with?"

"Happiness? Who is happy with their job? Every job has problems. I do not know anyone happy with their job. That is a fairy tale and you are dreaming again. You think being an artist will make you happy? Hah."

"Interior designer, Mama, not artist. I think Tato would have wanted me to choose something I liked to do, not just for the money."

Her mother slapped the bed beside her then winced.

"You okay, Mama?" It was obvious she was not. Her mother was pale and pumped full of painkillers. The nurse had told Luba that her mother had a nine-inch incision in her abdomen and that she would be groggy from medication. But now the grogginess had been replaced with the sharpness of a warrior prepared for last battle.

"Your father would have wanted you to make something of yourself, have a job that paid well so you could live comfortably," she said in a wheezy voice.

Luba didn't want to argue with her, especially now, but her mother kept pushing those damn buttons. A different buzzer went off in her brain. Aha, here was her chance to use that technique Bella had taught her. Luba closed her eyes, sucked in a deep breath, then exhaled it all. She could feel her mother's sharp glare piercing her eyelids. She took in another noisy breath.

"What are you doing?" she demanded.

"Breathing exercises," Luba said, breathing out again. "Something my therapist suggested for when I'm stressed."

"Why are you stressed? I am the one who is stressed around here."

"We are both stressed, Mama. Every time I try to talk to you, we end up arguing. That's stressful." Luba continued her breathing, but now she watched her mother's face closely.

"We are not arguing," Volya snapped.

"Then why are you yelling at me?"

"I am not yelling!"

Luba continued her deep, slow breaths.

"Stop that. You are being silly. What else do you talk to this therapist person about? I hope you do not say anything about our family." Her tone had mellowed a notch, but Luba could see she was still on edge. She had to remind herself that her mother was in pain. She would give her lots of rope.

"I don't have a therapist any more, Mama. But of course we talked about my family, and my history. I seem to remember you wanted me to tell the psychologist everything. How else was she going to help me?"

"So, how has she helped you? I see no improvement in your attitude."

"Well, I haven't tried to kill myself lately." A cloud fell over Mama's eyes, and Luba looked away. How stupid, Luba thought, why did she say that? Why did she let Mama get under her skin?

"You come all this way just to aggravate me, a sick woman? You may as well go back to Toronto. You do not want to be here, anyway," she said in a monotone, and continued to stare at the wall opposite Luba.

"Mama, I'm sorry, but I'm not going anywhere for a while. I came to see you." Silence. "So what do you want me to say? That I've decided to go back to a pre-med program so my mother can be proud of me? Even though I really don't like medical sciences, and I've never even wanted to be a nurse? It's taken me a long time to figure out what I want to do with my life. Sure I want to earn a decent living. I want to be able to support myself, and, eventually, I'll take care of you if you need the help."

"Hmph." She continued to look away.

"And while I've been learning more about myself, I realized that I don't know you as well as I should. And I know very little about Tato. I mean, if you were able to go to school like me, what would you have studied? And Tato, if he didn't get stuck in the Navy, what kind of job would he have liked?"

Luba stopped to let her questions soak in, in case her mother was listening. Slowly, Volya turned her head up to stare at the ceiling. Luba noticed that the dark circles under her eyes were more pronounced than usual, that the creases at the corners of her eyes were deeper and more numerous than ever. She saw Baba's face. But the nose—it was Ena's nose, Luba's nose. She took in another deep breath, then released it.

When Volya spoke, her voice was resigned, tired. "We never had a chance. Not like you and your cousins. After the war I went to England where I had a factory job in a cotton mill. I dreamt of creating beautiful clothes for ladies, for the English and the Americans. A fashion designer, I suppose, that was my dream. But the reality was so different, so cruel. Anyway, I do not want to talk about it now. I want to sleep." She turned her head away from Luba again, eyes closed. Session over.

She was running down dark alleys in a town that was familiar, but nameless. She was searching for a place to hide. She clutched a small bundle of towels to her chest. It was warm. A mewing noise spilled out from the bundle, then a small fist popped through. She tucked it back inside and it began to whimper. Where could she hide? She was so cold, she had to find a place soon.

Then she was sitting at a picnic table next to a beach where brilliant green lush grass and willows extended to the very edge of the water. Again, she could not quite place the lake that the table overlooked. There were huge piles of hot steaming food in front of her, and crowds of people on either side and behind her, pressing on her. She wanted to leave, felt the urge to stand up and start searching again. She had lost something. Her baby, where was her baby? She began to shout, but no one paid any attention to her. My God, did they not realize she had misplaced the baby? She had to run to the water, the baby was in the water, she was sure of it. But she could not move!

Luba's eyes popped open and she scanned the room in a panic. Her throat was parched and sore. Where was she? It was deathly quiet in that grey room. Her mother's house, her old bedroom. She dragged her prickly, cramped arm from under the covers. Nine forty-five. No one to wake her. She was alone in the house, now too big for her, including the small bedroom she slept in. Her mother would be in the hospital for another three days, and she was not looking forward to this next visit. Putting up with hours of verbal abuse from a drugged-up, whiny old sourpuss seemed more than any daughter should have to deal with.

Luba groaned and pushed herself up and out of bed. This place was too grim to stay in for long. The shower was not hot enough, as usual. As the water penetrated to her sleepy scalp, she gasped, remembering the lost baby at a picnic. Dreams were such bizarre phenomena. Little tidbits of reality tossed together like a handful of dice, then allowed to reassemble at random. The park with the lake reminded her of that walk she'd taken with Leo in early summer. And the feast on the table? Greg was forever talking about cooking, reading gourmet magazines, trying new recipes. Their families were obsessed with food, making it, serving it, pushing it on anyone they could drag to the table. But why in the world had she dreamt of a baby? She was never pregnant, though for a short, agonizing while she thought she'd been. She remembered reading somewhere that women who'd had an abortion or miscarriage could suddenly get depressed about the time they were due to deliver their baby. Well, that was not her. Anyway, she had nothing to be depressed about, except maybe her mother. Damn, why did she have to go get sick and need a hysterectomy?

When Luba tiptoed into the hospital room, soft snores floated up from her mother's bed. Good. She decided to sit and read her *Redbook* magazine. As soon as she made the first crinkly noise flipping a page, the snores stopped. Her mother made an "ugh" sound and fluttered her eyelids. Luba waited quietly until her mother turned her head and glints showed between her lids.

"Hi, Mama. How are you feeling today?"

She sighed deeply, ran her tongue over her pale, cracked lips. Luba found a cup of water on the side table and offered it to her. She sipped, not meeting Luba's eyes, then turned to face Luba.

"I do not like this place," she croaked.

"Aren't they treating you well?"

"No, no, not that. I want to go home. I do not want to die here." She spoke slowly, with determination.

"Mama. You are not going to die. The doctor said this was routine surgery, and you should heal just fine."

"You stay here long enough, you catch some disease, you will die," she said, her speech a bit slurred as if she'd been drinking. "When Mrs. Krokuv came in for a gall bladder operation, she was fine for two days, then got pneumonia and was dead five days later. I need to get out of here. You tell them, I have to go."

Volya's eyes were open wide, desperate. She grabbed at Luba's hand resting at the edge of the bed, and squeezed with a ferocity that startled Luba. Her mother was seriously frightened. Perhaps the painkillers were making her more paranoid than usual.

"Look, Mama, you aren't going to die here. But if it makes you feel better, I'll talk to your doctor, and the nurses. You're only in your fifties. Mrs. Krokuv was a lot older."

"No," she protested. "Only sixty-two. She was well until she had the gall bladder problem. And they told her the operation was good, she would be all better soon. They tell everyone the same thing."

Before Luba could counter, she continued, "I was so afraid you might die when you were in the hospital in Toronto. I have never been so frightened in my entire life. And I lived through some terrible times, when I was sure I would not survive another day. You cannot imagine. You cannot imagine the horror of losing your only child."

"I dreamed I did," Luba blurted out, then looked down at the magazine in her lap.

"What are you talking about? What dream?"

"Oh, it was only a dream, nothing important."

"No, I want to hear about it. You keep so many things from me. You are my only child, and I never know what you are thinking. And I may not be around for that long," she added.

What was it that Bella had told Luba? Share a few of the little things to help her mother understand Luba better, show some vulnerability to gain her trust.

"It was nothing, Mama. I just dreamt that I had this little baby, and I was looking for a place to hide, in some strange city. Then suddenly I was at a picnic, at a lake somewhere, and I'd lost the baby, and I was afraid she might be in the lake or something."

Volya gasped then squeezed her eyes tight as if in great pain.

"It was stupid, Mama, meaningless." But as the words came out, Luba realized she was wrong. Her mother had covered her face with her hands, an IV still attached to one of them.

"Mama? Are you okay? Should I call a nurse?" Luba stood up and leaned over, her magazine smacking the floor.

Volya shook her head but kept her eyes covered. After a moment, her hands slid down her face. Her nostrils flared and tears streamed down her cheeks. Luba handed her several tissues from the box next to the bed. Volya blew her nose and gave Luba such a morose look that she fell back into the chair.

"A long time ago, I nearly lost a baby," she whispered. "At a small lake."

"What baby?" Luba asked, her heart racing, afraid she might already know the answer. Was Mama finally going to tell her what happened? After all this time, all the denial, now, because she was afraid she might die?

Volya said nothing for a long time, staring at the ceiling. "I told you that once, a long time ago, I had a dream of being a fancy dressmaker, a designer. I thought about going to school. But I had so little schooling of any kind, and I was too embarrassed to let anyone know, or to start over with girls much younger than I was. They were so cruel to us sometimes, laughing at our accents, at our ignorance. So, instead, I concentrated on my job in the cotton mill, hoping for a promotion and more pay. I was so efficient, they gave me more responsibility all right, but the same pay. After three years they gave me a small increase in wages. I was disappointed, angry, but after the war there were few enough jobs to choose from, and when I looked around, I realized I was better off to stay where I was."

What did this have to do with a baby, Luba wondered. But her mother was talking, she was determined, focused on some endpoint, and Luba did not dare interrupt.

"Then just before the Christmas of 1953 I was finally rewarded for my diligence. At a day-end ceremony on Christmas Eve, I was given a small gold-coloured pin shaped like a spool of thread, and a five-pound bonus for being the most productive employee on my floor. Even the English women I had worked with all those years clapped begrudgingly when I accepted my award. I remember being nervous, standing in front of the big boss, Mr. Spencer. I was still in my work clothes, with a dirty apron and a red gingham kerchief that kept the hair out of my face. I must have been the same colour as the kerchief that day. When I finally looked up at this tall thin man, I noticed a younger version of my boss standing beside him. Both with the same sandy hair and freckles, loose pouting lips, and large ears. The younger one was his son, and he was staring at me, gaping in fact. I was very uncomfortable.

"Later my friends on the line teased me that Roger Spencer, Jr. was besotted with me. I pretended to laugh with them, and joked that he was only after my voluptuous body. Oh yes, I once had a figure that attracted all the young men. I know it is hard to believe."

"I've seen the photos, Mama. I know how attractive you were."

"Anyway, my friends were always trying to get me to go on dates, but I was not interested."

"Why not, Mama?"

She paused and gazed up at the ceiling again. "In Germany—during the war—I had some bad experiences. Let us just say my heart was broken and I did not believe I could ever love anyone. So I refused to date any of these boys and young men my friends tried to set me up with.

"But that Roger Jr. persisted. After repeated rejections, even to have tea with him after work at respectable restaurants or tea shops, he finally accused me of practising discrimination. Imagine! After all the discrimination I had suffered. Of course, I denied it, but he demanded an explanation. I was afraid of what he might say to his father, that I might lose my job.

"'It is not true, Roger,' I told him. 'I do not go out with any boys at all.'

"'Why not?' he wanted to know.

"'I am not interested. I do not need a boyfriend,' I told him.

"He finally gave up, and I was relieved that I did not lose my job. Instead, I learned he began dating one of the younger English girls who worked a different shift. When I saw the girl, I thought that perhaps I was just a little bit jealous. After a few months I forgot about the girl and Roger. I rarely saw him at work since he spent most of his day in an office next-door to the factory building.

"A year later I heard a rumour that Roger's girlfriend had been let go. There were whispers that she was 'in the family way.' Aha, I thought, I was smart to stay away from him. One of those playboys. Shortly afterward, he showed up again at my station, just as the whistle blew at the end of our shift.

"'Hallo, Volya. Haven't seen you in ages. How have you been keeping?' he asked, and looked woefully sincere.

"'Very well, thank you,' I said as I pulled on my overcoat, anxious to get away from him.

"'Well, that is wonderful to hear. Are you still breaking hearts, then?' he asked, and winked at me.

"I remember feeling most annoyed and snapped at him. 'Yes,' I said.

"'Oh, I am sorry, I did not mean to pry,' he apologized. 'Did you and your boyfriend part ways, then?' He would not give up.

"I did not know what to say and I did not wish to lie to him. He stood there, blocking my path to the exit. I had to watch while the other women filed past, a few of them smiling as they caught my eye.

"'Look, I know what they are saying,' he whispered. 'I need to explain to you. No one will listen. Look, Volya, you are a decent, level-headed girl, just give me a chance to explain what happened. I need to clear my name. Please, just listen, then I will not bother you. I just need to set things straight, and everyone knows you are honest and never gossip. Please hear me out, won't you?' At that moment I had a vision of a thin, gangly puppy that had followed me home, pleading with its sad droopy eyes for just one morsel.

"'Fine, I will listen. But that is all I can do,' I told him.

"'Oh, thank you, Volya. This means so much to me,' he said, gallantly bowing in front of me. We went to a tea shop two long blocks away. I was relieved that there was no one else I recognized at the shop.

"Once we had ordered our tea and scones, Roger placed his long spidery hands on the table in front of him. It was the same gesture I had seen when his father was about to launch into a speech on productivity and honesty, two of his favourite themes.

"'Volya, I'm going to be direct, so I hope I won't offend you. But the truth must be known,' he stated loudly, his chin jutting out.

"I remember glancing around nervously to see if anyone was watching this drama, but no one was even looking our way.

"'Sorry,' Roger lowered his voice to a whisper. 'Look, I know what they are saying. Janet was let go, that is true; and she was pregnant, that is also true. But I was not responsible. She dumped me. Yes, months ago. I mean, we still saw each other, but she was seeing someone else at the same time. And anyway, I did not know her in that way, if you know what I mean. It was not me,' he insisted.

"I remember wishing I could disappear right then.

"'Volya, you have got to believe me,' he said. 'I wouldn't do something like that. I am so sorry I got myself involved with that girl. But you would not have anything to do with me, so in misery I found myself another girlfriend. Who turned out to be a slut.'

"I must admit, his language was shocking.

"Then he said, 'I am so sorry, I have offended you, haven't I? I really did not mean to, I am just so upset. Here I am speaking my mind without any consideration of how you might feel. Please do forgive me.'

"Once again Roger left me speechless. Not that I had much experience with such things. He did seem earnest, so I wondered. He made it appear to be my fault that he got involved with this girl.

"So I said, 'I do not know what to say. Why do you care what the gossips might say about you?'

"'I don't care what they say. But I do care what you think. About me, I mean. I know you don't care for me, Volya, you have made it plain. But believe me, I still care very much for you. That will never change. Some people say that there is one special person for each one of us in this world. I think I have found her. Of course, I am brokenhearted that you do not feel the same way about me. I just wanted to let you know that I am not the cad people say I am. They don't even know me. You don't even know me, not really. So it is probably asking too much to have you believe my story.'

"The puppy dog act again. I wish he had not mentioned the one special person. I think that is what finally got to me, foolish and weak as I was.

"We had our tea in silence, then when I felt I could speak, I asked him what he wanted me to do.

"'Just believe in me, that's all,' he replied.

"'Fine, I believe you,' I said.

"That was the beginning of the end, I suppose. Somehow I convinced myself that I could come to love this man. He was so generous with gifts I had to ask him to stop. It seemed so wasteful, all the flowers, and wine I could not drink. You know how just the smell of anything with alcohol nauseates me, it always has. Roger told me that he could persuade his father to promote me, but of course I refused to allow that. Then for sure my co-workers would think I was sleeping with him, which I was not! I enjoyed going out to restaurants, but, I must say, I felt guilty when I ate roast beef. And when I met anyone from work, I felt lower than a snail. I supposed they thought I would become the next victim of Roger's charms. Still, he never pushed me. Only a small kiss on the cheek to say good night, holding my hand once in a while, all very proper. I was quite prepared to stop him in his tracks if he tried to go too far, but he never did. Not for the first few months."

Luba expelled her held-in breath—she knew where this was going; her stomach was already in a painful knot. She gulped quietly as her mother continued.

"After six months of dating, he asked me one evening after dinner at a particularly nice restaurant whether I had ever considered becoming more intimate. He was wearing his puppy dog look again.

"'No, Roger. This is something only for married couples. I am a Catholic, you know,' I reminded him.

"'Of course, of course,' he agreed quickly. The subject did not come up again until another month had passed. When my answer did not change, Roger's expression suddenly softened.

"'I knew you'd say that, of course, darling. I suppose it was just my way of being sure.'

"'Sure? Of what?' I asked him. I wondered if this was some sort of test.

"'Volya, do you think you could ever consider marrying me? Oh, what am I saying, I am such an idiot. I can't even propose properly. What I am trying to say, is, would you marry me?' Roger grabbed one of my very cold hands and grasped it between his own large bony ones.

"Although I had wondered if he would ask me, I was still unprepared. I did not know what to say to him.

"So, being such a fine gentleman, he said, 'I should not do this to you. Always putting you on the spot. Look, you think about it. You do not have to agree or disagree just yet. When you are absolutely sure, you can let me know.'

"I telephoned my friend Zora that same night and we had a long talk. She said, 'If you are not sure, do not marry him. Oh, but I do so want you to be married and happy like me.'

"'I know. I want to be happy, too. He has been so good to me. And I am twenty-nine years old this year. Who will want me if I turn him down?'

"'Do not think like that, Volya. You are an attractive woman. Lots of men are interested in you.'

"'Yes, an attractive, old woman.'

"By the end of the conversation, I was no closer to knowing the answer. But I knew one thing for sure—I did not love him. Was it fair or right to marry someone you did not love? It put me in quite a turmoil. The next day I avoided Roger at work. When I came home to my small flat that evening, I found a letter from Zenia. I tore it open, frantic for any distraction. It read something like this:

'My dearest Volya,

We are doing it! We are finally leaving this mosquito-infested hell-hole. Will be moving to Toronto, a beautiful modern city further east, with a huge Ukrainian community already there. That should be enough for Mama, but she says she prefers to stay back with Marko and Veronica. There is no talking her out of it. She says she does not want another big change so soon.

Bohdan has a job waiting for him and he found us a house in the city. I will also be working, but I cannot tell you what it is yet. It is bad luck to say when the contract is not drawn up and finalized. But it will be wonderful. I will be making as much money as Bohdan, maybe more!

You must leave England. You have no family there. You are not married, so nothing to keep you in that place. We will have plenty of room in the big new house we will start to build as soon as we arrive. It should be ready by spring and there will be a room just for you. Do not worry about the ticket, we will pay for it.

I hope you are happy for us. We are thrilled!

Big kisses,

Your sister Zenia'

"Mama would not move. I was not married. I read between the lines that I should come to take care of her children while she worked. Nothing to keep me in England. Nothing, indeed.

"The very next morning I sent a note to Roger asking him to meet me after work at a nearby tea shop. I remember his face seemed particularly long and narrow as I sat across the table from him. I think his big ears were even quivering.

"I was nervous, but determined. I took his huge puppy paws in my cold hands, forced a smile, and said simply, 'I accept.'

"For a moment Roger seemed stunned, as if he had not expected this verdict. Then a big grin cracked his face in two.

"'Smashing!' was all he said as he gripped my hands so hard it hurt.

"Then, lowering his voice, he said, 'Look. Why we don't we keep this to ourselves just for now. I need to give Mum and Dad a bit of time to get used to the idea, you know.'

"I agreed, because I did know what it was like. A middle-class English boy marrying a DP? He would have a lot of explaining to do. I remember wanting to cry, and trying not to, until the tea came. I gulped it down, burning my tongue, so when the tears came, I told him that the tea was too hot.

"In my bones I knew that it was wrong, agreeing to marry this man I did not love, then agreeing to sleep with him before we were married. But I had already humiliated myself beyond redemption. I am sure you can guess the rest. Four months later, when Roger still had not broken news of our engagement to his family, and I knew I was in trouble, I was not surprised when he told me that he was terribly sorry, but his parents simply would not agree to this marriage, and he could not break their hearts. He was their only child and heir. But that coward was afraid of being disinherited, or, more likely, he never had any intention of marrying me. I was just another naive woman in his string of conquests. I never told him about my condition, of course."

Volya sighed deeply, then winced. Luba sat frozen in her chair, stunned and sickened to think how ashamed her mother must have been, how alone and distressed, and probably deeply depressed as well. She felt the hate surging up from the pit of her stomach for a man she'd never met and never wished to meet. Her mother's eyes were red, the tears streaming again. Luba, trying to keep her hand from shaking, offered her the cup of water, and she sipped a little.

"One hot August day, I found myself in Blackpool. I did not have a plan. I was distraught and wanted to get away from the dingy little town where I lived. I wandered along the shore of a lovely small lake in Stanley Park. Zora had talked of it often, how much fun her family had taking a lunch, listening to music from the bandstand on fine Saturday afternoons. The Boating Lake, as it was called, was surrounded on all sides by brilliant green grass and swaying willows."

A picture flashed before Luba—the place in her dream.

"I watched the laughing families with their picnics, the children splashing in the water, the lovers rowing out, two by two. When the last of the picnickers and rowers had packed their baskets and stowed their oars, and I could no longer hear anyone at all, I stepped into one of the boats then pushed off into the calm water.

"I remember thinking that in the early evening, the colours around me seemed unnaturally vibrant. But the water was black, deep brooding black. I wondered if the Black Sea back at home was like this. When I reached the centre of the lake, I put down the oars. For once I had no fear of the depth below me, even though I could not swim. I looked over the edge of the boat into the rippling water, and thought of a young man I once knew, swimming like a dolphin. Perhaps he was down there, a merman, patiently waiting for me. After all, I thought, why had I come all that way if he had not called for me? I was possessed by ghosts. So I rocked that boat gently, then with increasing force, side to side, splashing myself. I fixed my eyes on the green, green bank for the last time, took a deep breath, and tipped myself into the water."

For a moment mother and daughter were silent. The tears on Volya's cheeks were replaced by drying salt tracks, while Luba fished for a hanky in her pocket to blow her nose. She could not remember a time when they had cried together without being angry with each other, except for her father's funeral. Yes, the man she really thought of as her Tato.

Roger Spencer. Luba didn't dare say that name out loud. She had wanted her mother to tell her about him, and now that she had, Luba was deeply disappointed. She hoped the ears were the only feature she'd inherited from that bastard. She always suspected he would be a let-down. So why did she push on Mama so much? To watch her suffer? Luba felt like such a jerk—first she'd put her sweet old Baba through the wringer, and now her mother. Maybe she'd inherited the jerk factor from him, her biological father. And yet, as badly as she felt for her mother, she felt a lightness in the room, that a thick, choking shadow had just been lifted from her mother's chest and she was able to breathe more freely. She thought back to Uncle Bohdan's words. Aunt Zenia had also banished an old demon and things were better for her now, he said. She, Luba, had done this, had made them open those bolted doors and let out the secrets that had been strangling them for years.

Volya whimpered softly.

"What is it, Mama?" She leaned forward in her chair.

"I am so sorry. I nearly killed you. I never confessed. I never told anyone. I promised this would go with me to the grave and I am nearly there now—"

"Mama. You are not dying."

"You had my dream, my nightmare. The lake, the green all around it. You were there with me. You remember. I am sorry you had to learn about this horrible sin." She sniffled. Luba handed her another tissue.

"It happens to lots of girls. Back then. Now. He took advantage of you when you were weak—"

"I was weak, yes, and proud. Pride was my downfall. I did not want Zenia to see what a failure I was. I had to prove I could make it on my own, have money, all the things she valued. And look what happened. No, my sin was when I tried to kill us both. That was the greatest evil. Some demon took hold of my soul and I lost my will."

She broke into renewed crying, quiet, no sobbing. Luba stared at her soggy hanky. She knew the blackness her mother spoke of. She couldn't believe how their lives had paralleled without even knowing each other's stories. How twisted, and yet miraculous.

"But, Mama, you didn't drown. Did you swim? Did someone fish you out?"

"Yes," she sniffed and blew her nose. "Yarko was watching me the whole time. He was sitting under one of those willows and saw me pacing up and down, saw me take the boat out. He saw everything. He worked on the boat yards out of Blackpool, and he was a good swimmer."

Luba nodded. "Okay, so he saved you, then you fell in love and came to Canada." Luba wanted to finish this story. She was getting depressed again.

"No, we did not fall in love. We both needed to leave England. It was convenient to go as a couple."

"Why did he have to leave?" Luba was happy to abandon Roger Spencer and pursue the story of a man she had, until a few months ago, considered her real father. The man who rescued her mother, and saved Luba's life as well.

"It is complicated."

"Why, Mama? You have to tell me everything, now you've started."

She paused for a long while. "He was, what do you call it now? Gay? The people he worked for found out and fired him. Just like that. He never did anything to anybody. Yarko was the most gentle man I have ever known."

"Okay, so you two got married and went to Canada," Luba finished for her again.

"No. We went to Canada. That is all. I borrowed his name, but I could not marry him."

Volya would not meet Luba's startled eyes.

"You couldn't marry him? Because he was gay?"

"No, not because of that. Not exactly. Neither of us was sure it would be right. He would be pretending to be someone he was not—"

"Which is what he did for the next eight years, isn't it?"

"Yes and no. It is very complicated, I warned you. I had already given my heart to someone else, someone I met in Germany during the war. We were going to get married, but the Germans took him—" she broke off with a strangled sob then clutched her stomach.

"Mama, you okay? Should I call for a nurse?"

Volya shook her head and waved a hand at Luba to sit down. Luba lowered herself slowly, still absorbing what she had heard.

"Mama?"

"Mm-hmm."

"I'm really, really sorry. I didn't mean to put you through all this—" Luba clutched her hanky more tightly, fighting back tears. "I had no idea what you went through. I thought I had a hard time. Mama, did you know, when I tried to—when I was in the hospital, back then, I was so depressed. Mama, I thought I was pregnant, too. But I wasn't, so don't worry. It was stupid. I'll never do anything like that because of a man again. They're just not worth it."

Volya stared at Luba with a puzzled look. "No, most of them are not worth it. But some are. A few. It is too bad Yarko did not like women that way. He was a wonderful man, like a caring brother. You will find someone special one day. Just do not be in a hurry."

"Don't worry, I'm not."

"Good. I want grandchildren some day. I was already thirty years old when you were born. So you have time, but do not wait too long—"

"Mama!"

"I am not well, you should not shout. I could die anytime. I think after everything I have been through, you could be a little more considerate. I want to hold a grandchild in my arms before I die—"

"Mama, you are not dying anytime soon and I'm not getting married. But if you'd like, I'll adopt an orphan. Greg and I can bring her up."

"Stop talking nonsense. Two cousins do not adopt babies. You would probably adopt a baby from Africa if I know you. We can send for a Ukrainian baby if you want to adopt. But you are talking crazy again. You will get married and—"

"I will not. Now I'm going downstairs to get a coffee. Can I have the nurse bring you anything?"

"No." The drug buzz had evaporated and her sullen face had returned.

"Fine. I'll be right back."

"Suit yourself."

"Mama?"

"What?"

"I love you."

She threw Luba a suspicious look, then her eyes filled with tears. Luba leaned down to kiss her cheek.

"I'll be right back."

"I am not going anywhere," she sniffed.

"I know."

As Luba stepped into the corridor, she threw back her head and shoulders and walked like Ena might: lightly, confidently, down the hall. Her bones were as hollow as a bird's, she no longer had to answer to gravity; her mother's confession had freed them both.

And she wondered, if her stepfather Yarko had lived how different her life might have been. Would her mother have been less bitter? Would Yarko have stayed with them, leading his double life? Then again, it may have been the perfect compromise for a man of that time and predisposition. No wonder her mother had never censured Greg or his lifestyle, in spite of her conventional Christian morals.

Luba pictured the self-portrait she'd been trying to complete in her mind. There were a few dark smudges in the background now, but that's all they were, nothing substantive. Your genes could take you only so far, provide a foundation and a few inclinations, perhaps. The character was applied in layers, and coloured by how you responded to the here and now. The painting would grow richer and deeper with time and would never be finished.

That's it, Luba thought, she'd paint a portrait of her mother over the holidays. She had a set of watercolours and paper at the house. She could start this afternoon while Volya was still captive in her hospital bed. Of course, her mother would protest, she'd hate the idea. A painting of a sick, old woman? Just the thing to light her fire, snap her out of the death bed act. Luba smiled. She had nothing to be afraid of any more; she knew her mother's secrets—some of them anyway—and in time her mother would know some of hers. No rush, just one brush stroke at a time.

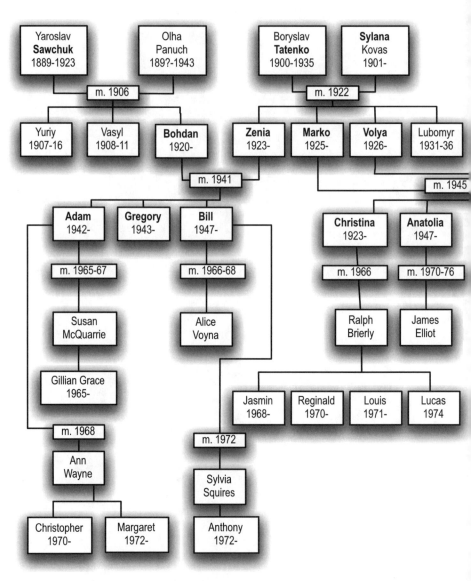

Gregory Sawchuk's
Genealogy Chart, 1977

```
┌─────────────┐  ┌─────────────┐         ┌─────────────┐  ┌─────────────┐
│   Vasyl     │  │  Bohdana    │         │ Volodimyr   │  │   Halya     │
│ Stachevich  │  │  Kripetz    │         │   Kassim    │  │    Bila     │
│ 1897-1949   │  │ 1905-1967   │         │ 1903-1966   │  │ 1900-1967   │
└─────────────┘  └─────────────┘         └─────────────┘  └─────────────┘
```

m. 1924

m. 1925

```
┌─────────────┐  ┌─────────────┐    ┌──────────┐ ┌──────────┐ ┌──────────┐
│  Veronica   │  │    Daria    │    │  Yarko   │ │   Ada    │ │  Kuzma   │
│   1927-     │  │   1929-     │    │ 1927-63  │ │ 1930-33  │ │ 1935-36  │
└─────────────┘  └─────────────┘    └──────────┘ └──────────┘ └──────────┘
```

m. 1955

```
┌──────────┐  ┌─────────────┐  ┌──────────┐      ┌──────────────────────┐
│ Zachary  │  │  Nicholas   │  │  Orest   │      │   Lubmyra (Luba)      │
│  1948-   │  │    1950-    │  │  1951-   │      │        1956-          │
└──────────┘  └─────────────┘  └──────────┘      └──────────────────────┘
```

m. 1970

```
┌─────────────┐
│   Phyllis   │
│   Martin    │
└─────────────┘
```

```
┌─────────────┐  ┌─────────────┐
│   Heather   │  │  Maribeth   │
│   1972-     │  │   1974-     │
└─────────────┘  └─────────────┘
```

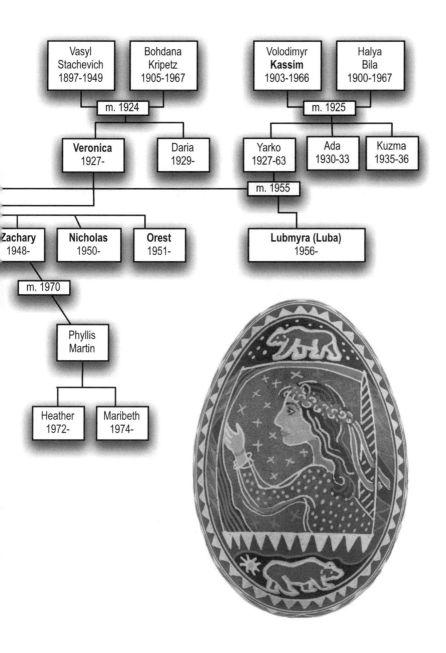

Acknowledgements

I am especially grateful to my editors, Melissa Carroll, who opened the blinds, and Richard Lemm, who provided me with new lenses. Thank you so much for lighting up my pages. Thanks also to the Prince Edward Island Council of the Arts for their financial support.

For their unflagging encouragement and love, I owe much to my writing group, those Wacky Writing Women of PEI. Thank you to all the readers of early drafts for their kindness and wisdom—Elizabeth Stevenson, Lesley-Anne Bourne, Liza Oliver, Shaena Lambert, and Brent MacLaine, and to Kathleen Hamilton who provided a stage for some of the characters to come alive.

Thank you, Lisa Chilton, for all the rich conversations about immigrants to Canada, and to Jean Kozelko for sharing your early memories of emigration, and those of your mother, dear Aunt Stephanie. I am also grateful to my parents, Olga and Walter, for deciding to settle in Canada and for teaching me the culture and history of our people.

My heartfelt appreciation goes to Laurie Brinklow for pushing this fledgling off the branch into the scary, empty air—the wings seem to be working. I am deeply grateful to my husband David Sims, a man of unending patience, who gave me time and space and a clean house to work in, and who believed this bird would soar. To everyone else who contributed in a hundred different ways, thank you for sending the wind.

Orysia Dawydiak was the first child born to immigrant parents who settled in Northern Ontario. She grew up with a foot in both worlds, on a diet rich in Ukrainian traditions and stories.

Her love of nature and animals led her to pursue a career in science. She works at the Atlantic Veterinary College in Charlottetown, and lives on a small farm on Prince Edward Island's north shore where she raises sheep and dogs. She writes books on livestock protection dogs, and has also written award-winning fiction for children and young adults. *House of Bears* is her first novel.

An excerpt from *House of Bears* was first published in *Water Studies: New Voices in Maritime Fiction* (Pottersfield, 1998).